RED
DIRT
ROAD

Also by S. R. White

Hermit
Prisoner

RED DIRT ROAD

S. R. WHITE

HEADLINE

First published in 2023 by
HEADLINE PUBLISHING GROUP

2

Cataloguing in Publication Data is available from the British Library

Hardback ISBN 978 1 4722 9115 8
Trade paperback ISBN 978 1 4722 9116 5

Typeset in 12.87/17.84 pt Adobe Garamond Pro by Jouve (UK), Milton Keynes

Printed and bound in Great Britain by Clays Ltd, Elcograf S.p.A.

HEADLINE PUBLISHING GROUP
An Hachette UK Company
Carmelite House
50 Victoria Embankment
London EC4Y 0DZ

www.headline.co.uk
www.hachette.co.uk

This book is set in October 2019, before Covid. But it was written during, and is very much formed by, the pandemic.
It is dedicated to the farmers of Australia who are, as Dana Russo points out, 'some of the best of us.' They not only feed 25 million Australians, but also tens of millions of other people throughout the world, despite working in a land of droughts and flooding rains. Something our politicians and journalists — of all political persuasions — would do well to remember and respect.

October, 2019

Annie Ogden always rose at five.

In summer it gave her a couple of hours' respite before the real heat arrived: a slice of cool serenity when she could move without feeling scorched. In winter the calm, crisp air was sharp on the tongue; the half-light held a peace that eroded as hours drifted by. In an ocean of scrub and stoicism, this time was her harbour.

She'd been up half the night and had a muffled, cotton-wool head that she knew would last until lunchtime. Her grandmother had raised five kids, working from dawn to midnight with three part-time jobs and six mouths to feed, but she'd always said it never felt like work. Her whole life had gone into it – the actual work was so sublimated into everything else that she never felt the difference. Annie was the same about her life here: it was so intertwined with 'work' that there was no border to cross.

Behind the pub, nestled between empty metal barrels and the pallets holding up a waning fence, an upturned tea chest and, right now, a mug of coffee. Not the standard dross she sold to punters but the good stuff she gifted herself, cold-dripped overnight in her own kitchen. The steam from the cup rose dead vertical, headed for a purple sky fringed by primrose yellow.

She was used to the vista in the east, saw it every morning. Three stained metal chimneys, yet to pulse with smoke from wood-burners, signalled the one-storey mid-sets that dotted Ransome Street, the empty blocks between them like the wounds from pulled teeth. To the right were four gum trees, holding on through the drought with Una-murra's gritty, instinctive determination. In the evening the white bark held the rays of the setting sun and seemed ablaze; at dawn the trees were jet-black silhouettes. To the right of that were –

To the right of that, something was different. New.

Seeping above the fence was a low, chilling black line. It ran in two gentle curves, split by a round shape the size of a football. It had never been there before, not in fourteen years of sunrise coffee and knock-off cigarettes.

She stood and had padded across to the fence before she thought. The sound of a nearby engine didn't reach her. Up onto a plastic crate, she could see beyond the fence into the back scrub and fully appreciate what stood before her. What had been draped, shaped, created – *curated*.

The metal frame was familiar: a basketball post gone wrong, large feet splayed for stability, arms reaching forward and up to support. Like dozens all over town. But this was different. Someone had stolen what should be there and left a hideous replacement.

Her husband was arranged in a swooping, drifting pose. He was veering in from above, poised to strike. He was splayed, desperate and bereft. He was just like the other one, a few weeks ago.

Tim Ogden was cold, sightless and quite, quite dead.

Chapter 1

'Russo.'

The instruction to come in was, as usual, a clipped bark.

Dana entered the office of Anton McCullough, her boss and district commander, as infrequently as she could manage. This suited them both. At no point did McCullough ever walk to the detectives' offices and he handled almost everything with an avalanche of curt emails. Her admin officer, Lucy, received no direct communication whatsoever from McCullough: any orders were passed through a channel of go-betweens, as if they all worked in 1960s East Berlin. Lucy had predicted that soon she would get instructions hidden inside a fake rock by a park bench. Dana's colleague Mike was better served, being compelled on a weekly basis to provide a departmental update. He'd offered to let someone else do it, but they'd all declared themselves too busy for the next seventy years.

Priorities were set by one man's whim. The district's management board was now moribund: McCullough wasn't interested in collegiate decision-making and simply gave out personal instructions without consultation or discussion. Any meetings were one to one, in his office. There was little doubt that he viewed this as decisive leadership, taking command of what he saw as a loose ship. He expected backing from a workforce that understood the necessary command structure of policing, but his lack of consultation meant that he had no idea how it was viewed. Someone had labelled him the *edict eejit*. It might have been Lucy.

McCullough's office, his for the next year or so before retirement, was devoid of anything personal or softening. Apparently, he had a wife and three adult children, but there were no photos. Apparently, he'd led mutual aid and partnerships in Thailand, Indonesia and Brunei, but there were no plaques or certificates. Foliage stopped outside his office window and, beyond one in-tray, there was no sign that any work was conducted in the room.

The man himself sat reading while Dana stood silently. The protocol now was to wait until McCullough decided to look up from whatever and address her. Others faced a similar process, but seemingly delivered with more professional courtesy. McCullough didn't like Dana's approach, personality or methods: he made that perfectly clear on every occasion. He let out a soft whistle as he turned the final page, as though a finance report held a twist he hadn't seen coming.

'The Lou Cassavette case,' he said, without looking up from the report. The one thing Dana liked about McCullough was that he always named a case by honouring the victim, not the perpetrator.

'Sir?'

'The accused in court yet?'

'Still on remand, sir. Psychiatric reports.' Dana slid into the same terse style as McCullough.

'Hmm. Shouldn't take long, but I don't like it. Confession, supporting evidence – it all stacks up. It's cut and dried. They knew exactly what they were doing, and people like that need banging up. I don't like 'em sliding.'

'No, sir. I believe it was the judge that ordered the psych evaluation.'

'Still on suicide watch?'

'Level five, sir, yes.'

McCullough's long-held view was that too many offenders 'walked' by faking symptoms. Dana felt that McCullough hadn't been directly investigating for years and had lost sight of the burgeoning mental health crisis. Every day, officers saw people who should be receiving health care and support but were on a waiting list that stretched a year or more. Life often intervened before then.

'The Monroe murder?'

'The trial starts next month, sir. On the fifteenth.'

The Monroe trial had been brought forward rapidly, after the golf-course intervention of a state minister. McCullough viewed it simply as paperwork to be processed – a rapist killed in cold blood. Dana saw a human tragedy, regardless of the victim's history. She was working twelve-hour days trying to comply with deadlines for evidence logs, audit trails and submissions.

McCullough threw the report into the in-tray and sat up straighter. His vague attempt at a smile was disconcertingly reptilian. A question slid out from the corner of his mouth. 'Ever been to Dutton, Russo?'

Dutton was one of the force's most isolated districts, a world of flat horizons and dust, rumoured to be riddled with corruption.

'Never, sir.'

'Well, you are now. This afternoon. Miriam's booked you a flight at two. Be on it. Here.'

He flicked a solitary piece of A4 at the edge of the desk. Dana came forward and caught it as it threatened to flop to the carpet.

'Dutton's a bloody mess, we all know that. Trent's good police, but he's surrounded by idiots out there. Ten weeks ago, they had a murder. Local farmer. Crazy MO and aftermath, so they hushed it up. Four weeks later, another one. Husband of the pub owner. Same MO. This all happened in a town called Unamurra. So maybe eighty people, two murders: they couldn't find a thing. Not one suspect. One of the

detectives . . . well, you can dig out the reports to read on the plane.
Solve their murders for them, Russo, so we can all get on with our lives
without Central crying like babies.'

Dana scanned the sheet, which contained less detail than she'd just
been told. At the bottom was a link to the files in the computer system. She must have frowned, because McCullough chuckled softly.

'You're probably asking yourself . . . *why me*? Have a think about
that, too. I expect you to solve that question, as well as the murders. A
couple of days should do it. And I mean a couple of days, Russo. Not
every performance review takes place in this building. Understand?'

'Yes, sir.'

'Hmm. Mike Francis's time is increasingly occupied with the Alvarez operation. So I can't have a detective who should be here going
walkabout like a headless chook. A couple of days, *max*. Get it done.
Heads up for you, Russo: Unamurra has no internet. So think
logistics.'

They both stared at each other for a second.

'Well, go on, then. Get packing.'

Chapter 2

Some people weren't made for flying, just like some were completely unsuited for ballet, brain surgery or basketball. Each dip or lurch from an air pocket, every variation in the drone of the engine, made Dana's heart flip. She stared at the propeller on the wing, trying to discern a tiny shift in the strobing that would herald imminent disaster: just one errant bird would do it, she thought. Frequent checks of her safety belt – she was the only passenger who hadn't released it as soon as they levelled out – didn't help. Breathing slowly and closing her eyes merely let her imagination wander. The insouciant chatter of other passengers frustrated her. She tried to bury herself in the information on her laptop, but it wasn't gelling.

McCullough had been matter-of-fact. He'd said Dana's flight to Dutton was already booked. Her return flight, she'd noted, was not.

Five months of McCullough had barely made a dent in her view of him. The initial impression – that he was a selfish, politicized ego who would drop his people from a great height whenever it suited him – hadn't changed. Her previous commander, Bill Meeks, was still suspended and, it seemed, beginning to accept that he'd never return. Collateral damage from a desperate fight to become the new Alpha dog at Central, Bill had been sidelined without a chance to challenge the allegations. Central was apparently muttering about a *dignified with-drawal* from his career. It had occurred to Dana in the three-hour drive to the airport that twenty-eight years of loyalty seemingly counted for nothing if your face no longer fitted: their treatment of Bill remained tatty, tawdry and unjust. Lucy had worked on with the stigma of impli-cation at her shoulder – she'd been a sacrificial pawn in the same sleazy game. She was outwardly back to her best but, Dana knew from their nightly phone chats, still gnawing on the unfairness.

Dana had packed what she'd hoped would be needed for up to a week. McCullough's sneering suggestion of a day or two seemed unfor-giving, designed to fail. The two previous murder inquiries had been perfunctory and lacking, but there was over a month of investigation in them: simply covering that work again would take the entire week. It had occurred to her that re-treading old ground might, therefore, be a poor use of her limited time. If nothing else, the distances were vast and she could eat up large chunks of a day simply getting from place to place.

If her attempted investigation went on any longer than two or three days, she'd probably have drawn a giant blank anyway. Then she'd have to slope back to Carlton and watch McCullough's face as he pointed out her inability to *operate beyond your comfort zone*. An extrovert detective with a burgeoning contacts list, a flair for people, open-natured bonhomie – a people person, in fact – would have done better: this would be the implication. It wouldn't be just a botched investiga-tion on her record, either. McCullough was looking to restructure and Dana was, she was certain, top of the list to be moved elsewhere. She wasn't sure she could manage the rupture to her life, or the distance from Lucy.

The plane hit a patch of quiet air and Dana managed to skim the gist of the case again, memorizing markers and noting some startling unanswered questions. The two detectives had covered most of the basics in a mechanistic way – items tallied and ticked, processes completed and simply filed. There appeared little thought other than what came next, or what might prompt a bollocking if it was forgotten. There was no analysis, no appraisal, no notes on likely suspects or motives. It filled paperwork but did little else.

Larry Muir had been the first victim, strung up in open country on a metal frame. His exact time of death was unknown, the body having been there seemingly for days before discovery. A local farmer, Muir had no obvious problems that would lead to this. Forensics were sketchy, with only one set of fingerprints and no witnesses. Everyone seemed to treat it as a bizarre one-off; the community wasn't ready for another when it came a month later. Tim Ogden was displayed in the same way, but with a location at the back of the town pub. Everyone lacked an alibi for each murder, because the first had a wide-open timing and the second had a twelve-hour potential window. Again, there was no clear motive for anyone around Tim's death. Background work had revealed no gambling debts, affairs or possibilities of blackmail for either victim. In such a small town each investigation had quickly run out of questions to ask, and people to respond.

The first hour in the air had yielded views of a tawny landscape still marked by greenery around the watercourses. Rivers seeped along the arcs and oxbows created when they ran in joyous, exuberant flood; dams held defiantly to the last dregs while surrendering long-drowned trees and crushed fencing. But not long after they'd crossed the solitary rail track that formed the border into Dutton District, she saw a huge mass of dusky nothing: no hills, no mountains, no trees. From this height the mottled surface resembled a dehydrated leather hide; the Dry was into its fourth year. Dutton itself was isolated but Dana's ultimate destination was the murder site, the town of Unamurra, a further two hundred kilometres along the only road. A settlement that was created because horse-drawn wagons had needed supplies to cross day after day of emptiness, Unamurra's relevance had faded once people no longer required blacksmiths. No modern necessity had replaced it.

The cab-driver was blessedly quiet, a middle-aged Indian man in a perfectly ironed white shirt, who drove with delicate sweeps of a hand and impeccable manners. The upholstery was immaculate, so much so that it felt vaguely plasticized. A prominent sign reminded passengers that *animals spit, humans don't*, but a second reassured that *people are joy*. Dana needed to re-gather. Her pulse was still skittish from the flight and, in particular, the landing. She knew the odds of having an accident and basically understood the rudiments of man-made flight. She comprehended it was fundamentally safe in the way she understood that venomous snakes sought to avoid conflict, huntsman spiders were God's creatures too, and lightning strikes were rare. None of this knowledge placated her. When the wheels had touched down and the plane failed to somersault, she'd finally breathed out.

Cricket commentary from overseas mumbled quietly on the radio: genial conversation drifting amid broiling Sri Lankan heat. The car, operating on its hybrid motor at these speeds, glided like a padding cat. Dutton didn't show its best face on the route from the tiny airport to the town. The abattoir was a rudimentary fabrication to the north side of the road, a web of cattle fences and two-storey steel sheds, sun-blasted but dormant. On the south side a collection of stores offered chainsaws, shade awnings, caravan repairs and welding services. An attempted *Eat Street* near the Federation-era post office had enticed only golden arches, several lofty silhouettes of chickens and a bottle shop.

The main street was, mid-afternoon, in drowsy repose. Many shops were closed – assuming they were ever open – and the only bank shut its oak doors as she passed. Verandas extended all the way from shopfront to street gutter: shade was cherished and the sun was an eight-month enemy. What struck Dana about the shop windows wasn't the old-fashioned presentation. What occurred instead, as a red light drew them to a halt, was that they didn't have many goods: shoe stores offered up three or four pairs, a cake shop presented two eclairs and a gateau. The displays were almost a facade of what every town had, but with a subtle indication that behind this was very little.

For four hundred metres through the centre of town, she saw no trees and no grass. Some country towns had enjoyed a golden era – literally an era of gold, in some cases – and reflected that temporary boom in the architecture of public gardens, town hall, banks or an incongruously large and ornate theatre. These statements were often overblown and vaguely pretentious with their wedding-cake aesthetic, but they also gifted those towns an air of civility and dignity. Dutton, however, had never had such a moment. Instead, it was a facsimile of urban life grafted on to an ungrateful land which tried to shuck it off at regular intervals. Nature's weapon of choice varied: nutrient-free soil, obliterating dust storms, life-changing but rare floods, blinding summer heat or – as now – years of drought. The land and the town fought an uneasy, desperate and silent struggle, each licking wounds periodically but refusing to buckle. The region suited empty landscapes and hardy, well-adapted fauna; the town was an interloper, its population aiding and abetting the trespass.

The taxi-driver broke his languid style when they stopped, scuttling to get her suitcase from the boot. He set it upright and extended the handle before asking for the fare. He seemed surprised when, after paying and tipping, Dana shook his hand and said thank you.

After the piercing glare of the street, the foyer of Dutton's police station was dusty, muggy, like the inside of a museum. Muted light slanted in through four clerestory windows, high set and cowering under the veranda outside. Dust motes sparkled and weaved in the diagonal beams. A bench had been bolted to one wall against tongue-and-groove panelling. Black and white floor tiles were scored by the tram tracks of recalcitrant furniture being dragged.

The reception was the standard mix of high-waisted bench – complete with scuff marks from a thousand boot caps – and Perspex sliding screens, set open a few centimetres for conversation to creep through. The space was designed to elicit basic details from the visitor while remaining essentially mute itself. In station foyers Dana could usually hear scraps of conversation beyond, muffled trills from telephones, a sense of half-hidden industry. Here, no sound but the rasp of a P-plater's exhaust from the street.

'Yeah, mate?'

The officer didn't look up from the journal he was perusing, flicking back and forth as though the contents made no sense. The pages were yellowed and the writing an elegant copperplate. Dana assumed it was an old ledger of some kind. His name badge read *Constable O'Brien*. He had sharp, matted hair like a pan scourer and breathed noisily, as if fuming at someone.

'Hello. I'm here to meet Constable Able Barella.'

O'Brien looked up at the voice, the manners, the invoked name. Presumably, those usually asking for Barella were different – or at least looked different. There was a short pause while O'Brien collected himself. Outside, the exhaust blared a second time and tyres squealed briefly.

'Really? Abe? Sorry, he's up at Unamurra.' O'Brien jerked his thumb over his left shoulder. 'About two hours thataway.'

'Yes, I know. He's meeting me here. My name is Dana Russo.'

The name should, she thought, have rung a bell. It wasn't every day someone traipsed across a chunk of continent to meet someone at O'Brien's station. A good cop, she felt, would have worked it out just from the suitcase. She spotted a printed email to his right and noted the double-strip of yellow highlighter that indicated it was high priority. She could read her name on the second line, in bold.

'Okay,' muttered O'Brien, seemingly unconvinced. 'Well, I can try getting hold of him, but, y'know . . .'

'Yes, I can imagine. He texted me before I got on the plane. He said he would meet me here at three o'clock.'

This time a smirk, as though Dana should have known better. O'Brien relaxed slightly and dropped his pen. 'Well, there you go, that's your problem. You're way early.' He pointed to the clock on the wall opposite: two minutes to three. It was above a poster of a haunted-looking teenager with sunken, surrendering eyes who was apparently missing. The teenager would be forty now, if she was still alive. 'Three means four, with old *Able*. His name's uh . . . what's the word? Ironic.'

Dana's observations continued to pile up in her mind: dissing a colleague to a complete stranger.

'Do you mind if I wait here, please?' She indicated the suitcase she'd left by the bench, which now loomed as a fait accompli for O'Brien.

He puffed his cheeks as though he couldn't care less, and flung a hand at the bench. 'Knock yourself out. I'd offer you some tea, but the water heater's just crapped out.'

'That's fine. Thank you.'

Thirty minutes later the main door opened slightly and a man stood at the threshold, looking back out at the town. His hand lingered on the door, holding it ajar. Dana saw short, stubby fingers, worried nails and the glint of a silver watchstrap below a denim cuff. After several seconds the man backed in, still staring down the street, and the door swung fully open. Dana recognized him from the e-pack Lucy had sent.

'Hey, Mal,' he called to the desk. 'That step's bloody lethal, mate. Someone's going to sue you one day.' Able Barella slapped some dust from one shoulder.

O'Brien shrugged. 'Well, I hope it's you, Abe. Because one, that means you've hurt yourself. And two, I know you can't afford a lawyer.' His pen veered away from Able, towards Dana. 'Visitor for you – been waitin'.'

Able turned and looked surprised, sheepish and open, all in the same expression. He had crow's feet around the eyes and scraggily coiled hair. He might have been thirty, or fifty. His wide mouth fell into a brilliant, reflexive smile.

'Hi, hi, Detective. Sorry I'm late. Local hit a cow.'

Dana shook hands and raised an eyebrow. 'With their car, or a lucky punch?'

Able stopped for a second with his hand still in mid-air, then laughed. 'Ha! Well, he swears with the car.' His hand reached to his chin, thoughtfully. 'But he could've punched the car as well, just to make his story stand up.' He nodded, eyes narrowed in mock-consideration. 'Yeah, hadn't thought of it that way. Good thinking. That's the kind of out-there approach you'll need, Detective.'

'I look forward to it. Please, just Dana.' She gathered her laptop bag and slung it onto one shoulder. 'Should I call you Constable . . .'

'Ah, crap no. Able. Abe. Whatever.'

'Okay, Able. Well, much as I want to get to Unamurra, I suggest we bottom out what we can with Forensics here. I don't imagine you have a big lab where we're headed.'

Able smiled. 'In Unamurra? Not big, no. Not at all, in fact. Not even a kid's chemistry set. Yeah, good idea. I'll take you through to Doc Mangold. He can, uh, give you some basics at least.' Able spotted Dana reaching for the suitcase. 'Oh, here, let me drive that. Comin' through, Mal.'

O'Brien buzzed them through, and Able parked the suitcase under the desk. After hearing *Detective*, O'Brien seemed contrite. 'Sorry about that. Didn't realise you were family.'

Dana deadpanned it. 'No. Forensics are this way?'

'Yeah, down the long corridor, turn left.'

They went through two fire doors to emerge into a long passageway that was half outside, half indoors. Dana guessed it had once been an alleyway that they'd semi-enclosed, a weatherproof cheat-route from the front office to Forensics and, she could hear, the motor pool. The air was saturated with the stringent smell of chemicals, recently sprayed along the base of the wall to stem inexorable pulses of bugs. She could see the smears from the sloppy application.

'You and Mal O'Brien are friends?'

Able replied back over his shoulder. 'Yeah, you could say that.'

He carried on walking for a moment, then half turned and addressed her a second time. 'Well, actually, *friends* is pushing it. Mal's a decent bloke when you get to know him. You need to take a blowtorch to his front panel first, mind. I've been working on him for about five years and I reckon we're just short of actual mates. But if I was ever in trouble in Dutton, I'd call for Mal.'

Dutton's station was about one third the size of Carlton's, Dana estimated, so she expected all the support resources to be proportionate. But the Forensics unit was surprisingly well served for a smaller regional station, with more equipment and space than Dana would have guessed. There was a main lab maybe ten metres across, with an examination table and a decent array of centrifuges and other paraphernalia. Beyond that, what looked like storage for exhibits and material, including the large silver door she'd hoped for.

Doc Mangold was sitting on a high swivel stool, clicking through an online form with an air of tedium. There was something of the *crow on a fencepost* about him. He'd carefully tended the hair above his ears because of its rarity value. Able made the introductions, then leaned back against a bench to signal this was Dana's run.

'I know you've spoken to Able about both deaths, Doctor, and I've read your reports, thank you,' began Dana. Mangold took off his glasses and regarded her with wariness. 'So I'll try not to trouble you with repetition. But I have a few questions.'

Mangold held up a palm and Dana surprised herself by stopping: it was a tactic she used in interviews, but unnerving when it was turned on her.

'Before you do, I think you should see the bodies. In full flight, so to speak. Might answer a few things for you. They're quite something.'

Dana glanced at the silver door and nodded, relieved. 'Yes, thank you. I wasn't sure if you still had them or if Central had picked them up by now.'

Mangold chucked his glasses on to the bench and shook his head. 'Those geniuses? Well, kiss goodbye to any more forensics when they show up next week. I have a very big freezer here, Detective. We, uh, *acquired* it when the butcher went belly-up in Unamurra. I can keep the corpses exactly as they were, hooked up and everything.'

He half jumped off the stool and began strolling towards the massive silver door jammed between two cupboards – practically a new room off the main lab.

'We've taken photos and video, of course. But when Central transport them they'll dismantle everything, throw bits away and pack the rest, and jam two bodies into one box for transportation. *Prioritize*, they call it. I mean you lose the uh, cinematic effect, when you squash them tight. We preserved them in here, exactly as. Have at 'em.'

He pulled back the door, which made a soft thump as the seal released, and Dana waited patiently for the mist to evaporate. It did so slowly, from the top down, giving the impression that each corpse was appearing to her from the gloom, moving forward for their moment. Despite viewing photos on the flight, at first she couldn't quite comprehend what she was seeing. Gradually, she put the puzzle together.

Angels. They were both angels. Dark, malevolent, but angels. Each corpse was staged in the same way – arms splayed in a curved lunge forward, tipped towards the observer like a giant raptor beginning its descent. They were falling yet floating upwards at the same time. The 'wings' of black leather, battered by dust, wind and sun, arched from the wrist to the spine. Thin cords tethered each corpse to the metal frame.

The images she'd previously viewed hadn't shown this level of detail. Two dimensions hadn't done it justice: the sense swept through her that a dead body was also at a moment of launching.

One expression came to Dana. 'Jesus.'

'I know, right?' muttered Able. 'Freaky as.'

She needed to be sure. 'Are they just—'

'Yeah, they are,' confirmed Mangold. 'Exactly like the Angels of Unamurra. Same posts, same binding, same wings, same posture. Everything. The real angels don't have faces, so that's different. But otherwise? Someone replaced an angel with a corpse. Twice.'

The Angels of Unamurra were an ongoing art project foisted on the town by a state government eager to pay lip service to helping remote communities through the drought. They'd been created and curated by Axel DuBois, a Québécois artist of questionable background who still lived in Unamurra although currently his whereabouts were unknown. The art moved irregularly about town, showing up where and when least expected. The angels were supposed to spark curious tourists, caravan-toting silver nomads and others. Many country towns in regional Australia got through hardscrabbles with a side-hustle of some public art – grain silo portraits or warehouse-sized murals. Just enough enticement to get fresh money into the town. Unamurra's angels were supposed to generate tourist dollars and go viral. The whole project was widely regarded as a failure.

The corpses here left more questions than she'd had at home.

Were they homage, or accusing pointer? Inescapable pathology, or misdirection? Why not hide the bodies in the vast desert? Why kill these two people, at these two moments?

Dana turned back to the corpses and looked more closely. Their nudity – the clothes being kept for analysis – gave them a strange vulnerability alongside the power. The wing bindings at waist, nape and wrist were crude: black twine wrapped and pulled tight. Nothing technical or difficult, no special materials. But then, DuBois liked to create using things people might have at home. The faces, except for the effects of freezing on the skin, were untouched. As always, an apparent dignity and placid acceptance that Dana envied; barely a mark to indicate anything beyond sleep. A small bullet hole at the heart was the only indication; a blood-bloom the size of a beer coaster was scarcely discernible through the frosting.

'Just one set of fingerprints?'

'Yeah, just DuBois as far as I've found. Which you'd expect – him being the artist, and all. They're on the frame and some of the bindings but not the body itself. There's nothing on those . . .'

'Except gunshot residue?'

'A few traces, yeah. So, fired from a short distance in each case – five to ten metres, depending on the wind. Hard to say exactly what the timescale is, especially for Larry Muir there. But a good guess is that whoever shot them was the person that framed them.'

She nodded. 'Identical methodology for both victims, Doctor?'

'Yup. We kept the whole thing under wraps when the first, Larry, was found. So not much chance of a copycat.'

It floated through Dana's mind that a murder corpse tied to a metal frame near the road, in a town that size could not be *kept under wraps*. A local farmer had found the first body. It was unlikely that he'd simply filed it away and never spoken of it.

Mangold flowed on. 'So, you know, same person we reckon. One bullet to the heart, clean kill. Standard forty-five, with a home-made silencer. I can match it when . . . *if* . . . you find it, Detective. I'd need the gun for sure; silencer would be a nice bonus.' He stepped forward and pointed at each stomach in turn. 'Hoisted up on to the frame using a thicker rope. Burn and slide marks on the ab muscles, showing how they did it. There's grooves at the top of the frame there, so it's like a pulley system. You just yank until the corpse raises into position. Dress the corpse with the wings, attach the twine at the contact points, more twine to bind the body to the frame, then take the thicker rope away. The same method DuBois uses for hoisting the angels – the video of him doing it is online, so it's anyone's business.'

She briefly wondered if they could track who'd viewed that video and maybe find a local IP address. The problem was there was no internet in Unamurra, apparently, so the IP address would be somewhere else – perhaps Dutton library. That would hardly narrow it down. But one way or another, chances were that the whole of Unamurra had watched that video somehow, somewhen.

Dana was mesmerized by the figures, the juxtaposition of falling dead yet taking flight, of life ebbing away amid new beginnings. The real angels, she thought, must be something special. She eventually glanced across to Able. 'The dead bodies: added where the frame happened to be, or was the frame moved into position beforehand?'

'Hard to tell.' Able pointed to the freezer, where some of the mist still roiled. 'See the bottom? Little wheels in the base – you can tilt it back and push it like a wheelbarrow. Like they have for netball, eh? Any adult could move them, even with the corpse attached: no special strength needed. Hard-packed ground out there, see? So no sign of when the frames were moved, or how much weight was on 'em.'

Dana could see it now. A frame with a corpse attached might weigh a hundred and twenty kilos but, even so, a reasonably strong adult could move it around, given it was tilted and on wheels.

Able stepped back and resumed leaning against the bench. 'Witness statements say the first frame – the one holding Larry Muir – had been near the road about eight or nine days, at the gate to Vince Reynolds' property. Vince didn't realize at first: his house is four clicks from the gate and he usually only leaves it every few weeks. He sure wasn't happy about hosting the frame. Some of them think it's a bad omen.'

Dana nodded. She'd read on the flight that the art project had faced significant resistance, mainly on the grounds that it was a crap idea and wouldn't bring money to the town. But some had felt uneasy about the iconography itself.

'Empty frame, of course, at that point,' said Able. 'They get moved empty all over town, all the time. Part of the art, right? Part of the *performance*?' An eye-roll indicated Able's sceptical view. 'Second one was different: Annie Ogden's old man, Tim? Out the back of the pub, near some scrubby ground. Frame wasn't there the day before, apparently. But that was on graded earth – tough to say where it was brought from, or exactly when. Thing is, these frames are all over the town, empty and full. There's—'

'*There are* . . . twenty-eight angels, but fifty-six frames.'

Able nodded. 'Yeah. Fifty-four frames, now we've got these two. DuBois had a hissy fit when we took the first one, I think that's why he's AWOL now. Like maybe some protest thingie: highlighting our lack of respect for his genius, or something. Dunno why twenty-eight angels, exactly.'

'It's a perfect number,' replied Dana quietly, still staring at the bodies.

'A what?'

'Perfect numbers: they're a mathematical sequence. Twenty-eight can be divided by fourteen, by seven, four, two, or one. Add those together, you get twenty-eight. To be perfect: all the numbers that can divide into it, added together, make up that number. It has symmetry.'

She moved closer to the corpses. 'It's DuBois' artistic calling card: using mathematical patterns. Bucky balls, Fibonacci sequence, that kind of thing. So they say.'

Able puffed his cheeks at Mangold as if to indicate the gap between a constable's pay grade and higher mathematics. Mangold grinned.

Dana stepped back. 'Doctor, any other signs of trauma?'

Mangold stopped grinning abruptly, as though caught out by teacher. 'A little. Both have slight bruising on the right knee or hip. It gets hidden by the frosting, there. But it's relatively minor, and not related to this.'

Dana paused before responding. 'Because . . . the bruises are old?'

'No, they're recent. I mean, recent when each body was discovered.' He pointed back to the two dead bodies. 'But, hey, shot through the heart.'

'Yes,' replied Dana. 'But shot through the heart while they were upright. Hence the bruises when they fell to the ground. Your hip, your knee: that's how you fall if you can't put your arms out. Plus, they fell *straight* down – no friction grazes from dragging along the ground.' She stopped momentarily and tapped her pen against her palm. 'So, first conclusion: dead immediately, not just dying. Second conclusion: not in motion when they were shot – no momentum drawing to a halt. So, either standing still directly in front of the killer or standing still facing the killer's general direction. Which one depends on how good a marksman the killer was. They were shooting with a handgun, so likely to be the former, not the latter.'

Another puff of Able's cheeks, this time of appreciation.

'They teach that kind of thing at Central, eh?' asked Mangold, seemingly irritated.

'I'm from Carlton. We feel the same about Central as you do.' Dana flipped forward, then back, in her file. 'Has anything further come back from Central on the ballistics?'

'Nope. Bit of a dead end.' Mangold jerked his head at the investigation report on a nearby table. 'Both bullets came from the same gun.
Like I say, a forty-five, but we have no way of knowing who has it.
Nearly half of the people officially living in Unamurra have a licence.
We've checked on each legal gun we could find in town and surround-
ing stations. Fifty-nine guns in total; nine of that calibre, but no
match. There might be one hidden, not registered, or it might be
someone who doesn't live there at all. Find me the gun, I'll match it.
But I doubt you'll ever find the gun. Needles, haystacks, et cetera,
right?'

'But you think there was a silencer?'

'Oh, for sure. Striations on both bullets say so. Probably a home-
made silencer, though, or maybe adapted. Not the markings of any I
can find in the database.'

Dana nodded. It struck her that the victims could have been murdered by a hidden shooter; they might never have seen their killer.
From behind a fence, for example, or undergrowth – if Unamurra had
any – or a room in a house. The silencer had been mentioned in the
crime report but buried in a longer, rambling paragraph. As though
the previous detectives didn't want to be seen to have missed it but
didn't want to draw attention to it, either. Most of the report had read
that way.

She pointed to the far bench. 'May I take some measurements,
please?'

Mangold frowned slightly, then shrugged and tossed over the steel
tape measure.

Dana nodded to Able, who joined her inside the freezer room. The
air felt not just cold but dry, fresh – clean. The mist was fully cleared
now, and she took a slow walk around the first victim, Larry Muir.
There was a small metal lip below his feet, his arches rested on it. If
there had been a horizontal metal bar at shoulder level, it would have

resembled nothing less than a crucifixion. That, she remembered, was part of the art's purpose: she'd read some snippets from Lucy's e-pack. From a distance the angels resembled Christ on the cross, but up close they did not. An accusation on *the modern tendency to deify the banal at a first and superficial glance*, according to DuBois' commentary on his own brilliance.

She took measurements from wrist binding to the base of the spine, and to the tether at the nape. She did so for both victims, while Able wordlessly held the tape as required. He watched her carefully, observing not only what she measured but how respectfully she approached the corpses, how she recorded the numbers, where she looked, and the fact that she touched nothing.

They stepped out of the freezer room. Mangold looked up from a booklet he wasn't reading. 'Care to clue us in, Detective?'

'Yes, yes, of course. I just need a calculator, please, if you have one.'

Mangold pulled one from the top drawer of his desk and, while Dana tapped buttons and chewed her lip, he raised an eyebrow. Able gave his catch-all grin, which might have meant anything from approval to resignation. Dana nodded at her own notes, then passed the calculator back to Mangold.

'Thank you. Sorry about that. It's not top secret, or anything. It's just when I do calculations, I zone out a little.'

'Calculations?' Mangold asked.

'I measured the distances between the three tether points of the wings: the triangle formed by the wrist, the base of the spine and the back of the neck. In the original Angels of Unamurra, those three distances make up a particular ratio, the golden ratio. Put simply, the two shorter distances should add up to the longer distance. The longest measure should be 1.6 times longer than the second longest, with the third longest making up the difference. Actually, 1.681, to be more precise.'

'Ookaay . . .' mused Able. 'And this matters because?'

'All the original angels have that same ratio; it's a ratio that crops up time and again in nature. You see it in the spirals of seashells and fossils, for example. It's also used in photography and painting. DuBois views it as a form of purity from God – a type of ideal – so it's in a lot of his work. It matters, at least to DuBois. And both these corpses have been staged with exactly that ratio.'

Mangold nodded. 'All right, but that would be luck, surely? Wouldn't it depend on the size of the corpses? Long arms or short body, tall or not, that sort of thing?'

'You would think so, yes. I did, before I saw them,' she lied. 'But, no, whoever staged these bodies adjusted them to create the exact ratio.' She pointed with her biro. 'For example, the binds are at the base of the thumb for Ogden, but up on the wrist for Muir. Also, because Muir is the taller, his arms are crooked at the elbow with a slightly greater angle. Both corpses have been adjusted so that the ratio holds.'

'What do we conclude from that?' asked Able. 'When I say "we", I mean you.'

'Hmmm. Well, before I saw the corpses, I'd have said the staging of the bodies was . . . not so much abstract, more rough and ready. Someone clearly didn't want to just hide the bodies out in the bush. That's a whole can of worms as to why not, of course. So, then their staging like this would be partly a matter of convenience. There were twenty-eight empty frames to hoist a body on to; if you wanted to flaunt it and didn't want to hide it, then those frames might seem fairly obvious locations.

'But now – with these ratios – I think it's slightly different. There seem to be two main options. One: that DuBois himself staged the bodies and can't resist using the golden ratio, or is unaware that he still defaults to it. Two: that someone wants to point the finger at DuBois and away from themselves. This kind of detail is the sort of thing

DuBois would do, so framing it with the ratio invites investigators to pursue him.'

Able glanced at Mangold and then back to Dana. 'You think DuBois is the murderer?'

'I suggested he may have staged the bodies, not necessarily that he did the killing. It's one option: it's viable because whoever put them on the frames used a key element of DuBois' artistic work around the world. That wasn't an accident. But it's just one option at this stage. At the least, we know the killer took DuBois' art seriously; maybe, precisely as seriously as he does.'

Able shook his head. 'Investigation didn't look into stuff like that.'

'It's not a criticism of those detectives, Able. There are a hundred and one aspects to look at, and this sort of thinking would be well down the list. That's what I'm here for: to come at things sideways so we can solve two murders. Isn't it?'

Neither replied; they looked to each other and back again. Dana noticed the beat that was skipped. 'Okay,' she rescued, 'I think I have enough for now. Thank you, Dr Mangold, for letting me see them. And for preserving them so well, I appreciate it.'

Mangold seemed surprised by Dana's offered hand, as though she was reaching from another era. 'No problem. Shout me if you need anything else, both of you. Oh,' he added, turning away as if ashamed to be relaying the message, 'just before you arrived, Judge Trent said he should see, and I quote, *whichever sticky-beak they've sent along.*'

'*Judge?*' asked Dana.

'Nickname for the big guy,' replied Able. 'I'll explain later.'

Mangold turned back and looked at Dana sympathetically. 'You'll love our boss just as much as we do, I'm sure.'

Chapter 3

Dana didn't want to embarrass Able by pumping him for information about the district commander, Leonard Trent. In situations like these, she'd learned, it was better to walk in without preconceptions. That way, her default of slightly naïve politeness was easier to project. So she trailed behind Able as they climbed the stairs, feeling the gradient in her plastic kneecap: she'd spent over an hour with it shoved against aircraft seating. Able knocked on the only mahogany door Dana had seen in the station. When a nondescript shout emerged, he opened the door and stood back.

'Detective Dana Russo from Carlton, Judge. Arrived just now. Taking her to Unamurra straight after.'

Dana noted the slight curve of Able's back as he introduced her, which hadn't materialized before. He spoke as though standing beneath a low ceiling and fascinated by the floor two metres ahead of him.

The office was dominated by the kind of large desk Dana associated with bank managers in the 1930s: fine workmanship and too heavy for three people to lift. One wall held certificates and photos to remind visitors of Trent's fine career, and therefore sense of worth. No ostentation, as such; but clumsily overt reminders of heft and authority. This was not an office where the incumbent ever heard his first name.

Trent was a tall, angular man with diagonal creases delineating a narrow mouth. His face looked *pulled down*; perhaps the legacy of a slight stroke. His hair was little more than a grey haze over his scalp. He sat back in a winged leather chair that was better suited to a gentleman's club in Melbourne or London. Behind him a four-panel window showcased Dutton's main street, which headed south in a blaze of dusted tarmac, chunky utes and the glint from metal roofs. Still no sign of trees.

'Russo. Hmm. Just you, then?'

It wasn't clear if Trent had been expecting more than one Carlton officer, or not. Dana had assumed he'd been informed that it was only her: he made it sound like a profound disappointment.

'Yes, Constable Barella and I at this point, sir.'

Trent didn't even glance at Able. 'Yeah, he's slightly better than Google Maps, I suppose.'

It always jarred with Dana when someone spoke about a person who was there as if they weren't.

'You'll probably know by now, Russo, but I'll reiterate it, in case you don't. We've already investigated both these crimes. Put two of my best on it. No lack of resources to back them up – you've seen we've got a pretty good forensics lab and an expert poached from City East. Despite the sneering from Central, we gave it a pretty good shot. People will feel patronized if you just cover the same ground twice. And they'll resent you behaving as if we're a bunch of bogans who couldn't find our arses with both hands, yeah?'

'Understood, sir.'

'What do you feel you'll be bringing to this investigation, Russo? Only your third murder, right?'

McCullough's metric. It was lost on Dana why some commanders counted the number of cases as an indicator of future quality. She'd seen experienced officers make basic errors and rookies have excellent insights, and vice versa. The two Dutton detectives who'd first investigated these murders had years under their belts but their efforts had been, in her opinion, perfunctory. Perhaps deliberately so. Trent had to comprehend this. She still didn't know for certain why McCullough had volunteered her. Except, most likely, the joy of seeing her face when he told her, the sublime satisfaction of imagining her various anxieties along the way, and the prospect of bathing in her subsequent failure. All within a few days.

'Constable Barella and I will both be new to most of the existing investigation. So, a fresh perspective, sir.'

Trent grunted and threw his pen on to the desk. It clattered against a glass tankard that had some sort of crest on it and currently held six biros, two highlighters and what looked like a Cuban cigar.

'Fresh perspective? Jesus. These murders are someone playing silly bastard, as I'm sure you've noted from the file. Don't be fooled by the decorations: killing is killing. Probably some idiot from away who's seen too many movies. I'll make sure you get any reasonable assistance, of course.'

Reasonable assistance meant next to none; she understood that.

'But as we found from the first investigation,' Trent barrelled on, 'there's so much space to bury useful evidence, so much time to escape or mess up the trail. Murders in this district only get solved if they're bloody obvious, or someone confesses. Otherwise they lay there for ever, unsolved.' He leaned forward slightly. 'They certainly don't get *investigated* to a conclusion. Ever. Right, Abe?'

There seemed some sort of blade behind the comment.

'Judge.' Able flinched, and didn't offer any eye contact. The reaction seemed to please Trent: he'd intended to wound, and he had.

Trent huffed, as if this was all too much effort. 'Apparently Central doesn't understand that fact, hence I lost one detective and another one had a tantrum. Hence . . . *you*. Does Carlton like being second-guessed, Russo?'

There it was: the bruised ego of a district commander being over-ruled. Dutton was likely to be Trent's last stop before retirement; these unsolved murders weren't damaging any future career, just tarnishing the present. That was sufficient, it seemed.

'No one likes a second-guess, sir. But that's not my understanding of why I'm here. If Central wanted that, they'd have sent someone from Ethical Standards. Sir.'

She'd now worked long enough in Carlton to understand both sides. On the one hand, Central needed results and were under con-stant state government pressure – rationalize, prioritize, sanitize. This manifested in a tendency by Central to use broad brush strokes, crude averages, and a premise that all regional and rural crime must be both rare and easy to solve. On the other hand, districts knew that any crime could be messy: they involved human beings, each more com-plex than any computer on earth, even when they were being an idiot.

Dana paused, in case Trent wished to object, but he sat impassively and watched her. Able shifted from heel to toe unobtrusively. 'As I understand it,' she continued, 'we have two unsolved murders and the two detectives assigned to them are unable to continue the investiga-tion. Hopefully Constable Barella's local knowledge and a new pair of eyes can help. Sir.'

Trent's eyes narrowed. 'All sounds very happy-clappy. I'm sure Unamurra doesn't get many people who talk like you. Got a suspect in mind yet?'

The question was odd: he had to know she'd seen neither of the crime scenes, nor talked to anyone in Unamurra. She wasn't sure there was a 'correct' answer to the query, just any number of poor ones.

'No, sir, I don't. I believe I was brought in to see the case from a fresh angle, so it would be counter-productive to have a favourite at the moment. Sir.'

Trent glared at her as though he were about to tee off, then seemed to think better of it. 'Ah, yes, I heard you were a stickler. Among other things. Though, if you're looking to save time and you really want to solve this, maybe you should look closer at this artist, DuBois.'

He pronounced it as *doo-boys*: she itched to correct him. 'From my reading of the previous investigations, DuBois had as firm an alibi as anyone and no motive. Sir.'

Trent grunted. Clearly he wasn't used to replies, let alone rebuttals. He glanced at Able, as if the constable should have trained Dana better before bringing her upstairs.

'We didn't get much chance to go hard at him before he disappeared, did we, Abe? Huh. Into the outback. Allegedly.'

'Allegedly, sir?' asked Dana.

'Yeah, well, no proof of that. Abe will tell you: since Frenchie went off in a huff, no one's seen or heard from him. He's from Quebec – he's hardly an expert in desert survival, is he? My guess would be that either he's died somewhere in the sand or someone's already offed him.' Trent looked past her shoulder and tutted. 'Don't give me some old crap about his stupid angels still moving around, Abe. For God's sake, no one has seen those things on the move, so anyone could have shifted them, eh? It's simple enough: kill Frenchie, then move the angels around a bit to fool *the gullible* that he's still with us. It's a theory to check out, Russo.'

'Yes, sir, I will.'

'Ever been to the outback, Russo?'

'No, sir, never.'

Trent paused and clucked his tongue against the roof of his mouth, as though Dana's travel history were one more insult. 'Oh, great, you'll be *exactly* what we need, then. It's another world out there. I haven't heard from your commander that you're one of life's great adapters.'

'We'll do everything we can, sir.'

It was the only thing Dana could think to say; Trent clearly wasn't going to admit to any deficiencies in the previous investigations, nor address any allegations of corruption. She hadn't expected hype about her work from McCullough, so that was no loss; all the same, it implied something about the politics of these cases that Trent had still accepted the offer of Dana's assistance. Perhaps Dutton were desperate to solve the murders and would take anybody, and hence take Dana. Or, more likely, she was here as a useful idiot, to stand atop what was already buried.

'Yeah, sure. Just remember, Russo, we have to police here long after you've swanned off to Carlton. So don't go trampling around annoying people. Type up your *fresh perspective* when you have it and send it here before your flight home. Clear?'

They both muttered at the same time: it came out as *sirJudge*.

'Righty-ho. Bugger off, then.'

As Able closed the door behind them, he gave his now-customary grin. Dana was admiring it more and more. There seemed to be nothing Able couldn't convey with it.

In their silence, the squeak of shoe on concrete stairs resonated. Dana didn't wish to tackle Able about Trent until she had a little distance and a chance to collect herself. It occurred to her that Able hadn't acquired a lot of allies along the way. He'd been marginalized from the two murder investigations on his own patch and now Trent appeared reluctant to back him in any way. Maybe both judgements on him were incorrect, errors of ignorance or personality clash. Possibly, Able simply had limited networks because he spent half his time beyond the outback – in the *outer-back* – and not schmoozing in stations and offices. Or perhaps both treatments of Able were silent warnings to Dana not to regard him as a partner, but instead as a resource to be tapped, then weighed and held at arm's length.

Before they reached the ground floor a door hinge complained and a voice resonated through the stairwell.

'Abe?'

They both looked up, Able with a slight sigh of resignation. Leaning over the bannister like a delinquent on a freeway bridge, a squat officer with heavy-set jowls looked down. His voice had a strange catch to it, as if permanently trying to loosen a lunchtime crumb.

'This the detective?' His voice echoed.

Ask her, thought Dana, *instead of talking around her*.

'Yeah, sir. Dana Russo, from Carlton.'

'Okay. A word.' He indicated his office with a jerk of the head. 'Not you Abe, just her.' The warning stalled Able mid-step and he shrank slightly as he went back to the half-landing. Dana swallowed and climbed the stairs, her kneecap grinding. The officer had already disappeared, assuming she would follow.

There were no introductions. She had no idea who this person was – there was no name plate on the office door – or his rank. In smaller stations she found officers were so used to knowing each other, and various members of the public, that they sometimes forgot the introductions. But others used it deliberately as a powerplay – so important, they don't need to explain who or what.

The office was a mess: files piled high and papers leeching from them. Two elderly swivel chairs were simply there to hold more files and block access to a whiteboard filled with what appeared adolescent scrawl. A computer monitor sat atop yet more paperwork. It all gave the impression of being very busy, constantly swamped – or presenteeism rather than performance. She glanced at the waste bin – a sausage roll wrapper and three empty Coke cans: junk food for someone manifesting maximum busyness.

'Close the door. Ta. You're on these two Unamurra murders, yeah?' His eyes were grey and heavy-lidded; his skin had never recovered from adolescent pitted acne.

'That's right, sir.'

Dana now noticed among the detritus a perfectly curated orchid on a shelf and a framed sketch of a finch on the wall. His family photo – a wife and three children at a theme park – faced outwards, towards the visitor, like a challenge. Or a justification.

He ran his tongue around his jaw, contemplating. 'Hmm. Read both the files yet?'

'Yes, sir, I have.'

Another pause, as if weighing up how much she could be trusted, or how easily she could be fooled. Ironic, she thought. That should be her call about him.

'Good. Then you know the standard of investigation that was accepted at the time.'

'Yes, sir.'

Dana's deadpan responses were giving him nothing. Although, if he was smart enough to pick up on it, they *were* telling him something: that she was savvy about keeping her cards close to her chest and taking all information offered as conditional.

'All right. I saw you going into Judge's office. Carlton tells me you're highly capable, but there's crap going on that you're not party to, and never will be. Hmm.'

He must have spoken to Mikey, she thought. McCullough would not use that descriptor of her.

He looked out of the window, as if the blinding light would guide him. His workspace endured the afternoon sun, but he seemed to have no problem with it; the window had no shutters or coverings. The sun bleached his view of the computer screen every day and this added to her perception that he was rarely here, so not as put-upon as he liked to advertise.

She'd assumed the undetected murders would have marked Dutton station in some way, especially those who'd worked directly on the cases. An unsolved double murder in Carlton would linger in the officers' minds, almost a sense of shame rather than regret. It would weigh down the air. But in Dutton, the scars were different. The two murders weren't burdens in the same way, instead, they were markers of how far the station and its culture had come. Or not. The cases, and their open status, implied who was winning in a power struggle.

'Word of friendly advice, Detective?' He said it to the window and missed her slight nod. 'Judge wants these murders unsolved – wants them *unsolvable*.' He turned back to her and tapped on a maroon diary for emphasis. 'It would suit him if you couldn't get further than his own people did. Your performance is a direct commentary on his – see what I mean? You're up means he's down. You're in means he's out. And so on. He won't lift a finger to help you. Nor will most of Una-murra, for that matter. Lots of motive behind that.'

He shook his head as he said it. Dana tried not to let her shudder through – why would a whole town not want their murders solved? And the atmosphere here at Dutton: it was reasonable to expect some professional resentment for having a go at crimes their colleagues hadn't solved – she'd anticipated that. But this station's unwillingness, this . . . *ennui* about the whole thing, it was more than mere pride. She was still missing some big picture here, and no one was prepared to show it to her.

'The reason Abe isn't in here with us, Detective? It's not because I'm a bastard. Abe's a decent officer, a decent person. Knows his community, I can't fault that. But . . . well, things aren't always clear cut, know what I mean? So whatever you were intending to do on this case, Detective, just do it yourself. Don't count on anything or anyone and don't be embarrassed if you get nowhere. It's pretty tough to solve after this time, to be honest. I mean, no weapon, no motive, no alibis, no witnesses and enough time for the murderer to go off anywhere in the world. Not good, is it?'

They both let the rhetorical question linger in the air. He seemed to be building up to something, while simultaneously trying to appear distracted and barely interested. He paused, carefully weighing his next statement, glancing up at her as he did so.

'It's like that test in *Star Trek*, that thingie . . .' He waved his hand, as though that always improved his memory.

'The Kobayashi Maru,' offered Dana.

A slowly raised eyebrow that seemed like forced surprise. 'Yeah, exactly like that. *Your* investigation is also a no-win scenario. Treat all this like a character test, a tabletop exercise. Got it?'

He held her gaze and she waited a beat to show him she took it seriously. 'I understand, yes.'

'I hope you do, for everyone's sake. I won't lie to you, we've handed you a can of worms. There's stuff here that's way above your pay grade. We've kept a bit of a lid on these murders as far as the media is concerned – to be honest, city journalists can't be arsed to do any more than phone us occasionally – but we can't afford to have it blow up into something bigger. That is not in anyone's interests, all right? So, gently does it. Don't go in waving a big stick and don't make a fuss if you can't get it done. In terms of your career, Detective, this is a box tick that says you took part. It's not a bloody crusade, eh? Good.'

He looked around the desk, as though an end to the conversation would magically materialize, then patted his breast pocket like a smoker. When he spoke again, he didn't look up.

'There you go then, I've done my civic duty. That's it, mate, that's your lot. Leave the door open, eh?'

Chapter 4

Once they were on the ground floor, Dana turned to Able.

'Who was that I just met, Able? He didn't introduce himself.'

Able held a door open for her. 'Ah, yeah, he does that. Graeme. Inspector Graeme Cronin. Been here since year dot. Judge is always trying to retire him, but he keeps getting another fixed-term contract, and another. Has a lot of mates in Central. That's why they're on separate floors. Judge can't stand him.'

'Hmm. I see.'

That fitted. And not just Cronin's mixed messages and need to personally tell Dana the lie of the land. No, the whole thing: this was a station riven by a power struggle. People constantly choosing sides, or having to appear to choose. Everything seen through the same lens of *my way or his way*; a fight for resources and kudos; wasted effort undermining the other. She'd seen it in Central departments sometimes, but it seemed more egregious at a district command. There was no way for anyone working here to avoid it: they would be political activists and card-carrying members whenever they were here. Perhaps another reason for Able to be rarely in station.

'Did he say anything useful?'

Able didn't appear to be fishing, but that could have been his open features. His face said he was incapable of guile and simply asked honest questions. But Cronin's warnings – that even *he* couldn't tell which side Able was on, and that there were definitely two sides to choose from – had wormed their way into her thinking.

'Not really. I didn't get the impression that he was bowled over by the standard of the first investigation. But I wasn't convinced he was enthusiastic about our chances either.'

Able nodded, as though he heard that kind of appraisal regularly. Dana felt the need to drag the conversation back to Trent. 'Your big boss went to the same charm school as mine. They should both get a refund. I can see why he and McCullough get along. So, he's called Judge?'

'Yeah, yeah. I don't know who started that. Everyone's called him Judge for as long as I've been here. He thinks it's because he's the big man in town – you know, the face of the law, more than his job? Actually, as you've just found, it's because he makes snap judgements about people, then holds to them for ever.'

The acidity of Trent's remark about unsolved murders floated past her. Some damaging history between him and Able? No, she thought, not quite. There was something malicious behind Trent mentioning it, but it was more oblique. One particular case, perhaps.

Dana nodded. 'So he won't change his mind and send me a card and flowers at Christmas?'

Able gifted her that dazzling smile. 'Aah, nah. Nah. Don't wait by the mail box, anyway.'

They collected Dana's suitcase. O'Brien had made himself scarce when he saw them approaching.

'I upset Dr Mangold earlier, didn't I?' asked Dana.

Able chuckled and held another door as they moved out into sunshine. 'God, no. Almost the opposite. Look, Doc Mangold used to be top notch; deputy head of Forensics up in the city, bit of a star.

Brought down by some scandal. Two married people who weren't married to each other, plus one hot tub. Not quite chased out of town with a shotgun, but not far off. Transferred big-style and hunkered down. What I'm saying is, he has skills he doesn't need here, doesn't get asked to use. The Judge treats him as a smart-arse nuisance and he plays up to that, I reckon. No, I think you arriving just made him raise his game, and now you've caught him off guard. He'll like it. Don't be surprised if he burns the midnight oil and comes up with something else tomorrow.'

They stopped to allow a patrol car to reverse. The driver tipped a greeting in Able's direction as he passed. The sun was strong and direct here, much warmer than earlier because the motor court was sheltered. The revving of an impact wrench punched through the relative calm.

'Neither of the detectives who investigated this are here now?' asked Dana.

'That's right. Andrew Carver left on medical six days ago, now fishing somewhere in the Top End. Jason Milford – he was lead detective – well . . .'

The report had been mercifully brief, yet precise: Milford's shadow launching sickening loops over his kids' bikes.

'Yes, I'm sorry. That was awful.'

'Yeah, yeah it was. And, of course, left a big bloody cloud over the investigation. Some of the stick we're getting today from the top floors? Because of that – because we remind them of that. People here make up their own pictures of Jase. We're helping them to do it. But hey, if not for that investigation, you wouldn't have had the pleasure of meeting me, eh?'

Able was parked out on the street in a bug-spattered Landcruiser which was, she noted, a diesel. She guessed Able didn't chase anyone as such but racked up the mileage ploughing between Unamurra and

Dutton and further out into the bush. Diesel made sense. The car was ostensibly white but mainly dusty orange. The luggage area was filled with survival gear – water, some maritime flares, food, radio equipment. The roof rack held spare canisters of fuel, ropes, a run of chain and what looked like some kind of packed tent.

The car was tidy enough inside, and it came to Dana as she sat that Able might have cleaned it up, hoping to give a good impression. Able opened up the armrest and offered a bottle of cold water; the centre console was insulated and chilled. The view ahead was bordered by an old-fashioned strip of blue tint at the top of the windscreen; a Chinese Lucky Cat gave frictionless greetings from the top of the dashboard. Headroom was mighty – Able could have driven with his hat on.

'Do you think your Judge actually wants these murders solved?' she asked. The question was sparse and polite but shimmered with meaning. She wanted to know, for starters, if Able and Cronin were of the same mind. Able started the engine, then puffed his cheeks, his default reaction whenever the grin was resting.

'Dunno. That would be my honest answer. We get three or four murders a year in Dutton district, average. As Judge said, most get solved because they confess: bloke walks into a pub and says he shot his mate, that sort of thing. Or, given the population density, it can only be one of three or four people and the guilty one folds early on. Maybe Judge wants them solved because he wants them off his books, and Central off his back.' They swung out into the street, looking to turn right, and waited for a delivery truck to pass. 'On the other hand, smart money says Judge wants you to do the minimum and go away. 'Course, that would boost him: *See, these murders really are impossible to solve, so we're not just a bunch of idiots out here after all.* Your failure would make everyone else's look reasonable, wouldn't it?'

Dana took that in, along with the insinuation that drifted around the car.

'Whereas,' he continued, 'if you solve them, does it make us look like morons? Does it make him look a bad commander? I mean, he hand-picked two detectives and they got nowhere, then a fresh face out of Carlton solves it in days. Judge can't come out of that well, can he? Would that encourage Central to chuck people at us every time they think we're bogged down? Like Judge said, no one likes being second-guessed. So, as I said – dunno.'

'What about you, Able?'

Most officers would have baulked at the question: the implication that a police officer might accept unsolved murders on their piece of earth. Able seemed to view it as a necessary line of inquiry.

'Me? Two people I knew and cared about were killed. On my patch. If you solve it, I probably look a dick to everyone, since I'm supposed to be the local law. On the other hand, I have no career as such, I have a job. Like Judge quickly noticed, I'm pretty average away from my home paddock – not motivated, really. I stand out because I'm clearly not where I want to be. Luckily, no one's itching to take my beat. It's handy for Judge – and for me – if I stay in Una-murra, so I doubt I'd be moved if they thought I'd dropped the lollies on these murders. But yeah, I just want them solved anyhow, by any-one, thanks.'

Dana nodded. Able had *forgotten* to mention that he hadn't been invited to participate in investigating two murders on his own ground. In fact, he'd been deliberately excluded. She'd have to tackle that potential issue, but not yet. It might indicate he was on the take and the two detectives felt his involvement would warp or derail their efforts. Alternatively, it might be the opposite; he would be by-the-book and wouldn't cooperate with their shortcuts and omissions. Perhaps, given that they had no strong suspects, they'd even wondered if Able was involved in some way. At the very least, she thought, detec-tives from Dutton should have wanted to tap Able's knowledge and contacts, his ability to smooth down the ripples caused by the investigation. They hadn't, and there was a reason for that.

Dutton existed by supplying a huge but sparse area with the essentials and limited public services, and from hosting the abattoir. The latter was working part-time through the drought, the company redistributing staff elsewhere in the state if they wanted to keep a job. It dragged the town like a chain, when it used to be an economic engine. The council had pasted murals in all the empty shop windows to fool a quick glance.

Able eased them slowly towards the edge of town through broad streets built wide enough to turn a wagon train and now split by rows of palm trees. These had desiccated in years of feeble rain, dropping shrivelled brown fronds, and now bristled in a chilly westerly that skimmed the roof of the car. The bowling green of artificial turf, the school playground, the empty skateboard park, all rested under giant, rippling shade sails spattered by bird droppings. Water was too scarce to waste on cleaning them. Not just because it was, but because the optics of spraying precious water to clean a sail would be political suicide. Out past a servo with stupefyingly high bowser prices and a closed car wash, left at a roundabout that someone had recently ploughed across, and away past a sign that said Unamurra was 189 kilometres away. No town or landmark was indicated beyond that.

Within five kilometres they'd shed most signs of eucalypt, mulga or any other foliage. The road held periodic tyre marks – nocturnal doughnuts made by bored teenagers to impress each other. What houses existed were set way back from the road; approached by a ribbon of powdery ochre, bookended by rusting water tanks and deliberately built up on earth mounds, huddled beneath the few trees that could be reared by artesian pumps. Occasionally a desert oak clung tenaciously in the middle of a paddock, tilting itself away from the prevailing wind. Any grass had been seared and baked long ago and might as well have been plastic. Barbed-wire fences had sagged from lack of maintenance, troughs rusted and listed. Everything had a grim air of hanging on. It was farming by fingernail.

Able tapped out a stick of gum and popped it, offering the pack to Dana.

'No, thanks. Takes about two hours to town?'

Able nodded and grunted. 'As long as we don't hit a camel, yeah.'

'More likely than kangaroos, then?' She glanced across. 'Or cows?'

'Ha. Camels – millions of the buggers around here. They have more road sense than 'roos, but they're a hefty strike, that's for sure. Plus, they act like they own the place, like you wouldn't dare. So, what do you need to know, Dana? What can I tell you about Unamurra?'

Dana already had a headful of stats and data from Lucy, including the current file on both murders, but this wasn't really about gaining information. 'Hmm. Let's start with the basics. Population eightyish?'

'Officially, eighty-two. Which I thought was why there were twenty-eight angels, to be honest. Reverse the numbers, yeah? But really, maybe fifty.' Able paused as he scrunched the gum wrapper, then scratched his calf muscle. 'We've got about a dozen working away on farms interstate; some others have taken fly-in fly-out mining jobs. FIFO's the only way they can make a real buck at the moment. We see those three or four times a year. Five school-age kids, but they're away at private school; you won't see them. Then there's the usual turnover: people away visiting rellies, or sick in hospital, or dying in a hospice somewhere.'

Like any community, thought Dana, when things slide this far. Those that could go elsewhere did so, even if they meant to return. But there was a vicious slope. Once robbed of the young and talented and a critical mass of bodies, the place could never regain its footing.

'You're not a healthy bunch, then?'

'Ah, nah, we're not. If we catch something, we generally just plough on and see if it drops us. Yeah, plus, we have a limited diet, but plenty of booze. No actual alkies, I'd say, but a few coming up on the rails: Annie has to watch 'em. Pub's the biggest thing in town, you'll see.'

She'd taken a virtual skid through Unamurra online while waiting for the Dutton flight to board. Viewing the entire town hadn't taken long. Two skinny verandas' worth of main street; empty and abandoned versions of bank, butcher, pharmacy and bakery, now all residential; five off-streets of sun-smashed one-storeys running for the horizon; a water tower pock-marked by BB pellets; a store that also sold petrol; and the pub. All in razor-sharp focus. Strong light and deep darkness went side by side in Unamurra.

'Any internet?' She already knew the answer.

'Yeah, good luck.' He shook his head. 'It's supposed to come from a satellite. But, I mean, us and every other remote community's chasing that one satellite, mainly at the same time. You might download a photo. Or, if it's a bad night, you might not. Most people don't bother.'

Dana had already factored that in. She'd planned the logistics while she prepped back in Carlton. Lucy knew to mainly text and not to bother with graphics or video footage. Able tried to atone for the internet. 'We've got mobile phone, though. As long as you speak or text and don't stray from town – two kilometres and you're done. Whatever generation of mobile it is for data, we're about three behind that. The town name, Unamurra, it's an old indigenous word.' He lowered the volume. 'Means *place that needs faster broadband.*'

Dana laughed and leaned back again. 'For half a second, I looked like I was about to believe you, didn't I?'

Able grinned. 'Walked right into it, yeah. Nah, no one really knows what it means. Probably several words that got jumbled, way back when. Most names around here are like the rest of Australia – stupidly literal. That dip over there? Deadman's Creek. Guess why.'

'Going out on a crazy limb, it's a sometimes-creek where a man died?'

'Bingo. I mean, Australia has mountains of snow we call the *Snowy Mountains*. A beach that's ninety miles long? That'll be *Ninety Mile Beach*, then. A big desert full of sand can't be anything but the *Great Sandy Desert*, can it? Jeez. I'm just amazed Unamurra isn't named *Human Settlement*.' He squinted and took a long look in the rear-view mirror. 'What else can I tell you? Apart from me, the only public service is Nonnie Scott, who's technically a nurse.'

'All right, I'll bite. Technically?'

'Hmm. Well, the Medevac helicopter's in the city – too far away for us. It's ninety minutes – *minimum* – for the nearest ambulance to reach us from Dutton, so the health department tried to persuade someone with nursing skills to live here. Nah. No-go. They won't come. So we have Nonnie, who *was* a nurse. Got barred for malpractice – drunk on duty. Then the ban got magically lifted, for as long as she stays in Unamurra. If she tries to get into Dutton Hospital, she's struck off again. They pay her as if she works five hours a week, which keeps her as *relaxed* as she likes. But she's really emergencies only, for everyone's sake. Town gets someone with some clue, which can be handy. Accidents and the like.' He paused and rubbed a three-day growth. 'She can't prescribe, except for herself.'

Dana took that in for a moment. 'She'd be the local drug dealer, then?'

Able gave her a sidelong look. 'Interesting thought. Because?'

'Because it would be very difficult for an out-of-towner to do it. They'd visit occasionally and you'd notice the spike in activity. It would be everyone's business in a heartbeat. You don't get enough visitors for strangers to blend in and besides, there aren't enough locals for a viable market to attract an outsider. Plus, your Nonnie might be thought to have potential access to certain legal drugs – diazepam, opioids, and so on. And maybe some old blank prescriptions she could use for barter.'

Able smiled and nodded. 'Yeah, spot on. I keep a bit of a lid on it, and we've had some, uh, conversations about where the limits have to be. Kids – on the rare occasions they're in town – the harder stuff; that kind of thing. She mostly deals in pick-me-ups for truckies, I think. Not that that isn't dangerous, I get that. But I haven't bothered to work out how she's doing it, to be honest. Some kind of drop point off the highway, I'd guess.'

Of course, thought Dana. If he ran Nonnie in for the drugs, the town would have no one with medical training. Anyone with something serious and sudden could die, partly because Able had wanted to beef up his monthly statistics. Policing discretion was always about trade-offs, but out here the calculation was on a whole different scale. Able clearly understood how to play a longer, wider game.

The geography was unyielding. A horizon that ran flat and true; nothing taller than a dog, occasional dips in the ground as though the earth had given up. If she looked closely she could see alarming craters, places you could hide a bus. From inside the car it all looked hot, because it was so dry. But the brain was fooled. The day was chilly and might drop below zero tonight. Drought meant simply a lack of rain; it didn't automatically come with raging heat. They hadn't seen any livestock in twenty minutes. The road was like a bullet's trail.

Dana leaned over slightly towards the centre console. 'The satnav says straight on here,' she said, grinning.

Able chuckled. 'It would. What about now?'

'Straight on.'

'Now?'

'Straight on.'

'Now?'

'Wait a min—no, straight on.'

They both laughed.

'So how long have you been here, Able?'

'In Unamurra? Uh, well, born here. Grew up here. Dad was the town mechanic, back when we had one: all Swarfega and sweat, he was. I had a spell in the city – hated it. Been posted here eight years. No one else wants to come. We're not quaint enough to balance out all the crap. I don't just do Unamurra – got a whole sweep of back country to my name as well. Twenty-six stations – nine cattle, twelve sheep, five mixed. Area the size of Belgium, so they always say. But with more flies.' He glanced to the mirror again. 'Oh, hang on, I'm just pulling over, let this B-dub past.'

All Dana saw in the wing mirror was an approaching maelstrom of blood-orange agitation. She couldn't see the B-double road train until she got a sunlit flash from the chrome grille. This far away, it was silent. Many trucks were doubles but, out here, they often hauled triples. Like three full-to-bursting buses chained together, barely contained mass and momentum on a road hardly wide enough for a car. Dust reared and twisted behind it as it approached. Able got about thirty metres off the tarmac and waited.

'Do you get many?'

'One or two a day at most now, more when it's a wet year, but. As you know, that doesn't happen any more. This highway cuts off a corner for 'em, but the traffic's still limited. Especially when the livestock's not moving.'

Now the truck's image loomed larger and their wing mirror began to shake slightly.

'Jeez, he's travelling.'

'Yeah, they've got electronic limiters to restrict the speed, but there used to be ways and means, so they tell me. Not so much now they rely on satnav – spy in the cab, and all that. Truck like that sits on cruise control for hours at a time if it can.'

'Can they make a living?'

Able shifted in his seat to get a better view. 'Well, every time he changes gear, it costs him money. Every time, up or down. Or her, excuse me. If they have to really slam on the brakes at any point: hmm, they just lost the entire profit for the trip. Flat-spots the tyres, see; have to replace some or all – and there might be thirty-six, forty of them. So then they've driven four days and nights for absolutely nothing. Most of them scrape by, really, but they'd never want to do anything else. Best thing to do is pull over, let 'em get on with it.'

The truck was screaming and hammering past the point where they'd left the tarmac. The driver gave a blast on the horn, by way of thanks. It disappeared ahead of them, swallowed by the vortex it had created, hurtling beyond a cloud of its own making. As Able waited for the dust to subside they shared swigs from a water bottle. He spat the gum into a tissue and pushed it into the door pocket, where it snuggled with the rest.

Back on track, the tarmac suddenly halved. No longer wide enough for two cars to pass, it shrank to a thin strip of bitumen down the centre of the road, bordered by creeping sand that swayed in winds and backdraughts like a shallow tide. They could see the tracks made by the B-Double, too wide to hit anything but dirt.

Dana's eye was drawn by a flash of dark blue. 'Is that a car over there?'

The carcass was nose-down into a shallow crack in the earth; the rear end was airborne, as if the wheels might still be spinning and the driver crawling away, bloodied and concussed. The temperature in the Landcruiser dipped noticeably.

'Yeah, was. So yeah, that Falcon just pulls off the highway one day, plugs in the dirt; driver walks off into the wilderness. Never found him. That was, uh, seven years ago last month.'

Apart from the deflated tyres, it looked almost driveable. The chrome still gleamed, the paint remained solid beneath accumulated dust. Able shook his head, suddenly wearied. 'Things last for ever out here. It's a bloody curse.' A pause. 'Except for people, of course. They don't last long enough.'

Dana let him sit with that thought. He rested his wrists on the top of the steering wheel, rubbing his ring finger. The car's engine mumbled and the plumes from the B-double faded. A fillet of cloud was starting to rise in the west.

Dana looked out of the window while she gifted Able as much space as the car would allow. The landscape made it so easy to hide a body, she thought; gullies and overhangs and holes in the rock, and vast tracts where no human would ever tread. So why put those two bodies in plain sight? And why dress the scene – why make them angels?

Able kept his eyes rooted to the road. After forty minutes he finally eased back and relaxed. He nodded, his voice barely audible above her silence.

'Thanks, Dana.'

They trundled on through occasional whirls of dust as the wind picked up. Only now did Dana notice the puffs coming through the air vents. She realized that by the time she got to Unamurra she'd probably be coughing. The land seeped in everywhere, clawing back, undermining. It seemed to her that it wanted the people gone. She could already picture her limited time being chewed up by the vastness and the hours it took to cover it.

'Do you have a theory, Able? About the murders?'

Able looked dubious. 'To be honest, I don't have a clue right now. Had a favourite suspect for a few weeks, but that's gone down the toilet and, anyway, I had no real evidence. Look, I worked a few murders when I was in the city. They were easy. Simple, almost. Judge says most of them are obvious out here, but the same's true in the city, really. Bloke dies, and you find he was a drug dealer. Well, duh: it was a competitor. Woman dies, in her own house. Well, duh: it was her partner. And so on – easy as. But these?' He shrugged and re-gripped the steering wheel. 'I'm not seeing the motive, that's one issue. I mean, there's a few spats over sport or politics in the pub, sure, but Annie puts them on zero rations for a week and they come back with their tail between their legs. So I can't see an argument getting out of control, not that way. Has to be something different to motivate a killer, but I'm stuck for seeing it.'

'Relationships? I see there are roughly three men to every woman, as a ratio.'

Able rubbed his stubbled jaw and the scraping sound set Dana's teeth on edge. 'Yeah, that's a bit misleading. Makes Unamurra sound like a town it isn't. Most of the blokes here are old and past it, pretty much gave up on that long ago. In fact, I suspect some moved here for that reason. Life with us just doesn't revolve around romance or sex. Anyway, Tim was married to Annie; Larry to Sarah. Even so, it might be a possible for one murder, I'll grant you, but not for two. If you killed the guy who was moving in on your wife, there's no need to double-down with a second one, eh? And it's unlikely you'd dress the corpse like an angel and parade it. Nah, what you'd do is, you'd *disappear* the guy in the night. Everyone would think he's shot through and he's on a beach someplace, or he wandered into the desert. So, crime of passion? Nah, it doesn't have that feel, does it?'

No, she thought, it did not.

'It could be anyone in town, for any reason,' continued Able. 'All the bets are off out here. The scale's different, see? I mean, you can wind someone up in a city but never see them again. Do that here, they're in the same pub, the same shop, the same street, every bloody day. You can't miss 'em. Insults, imagined insults, problems, misunderstandings . . .'

'Everything in Unamurra gets magnified by the isolation.'

'Exactly. Yeah, exactly. So we've got fifty-odd suspects, assuming we disregard anyone coming through.'

There was often a tendency in small communities to regard *trouble* as the outside pushing in, not the inside pushing out. It wasn't xenophobia, Dana felt, more that local people believed they knew and understood their community and the crime simply jarred with that perception.

'Should we? Disregard them, I mean?'

Able peeled another piece of gum with one hand and popped it. 'The locals often say the killer must be a drive-through. Mainly because that's less scary than the idea that it's one of us. Less likely there'd be a third killing, as well. But no one remembered hearing an engine around those places at the right times. And they might hear it – sound really carries out here.'

She could imagine. Engine noise would skim this flat, stark surface like bird-cry on a lake.

'Plus,' continued Able, 'I've already researched the trucking companies. No one was hauling near Unamurra on both occasions. Once, maybe, on the right day for Larry Muir at least, but not twice. We don't have an accurate time of death for either body, I know, but all the same. Trucks' satnavs say none of 'em have actually stopped in town for over three years – just rumbled through each time. So yeah, I'm ruling out a team of truckies who can fool their navigation system, commit one murder, then alibi out for the other murder. Almost no one else comes here, Dutton police included.' He shook his head ruefully. 'Much as it worries the locals, it's most likely one of us, for sure.'

Dana turned back to the scenery. She felt almost obliged to go along with that thinking, because if the killer was from out of town then she had literally no hope of finding them. A stranger sneaks in under darkness, headlights off and purring on near-idle. The stranger kills, stages the corpse, then either goes straight back towards Dutton or drives further, deeper into the wilderness. That stranger would now be long gone. In the period since the most recent killing they could have driven to any corner of the entire continent, with nothing currently connecting them to the town, let alone a murder.

No, she had to rely on the killer not only being *from* Unamurra but *in* Unamurra. Right now. Waiting, watching, hoping Dana wouldn't get any closer than the previous investigation.

'One odd thing that struck me,' she said, 'and I don't think the previous investigation covered it properly. In the twenty-four hours before Tim Ogden's body was discovered, no one reported him missing. Did he often go AWOL for that long?'

'Ah, yeah. Well. The day before, that was Annie's busiest day of the month. They get a food delivery every morning and dairy every few days, but once a month they get all the other stuff: the bleach, the toilet rolls, the notebooks, garbage bags – all the non-foodie stuff arrives on the one truck. Big day of inventory, pricing goods, checking, putting on shelves and all that. Means she wasn't giving Tim's whereabouts her full attention. She closed up the pub last thing, too, so it was an eighteen-hour day for her. I guess she was just knackered. Tim had that day off because he'd worked six in a row before that. Apparently, when he's on a free day he has a good old lie-in, then potters about the apartment playing video games and so on. Not unusual for him to be invisible on his day off.'

Dana could just about picture that, although it still seemed odd. Some couples simply operated that way; they orbited tangentially, coming into contact for periods but out of range at other times. 'Okay . . . but at the end of that day?'

'Yeah, I don't know if they asked her. Annie doesn't respond well to delicate questions, but if they did ask it was off the clock and off the record. So maybe Tim and Annie have separate bedrooms in that apartment? Never met anyone who's been allowed in there, so I couldn't say. Lots of couples do that, though, especially when each half of the couple works shifts. So maybe she just crashed out exhausted and assumed he was in the other room.'

Alternatively, thought Dana, Tim may have been at someone else's house. And maybe the someone had good reason not to volunteer that information.

'What Judge Trent said – about Axel DuBois. How do you see that, Able?'

'Axel? Yeah. I think that might be a case of just blaming the stranger in town. Judge wouldn't know up from down in Unamurra. As far as I know he's never been here in his life. There was talk that the investigation should have looked harder at Frenchie – each body was on one of his frames, and each body was set up to look like one of his angels. Hard to say what the detectives were thinking, but the case file barely mentions him and some of the data about him is . . . well, not quite hidden, but takes a bit of finding. Personally? Nah, I don't think so. Bloke has a big ego, that's true; but killing two people and then pointing the finger at himself doesn't seem likely.'

Although, thought Dana, it would be a very good double bluff. It seemed so implausible, as Able had just said, that it would be highly effective. 'Able, in town, how many people have a car? Or access to a car?' She framed it that way in case people shared. They might need a car only intermittently.

'Well, now.' He paused while he added in his head. 'Four cars. Annie and Tim had one each, doubled up as delivery for the shop. So . . . five, if you include this one. But that doesn't count the farmers. They might have two or three vehicles of various kinds on their station, more, some of 'em. Remember, their station might be a day's drive from Unamurra. But in town? Yeah, four. 'Course, you might borrow one of those for a day, so *access* is a slightly elastic thing, I suppose. In

Dutton, our boys and girls don't really get agitated if you're driving an Unamurra car, but you don't own it, as long as you're a local. They get it, see – out here, police discretion works a bit differently than in the city. That car might be the only way someone can get to hospital, or see a dying rellie, or whatever. Can't be too tightly wound about stuff like that. Not here.'

Dana chewed on that. In a place as isolated as Unamurra, it really mattered who had mobility. Not just to get to Dutton or further afield, but simply to get far enough into the bush to dump a gun or any other forensic evidence. In practical terms, merely walking a kilometre into the desert at night would permanently hide it. But this wasn't about practicality. Out here, it was all psychology. Unless they had a socio-pathic absence of nerves, having the gun in question just a few minutes' walk away would still leave the killer jittery. It was irrational, but the fear of exposure would linger. Whereas if they'd driven fifty kilo-metres and buried it away from the road without being seen, they would be much calmer.

Unamurra didn't run on oil, iron ore, bauxite or even cattle. Una-murra would run on a unique psychology of living there. That, Dana felt, would be the key.

'So how do *you* see the case? Now you've had a taster of our beauti-ful country?' Able raised an eyebrow as he asked.

Dana considered for a moment. She'd been able to glean very little before she left Carlton about accusations of corruption in the Dutton district. Maybe Lucy would have more when she got back into tele-phone range. Ever since Dana had joined the force there had been chatter about Dutton: cosy relationships with politicians, blind eyes for the errant teenagers of local worthies, brown paper bags and dipping hands. It was almost a byword for a stereotype of sleazy, nudge-and-wink, bumbling rural policing long on mateship and short on professional integrity.

But proof to back up the claims was practically non-existent. There had been no major case that she could recall. Many seemed to take the view that Dutton must be corrupt because it was small. Isolated rural areas were assumed to be tainted by low-level mischief because, in urban eyes, *everyone knew each other's business*. Just like any rural murder, to any briefly visiting journalist, automatically made such a town *a community united in grief*. Much of the corruption innuendo appeared merely snobbery from Central, part of a wider trend of urban sneering towards regions. It was always easy to throw vague accusations about people outside the city from the comfort of the city; a lot harder to provide verifiable evidence.

All the same, Mike had suggested before she left that, on this occasion, there *was* considerable room for doubt. The murder investigations were demonstrably sloppy, not just in the actions and conclusions of the detectives but through feeble oversight. It was hard to escape the notion that at least some of that was deliberate. Perhaps the shortcomings didn't extend further than Unamurra's failure to cooperate and the detectives had simply recognized a brick wall when they ran into it. Maybe omissions were a tacit admission that they'd handled it badly. Possibly not. Either way, at this point Dana couldn't decipher who she should trust and who she shouldn't. However, she'd decided on the flight that she ought to at least try trusting Able Barella. Without his active assistance the investigation would go nowhere anyway.

She really needed it to go somewhere. She felt – without any tangible evidence – that McCullough was looking to move her away from Carlton. He never said so, but it permeated his decisions. She was desperate to stay: it was her home, her life; it had Lucy in it. She didn't have the will or the energy to rebuild again. But McCullough didn't rate her, didn't like her style and didn't agree with her methods. There was nothing partisan, or misogynist, or homophobic about it, he displayed no interest in identity politics whatsoever. No, McCullough simply had a view of what a detective should be, and Dana wasn't it. He regarded *introvert detective* as an oxymoron. If that was so, she needed a result here and needed it quickly, and not just to solve a murder. She had to show she could cope without Mike or Lucy, without the comfort of familiar surroundings and a home town, without a support team.

'We have two murders: one of them ten weeks old, one of them six weeks ago. They were investigated in a flimsy, haphazard way that may well have tipped off the murderer and steepened our odds.' She glanced at Able but he remained silent. 'One of the detectives is dead from hanging; the other is somewhere in Kakadu annoying crocodiles and won't talk. There is no apparent motive for either murder. There is no weapon extant, and the killer or killers have had at least a month to dispose of the gun: in an empty region the size of Belgium, where we'd have no realistic hope of finding it. Let's assume for now there are no drive-throughs. We still have over fifty suspects in town and, since we don't know exact times of death, not one of them has a worthwhile alibi. Is that about right, Able?'

The trademark grin, and a scratch of the stubble. 'No motive, no alibis, no weapon, no witnesses. Yeah. See, put it like that, it doesn't sound so easy. Not what you signed up for, eh?'

Dana sat back a little. 'Oh actually, it's pretty much the kind of scenario I was expecting. But we're better off than I thought when I was boarding the plane.'

Able took his eye off the road for a moment. Not a great risk when the nearest vehicle was ten kilometres away. 'Wait, better off? How?'

'Well, having the bodies in the freezer and rigged up as they'd been found, that was a real bonus. I wasn't expecting that kind of front-row seat.' She paused, and started counting off points on her fingers. 'Second, I wasn't certain until we spoke to Doc Mangold that the killer used a silencer. The investigation report underplayed it so much I wasn't

sure it was true. A silencer tells me something. It's unusual and therefore significant and, if it's home-made, then of course someone made it.
Third, I thought Unamurra would have more through traffic so I was
expecting more suspicion to fall on people who'd had the opportunity
to disappear. With little chance of it being a drive-through, we trim the
range of suspects. Also, Unamurra is slightly more isolated than I'd
thought. Not that I hadn't looked at the map, but it's remote in that I
sense no one from Dutton seems to *want* to go there, regardless of the
distance. So that also narrows the field. Finally, the population is two
thirds of the number I was expecting. The town's structure of relationships may be a bit clearer than I'd thought before I met you: I reckon
you could probably draw it on a sheet of A4 already. So that gives me a
better sense of who and what – who might do something about someone else, or with someone else, or for someone else, and who definitely
wouldn't. Which also cuts the number of suspects.'

Able puffed his cheeks. 'I had no idea you'd be such an optimist.'
His eyes narrowed slightly. 'What about this corruption angle? Isn't
that why they sent you in the first place?'

That skipped beat between Able and Mangold flashed through her
mind. She had no idea what anyone had really been told about her
arrival; it might be best to still keep it that way and operate in blissful
ignorance. At the very least, it might make some people complacent.

'Yes, apparently it is. Some people think the homicides weren't
solved because they weren't supposed to be solved. I only spoke a
dozen words to my commander before he literally sent me packing, so
I know almost nothing about the bigger picture here. Not interested,
to be honest – politics isn't my sport. I'm no good at it. My only brief
was to solve the murders. I'm not here to criticize what went before,
apportion blame or uncover misdeeds – unless they pertain to the
murder investigations.'

'But you think they do?'

Able's eyes sparkled when he got down to the fine grain of crime detection. He defaulted to the wide grin and the easy manner, especially if he felt outgunned. But beneath that armour he was smart, resilient and a good potential ally. He was a natural for law enforcement, she was relieved to note. Time to jump, and hope there was a parachute.

'Hmm. As you've probably guessed, Able, I'm already all-in on trusting you as much as I can, and not trusting anyone else at all. If I'm wrong on that score, then I'll hit a big fat zero and go home having failed. I'm banking on your integrity because I trust my instincts. So . . . here's the bottom line.' She turned towards him. 'I think the errors of investigation are more likely of omission, of overlooking and turning the other way. My reading of the files is that the basics were covered in both cases, but little more. That said, I'm perturbed that you were sidelined in both investigations, because that seems to me a big mistake. But the motivation for those errors is beyond me and my timeframe. Regardless, Carver and Milford did an okay but limited job. It might have been laziness, lack of training, being warned off, whatever. But I believe both murders can be solved. And I think, between us, we can solve them.'

'That'll do me.'

This smile was the same yet different, broader, deeper, more heart-felt. Apparently he had more than one, after all.

He leaned towards the steering wheel and pointed. 'Ah, there, off to the left. Behold, mighty Unamurra.'

Chapter 5

The road carved an elegant, sweeping parabola to the left, climbing slightly as they neared Unamurra. The rise was almost imperceptible, but would save most of the place from the once-a-decade biblical flooding the region experienced. The geometry of the town was apparent before they reached it: either side of the main collection of buildings ran low escapee streets, partly built and partly barren. The solitary structure beyond two storeys was the water tower, loitering on stilts and offering the only bloated curves among right angles and diagonals.

Dana's eye was caught by a flash of green from the edge of town, which disappeared as the road dipped behind a mound. It came to her that, after two hundred kilometres of sand and parched earth, she was seeing things.

Able grunted. 'Your welcoming committee, madam.'

Dana peered intently, trying to discern what he meant. At first she missed it, her eyes unused to such vast distances and flattened angles. Gradually, the semblance of an image shimmered into focus. To the left of the road, barely ten metres past the town's sign, perhaps twenty angels lined the road as a Praetorian guard. Able knew to slow to a halt without her asking.

The engine ticked as she took in the line. They were set millimetre accurate; not a vague sort-of-straight but a rigid, military cohort in perfect formation. Much as they were incongruous, they struck her as being exactly where they should be. They weren't blending in, yet it seemed as though they'd always been there. Wherever they happened to stand, she reflected, they felt as if they owned that landscape. DuBois had imbued inanimate objects with authority – she could see that through the glass.

For some reason, she expected noise when she got out of the car. A background, a soundtrack. The moment seemed to merit that. But she was struck by the silence. Able stood by the car, wary of moving too close. She would have to ask him about that. It appeared beyond simply deference to her, or to the art. More like a penitent quivering before God.

The two dead bodies in Mangold's freezer hadn't been angels, they'd been grotesque deformations of the concept. No wonder, she now appreciated, DuBois might feel personally slighted; they'd been an insult to his art. These angels held less humanity but more emotion than the two dead bodies.

She stood silently and let her own reaction wash over her. It came in waves. First, a slight shudder, as she often felt when standing before works of art, a semblance of the artist's efforts or passion that seared through her. She liked art from scarred, damaged minds; she felt the connection. Her take was that DuBois was incandescent about something, enraged to the point of apoplexy, but able to communicate it only by building and moving angels. Such anger was not transient, it was about something huge and severe, ongoing and life-changing.

After that, she felt a quiet awe. The beauty of each piece took over from the hot blast of rage that created it. They had a power held in check. DuBois had chosen well: these angels were the muscular transmitters of his emotions yet they held the serene command to do so.

She walked slowly towards the first in line. Her footsteps crunched on the sand that fizzed across the tarmac in the breeze. Part of her expected the angel to swivel its head and regard her with . . . what? Menace? Dismissal? Something, she believed, less than respect.

This close, she was struck by two aspects. First, by their height: the bodies in the freezer hadn't overwhelmed as these did. The angels made her shudder and doubt; while they were human-sized, their wingspan neared two metres and they started a metre off the ground, looming over whoever was nearby. It gave them stature; they had a brooding presence beyond their physical size.

Second, while almost every part of them was dust-mottled and windswept, the heads seemed alien in their pristine gloss. The Angels of Unamurra did not have faces, or hair, or human skulls. Instead, their heads were bullet-shaped and obsidian, completely bereft of feature or expression. The head sloped down towards the viewer, who was skewered with a sightless gaze, it added to the intimidating majesty. The angels were not abstract concepts of people, they were always intended to be another species, delivering judgement on the humans beneath them. The jet-black surface of each head appeared devoid of dust; it shone in the fading afternoon sun, polished so finely that blown sand fell away, leaving reflected light to fire in all directions.

Twenty angels in a row, mutely observing the passing world. Set for a reason. She walked up and down the line, looking for the track marks. Nothing. Breezes had whipped the sand across them for hours. Presumably, then, brought down the road some time earlier: which must mean witnesses on the three hundred metres from the first buildings to here. It would have taken at least an hour to set this up. She imagined a small crowd spilling out from the pub to observe, leaning on the columns of the porch and leering at the puffing artist moving to and fro. She pictured DuBois sweating and cursing in the swirling dust, ignoring the catcalls and wisecracks, answerable to no one, going about his meticulous craft. There *must* have been witnesses.

Able read her mind and called over to her from the car. 'They were placed overnight. I already asked this morning. No one saw anything. DuBois started fitting new wheels on the base, see?' He pointed to the splayed legs of each frame. 'Rubber compound, almost completely silent.'

Dana nodded and looked back along the line. She might be witnessing the handiwork of a killer – her admiration for the angels shouldn't divert her from that possibility. Aside from his potential role, she really wanted to meet DuBois; she felt he had something to tell her. Not, she believed, chapter and verse; more that he had an impression of this town – an insight – that she should have. Perhaps he would share it. Or maybe he'd laugh and tell her to work it out for herself.

She walked back towards the car. 'Does anyone else move these angels?'

Able regarded the figures as though they were snarling, drooling dogs, savage and unpredictable. His hand shook before he gripped the top of the car door, hoping she'd misinterpret the gesture as casual.

'Ah, no. It's not advisable. When he first set them up, one of the local geniuses thought it would be funny to move a few. When that bloke woke up the next day, someone had covered his entire house with white paint, and superglued every door and window. Took us ages to get him out, had to chisel the door open. House still looks bleached. A week or two after that, someone else moved one. Just one, about five metres. It was right by their front door and it was freaking them out. Next morning, they stepped out and walked into a buzzing kangaroo corpse. Hung from the door frame, flies and maggots and all.'

'A dead kangaroo?'

'Yeah. Not butchered for the occasion, it was roadkill. All the same, some of us reckoned the 'roo had been moved ten clicks to be there. So, you know. Not advisable to dick around with his art.'

'And all that was definitely DuBois?'

'Uh-huh. Well, I asked him each time, and he just shrugged and laughed. So, legally, no proof . . . but yeah. No one touches his angels any more. They just wait quietly until he chooses to move them.'

Power, thought Dana. The power to put his messages wherever he wants, whenever he wants. All the same, they weren't being heeded. Otherwise, why would he continue to send them? Something was blocking them; that, or the town greeted it all with a studied indifference.

'Does DuBois do this pattern a lot?'

They got back into the car. Able was clearly glad to have metal between him and the angels. 'Straight line of twenty? Guard of honour into town? Nah. This is the first time. So you should be honoured, Dana. Or worried.'

She stared at him. He looked out of the side window, knowing he was being watched. After a couple of seconds he turned back. 'What?'

'Your reaction to them; it was . . . interesting. You don't like them?'

'Not . . . not really, no.' He fiddled with the gum wrapper again.

'Correction: you fear them. You know they're just a collection of metal and plastic and leather, but you feel something visceral.'

He gave a weak facsimile of his usual grin. She contemplated, simply from compassion, letting the subject go. But no, he'd demonstrated a foreboding that she felt herself, despite her admiration.

'Yeah, well. The short answer is, they give me the creeps, eh.'

'We've got time for the long answer.'

He put both hands on the steering wheel, as if he was determined to set off and disregard her question. But he didn't get further than staring ahead.

'I'm not judging you, Able, I'm interested.'

'Hmm. Okay. Well, part of it's practical, I suppose. Those things move all over town, at various times. Out near a couple of the stations, too. All the locals here just shrug and think it's all random, as if

DuBois shoves them wherever he fancies for no reason. But that's wrong. He's very particular about it. Always. He's not playing games and he doesn't stick them somewhere just to make a pretty pattern, or piss someone off. He's trying to communicate.'

Yes, thought Dana, glad they were in agreement. DuBois was supposed to be off the radar somehow; although how he could survive in such a hostile landscape was beyond her. Regardless, he was apparently skulking back into town to move them, to make a statement. He was seemingly risking something to leave that statement – which gave the communication some additional weight. Or made it a more formidable diversion.

'But beyond the practical?' she prompted.

'They . . . look, I'm not a believer in spirits. There, said it.' He checked both wing mirrors, as if elders would emerge from the sand, beset by wrath. 'I don't diss what my rellies believe or anything, but for me a rock is a rock, a tree is a tree and a snake is a snake. So I'm not really open to anything . . . you know, supernatural or anything. But these angels, there's something odd about them.'

'Otherworldly?'

'Yeah.' He glanced across and nodded. 'Good with words, you, they said you were. Yeah.' He stared ahead again, past the angels and towards town. '*Otherworldly.* I know what you said – they're all metal and plastic and leather – I know that. But when you get near them, it's like they've got something inside. Moving parts, a heart, I dunno. *Something.* And it's like they're constantly passing judgement. They look down *at* you and they look down *on* you. You're lesser. You're the judged. And something usually comes after judgement: punishment. So I'm . . . I'm waiting for their punishment.'

She looked back at the sloping obsidian, the magisterial spread of the wings. She could see what Able meant. It was beyond verdict – it was a sense that they were about to exact retribution, somehow, for something she couldn't yet fathom and in a way she couldn't predict.

The angels were on the cusp of flight. The town was on the cusp of something much darker.

They drove on towards town, a slow cruise with Able leaning an elbow on the window frame. For two hundred metres. Then, they slowed again.

The glimpse of green. She wasn't going crazy. 'Is that a *lawn*?' She felt stupid for asking.

Able grinned. 'It sure bloody is. I'll show you.'

It was, indeed, a lawn. She'd thought as the car rolled to a halt that it must be artificial grass, albeit a deeper shade and more subtle texture than the light green carpet she'd seen at Dutton's bowls club. But no, it was indisputably the real thing.

They crossed the road. Able didn't bother checking for traffic, but she did, feeling like a naïve visitor as she realized. Ahead was the ANZAC memorial, a narrowing column of beige stone two metres tall topped by a small pyramid. She dredged from somewhere a technical name – a square frustum. The names of the wartime fallen reached one third of the way down the column; the forefathers had future-proofed their respect. Beyond the obelisk two steps led down to a patch of smooth, beautifully maintained grass about the size of a tennis court. Around it, stone benches and picnic tables, several covered by slanting metal roofs for shade. The whole thing was immaculate and totally incongruous under desert skies.

Able had noticed her hurried limp as she'd crossed the highway. 'I was wondering back at the station: what happened to your leg?'

Dana patted it. 'It's a plastic kneecap. As long as the killer isn't Usain Bolt, we'll be fine.'

'Huh. He runs quick, but he doesn't run far; I'd catch up. Seriously? Plastic?'

'Yes. Well, two thirds of it is, anyway.'

'Ah,' he grinned, 'so you're a cyborg. Fair enough.' He stood before the lawn and spread his arms like a true believer. 'Eighth wonder of the world, eh?'

Dana smiled. 'It's remarkable. What's the story?'

They began a slow circuit in and out of the shadows created by each picnic spot. The wind picked up and carried the incipient chill of early evening.

'Ah, well, until about a decade ago all this space in front of the memorial was dust. Just a scrubby bit of sandy ground. Someone came back from an outback town someplace else and said, 'Hey, over there they have real grass in the meridian strip, a line of it down the centre of the street.' They said we should do that here, but Dutton council nixed that: road trains didn't like it, apparently – made the road too narrow to 'em. So we went for the next best thing.

'Each property in town sacrifices three litres of their water allocation a day. There's a water committee here and they're plenty fierce. Anyone who operates off tank water – only three of them left, mind – they have to physically bring that water and put it in the container over there. Add up the whole giant city: seventy or so litres a day, plus sunshine and some animal crap, produces this. Old Henry Beattie looks after it. Having this lawn means we can always walk around in bare feet, cool grass on our skin, getting wet when there's a dew. It's a luxury. You don't realize that until you don't have it. Like most things. We did it mainly for the kids, I suppose. 'Course, there aren't any here right now. When Henry's fixing to cut it, he puts up an orange notice in the pub window. Then we all come down and have a picnic the moment he's finished: just drink in the smell of freshly mown, juicy grass. One day we won't have to water it. God'll take over. But until then, it's on us.'

Around Carlton and Earlville, thought Dana, people usually cursed water. They got large amounts at inopportune times. It created vast clouds of mosquitos year round, it smashed infrastructure and ruined crops, it made entire districts impossible to farm. People had drowned in swamps only a few kilometres from her house. Same continent – same *state* – opposite lives.

'It's truly a thing of beauty,' said Dana. 'It looks like it needs a cut pretty soon, yes?'

'Week after next, they reckon. Big news all over town.'

Chapter 6

'Could we stop round the back, please?'

Dana pointed at the pub and Able frowned for a moment, before catching on. 'Ah, the second body dump?'

'Yes. Thank you.' Dana found it hard to believe Able had forgotten where Tim's dead body had been so recently found.

Able swung the car off the road and it bounced over a couple of ruts before he could turn behind the pub. The building had a flat roof that reached out towards the horizon. Several licks of bitumen had lifted and curled. It ended with a cement toilet block and a loosely fenced area that held metal barrels. The block had a scuttling lizard on the wall, which grabbed her attention when it fled for the shadows. There were scuff marks in the dirt where staff had manhandled full barrels into the pub – crescents showing the curved path towards the sliding doors. To the left of that, the rear of the building itself had a run of wooden stairs leading up to a first-floor balcony of sorts for the apartment: three empty terracotta pots and a broken camping chair that listed to one side of the back door. At the foot of the stairs the pub kept various detritus: milk crates full of used glass bottles, an old fridge, empty pallets tipped onto their edges, and an upended tea chest. The fence containing all of this was sturdy on the east side, but north and south were flimsy efforts and perhaps one strong wind from horizontal.

They stayed in the car. Dana tried to imagine who and how. It wasn't gelling. She couldn't picture the back of the pub in normal times, so she couldn't tell if a detail was jarring now. Sometimes a crime scene or body location had a feeling about it, a sense of why it had been chosen. Perhaps it was the flatness of the general terrain, but she couldn't pick out why this spot was so special.

'Annie was sat on that tea chest there.' Able pointed. 'Sunrise, or just before, actually. She has a coffee there first thing, always has done. The frame and body were right in front of the bonnet here, about five metres ahead of us.'

She strained to focus on the sand. 'No telling when it was put there?'

'Nah. According to the bar staff, it wasn't there at ten the night before, because they'd have seen it when they cleared some barrels and threw out the empties.' He grimaced. 'That may or may not be true. There's no streetlights here and there was no moon that night. They were focused on finishing a shift, not keeping an eye out in case a corpse appeared. Anyway, at dawn, Annie sees her hubby up on the frame, just as Declan comes round the corner here, like we've just done.'

'Declan delivers the milk?'

'Yeah, every three days. Dairy stuff of all sorts, actually: cheese, yoghurts, butter and whatnot. He brings the post and the medicines as well. He's a solid bloke – been doing this run for five years. Steady as; not the type to panic, or make up crap later. He must have seen it the same time Annie did. She was still staring at it from her back-yard fence. She went in and called Dutton police. He did the smart thing and put a load of witches' hats in a circle around it. Big fan of *CSI*, apparently.'

Dana smiled. 'Usually that's a curse, especially if they're on the jury. They expect 3D computer graphics and lasers everywhere.'

'Yeah, well, as you can imagine, the whole town wanted a look-see. We're not immune from people taking photos instead of helping. A few of them wanted to bring Tim down, preserve his dignity, but wiser heads prevailed. Annie was shell-shocked. That was the word everyone used.'

The phone records backed up the summary. Within fifteen minutes of that initial call to Dutton police the tower logged twenty-two mobile phone calls from Unamurra locals to relatives and friends. Bad news travelled fast.

'Did anyone mention someone seeming . . . suspicious?'

'Anyone having an inappropriate reaction? Nah, not that we found, at any rate. Of course, Axel DuBois wasn't there, was he? Anyway, they all had a good long look at each other, no doubt. Must have thought one of their own had done this one, even if Larry Muir's was a bit more mysterious.'

'They thought it was two different killers? That's interesting.'

'Hmm, okay, maybe *thought* is a bit of a stretch. Knee-jerk reaction, more like. Even though the staging of the bodies is identical, some of them didn't know all the details of Larry Muir. I saw your sceptical look when Doc Mangold mentioned keeping it all hush-hush after the first body. Yeah, you're right: you can't, not in a one-horse town. But we did our best. So some of the town didn't know quite how identical this one was. Annie did, though, poor sod. A few others as well.'

Again, Dana found it hard to picture the scene, and that was always a disadvantage. She was on the back foot here; no knowledge of what was out of place, no feel for the town or its people. She needed to make that an advantage, not a handicap.

'Dutton police would take, what, two hours to get here?'

'Yeah, about that. They alerted me on the sat phone straight away, hoping I was in the neighbourhood, but I was around two hours away as well. On my way to do a sweep of outer Belgium for a few days, so I'd started out maybe 4 a.m. Had to turn around and come back. Annie opened up the pub and gave everyone a free drink, on account of the shock. She put Macca out the back to tell everyone to bugger off if they lingered. So the scene preservation was surprisingly good.'

'What do you make of it, Able? The positioning of the body?'

'Well, the staging on the frame suggests the same killer, obviously. Hard to see two different murder scenes would be identical to that level of detail . . . *accidentally*. Like you said back in Dutton, that special ratio, the calculations and all. As for the location? Hard to say. Everyone knows Annie gets up at dawn and has a cup of coffee, so I don't think that bit's going to narrow the field. I'd say it's especially cruel to sling the dead guy up where his wife is bound to see him . . . bound to be *first* to see him. Bit brutal, eh? Have to think it's someone who's really got it in for Annie, to do that to her.'

It was hard to disagree. On a basic level Dana still couldn't see why anyone would display the bodies rather than hide them in the vastness of the outback. On a deeper level, making sure the widow was the first to see the dead body was callous, and spoke of a personal enmity that had surely been noticed by someone.

'And who has really got it in for Annie?'

'Ah, don't think I haven't chewed on that. Look, I'm sure you'll meet her soon enough, so you can make your own judgement. But basically, Annie's a force of nature in this town because she owns the shop, the pub and the petrol. That puts her front and centre not just for people who have a grudge against her but anyone with a whinge about the town generally. So anyone who doesn't like their life, anyone ever ejected from the pub, anyone refused credit at the shop, anyone whose footy team just lost, anyone who has a strong opinion that goes against Annie's. She doesn't back down much, Annie. The field's wide open on people she's pissed off, in a general sense, like. Or are otherwise pissed off, of course. But going to this extreme? Nah, can't think of a one.' Able turned to her. 'What do *you* reckon, Dana? First thoughts?'

'Broadly the same as you. Someone knew Annie's timetable, because this was left for her to be the first to find it – they had a choice of dozens of frames all over town. So, specifically aimed at her and, as you say, notably cruel. There's nothing else intrinsically important about this spot, though, whereas the siting of Larry Muir at the entrance to the Reynolds property may be significant. It's possible there were two different thought processes, even if the killer was the same. Larry was perhaps positioned to point a finger towards Reynolds, but Tim was positioned to be cruel to Annie. Hmm. I'll have to ponder that a bit. Thank you, Able.'

The Landcruiser drew up as a gust of wind pirouetted across the street, the whisked dust disappearing through a gap between the former butcher's and the converted post office. Just for a moment, squeezed between the buildings as it whirled, the shape of the eddying sand seemed almost familiar, almost human.

They were parked outside Able's place, a former servo with the metal shutter down. Above it there was a faint vestige of art deco in the slashing diagonals and underlining of the word 'service', now slowly being obliterated by the blistering of orange paintwork. Dana had a sense that Able still took the word seriously and at face value. Above the lettering, four square windows blinked across the street and reflected the gathering crimson to the west. Next to the metal shutter was a battered wooden door in a faded green, a vertical mail slot glinting in the fading light.

'Abe, son. Where the bloody hell were ya?'

The call came from three doors down. The old man had a stoop, permanently bent knees and simian-hanging hands. His mop of silver hair flopped either side of a vague centre parting. A prominent top lip pulled his features down into a grumpy resting face. From a distance his gender would have been hard to distinguish: his body was soft and doughy.

'Sorry, mate. Had to go into Little Big Town, pick up a friend.'

The man shielded his eyes from the lowering sun. 'Ah, the detective from someplace silly. Where is it, darl?'

'Carlton,' replied Dana. 'And yes, it's a very silly place.'

The man swatted at something; a fly, a vague sense of faux pas. 'Ah, no offence, like. The name's Sandy. I know; live in the outback, called Sandy. Heard 'em all before. Anyways, Abe was supposed to help me cart this stuff round the back.'

'Yeah, yeah, I was. Uh, pop round in a bit, mate? Got to get Dana here settled and all.'

'Hmm, let me check my diary. Prime minister can wait, the queen's never on time. Yeah, I'll fit you in between all my other appointments. Oh, welcome to Unamurra, young lady.'

He tipped an imaginary hat and strolled off towards his home, kicking an errant stone to one side and watching it ping against the side of his house.

Able raised an eyebrow. 'Sorry about him. Got no brakes in his brain, eh – it all flies out as soon as it comes to him. Sandy runs the Men's Shed kind of thing. Got a shed out the back and we all use it as a workshop. You know, pop in to use the tools, repair stuff. He's got the oxy tanks and the welding apparatus, if you need it.'

Dana's mind clicked a gear. 'So not just carpentry, then?'

'Oh, no, bunch of us can turn our hand to most things. Have to, really. Two hundred kays each way to Dutton – tough to get a tradie to call in for a quick job. Nah. Metalwork, bit of upholstery, joinery, anything really. Sandy never locks the place, so we can dip in and borrow stuff whenever.'

'He never locks it?'

'Nah. Why would he? Sorry, I'm supposed to dish out crime prevention advice, I know. But this is Unamurra. Maybe only half of us even have a key to our home. More likely Annie has one, to be honest.' He turned towards his front door. 'Here we go.'

Dana looked skyward for a moment. A workshop that could be used to make a home-made silencer. With no locks. And no one keeping tabs.

Able took her suitcase and opened the door. The stairway seemed unnecessarily narrow – almost designed for a child. Able huffed and puffed ahead of Dana and the door closed softly behind them.

They emerged upstairs into one large room around six metres square. Table lamps were already on, splitting the room into four hazy circles of influence: a couch staring at a blank wide-screen, a blond-wood dining table covered in a loose spray of files, a kitchen of dark wood units and, in one corner, a study with a desktop computer, filing cabinet and swivel chair. Apart from the files on the dining table it was neat and ordered. Next to the fridge was a short alcove, with two doors leading away, Dana presumed bedroom and bathroom. The furniture was seventies but sturdy.

'You'll be pleased to know I'm not a slob, then,' ventured Able.

'I never doubted you. This is nice. Was it like this when you inherited it?'

Able left the suitcase next to the fridge. 'Ah, is that a famous Russo deduction? Go for it, Sherlock.'

Dana leaned against the newel cap, primarily for the rest; her kneecap fizzed from the minor climb. 'You said earlier your father was the mechanic for the town, back in the day. I can see a photo of him there' – she pointed to a frame above the desk – 'working on a V8.

Same smile; you definitely inherited that. Those are Carroll Shelby stripes on that bonnet, so a Ford man, not Holden. This garage closed for business some time ago, judging by the external paint, yet you still live above it. Hence you own it and inherited your dad's place.'

'Very good. You recognise specialist Ford livery from ten paces?'

Dana smiled. 'My dad built roads for the county. He spent all day every day looking at cars going by. When he got home he'd read about them. I know my Hofmeister Kink from my opera window.'

Able gave a theatrical bow. 'My kind of detective.'

Dana laughed. 'Plus, I had my colleague Lucy send me details of all the property ownership in the town while I was flying to Dutton. You own this place outright?'

'I do. No mortgage on it. Unfortunately, it's worth about four bucks. Retail.' He reached around the kettle to switch on at the socket. 'And until you told me about this Lucy, you seemed like a magical cop from the future. Now, I'm afraid, you're just human.'

Dana shrugged. 'Yes, let-downs and I go hand in hand. Sorry about that.'

Dana stalked outside at the rear of the garage, phone at her ear, waiting for Lucy to pick up. From the back, the buildings of the street lost their uniformity and identity. Instead, various owners had added a ragtag of lean-tos and the barely-standing, using whichever materials were to hand. An outbuilding had wooden lapping that had aged to a silver patina; a fence was four panels of Colorbond, each a different hue; some decking had been attempted but had backfired – when the cash ran out, it left jagged teeth of planks biting into thin air. That hadn't stopped the owner placing four plastic chairs and a metal table precariously close to the edges.

There was no street behind the garage, just a dusty area that could be used for parking, with an ill-defined transition to scrubland and wilder bush beyond. While she gazed at a sliver of Belgium and pondered, Able was upstairs calling Vince Reynolds and organizing an immediate interview. The Muir property was a two-hour ride. Dana had thought it better today to visit Reynolds' place just outside town. That way, she'd have seen both body locations by nightfall, if she achieved nothing else. Distances out here were unyielding – a tangible obstacle she couldn't bypass. She could lose most of her time sitting in a Landcruiser. The air temperature was fading fast. Able reckoned a frost tonight.

Dana had a strong signal for the telephone, even if it was old-school and could only deal with voices and texts. Lucy picked up on the seventh ring.

'Howdy. Plane didn't crash after all, then? Or have you just crawled from the wreckage and your first thought was to ring me?'

Dana couldn't help but smile at the mere sound of the voice. 'Ha-de-ha. I have an eminently reasonable concern about things being in the air when they're heavier than air. Despite your many vociferous claims, Luce, you are not a highly qualified aeronautical engineer and so can't convince me otherwise.'

'Sceptic. How's you?'

'Okay, okay. Well, actually, a mixed bag. I'm increasingly certain I'm on a hiding to nothing here. I've been in Dutton and now Unamurra. I doubt half of the hierarchy in Dutton want the murders solved. Not forgetting the Unamurra locals – they gave the square root of nothing to the previous investigations. And of course, no witnesses, no motives, no alibis, no weapon. If they had creeks here, I'd be right up one.'

'Should I send you a paddle?'

'Send two.'

'I call those things mere crimps, Dana Russo. For a detective of your pedigree, they're slight bumps in the road. Did the property data get through?'

'Yes, thanks.' Lucy had sent a pile of reports that had arrived as Dana touched down in Dutton. Dana nodded thoughtfully at the ground and scuffed an errant stone into a ditch. 'Yes, very interesting. It's a strange place all round, this. I'll fill you in later. Do you have some spare capacity?'

'Yeah, pretty quiet here. McCullough's up in Central for two days. Mikey's interstate working on the Alvarez. I'm the queen of an empty office. So, *á votre service, chérie.*'

Dana smiled and scratched a further note on her pad in Pitman. She'd decided shorthand was safest here. Chances were, no one would be able to quickly transcribe her notes if they saw them. 'You're always the queen, Luce, no matter who's there. Okay.'

She reeled off a list of data for Lucy to chase, constantly aware that it had to be something that could be transmitted via a long text or wait for a conversation like this. In fact, Dana focused mainly on specific questions that produced exact answers; she felt that was a better fit for the circumstances. If anything, she reflected briefly, being unable to organize armfuls of data was sharpening her act. Getting precise answers required her to think about the questions, the underpinning assumptions she was using, the route map to success. It was already shaping her thinking, and her trajectory.

'Eight bios – might take a little while. I'll text each through as I get it done. I take it all that lot is about focusing the investigation?' asked Lucy. 'Narrowing down the suspect list?'

'Yes, but it's not easy. Just thinking about the number of people who can shoot a gun well enough makes my head spin. The shot was from relatively close range but more than a couple of steps. That's as good as those forensics get. It wasn't a difficult target on either occasion. That allows for the majority of Unamurra, plus almost everyone on a station within eight hours or so – around ninety people. Not counting anyone from Dutton. That would add hundreds more. The majority of those ninety will have met both victims, either occasionally or often. And motive's just as flaky: who knows what might set off an argument? I've known people killed because someone imagined that someone said something which implied someone else wasn't all they might be. The link can be that tenuous. So, it's not easy.'

'Where to start?'

'Well, the two widows, obviously. They're involved, even if they don't want to be. And I've just been to the location of the second murder – round the back of the pub. I'm off in a minute to the station where the first body was found, see if I can glean any more from that. So that will cover both body sites. Aside from that, I'm currently open to suggestions.'

'I'm just reading the case files now. You know me, somewhere between intellectually inquisitive and just plain nosy. I see a lot of gun-testing going on, to no avail. The first investigations got nowhere, did they?'

'Yes, true. They did a lot of the fundamentals: ballistics, phone records, witness statements, door-to-door, and so on. But the way they did it seemed careless and superficial. I'd like to use what they did as a basis, if only to rule some people out. But there are some shocking omissions in there. No one's chased up the location of cars, for example. Lots of people give vague alibis that aren't cross-referenced, even with other alibi claims. Some vital aspects are buried in long paragraphs, or in the appendices, or referenced obliquely rather than directly; for example, the detail about the silencer. It's hard to see the first investigation as a building block. More like a roadblock.'

'Does your local man have ideas?'

'Able? Hard to say, exactly. We're at an early stage, he and I. It's disconcerting that he wasn't involved in the investigation, but I haven't bottomed out why that occurred. He certainly seems to know the town well enough, and I understand he had some theory or other, although he discarded it. But whatever the reasons, they deliberately ignored and sidelined him. I'm trying to play it like a fresh start, but it isn't; it's full of resonance, old wounds and scars.'

The pause told Lucy that Dana was feeling the pressure of a seemingly impossible case, a recalcitrant town and the silent shadow of McCullough's expectations. Sometimes Dana's brain needed pulling from its own thoughts.

'So, Unamurra's as weird as it looks from space, then?' she asked.

'Yes, in many ways. One shop, one pub, two petrol pumps and about fifty people actually here. Oh, and an immaculate lawn.'

'Yeah, sure.'

'No, truly. If I could send you a picture, I would. A big stretch of lawn by the ANZAC memorial; it's very impressive. I'm meeting the curator this evening.'

'Label me stunned. Is that your lot, madam?'

'It is, Luce, thank you. How's Tubs?'

Lucy's dad had been in a coma long term after an industrial accident. Lucy tended him day and night when not at work. Her devotion inspired, and broke Dana's heart.

'Oh, same old. We're reading *Moby Dick* now, so that might keep us going a while.'

'Ah, an excellent chance for your comedy voices, then?'

'Oh, definitely. All seafarers will have the same pantomime-pirate voice, and all the other accents will be West Country England, despite the Nantucket setting. Tubs will love it. Laters, chick.'

'Bye.'

Dana turned back to the wilderness. A kite screeched as it turned, kissing the thermals as it circled away and faded into the sky. Something that ate nothing but carrion: it was the only bird she'd seen for an hour. What, she wondered, would make fifty people stay here?

Clearly, the town had long outlived any ambition it had, yet fifty-odd souls still called it home and wouldn't leave. Even with two of them murdered, they remained. Perhaps they all knew who'd done it, and why, so they felt it was all over and the rest of them were safe. Or maybe they had no clue. Their easiest answer to that uncomfortable and unpleasant idea was to ignore it.

Chapter 7

Dana was re-reading some notes before they set off to see Reynolds. Able was trying to put the door back on his tumble drier. She didn't ask how it had detached. Dana heard scuffed steps outside. She was surprised at how sound travelled. The steps halted, there was a rasp of breath that was audible, then –

'Abe. Open up. Got frozen stuff here.'

The voice was muffled by the front door and the stairwell yet pierced the space with ease. A gravelly, twenty-a-day tinge, a voice used to being recognized and heard. There were twenty-one women officially living in Unamurra, but Dana had no doubt who this was: Annie Ogden. The knock was similarly stifled, but clumsy. Annie was kicking at the door.

Able scooted – there was no other word for it – across the room and down the stairs. Dana heard him open the door and then, instead of a greeting there was simply a 'here' from Annie, followed by a rustle of cardboard and an *oomph* from Able. The two sets of footsteps up the stairs were different. Able clumped and seemed to be struggling with balance a little; Annie moved evenly and crisply.

Dana made a deliberate effort not to look up and continued to read from her laptop. She already had some impression of Annie's role and place in the community from the original investigation notes.

Redoubtable pub landlady, owner of the accompanying shop and petrol pumps, dispenser of discipline within her own establishment. After
four years of drought she was now owner of the only surviving business in town: she'd outlasted the butcher, the bank and, of course, the
garage. The way Able had responded to her voice at the door was practically Pavlovian. These things all said that Annie mattered.

Dana had seen photos, because Annie was the second victim's wife,
but three dimensions were always different. Around fifty years old,
Annie entered the main room as if she owned it. She was solid, chunky;
she leaned forward slightly as if her spine was permanently fused that
way. She wore black corduroy trousers and a knitted sweater with a
distinctive goanna logo. It looked cheap enough but, Dana knew from
a magazine article last week, wasn't. Annie's hair was short but thick,
a relatively unkempt salt-and-pepper splodge, it was *low maintenance,*
but her eyes would, Dana believed, blaze at anyone who suggested
that. Annie had strong forearms she'd presented by rolling her sleeves.
Her eyes were dark and held below thick eyebrows. She looked to
Dana like a stolid woman in a Russian melodrama: no-nonsense, formidable, capable of withstanding almost endless privations without
complaining once. She stared at Dana and was not, Dana surmised,
impressed at all. Annie looked glad not to be impressed.

'So you're the detective, yeah?'

She made no move towards Dana, instead stepping back slightly
from the table. Dana guessed a handshake was out of the question.

'Dana Russo, yes. You're Annie Ogden?'

The question was passive-aggressive provocation; Dana had felt an
impulse to get her jab in first, or at least to hold her ground. Annie
appropriated space in a house that wasn't her own – *like she was walking on to a yacht,* came the unbidden lyric. It was something Dana
would never do, and she wondered why Able allowed it from Annie.

Annie was slightly affronted that her identity needed confirmation.

Possibly, thought Dana, in a small town like this they get out of practice, fail to realise that not everyone will know them. Or, more likely,
Annie had a big ego. There was no answer to Dana's question. Instead
Annie turned to Able, who'd deposited a dozen or so frozen-dinner
cartons on to the counter, then back to Dana.

'We have rooms at the pub, you know. Youse could have put some
money into the local economy, couldn't you?'

It sounded aggressive, but Dana sensed that almost everything
Annie said would carry a combination of volume and abrasion that
would be forever combative. When it didn't sound that way – *that*
would be the unnerving tone.

'Yes, I could. Since I'm here to work, this suits me better.'

Dana's voice was even and controlled. She noted the very slight
raising of Annie's eyebrow.

'Who gets the couch, Abe? You, or her? Or . . .'

'Me, of course.' Able rushed to fill the tail-off. 'Obviously. Age of
chivalry isn't finished yet, Annie.'

Annie's grunted reply could have been anything from mild agreement to dismissal. She turned back to Dana, who hadn't moved since
Annie entered the apartment.

'Annie, I need to talk to you a little about Tim, please,' said Dana.

'Yeah, thought you might. Okie-dokie.' Annie moved towards the
table and hitched up her sleeves. She called over one shoulder. 'Abe,
you've got someplace else to be, I bet. Women here chatting, and all.
I'm sure you don't want to hear us gassing, do ya?'

Dana waited for Able to baulk at being thrown out of his own
home, but the acquiescence was instant. Able looked around for a
small rucksack and shouldered it while Annie sat. 'Yeah, yeah. I'll pop
in on Sandy, get that stuff moved.'

The two women looked at each other as Able descended the stairs
and went out. The silence crackled slightly. It seemed to Dana that

Annie didn't like any intelligent women setting foot in her kingdom. Even in a town of fifty, someone had to be top dog. Annie seemingly had a rivalry with Able about who wielded the most influence in Unamurra; now she saw Dana as some kind of challenge.

Annie's voiced dropped to something near a whisper. *Quiet* was indeed unnerving. 'Okay, Detective from Carlton. Fire away.'

'I only know a few details about Tim from what's in the file. What sort of person was he?'

Dana felt most wives would respond instantly; positive or negative, their response would come straight away. Annie considered it as though it was something she'd never pondered before.

'Good bloke. A good person.' Annie tapped the table with her finger for emphasis. 'Better than me, in fact. I know, hard to believe, hey? But he was. Straight up and down the line; didn't start fights, got on with it. Some little blokes, they're all in your face, trying to prove something all the time. Tim wasn't like that. Me and him, we went all right. Got ourselves straight early doors – that's my tip, as if you're looking for one. Each of us had our strengths and weaknesses, worked out early which was which.'

'What were his strengths?'

'Loyalty. Which is actually pretty rare in this world. And this town, come to that. People just want to run the first time things don't go their way, don't they? Cave in, make a break for it, blame someone else – anyone else. They whine and moan about how things didn't happen the way they wanted, but Tim had enough backbone to see the long term. Didn't wander off at the first argument, didn't have to win all the time. That's blokes generally, see, gotta have the last word, or feel like it's a victory. Half this lot in town, they sulk if you don't let 'em win an argument. I've learned to tone it all down. Didn't have to with Tim. I could give it both barrels and he'd still stick around, and we'd get on with it.'

Although, reflected Dana, even if that were true, it might not have felt that way to the rest of the town. Or to Tim, for that matter. 'You had a lot of arguments?'

'Ha. Not really. Just, you know, we work together and, since I own the place, then I suppose, technically, I'm his boss. While we're working, like. Not always easy. But like I say, we get on with it.'

'And what was his biggest fault?'

Annie glanced to the window and back. 'This is you investigating, or you being nosy? Coz I've noticed with cops, they get the two mixed up. Start delving into your private life, claiming it's all so very necessary.'

'He's been murdered, Annie. As a professional, I'll ask any questions that I think will get me closer to the truth.'

'Will you now?' Annie smirked, as though Dana was a schoolgirl debater operating above her ability. 'Okay, then. Tim's biggest fault? Actually, like you, he was nosy. Loved gossip, could listen to it all day. It made him a lazy barman because he was always gassing instead of, uh, encouraging further purchases. I had to put him on the barrels and the cleaning to get a day's work. If he was in the bar, he was chatting. Didn't have a strong grip of what was private and what was his business. That kind of thing.'

'I see. And who do you think would want to do him harm?'

'Well, there might be a few who want to 'do him harm' as you so quaintly put it, but that's a long way from killing him. Frenchie – he's got to be favourite, eh? Tim was strung up on one of those angel frames, after all. In the same pose as an angel. And while Frenchie doesn't talk about his past much, I reckon he knows which end of a gun to point. So, I dunno, maybe Tim landed in some trouble with him, eh? Bloke doesn't like a lot of personal questions, and Tim was a bloody sticky-beak. Would explain a lot.'

Annie's voice softened momentarily, becoming almost dreamy for a second. 'What you don't get, Carlton, is that this is an odd community, a one-off. No point comparing it to back home. If you moved here, lived here, you'd have another approach. This town's my heart and soul, I fight for it. And it's small enough that I can make a difference here. That's not usual. That's not most Aussies' experience. They live in a town or a city and they have hardly any say. Unamurra's unique. You'll find that out if you stick around long enough.'

Annie got up and wandered over towards Able's desk, another assumption of space and right. Perhaps they all did this, thought Dana – in and out of each other's homes and less prissy than most about privacy. Annie flicked at a calendar behind the desk lamp and spoke to the wall.

'Why did they choose you for this gig? Didn't need someone who speaks like a dictionary, eh. Got no connections here, have you?'

She wanted Dana to turn around in the chair, to squirm to retain eye contact. Dana looked squarely at the stairs and let her voice carry over her shoulder.

'You'd have to ask them why they chose me. Police officers don't always get the whys and wherefores, they just get told.'

The truth was she didn't know. McCullough had challenged her to work it out, but she hadn't yet given it much thought. She had a vague sense that she'd been picked to fail, selected because of her expendability – a suitable sacrifice that would please McCullough and appease Central. She *did* know this trip was all borrowed time – McCullough had little patience and wanted nothing but results. According to Lucy, the rumour was he was planning a full-scale review of crime investigation in the district, meaning Dana and Mike were front-row risks.

Annie swooped back into the chair, elbows claiming half the table and knocking against Dana's laptop.

'You an expert on murder, then? Done lots, have ya?'

'Very few officers have investigated lots of murders, Annie. It doesn't mean they can't solve the next one.'

Annie rolled her tongue around her jaw. 'Yeah, sure. I watch a lot of crime stuff on TV. All those British ones with the posho accents and the drizzle. You'd fit right in there, I reckon, way you talk. I saw a doco on one guy, Gary Something; he's solved loads of murders, eh. Was expecting someone like him. You're not like him, though, are you, Detective from Carlton?'

'Gary Jubelin, yes. He's not a police officer any more. Very few people have his experience. As I say, you can expect a professional investigation, Annie, into who killed your husband. A fresh perspective.'

'Yeah, right. You and Abe gonna smash it? I want to have faith, truly I do. This town's suffering enough, what with the drought and those crappy angels. But I can't see you getting far, either of you. I mean, if I'm putting someone behind the bar for a few shifts, I don't want someone who's barely done it. Nah, I want a track record. *Fresh* doesn't pour many rounds, eh?'

'What did you do before you ran the pub, Annie?'

'Me? Ah, this and that. Nothing major. Like most people in the pub game, knocked around doing all sorts for a while. You need a broad set of skills, don't you? So, you know, all experience comes in handy sometime. Looked after me mum for a few years. Her last few years.'

Dana doubted that was the whole story. If nothing else, Annie would have needed to raise capital to buy the pub and the shop.

Annie tilted her head. 'I just can't picture you running down a killer.'

'Well, it's happened before. Twice in the last six months, in fact. If it's any comfort to you, I've solved every murder I've investigated.'

'I'm not comforted by that, nah. Like I said, I'm all about the track record usually. But for some reason, you don't fit.'

The stare sucked the oxygen from the room.

*

Able made a deliberate noise as he came in, huffing and sighing and making sure the door closed with a solid thud. They both listened to his steps as he climbed the stairs. He acknowledged them with a sheepish grin.

Annie's 'insight' into Tim was little more than Dana could have got from Able. Maybe less. Perhaps, Dana thought, she was judging too harshly. She, of all people, knew tears often meant nothing. Not everyone showcased their grief with crying.

With Able back in the room Annie was more performative.

'You're definitely gonna solve Tim's murder then, eh?'

'We'll be doing our best, between us.'

Annie stopped for a moment, then eye-rolled. 'Hmm. It was weeks ago, and none of youse have got anywhere, from what I can see. Don't get why it takes this long, or why it's this hard. Only fifty people here, eh? Well, you'd better be hotter stuff than you seem, mate.' She tilted her head at Able. ''Coz Abe, he bloody lives here and he can't solve it.'

For the second time in a day someone was demonstrating low expectations of Able. For the second time in a day Dana couldn't tell if it was justified. Perhaps the town saw Able as an amiable but plodding presence, a *nice bloke* who was limited and ineffective. Or maybe they had some other reason for doubting him. She was also conscious that she needed to set some parameters with Annie.

'Able's a very capable officer and knows this area better than anyone. He wasn't part of the first investigations, so you don't know what he might achieve. However, I'm willing to bet, Annie, that these murders can't be solved without his considerable help. That would make him invaluable, rather than someone to have a go at, wouldn't you say?'

Annie stiffened initially, mouth open for a retort. Then she thought better of it for some reason. Instead, she smiled slightly and nodded.

'Ah sure, back each other up. I get it. *Code blue* and all that. Good for you. Mate.' She rose and turned sharply on her heel. 'Anyway, Abe, drop in the money when you're passing. Happy huntin'.'

She plodded back down the stairs, eyes fixed ahead as she shrank from view. Her footsteps stopped, four steps from the bottom. She grunted once, then carried on to the doorway. Neither Able nor Dana spoke, or moved, until they heard the door slam behind her.

There was a sense that something important had taken place, even though nothing had seemed irrevocable. As Dana had guessed would happen, it was marking out the first few lines on the pitch. She wasn't sure exactly what to make of it.

Able waved a hand at the space Annie had occupied. 'I haven't formally introduced you. Annie Ogden, Detective Dana Russo. Dana – meet Annie.'

Dana smiled. 'She didn't spend a lot on etiquette lessons, did she?'

'Law unto herself.'

'I'll bet.' Dana let that hang in the air for a second, until Able averted his eyes.

'Thanks for the back-up,' he said to the floor.

'You're welcome.' Dana sat back, pondering how far to push. 'I let it ride with Judge Trent, because he's your boss and I wasn't sure of the lie of the land. But Annie there? That wasn't two old friends messing around, was it?'

'Nah. Nah, it wasn't. Still, hard to poison frozen food, so I think I'm safe for another week.'

He turned and began shoving the food – mainly pizzas and pies – into the freezer.

'What's she got against you, Able?'

In her mind she summoned her own mystifying answer: *everything*. She flitted back to the conversation at the rear of the pub: a potential killer with a reason for being notably cruel to Annie.

He stopped, blinked at the vapour escaping the freezer and took his time to gently swing the door shut. When he straightened up he looked arthritic in a way that he hadn't all day. Dana was beginning to appreciate that how Able moved at any given moment told a story. The supine shuffle at Judge Trent's door, the slow recovery of poise now. They spoke.

'Ah, well. All that data your Lucy sent: you already know I own this place outright. The bank and the butcher's, Annie turned those into houses and rented 'em. She wanted to buy this a while back. I didn't sell.'

Dana estimated that he'd summarized a long war, probably guerrilla tactics and sniping rather than a full-out confrontation. She also felt that he and Annie had locked horns over many things. They were the duopoly of this town, fighting each other for status. But Able wasn't fighting very hard – he had no pride to preserve. Annie had the upper hand, it seemed.

'I see. What did Annie want to do with this place, do you think?'

Able spread his arms theatrically, a gesture that said he was already tired of talking about it. 'Dunno. Maybe there's a ton of oil under it. Who knows with Annie? She wants what she wants when she wants it.'

'And always gets?'

'Pretty much, yeah.'

'But not this time? Not from you?'

'Nah. Dad's place – can't give that up.'

The way Able turned away and fussed with nothing on the kitchen counter told Dana to withdraw. Now was the time to give Able some space and dignity. Instead, she reflected on the question she'd withheld: what did Able have against Annie?

Chapter 8

The road to Vince Reynolds' property was rail-straight. It rippled in a series of mild undulations and haze that telescoped the range; at any given point, it looked half the distance it was. Dana found herself again disoriented by the flatness of the terrain, the size and curve of the sky and the absence of any features to aid her perspective. She was used to three dimensions, but this landscape always felt like two.

This was a 'quick trip', in Able's view: it might take an hour of driving each way. Dana was assuming she had two or three twelve-hour daylight blocks to solve the case. After that, McCullough would wield a metaphorical hook and enjoy telling her how detectives who can't network can't solve serious crime. Followed by a pink sheet identifying her new work location on the other side of the state. Cops in this state were terrified of pink sheets: they ruptured marriages, fractured lives and left trails of resentment.

'Vince Reynolds' station is only cattle?' she asked.

A pause from Able, wondering where she'd acquired the information and how quickly she'd assimilated it. She seemed to have memorised the stock preferences of all twenty-six stations in Belgium on a first read.

'Sorrento? Yeah. He dabbled in camel farming a few years back, but it bombed. You need to be able to milk camels to make a buck. He could never get it right. So yeah, all cattle. What's left of them.'

She nodded. The first investigation had assessed whether the location of Larry's body at the entrance to Vince's station was significant. Yet, as so often with those investigation reports, they were opaque; there was little concrete evidence about Vince's potential involvement. Dana found it hard to believe the location was entirely accidental.

'Their farms share a boundary and they've both been here a while. Vince and Larry Muir knew each other pretty well?'

Able smiled. 'You could say that.' He shuffled in his seat and tapped the steering wheel. 'They moved here within about a year of each other. Vince bought Sorrento, then Larry bought Pelligrini. Not really rivals, as such. It doesn't work like that here. One farmer doing okay doesn't really stop another farmer doing all right. But all the same, in the good years there's a bit of ego going on. Except with those two, it seemed more personal. More bite to it, you know? Something underneath, some scars they both had that they couldn't stop scratching. I never got to the bottom of it. Might be they forgot themselves, by the end.'

Dana tried to absorb it. She was searching for a catalyst that caused someone to kill Muir: it might well have been set off by Reynolds, even if he wasn't the killer.

'Was there any particular disagreement, before the murder?'

'Oh, they were always at it. Constantly. Fights about stock, water, fence repairs – anything, you name it. About five years ago it was getting out of hand, you know? Brandishing shotguns, threats. Urgh, was taking up a lot of my time.' Able shook his head wearily at the mere recollection. 'I'm halfway across Belgium there, and I have to come back because of those two. So Annie comes up with the solution. The Book of Feuds.'

'The what?'

'The Book of Feuds. It was an exercise book, an actual book. She kept it above the bar. If either of them had a whinge, they came to the pub and Annie carefully wrote down the accusation, see? Then she called in the other one, he had his say, and she wrote that down. Then the Council of Feuds – me, her and old Henry Beattie – we sat in judgement. Whatever we decided, they had to agree to it. No ifs or buts; or I arrest them both and they can cool down in a cell in Dutton while I misplace the paperwork.'

Dana smiled at the window. 'That's actually very, very clever.'

'I know, right? Annie's idea totally, I can't claim any credit. Took the heat out of everything, let people back down without losing face. Plus, they had to think twice about bringing their little whinge to the Book of Feuds, where the whole town could read it. I mean, better be worth looking like a loser to everyone, eh? Bright girl, that Annie.'

Dana allowed a pause that suited Able, and he nodded at the implication.

'Yes,' replied Dana. 'Yes, she clearly is. And they stuck to this?'

'For five years, yeah. Until last month, when Larry turns up as a dead angel, like you saw. Parked on Vince Reynolds' land, too, by his main gate. No more Book of Feuds.'

She thought for a moment. 'Where is the book now?'

He squirmed and re-gripped the wheel unnecessarily. 'Yeah, about that. She burned it. Annie. The day they found Larry Muir. Said it wasn't needed any more, reminded her of Larry.'

'Hmm.' It was more than inconvenient. The book was the first new potential evidence source Dana had discerned since she'd arrived. 'And what did you make of that, Able?'

He took his time liberating a fresh piece of gum. She was getting used to his body language displaying his level of discomfort with a conversation. In the car, he had less room for manoeuvre and so used silence to the same effect.

'Ah, I told the first investigation about it, but they didn't seem bothered. There's nothing about it in their report. No one seriously thinks Vince Reynolds killed Larry. The pair of 'em beefed and bristled, is all. At worst they could maybe have had a blue, but I never thought it would even come to that. Larry would have mashed Vince. I think they both knew it. Might accidentally shoot someone in the foot – possibly themselves – but not murder. So the book would only go to state of mind for Larry, really.'

He looked across, as though he needed to see her nod. She stared out of the side window instead, knowing that would enforce the follow-on.

'Anyway, I'd read it a couple of days before Larry died. Nothing dramatic.'

She waited, giving him the opportunity to expand, noting that he didn't take it. While they were cooperating in this investigation, both were holding back, she comprehended this. The trick, she thought, was to understand why the gaps existed at all, and why exactly there.

'What was their last feud?'

'Oh, a timeless classic. Something to return to when other rows ran out of steam. There's a big dip in the ground on the border between their properties. They both called it Bulrush Gulley, but I've never seen a map that names it. Anyhow, it's pretty deep and there's something about the geology – when it fills with water it stays filled; doesn't soak away. So if it ever rains again, it's a vital resource. Would have been a lake the size of, oh, ten footy fields, maybe? They both claimed all of it, of course.'

'What did the map say?'

'Ah, well. Larry and Vince each own about five per cent of Belgium, so sizeable chunks and all that. But the gulley's right on the border, and the official map covers the entire gulley in the felt-tip marking the border line. So, technically, they'd each own half. Couldn't be bothered to share, though. That's what the Council of

Feuds had decided, but they were both grumbling at the time. Here we go.'

They pulled off the bitumen at a boarded-up post box – a rust-mottled old milk barrel with 'Sorrento' and 'Reynolds' painted scratchily on to it – and drove three hundred metres up a dirt road, halting at a wide turning area of packed sand and loose stones. There was a traditional ranch entrance, unsophisticated logs forming an arch of sorts with the Reynolds name burned into the top bar like a cattle branding. A metal gate closed off progress to vehicles. Able pointed to a small mound of disturbed soil about six metres from the entrance.

'There. At first just an empty angel frame, for a while. Reynolds only saw it once but, like I said, no one wants to upset DuBois so he left it alone. Somewhen after that, Larry Muir is hoisted on to it. Then Reynolds needs to go to town again; that's when he sees the dead body. Hence no really accurate time of death, no alibis, no footprints or tyre marks – nothing.'

Dana glanced over her shoulder and back towards the highway. Fair point, she thought. It was too far from the main road for anyone to see that there was a frame, let alone a corpse. Drivers would need binoculars to see this spot from the highway, but even in the late afternoon they hadn't passed any vehicle since leaving town. She'd thought previously that someone must have seen something. But now she had to revise her concepts of what might reasonably be expected.

She turned back to Able. 'No one else came down this track during those days? Visitors for Reynolds? Deliveries? Someone working on his land?'

Able sat back and puffed, as if explaining this was too sad to contemplate. The air conditioning surged and subsided. 'Yeah, deliveries all go to the pub and shop, then people collect. Not just mail, either – prescriptions, too. Only Annie and Tim are authorized to hand those on. Annie writes the date and time of collection in a book. Reynolds gets visitors occasionally but not often. No one works on his land, because . . .'

Dana would have sworn Able was close to tears. She pretended to brush something from her jeans, just so Able would know she wasn't staring open-mouthed.

'Ah, look, the drought has broken Vince, poor bugger. I wouldn't even call him a gentleman farmer these days; he does nothing, you'll see. He collects his supplies from town for a while, picks up his post and medications, buys as much alcohol as Annie will sell him, and retreats back here. A week or three goes by, he does the same again: rinse and repeat. Been like that for over a year. Larry Muir took the piss at first, but he soon stopped that. Kicking a bloke when he's down – even Larry had standards.'

Dana opened the gate and held it while Able drove through. The dirt was tightly packed and she could see why forensics would have been limited. As she climbed back in the car she took a further look at the location of Larry's corpse, hoping for some semblance of meaning in the choice, but it wasn't coming to her. Insight was close by, but it skipped away from her and wouldn't play ball.

They both felt the bone-buzz as they drove over the cattle grid, before the Landcruiser picked up speed and scuffled along the poorly maintained dirt road. It followed the contours of a dip that probably became treacherous during flood, before giving a first glimpse of Sorrento. The station hunkered down below a rusted set of flickering blades and the fading sun caught them as they turned idly, firing spinning shards of light at the car. If there was any water remaining deep in the ground, the machinery looked too exhausted to pump it.

Behind the house itself was a disorganized set of metal sheds and gated pens, solid grilles and gates. In the late-afternoon light they resembled skeletal ribs, needing meaty flesh to make them whole. There was no sign of livestock. Instead the place spoke of a withering and tenuous clutch at land that had turned its back on Reynolds and callously left him to perish.

The farmhouse itself held to a remnant of better days. The front door looked like some kind of Indonesian teak and was framed by two columns of sandstone. A veranda led around each corner and disappeared from sight at the back. A child's swing by the driveway made Dana catch her breath. As they approached, the door opened and Reynolds came out to meet them. He held to the door frame as if he'd capsize without it, then scuffed his way down some steps towards the Landcruiser.

After they'd parked, Able rushed out of the car, determined to be the first to greet Reynolds. Their hug was long, close and heartfelt, so Dana hung back until she was introduced. Reynolds' handshake was sharp, terse as he looked away. His large checked shirt was frayed on one cuff and his jeans were damp near the ankles. He was swamped by his clothing, his face a map of blood vessels and anxiety. He wasn't hard to read – a deeply depressed heavy drinker who wore his desperation on his features.

They sat on the veranda, observing the sun as it dipped. Reynolds seemed impervious to the sliding temperature, a booze-coat fooling him it wasn't becoming cold. The child's swing haunted Dana's vision; she kept flicking glances. Vince Reynolds didn't have kids. His wife had died in childbirth nine years ago, the baby daughter failed to survive the day. Dana had shuddered when she'd read that in Lucy's notes. It seemed such a *medieval* cause of death, so far in the past yet still extant. Clearly Reynolds had installed the swing when Claire had been pregnant then couldn't bear to take it down afterwards. Thus it stood now as memorial, taunt and curse. Reynolds poured rum into a porcelain mug from Brisbane's 1988 Expo. The bottle had run half its race already.

'Mr Reynolds,' she began, 'I'm looking into the two murders, Larry

Muir and Tim Ogden. Could you describe finding Larry's body, please?'

Dana didn't want to waste precious time asking the obvious, repeating what the previous detectives should have asked, and maybe did. But the earlier investigation's narrative had started with Able reaching the crime scene; it ignored anything prior. She needed to ground herself in this crime scene in the way she had behind the pub, the site of Tim's murder. It was a baseline for her not just forensically but emotionally. She wanted to understand how that moment had felt for Vince.

'Yeah, okay. Well, I'd seen the frame up there six or seven days before. Morning, that was, on my way into town, coz I had some tablets to pick up. Angina, see? Anyway, the bloody frame was by the gate, so I guess Frenchie stuck it there himself and all. It was unusual to see one out of town, but I didn't pay much attention. If you leave 'em alone, he moves them after a while. If you touch them, he comes over all fascist about it, eh, Abe?'

Able nodded sagely. Vince wiped his lips with his wrist.

'So, must have been a week later, I go to town again. Food, this time. And the uh, critical supplies from Bundaberg. Frame wasn't empty any more. I was driving towards it, thinking Frenchie had added an angel and wasn't that a waste of his bloody time, out here where no one would see it? I'm sure you see dead bodies all the time, Detective. But, you know, all done up the way he was, it didn't seem real. I thought I'd puke, but I managed to hold it back. It was weird, I was only twenty or thirty metres away when I realized it was Larry. He can't have been there long because the birds hadn't really started. In fact, nothing was moving at all — no breeze, no insects, nothing. Like the world took a breath. I'm not religious, but I crossed myself anyway, be on the safe side. I did look about, but I couldn't see anyone.

'I drove around the clearing, through the scrub, in case there was evidence and whatnot. Been around Abe long enough to know the drill. Saw Larry had a bullet in him, any rate. Poor bastard. High-tailed it to town and got Abe, who was being a lazy bugger and having a lie-in.'

Vince nodded at the ground. It was enough for Dana to draw some mental pictures.

'Thank you. Did you hear or see anything in the day or two prior to that?'

'Nah. Nah, I was on a bit of a bender before that day. Bad anniversary.' He nodded to the swing and swallowed hard. 'So nah, wouldn't have known a thing about it. Poor Larry. There's dyin' and there's dyin'. Wouldn't wish that on anyone. Like I said, you must see dead people all the time, but for me? Shaking like a leaf all day, don't mind admitting it.'

'Larry Muir and Tim Ogden – exactly how well did you know each of them, Mr Reynolds?'

She shared a look with Able. She knew they'd already discussed this in the car, but Vince needed a way into deeper conversation. If he lived an isolated life with little chatter with strangers, the segue had to be created for him. He'd gabbled when he was talking about finding Larry Muir, but much of that was delayed shock, even now – the tremor in his voice lingered. She suspected he'd clam up after a while, simply from lack of practice.

'Vince, call me Vince. Jeez, you're not having tea with the queen, mate. Ah, well, Tim not so much. Saw him in the pub sometimes. I never got a full handle on what he actually did. Just skivvied for Annie, I guess. I mean, arrange your marriage how you want and all that, but Annie ran things and Tim just ran around at her feet. Always felt . . . *undignified*, yeah, Abe?'

He leaned forward for Able's confirmation, which came via a silent grin and a barely perceptible nod.

'Yeah, seemed to me Tim did whatever Annie couldn't be bothered to do. Out the back changing barrels, running errands; did a lot of cleaning, did Tim. Christ knows what kind of pre-nup those two had, coz I guess Annie's worth a bob or two. But yeah, reckon that doesn't matter if he goes first, eh. Larry? Ah, well, that's a bit different. You know about . . .'

He glanced over to Able.

'Told her about the Book of Feuds, mate, yeah.'

'Ah, okay. Good, I s'pose. Yeah, me and Larry just got into a situation where we always saw the worst in what the other one was doing. Half the time I was doing nothing wrong and he'd get all riled up; if I'm honest, the same in return. Sometimes, I liked it. You know, as things started going south here. I could vent a bit with Larry. Felt like a freebie, somehow. But lately, yeah, he got all serious. I think his place was in trouble – not like mine, I grant you – and he was arguing with Sarah a lot. So he was, uh, especially testy.'

He paused for another swig.

'But, interesting thing. Knew him for twenty-six years; never set foot in his house. Not once. Sarah kinda couldn't stand me, that's part of it. But even so. Never the offer. Never "have a beer" or "stay for dinner": just had to say my piece and bugger off. Both of us, me and Larry, we're fine with all the other farmers, and the townies. Just each other caused the problem. Couldn't stop it, somehow.'

It was useful background, but it wasn't where Dana wanted to take the conversation. However, it had kept Vince talking.

'It must be very difficult, I imagine. Being in a drought, like this.'

Reynolds looked at her sharply. She hadn't thought him capable of such quick, precise movement. He considered what she'd said, then raised his mug and gave her a weak half-smile.

'You didn't say we're in the *middle* of a drought. Thank God. Thank *you*. You get it: how do we know if this is the middle? Maybe break next month, could go on for years. That's part of the problem – we can't be sure.' Reynolds' voice was the gentle belligerence of being half cut; slightly too loud and too aggressive for the occasion. 'Drought is death by asphyxiation, Detective. Chokes you, gently takes everything that keeps you alive. Slow and deadly, not neat and quick.'

He waved his mug vaguely at the horizon and they all watched a splodge of liquid launch at the dust. Reynolds didn't seem bothered at the message of gorging on Bundy all afternoon, nor at the waste as it seeped into the soil.

'I mean, every other natural disaster *is* quick. And forecast. No one gets flooded over a period of five years, do they? You usually get a day or two's notice of the rainstorm or the rising river, then it's on you. Time enough for most people – if they've got sense – to get out of the way themselves, save their prized possessions or their stock, at least stop the worst of it from affecting their livelihood. Same thing with cyclones. They get trailed for at least a week before they arrive. Get out of the way, follow the instructions. And that's assuming you live in the quarter of the country that get them – most people don't.'

He was strident but not likely to spark fully, Dana calculated. In other words, he was open to prodding.

'Bushfires?'

He gave a her a sly glance of appreciation. Perhaps, she thought, he simply isn't used to speaking to people. Or, possibly, the listener actually paying attention was a rare icing on his cake.

'Well, *slightly* different. Good point. But ah, we could argue all day how much of those is natural disaster, how much is human stupidity, couldn't we? Bit of a can of worms having that chat, these days. But yeah, they can leap up out of nowhere, I suppose. Even so, there's usually warnings – dry spells, days of total fire bans, people telling you to watch, act, evacuate; it's over in a few days and there's usually help before and after.' His blasé summary of lethal events hung on the evening air. He seemed to finally consider what the listeners might think of him. 'Not saying all that isn't God-awful, or deadly, just . . . not the same.'

He hauled himself up from a slump and became more focused, more animated. His voice steadied and his choice of words was more forensic. Again, a gesture and the waste of precious rum.

'No, drought's different. It's a day-by-day squeeze. It looks, feels, exactly the same from one day to the next. There's nothing to run from, no instructions to *leave now*. You never know that *this* is the day you should pack up, or sell your stock, or cash in. You only know looking back – you realize that two years or four years ago, you should have done all that. So drought's almost mocking you, isn't it? Making a fool of you for not seeing it all coming, for missing that tipping point, for being an optimist.'

He seemed satiated at that point. They all watched the sun tip at the horizon, flickering through the spectrum as it died. Dana was about to ask another question when Reynolds resumed, with no prompting, as though his pause had been one brief intake of breath, not five minutes of fuming silence.

'Then there's the fact that it most directly hits one group – farmers. Oh, there's fallout on the whole community, no question, but the hardest, deepest punch is into a farmer's gut. Not just because they're losing money, or stock, or crops. No, it's because the farmer feels history more than anyone else. They'll have weather records for that land going back decades – maybe a century or more. Those notebooks in a drawer, written longhand every day for generations? They are very. Bloody. Heavy. They shout that farmers before now had it harder, for longer, without all the mod cons, and *survived*. So the modern farmers, they look at those records and think they're a failure: not hard enough, not smart enough, too soft, too foolish. And if those records were made by their dad, or their granddad? Well, Jeez, add another layer of self-loathing to it. Because now they're trashing a legacy, aren't they? Can't keep the family farm going, when others had it tougher before them? They feel they've let everyone down, up to and including people who are long dead. That's real pressure. No wonder so many of us top ourselves.'

He paused for a moment and ran his hand across four or five days of stubble. 'Ah, crap. I didn't—'

'S'all right, mate.' Able squinted at the car and blinked.

Reynolds took a large swig just to relish the burning sensation. His voice came softer now, reached deeper because of it.

'Nah, drought's the worst. Fire and flood? They're like taipans: a quick snap and it's done. Drought's a python. Soft little contact you don't notice when you're asleep, then it quietly squeezes the life out of you. Comes a point where you can't scream, then you can't move, then you can't breathe. Slow as it likes. Drought has all the time in the world, but your life collapses one day at a time, one minute at a time.'

They all soaked up the implication and gave Reynolds' speech due respect. He harrumphed, took another slurp, and nodded at the ground.

'I looked up the rain records for Dutton before I flew out,' said Dana. 'Is it the same here?'

'Well, Little Big Town usually gets a bit more than us. Something to do with the weather fronts, the way they curl as they cross country. So whatever they get, knock off about ten per cent.'

'Ninety per cent of nothing is nothing.'

Reynolds smirked. 'There you go. In theory, I still have plenty of cattle, but only sixty of them are here. The land, plus the bales I buy in, can only support that many. The rest are interstate; I pay to have them kept on farms that actually have grass. Those farmers do a decent job and they're good people; I'm not getting screwed or anything. But the numbers don't stop, do they? Not the bills, any rate. I went backwards every day. Used to have the laughable hope of building the herd up later on. After, you know, all the rain we need for a decade falls in a month.'

Able lightly touched Reynolds' elbow, a curiously intimate and subtle gesture. She noted Reynolds' ease with it. These two went way back.

'Only takes one monsoon event, Vince.'

'Yeah, I know, Abe.'

Dana thought about how to introduce the next element. Lucy's foraging had given her a way in, establishing the issue but not all the parties. Dana didn't want to lay out her cards at this moment. She wanted to know how much Reynolds wished to be public, and how much he still wanted to hide. That mattered – what people in Una-murra tried to keep cloaked was, she felt, critical.

'But your circumstances have changed? *Of late?*'

Reynolds caught his breath. He used more rum to regain his balance, appraising just how much she knew and recognizing from Able's surprised grunt that she hadn't shared with the constable. She was giving him room – if he wished – to retain a secret.

'Yeah. Actually,' said Reynolds, 'I've just sold.'

'*Sold?*' Able leaned forward, elbows on knees and rubbing his ring finger, staring at the dust because he didn't want to look his friend in the eye.

'Yeah. Sold up. The whole thing. All the debt, interstate stock, too – the whole caboodle.' Reynolds squinted at the sunset. 'Oh, I'm staying on short-term, renting back; keep things ticking over while I sort out my next step. But in a few weeks I'll be shifting my carcass.'

'Who bought it?' asked Dana. Good detectives rarely asked a question unless they already knew, or suspected, the answer. She could narrow it down in her own mind but would need Lucy to hunt for confirmation.

A long pause and a swish at a mozzie that might not have been there.

'Ah, anonymous buyer. Not allowed to say. Confidential – it's part of the contract.' Another pause. 'No point trying to look it up, neither. All done through companies and nominees and such.'

Dana reflected that, at the very least, she should now be certain that the buyer was Australian. If they were foreign, they'd require the permission of the federal government: farms were sensitive national assets. The *quid pro quo* for that permission would be transparency from the ultimate beneficiary. So genuinely anonymous buyers were always Australian and therefore, potentially, could be uncovered by Lucy.

'You sure that's what you want to do, mate?' Able's voice was gentle yet searching.

Reynolds put the empty mug down carefully on the soil, leaned forward and clapped his palms free of dirt.

'Yeah. Yeah, actually. Had a gutsful. Been trying to hang on, but, you know, gets you in the end, eh? Yeah. Feel pretty peaceful now it's gone through. Didn't think I would, but yeah. *Peaceful.*'

His voice drifted off on the final word, and Dana felt a chill in her blood. Reynolds had the same kind of faux tranquillity that came over hypothermia victims at the last, a floating absence of feeling that they misunderstood as benign. Reynolds, she believed, wouldn't last three months after leaving this property. She sensed Able had the same perspective and saw his eyes prickle as he realized it too.

Reynolds rose silently and patted Able's shoulder as he passed. Dana and Able still hadn't spoken when the farmhouse door closed with a soft *pffft*.

Chapter 9

The car felt too small for their emotions. Dana's shudder of empathy was dwarfed by Able's nascent grief for a friend who hadn't passed yet. Again, an absent-minded touch to his ring finger. She gave him time, until he nodded twice at the windscreen and offered her some gum.

'No, thank you, you're good. I'm sorry, Able.'

'Yeah, well. Nothing to be done. Can't save him from his own mistakes, eh. He'll do what he thinks he wants. Truth is, he'd have been turfed out by the banks before long, probably with less money in his pocket. At least this feels like going on his terms. It does to him, anyhow.'

She thought he'd want to say more on the subject, if only to give it voice and oxygen. But instead Able came at a different issue. 'Can I ask a question?'

He asked for permission as though they had a hierarchy between two people. As she'd witnessed with Judge Trent, Able had a default of observable deference when he felt on the back foot.

'Yes, of course.'

'So you've explained why there's twenty-eight angels. But why are there fifty-six frames? That's not a thingie – a perfect number, is it?' He glanced across at her head-shake. 'He only needs a few spares, doesn't he? Not twenty-eight.'

It was a good question. It was one she'd asked herself back on the plane, when she'd read some background on DuBois.

'Did you ever ask DuBois about his art?'

'I tried a few times, but he was, well . . .'

Constantly angry. Dismissive. Condescending. Contemptuous. All of the above, if Lucy's e-pack notes were a fair reflection: the flight had given Dana time for a potted history of DuBois' art . . . and his reaction to critique. She opted for something more diplomatic.

'Opaque?'

Able snorted. 'I was going to say smart-arse. He said it wasn't his place to tell me what to think about the art, it was up to me to look properly and feel it for myself.'

'Ah. Yes, he probably would.' She nodded. 'You're right. In a technical sense, he doesn't need that many spares in case some get damaged. But the extra frames form part of the art, don't they? I mean, they're all over town, just like the angels.'

Able frowned, as if this wasn't computing. The first investigation hadn't bothered much with DuBois; the siting of both corpses on his frames seemed to have been taken as simply an ad hoc measure. There was no evidence the two detectives had looked closer, searching for further meaning. They'd established a rough alibi – pub, shop and home were the only viable options, just like almost everyone in town – and had no inkling of a motive, so they'd parked DuBois somewhat. Dana suspected they found a conceptual artist tricky to fathom and stuck him in the *too difficult* box. Dana could try to find him, but had no idea how to start in a desert the size of Belgium. Better, she felt, to focus for now on what was tangible and reachable and see where that took her.

'Look,' explained Dana, 'if he has one frame per angel and a few spares tucked away in storage somewhere, you don't consider the frames at all. They're just a means of hoisting the angels up, to make them seem bigger and more imposing. You take the frames for granted. Whereas if there are empty frames dotted around town and often moved, they act as a constant reminder. Then you also think about the frames: they look odd to you, standing there empty, and you subconsciously wish for them to be filled. With no angel on them, they look like stick figures with their arms out, beseeching, wanting fulfilment. He's given you something that feels unfulfilled and that taps into your wish for more.'

She glanced at him to see if this was sinking in or resonating. He stared resolutely ahead. She summarized a view she'd read in a magazine article written by DuBois' sister.

'DuBois isn't really a fan of the modern world – he feels we've gone off the rails. A lot of his work is supposed to be warnings of various kinds: he's telling us how to change course. DuBois believes we're constantly longing for what we don't have. So if we get a nice house, we want a spare bedroom for guests. Then we want a home office. Then a media room. Then a pool, and so on. By creating the empty frames he invites us to think about why we're never satisfied, why we always want something more than we have, and whether that's a good thing or not. I believe that's the idea.'

At length, Able shook his head. 'Why didn't he just say that when I asked? He's a dickhead.'

'Hmm. Partly, because he's an artist. That's how he expresses himself. So he won't say much out loud. He wants to – *needs to* – communicate through art. It's a restriction in his life but also a compulsion. He wants you to arrive at those conclusions yourself, because that means you've engaged with what he's done. But as you've now demonstrated, people don't always go where they're led. That means DuBois gets annoyed that people don't appreciate his work, then it all gets a bit fractious. Public art is like that – you put it out there, but most people don't dance to the tune you've provided for them. It sort of goes with the territory; it's an occupational hazard. But DuBois seems to have taken this one to heart. Maybe that's why he still lives here. There's an element of masochism to that decision, I'd suggest – sticking around in a place that doesn't understand the art he's made.'

She was fishing. Able bit.

'Ha. Well, he lives here when he's here. Spends his time out in the bush now.'

Dana had wondered why DuBois hadn't gone to the city in a huff. She'd read his contract. He wasn't obliged to stay in Unamurra past the opening ceremony six months ago. Remaining here couldn't be anything other than unfinished business of some kind.

'Then he's embedding himself in the environment, soaking up what it has to offer. That's what he'd claim, anyway.'

'Yeah, nah. He's hiding. Has been for weeks. I have to wonder *why* he's hiding. What, or who, is he avoiding?'

The two concepts were clashing: DuBois staying when he could easily leave, and DuBois hiding when he seemingly had no reason. The two things were both true, she reasoned, and happening at the same time. The juxtaposition seemed important but, like so many aspects of this town and this case, she was having trouble seeing through it.

'Second question?' he offered.

Again, undue deference, she felt. 'One's normally my limit, but seeing as it's you . . .'

'The wings,' said Able. 'Where did whoever get the wings from?'

'Sorry?'

'It occurred to me when I was driving down to pick you up. I should have mentioned it in Dutton station – Doc Mangold might have had a theory. We know there's twenty-eight angels, right? Each angel has a set of wings; otherwise they're just, you know, weird torsos. But there are still twenty-eight angels in town, as far as I know. They all still have their wings. So the wings on the two bodies – where did they come from?'

His logic drew her up short. In the few hours she'd had to skim through the case files she hadn't got to that notion at all. It was a good question. One that had only one viable answer.

'DuBois, I suppose.' She felt a catch in her throat, as if she didn't want to admit this. 'He probably has the only access to wings. Which means . . .'

'He was involved in the dead bodies?' Able glanced across. He was being polite about it – this new kink pointed the finger at DuBois as the murderer.

'Has to be, doesn't he?' she agreed. 'We know DuBois hates anyone interfering with his angels – hates it with a passion. I don't see how anyone else in town could reasonably have got hold of more wings. He'd hardly donate a couple of pairs, would he? Unless . . . unless whoever it was simply stole them, used them on the dead bodies, then DuBois came along and replaced the wings that had gone. Maybe.'

They both chewed on that for a moment as they rumbled to the final ridge and Unamurra came into view. They reached the two-kilometre pole and, like clockwork, both their phones buzzed as they came within signal range of town. Dana read and then looked across.

'I've got one from Doc Mangold and a few from Lucy. You?'

She could see an entire screen of bold headlines, but Able chose to share just one.

'Half-price pizza at Dutton RSL. Only a four-hundred-kay round-trip for a Hawaiian.'

She grinned. 'Able Barella, I'm surprised and disappointed. Surely you don't sanction the mixing of meat and fruit on a pizza?'

Able shrugged. 'It would be one of my five-a-day. What did the Doc want?'

She scrolled as they came on to the main street. 'Ah. He did some extra chasing on fingerprints with Interpol. He confirms that the only marks on the bodies and frames are from Axel DuBois. The only ones. In capital letters, bold.'

Able turned into the main street and slowed to a gentle cruise. Everything looked closed; even the pub door was shut for now. The shop had background lights on, but there was no sign you could buy anything this evening. Dana thought back to Able's comment that Annie made up the shop rules as she saw fit. Presumably, that included opening hours, too.

'Hmm,' reflected Able. He was adding the confirmation from Mangold to their discussion about the angel wings. 'Well, his prints ought to be there, seeing as he's the artist and all. That doesn't surprise me. Expected to see some others, maybe. Mangold said it was only DuBois' prints, back when the first investigation came knocking. But he's been doing some extra work on some of the more difficult surfaces, since he heard you were coming.'

'You said he might have been inspired to raise his game. I agree – there might have been other prints, even if they were smudged or partial. I don't think it puts DuBois any more in the frame than before, though.'

'Nah, not more, not less,' replied Able, swinging a U-turn and stopping outside the garage. 'But all the same. His art. His frames. His fingerprints. His access to those wings. He's got his imprint all over both murders, hasn't he?'

Chapter 10

Dana paced again at the back of Able's place. The cloud was drifting in and the breeze had died a little. She'd found herself paying inordinate attention to tiny shifts in the weather patterns ever since she arrived. Something about the size of the sky and Unamurra's dependence on every nuance of isotherm and pressure system made it compulsive. It felt as if the whole town was looking up, begging for release, and she should somehow take part in that. In Carlton she'd barely check if it looked like showers; in Unamurra the important landscape was always above her and she acted accordingly.

She still didn't have a proper read on DuBois' place in this town, or in these crimes. As Able had rightly pointed out, DuBois was inextricably linked to both crime scenes and both bodies. He had the means of committing each crime, knew both victims to some degree. Now he was out in the wind, deliberately avoiding everyone. But, like almost everyone in town, he had no concrete alibi because the windows for killing and staging the bodies were each at least twelve hours. Like almost everyone in town, he had no discernible motive for even disliking each man, let alone murder. Milford had described him as *incidental*.

The first investigation had finally interviewed him, but it had been cursory – mostly concerned with background on how to hoist a body onto an angel frame. The detectives could have simply watched an online video in Dutton: they raised little for DuBois to account for besides that. She felt that was an error – though not necessarily because DuBois was guilty. Logic made him a strong runner, but her instinct refused to fully buy into it. She had no idea why.

'Hey, Dana.' Lucy's voice lifted her.

'Hey, you. What am I missing back home?'

'Oh, big things. Mighty things. It's all changed in a heartbeat. You won't recognize the ol' place. Miriam might be getting a new puppy; I've heard *all* about that today. But worse than that . . .'

The change in tone gave Dana fair warning. 'McCullough? What's he done now?'

'He's *visited.*'

'Seriously? In the office?'

'Yup. A rare sighting. I got myself a cuppa and when I got back, there he was. Lurking. He fidgets, chick, I don't like it. Kept looking down, like you and Mikey would rise up from the carpet, then up, like you'd both abseil in. Anything but look at a person in the same room. I swear, when he retires he could make a very good living in hospitals, hiring himself out as a human emetic.'

Dana snorted, but she could tell Lucy was rattled. Not much pulled Lucy off balance. 'He said something, Luce, didn't he?'

'Yeah. Well, words slithered out. I'm not sure public speaking is his forte. He said he had Central's blessing for a District Scrutiny.'

Dana shuddered. A District Scrutiny happened once in a blue moon. The local commander had to convince Central that the district was in such a parlous state that he should be allowed a free hand to practically reinvent it. Human Resources and Legal loved the District Scrutiny, since it provided cover for drastic changes that couldn't be challenged in tribunal – the Scrutiny was its own justification.

'Pink sheets a go-go?' asked Dana.

'That was the implication. I had to wash my hands after he'd gone.'

'I know the feeling. Any indication when he would start?'

'Nada. I think he likes holding the sword over the innocent, doesn't he?'

'Absolutely.'

They both understood the implications. Lucy was tied to the area by her circumstances and would be unlikely to get a similar job anywhere local. Dana was terrified she'd be moved across state, away from everything. Away from Lucy.

Lucy sighed. 'Aargh, I can't afford to think about it any more. Tell me you have something interesting for me to do, chick.'

Dana smiled. 'A couple of things, yes. Thank you for those bios – I've read six of them. These people aren't just strangers to me, they're strange, so having some background data really helps. Stuff for you to do, yes. First, can you check the system for an unsolved murder? It would have been in the last eight years or so, either in Dutton itself or further into the outer-back.'

'Okay . . . please hold, madam . . . your call is *impertinent* to us. Ah, here we go. One from nine years ago. In Dutton. Let me skim the details for you.'

Dana swirled some sand around on her shoe, watching the way it behaved as it trickled. Sand and snow: two things that weren't liquid but could act like it.

'Okay. The deceased was a Kendall Hendricks, twenty-five, shop assistant at the local Woolies. Killed by persons unknown as she walked to her car at 8 p.m. September 25. Stabbed twice – the one on her right arm was thought to be a miss, or her defensive reflex. Second was in the stomach: near her heart, but not near enough. She took two days to die in hospital. Jesus, that's awful. How did you know there'd be an unsolved there?'

Dana felt a ripple of ice slide through her body. She knew what was coming next, but had to confirm it.

'Someone mentioned something today. Can you check . . . if there's an involvement by Able Barella, please?'

'Sure. Wait, that's your . . . sure. Hang on . . . yeah, here he is. Deceased's fiancé. Christ. He was posted to City at the time. Came back and he was by her bedside when they turned off the machine. He was her only family, apparently. She was adopted as a kid and those parents were already gone.'

'The investigating officers and district commander at the time?'

'Commander was Trent – he's been there much longer than that. Detectives were Morgan and Milford. Does that mean anything to you?'

Her stomach twisted at the recollection of the conversation in Trent's office. The callous indifference Trent had shown, the crude kick in the guts he'd administered as a mere aside. Able had taken it without retort: he was strong. But something had made Trent believe he could dish that out without fear of a comeback. It might be simply arrogance, she thought, but it said something about Able's reputation as well. And, since that moment, the gold ring Able touched whenever he drifted into melancholy.

'Yes, it does. And I think it still means a lot to Able, as well. Okay, thanks for that Luce. I won't need anything more about it for now, but please archive the file just in case. Ah, what else? Yes, the farm. You'll recall from the data you sent that there's a station out here called Sorrento? Owned by Vince Reynolds. He says he's sold it very recently, but he won't say who's bought. I'd like to know, please.'

'I assume that information isn't going to be lying on the ground, waiting for Lucy Delaney to pick it up?'

'No, someone's trying to bury it. So I imagine you'll need to dig.'

'Shall do. Anything else?'

'A couple of kites to fly, please. The first investigation mentioned Larry Muir's wife and some visits she made to the family solicitor, but it just has dead air about what was discussed. One of many loose threads in their report. Can you dig in and around that, please? There might be nothing, but I need to cover bases and I'm visiting Sarah Muir tomorrow morning. Also, Unamurra is too small to have a councillor, but I think their local government business is done in Dutton. Can you ferret around for anything relevant? This town doesn't seem to have a future, but presumably some local worthies have floated some boats at some point. They can't just rely on some art to lift them out of the drought. Finally, I don't know how they operate their water here. It gets delivered and put in the big tank, I know that, but they seem to have some local group deciding how it's used. Anything you can find might be a help. Thanks, Luce.'

'Oh, I like a good ferret. So much better than a rummage. How's it going out there?'

'Strangely. It's going strangely. As if they don't mind who did it, or don't care if that person might be walking around freely.'

'Hmm. Do they seem scared of the killer, then?'

'No, that's a weird aspect. No one's telling me to leave it because they think I'll spark more violence if I pursue it. It's not the silence you get when people fear retribution and pull down the shutters, not at all. It's more insidious than that.'

'So that's a clue, chick.'

She nodded. Lucy's insight was keeping Dana sharp, as if the analysis from a distance was even better than she could muster here, inside the enigma.

'Yes, it is. I know what you mean. But it's such an odd thing that I can't quite make use of it. Yet. Speaking of odd – these angels. There was a line of twenty at the edge of town when we drove in.'

'A welcoming committee?'

'That's what Able said as well. They didn't seem very welcoming.'

And, she reflected, Able hadn't seemed reassured by the welcome. His explanation of his reticence had been useful but partial. She felt there was even more to it. Able might have feared that DuBois was the killer and the presence of a row of sinister angels was DuBois' way of telling the town he was still around. Which might also explain everyone's reluctance around solving the case.

'What are the angels like? I've seen the photos, but what are they like in real life?'

'Wow. They're just . . . wow. It's a shame they're all the way out here because they're magnificent. I hadn't imagined he'd be this talented. Perhaps if you put them inside a gallery they'd lose some of their power; it might be that they only work in this town, at this time. But they are tremendously impressive, intimidating.'

Beyond the technical and artistic ability, Dana thought, DuBois was also demonstrating some form of tenacity. He was sticking around in a district where he felt he needed to be in the desert, not the town. Staying here was important to him, but the *why* remained inconclusive – at least, to her. He could be remaining to intimidate the town into silence, ensuring the Detective from Carlton went home empty-handed.

'Luce, sorry, another request. Can you dig deeper into DuBois' background, please? All the way back, as far as you can get. He's a bit enigmatic and he seems to have breezed into Unamurra on the back of this artistic project. In that sense, he arrived out of a clear blue sky. I'd like the measure of him in case I bump into him at any point, or he looms even larger further down the track.'

'Yeah, no problem. He's from Quebec, but I think I read he was from Europe originally. I'll hunt him down.' Lucy paused. 'It's not just the fact that you're miles away, but you sound a bit distant.'

Dana sighed. 'Yes, I am. Sorry. It's just that this place is so weird to me, so far off my usual scale. I've got a horrible feeling I need to really understand this town to make progress, but I might be the last person who would understand it.'

'But you're solitary, and surely all those people are solitary, too?'

'Yes, good point, but it feels different to that. I just haven't been somewhere quite like this, and it's throwing me. Talk to me about something normal, Luce.'

'You don't feel normal there?'

'No, I don't. I mean, partly it's me being a fish out of water. I'd factored that on the journey to Dutton. But it's more than that. There's a vibe, a sensibility – something. There's a sense that the whole place is tilted – not grotesquely, like a hall of mirrors, but subtly.'

'Okay. Well, here's some normal for you. I'm making spag-bol and speed-reading a Grisham, but I've currently got half an eye on a home-shopping channel, if that's a help.'

'Ooh, what are they desperately padding out to an hour?'

'A necklace. Poor bugger has been forty-four minutes on this diagem necklace, and he's flagging. Oh, no.'

'What?'

'He's brought out the ruler.'

Dana laughed. 'Oh, game over. Stick a fork in him, he's done. All out of chat now. I bet he does it in metric *and* imperial.'

'He has, he has. I can't watch any more carnage. A man with a Botoxed face just shot his own career.'

'Thank you, Luce.'

'You're always welcome, chick. What's next on your agenda?'

'Ah, we still have a last bit of daylight here. So, a chat with the man who made the desert bloom, I think.'

'Laters.'

Chapter 11

The light was fading more slowly than she'd expected; dusk was grey and gusty. The Beattie residence was halfway down Ransome Street. To its left a grassless vacant lot showcased a rusted lawnmower, its handle covered by a dust-blown old towel anchored by two clothes pegs. The blades held wind-whipped cobweb from a golden orb which shivered as the breeze permeated its work. At the front fence the empty lot had two vertical posts: remnants of the decades-ago attempt to sell it. To the right, a presumably disused cottage hunkered forlornly. It had an always-distressed look, a sense of being discarded practically at birth – left to lizards, insects and the blown sand that encroached through its cracks and splinters.

Henry Beattie's house was only slightly snappier. Unlike its neighbour, it offered revealing glimpses of previous care. It was a home that had once been neat as a pin but had deteriorated when only one person was paying attention. The paint applied with meticulous accuracy was now faded and bird-stained. Attempts had been made at a garden, but now it shrivelled away from light and heat. Hanging baskets held powdery soil and tendrils so brittle they would snap in a man's fingers. The siding planks hummed in the shimmering wind, vibrating against the framing as they tried to drift away. On the porch, three chairs faced them, upright dining chairs from a 1970s set, the wicker seats fraying and bursting.

'Ah, good, he's in, then.' Able swung open the metal gate, which twisted to an unruly angle on its only working hinge, and let Dana go first.

'Were you anticipating he was dining at the country club or holding court in the casino?' asked Dana over her shoulder.

Another Barella grin. 'It's the lowest form of wit, you know that, right? Nah, it's the chairs. I should have explained before. An Unamurra code – we have a zillion of 'em. Everyone has chairs outside their house, see?'

He pointed with a sweep to the seven homes within sight. Each had a motley collection of seating on their veranda. A few had chewed-up old armchairs, but most were spartan wooden chairs of varying rigidity. A couple faced the house, not the street.

'Yes, I see. Very public-spirited. Very communal.'

'Ah, well, that's the thing. If all the chairs face the street, it means you're welcome to rock up to the home and knock. They're up for a chat, or a visit.'

She gave a sidelong glance. 'But you do always knock?'

'God, yeah. Once you've seen an oldie wandering around stark naked and itchy, soon puts you straight on that.' He briefly mimed vomiting. 'Anyway, the chairs. If any face inwards, that means they're either not at home or they don't feel like chatting.'

'An interesting form of etiquette.'

Able shrugged. 'I think it makes sense. Used to be, people just barged into each other's homes any old time. I reckon we're more about personal privacy now. So this is some kind of compromise. There you go, I can see Henry's in the kitchen.'

Able knocked and stood back from the door as Dana looked past the chairs to an old dresser by the corner of the house. She wasn't sure

if it was standing outdoors because Beattie intended to restore it or
chuck it: either option looked viable. Beattie answered the door while
drying his hands on a tea-towel.

'Abe, mate. Who's the newbie?'

'My detective colleague, Henry. My esteemed colleague.'

'Oh, pardon my French. Hiya.'

'Is the jug on?' Able asked.

'Yeah, it can be. Come on in, both.'

They entered a large room. The floorboards were rough-hewn and
laced with knots: Henry was barefoot, so presumably his soles were
leathery by now. In front of a fireplace that held an immaculate pyramid of logs was an elderly rug. The ends were shucking their braids
and the centre was worn to the point of transparency.

Off to the side, Dana could see one closed door and one open. The
latter showcased an elderly top-loader crowned by a rotund, striped
laundry bag. To the other side, two closed doors. The main room had
a kitchen that Dana reckoned to be 1960s at best; squared-off wooden
units with metal ellipses as handles, all clumsily painted in a vaguely
nautical blue-and-white combination, the work surface Formica and
edged by a metal band. The wall units above the sink had sliding glass
doors with a wavy pattern etched in. The fridge clearly weighed a ton.
It was retro without being ironic and a corner had two wooden wedges
underneath to keep it level where the floorboard had yielded.

The dining table was off to one side. It had the missing chair to
match those outside, but this one was in better shape. The sofa was
harsh cloth with a red-rose motif, almost abrasive, with a white linen
cover slanted across the back. The television was a small, modern flat
screen, the cheap, brandless type used in rental apartments and
motels. It had a plethora of thick cables running via a box to the wall,
where they slithered outdoors. Dana couldn't recall seeing a satellite
dish on the roof, but perhaps it was around the back. All the curtains

were faded and, at the rear of the house, they'd fallen off the runners at one end.

No sense of progress or trajectory pervaded the room; it reeked of inertia. A home, she surmised, of someone who was surviving rather than living. A person who couldn't bear to go backwards or forwards but hated where he was.

Henry Beattie was a tall, rangy mess of stiff limbs; he shuffled on legs that barely bent. He wore dusty jeans, and several buttons of his striped shirt were open despite the cool weather. When they'd stepped past him into the house Dana had spotted the top of a surgical scar across his heart, camouflaged by mottled skin, grey hairs and a pre-melanoma. Two decades of cattle farming had made Beattie robust, fixed in posture. But retirement had created sclerotic movements. Unable to work land he'd cherished, he was now calcifying.

Beattie did the honours while he gassed to Able about footy. Dana took a closer look at a set of photos on the wall. At last Beattie slumped into a denim-hued armchair that had a coffee stain on the right arm and a worried hole on the left arm. He'd set some solid builder's tea in front of Able, and a freshly opened bottle of water for Dana. He suggested a glass with an incline of the head, but Dana politely declined.

'No thank you, the bottle's fine. Mr Beattie, my name is Dana Russo. I'm a detective investigating the two homicides here in Unamurra. Able Barella you know, of course.'

Beattie's eyes were, for want of a better description, *murderous*. He squinted no matter what the light, but his stare was electric just the same. Up close his eyes seemed more yellow than any other colour, a sparkling gold that radiated ferocity despite his languorous body language. Dana had a sense of being pierced and pinned. Beattie shuttered his gaze across to Able, then back again.

'Yeah, Abe mentioned something was coming up. But those two killings have been investigated.'

In a town of fifty souls, the arrival of an out-of-town detective for two murders wouldn't be a passing comment he'd barely recall; it would be front page, bold type. Dana was always suspicious of those who dissembled before the preliminaries were done: it spoke of both major motivation and a lack of patience. In addition, she noted, Beattie had stated the end of the investigation as a fact, not a question.

'The investigation is ongoing, Mr Beattie. Perhaps you could begin by telling me when you moved to Unamurra, and why?'

Beattie was clearly not used to hiding his emotions. He raised his eyebrows and grunted. 'What do you want to know that for? Not a suspect, am I?'

'Mr Beattie, I'm asking you for some general background, please.'

They stared at each other for several seconds. Beattie glanced at Able, seeking . . . what? Permission? Reassurance?

'Yeah, okay. Oh, and stop calling me Mister Beattie. You talk like a tax inspector or a dentist and I don't like either of 'em. Henry's just fine.'

'Of course, Henry. When did you move here?'

'Uh, 2000. Just before the Olympics. Because Jane, my wife back then, she wouldn't come until the new year. Paranoid about that millennium bug, remember?'

'I do, yes.'

Henry nodded and looked again at Able, as though inviting him to intervene. Able leaned back further against the sofa.

'So once the toaster hadn't tried to kill us and there weren't zombies in the streets, it was February 2000 when we moved here.'

'And why did you come?'

'Ah, well, two reasons. First, her brother Alfie was living here then – in this house, in fact – and he had chronic asthma. I mean, *chronic*. He moved here for the dry air, see? Ahead of his time, wasn't he, Abe?'

Again an appeal to Able, who gave one of his trademark grins, arms folded. Dana noticed the attempts to marginalize her. It didn't feel aimed at *her*, as such, more at anyone who was an other, an outsider.

'Anyway,' he continued, 'she wanted to nurse him and that – they had no one else but each other by then – so I pretty much tagged along. She promised me a workshop out the back. How could I refuse? Well, four months later Alfie up and died on us. Then Jane hotfoots it to Sydney and I . . . decided to stay.'

There was clearly a story within a story there, but Dana decided to let it lie for now.

'You said there were two reasons?'

Henry grimaced and glanced at a broken clock on the mantelpiece. The wall plaster had a long crack from the clock up to the ceiling. The house was tugging north and south at the same time, unable to form a consensus on how to fall apart.

'Yeah, well, if you're asking everyone this, most of them'll give you the same answer. Cheap. It was bloody cheap to move here. We're mostly on pensions, fixed incomes here; we need low outgoings. People think boats, caravans, motor homes. But that's false economy in the long run; they need maintenance, servicing, they can turn into a money pit. Most of us did our homework, see? We all sold up some-where else, came to Unamurra – gave us some money in the bank. Some, uh, *rainy day* money.' He smirked at Able again, who gave a nod back. 'Owning one of these places costs next to nothing, really.'

What Henry had said wasn't strictly true: Lucy had already pro-vided data that contradicted him. He'd left out salient details that transformed what he was inviting Dana to believe. She could see from the thump of his Adam's apple, from his glance at the floor: he knew. Henry was hoping she wouldn't push it, but the fact that she under-stood that meant she didn't have to.

Her degree was in accountancy, not economics, but she'd read enough property pages to have a follow-up question.

'I see. But that's a one-way ticket, isn't it? Prices here don't rise, they drop. Everyone wants – or needs – city life and city jobs. That's where the young people go, the migrants; they push up rents and prices there. The longer you stay here, the more difficult it becomes to ever return to the place you left. Or go almost anywhere else. Don't you end up stuck here?'

Henry's face faded to a pinkish hue of grey. The side-glanced bonhomie with Able had vanished.

'Yeah. Yeah.' He looked at his hands for solace. She noticed no callouses, no nicks or plasters. Presumably the workshop now lay fallow. 'Yeah, you could say that.'

She could ask him about the divorce settlement. She could push further on when he'd sold the place he still lived in, how he came to be a tenant. But she didn't know how much of that was known to Able. She sensed it could simply be a humiliation for Beattie and a self-defeating temporary gain for her.

'I saw your lawn on the way in, Henry, at the ANZAC memorial. That's mighty work.'

Henry tried to wave it off but couldn't conceal the smile of pride. Three of his teeth had chipped and remained unrepaired.

'Ah, well. We're a bit of a community here. Have to be. So far from anywhere else. Everyone lends a hand, you know?'

Her own neighbours were friendly enough, in the sense that they would hold a chat of one to three minutes' duration. A discussion that required them to give nothing of themselves but instead spread some minor life-froth around until everyone agreed they were terribly busy and had to go but hadn't this been nice? So, no, she didn't have any first-hand comprehension of Unamurra's community dynamic at all.

'Is it a lot of upkeep?'

'Yeah, nah, not really. Water it every day, that's a bit of a habit. Wander down when the sun gets low, stand about with a hosepipe.

Just got back, actually. When the kids are around town some of them come down and give it a go. Novelty, I guess. When I have to feed the grass I wait until midnight. Not that we have many birds now, but a couple can bugger up your plans.'

'Do you ever see anyone, at midnight?'

'Not usually. Annie closes up the pub around eleven and there's nowhere else to linger. Sometimes she's sittin' on her veranda out front. Insomniac, I think. Oh, and our resident artist. Not lately, of course.'

'Axel DuBois? He's a night-owl?'

'Ah, sure. Well, Frenchie comes and goes as he pleases. Sometimes I saw him regular, then other times not for ages. Law unto himself.'

An unusual description to hear twice in a few hours.

'What was Axel doing at that time of day?'

'Usually dragging one of those bloody frames around. Muttering. Sometimes he waved, sometimes he flipped me the finger, sometimes nothing. Never really got to grips with him, to be honest. You, Abe?'

'More finger than high-five, I reckon.' Able grinned.

Again, Dana detected a sidelining, a wish to talk around her rather than to her. It wasn't that Henry had anything against her per se, more that he felt hemmed in and looked to the familiar to offer him a way out.

'You were in the army, Henry? So Able tells me.'

Able adjusted his posture: he hadn't mentioned Henry's background. Just for a split second, Henry narrowed his eyes, as though he didn't appreciate the scrutiny. He covered it in a slow blink, but she noted it just the same.

'Yeah, well. Came from a town not much bigger than this one. Wanted to see the world.'

'And did you?'

Henry gave a thin smile. 'Ah, well, bits of it. Went some places, got shot at, came back. Not much of a holiday.' Again, he regarded his callous-free fingers. 'Vietnam finished it all off for me. Never again, eh.'

Dana had already read Lucy's précis of his service record – it was more than he was telling. She gave him a chance to hide himself in the general wash of army life. 'You were infantry?'

He grimaced. 'God, no. Those boys were cannon fodder, poor bastards. No, I did basic training, but then they moved me into maintenance and ordnance. I was quite handy, see. The army likes young men who are handy, eager. We're useful. Army just batters everything it gets its hands on, then expects someone to fix it. Instantly. At zero cost. And under fire. Yeah, electrical stuff, mainly. Bit of mechanical.' He swallowed and glanced at the window. 'It's why I got on with Abe's dad, eh?'

He'd directed the remark at Able, who nodded sagely but stayed silent. Dana considered what drifted beneath that surface. Able's reticence now had a slightly different tinge: more active, more difficult to perform. He glanced at the wall of photos. The air in the room hummed briefly.

'And then, farming?' she asked, letting them both off the hook because she had what she wanted.

Beattie shifted again in his seat, looking uncomfortable with the direction of the questions. He drew his legs towards him, giving the impression of something forcing itself to coil, and closed his fists.

'Jeez. How do you know all this crap?'

He'd deliberately softened his voice, so that any objection from her could be batted away. But she grasped the implication – Beattie had all his shields up.

'Just standard background, Henry. There are fifty-odd souls here, and I didn't know anyone until I arrived. It's what you would do if you were me, isn't it?'

She calculated that the blade would dig just under the ribs. Beattie was out of practice when it came to swallowing a reaction.

'*If I were you*, Detective? Well, I wouldn't be wasting my time in this little town chasing ghosts. It's all over.' Those eyes came at her, full-beam. 'We don't want any more investigating, didn't ask for it. No one wrote to the papers, or rang their MP, or anything. It was investigated. They didn't know who did it.'

His rising, urgent voice echoed off the barren walls. Dana looked at him evenly. Able squirmed. Beattie breathed through his nose but couldn't hide the belligerence.

'Why wouldn't you want to know who did it?' she asked calmly. 'Don't you feel unsafe, with a murderer out there?'

'Unsafe? Jesus, what would you know about it, eh? Carlton, right? Do you feel unsafe there? What, two murders in the last six months you've had, isn't it? Yeah, I read the papers. Same as here, then? Bet you don't go around your town shaking like a leaf.'

She noted that Beattie had claimed virtual ignorance about her arrival but remembered her home town, and Carlton's crime rate, without a hitch.

'No, I don't. But those suspects in Carlton are in custody. The murders may well have been solved. These haven't been solved yet. So the question remains, Henry.'

'We're two hundred clicks from anywhere here, aren't we? Bet you had a bit of a gulp on the journey, eh? Take a look at isolated communities in this country, Detective. Any state you like, I'm not picking on any group, here. I talk with Annie about this all the time; she knows stuff, she'll tell you. Take a long, hard, bloody honest look. What do you see in those places, eh? I'll tell you what I see. Drugged-out kids chroming on paint and torching cars. Dads who get smashed and beat the crap out of their partner, their kids. All the women in a settlement with their front teeth missing, kids with sexual diseases. Little children who should be taken into care passed around like a toy. I see vandalized property, teenagers hanging on street corners, illegal grog in the boot of a car, crystal meth. I see police who can't control the

town, cars parked behind barbed wire to stop them getting stolen. I
see people with nothing, but they're still having that nothing stolen
from them or wrecked, just for the cheap thrill of it. That's what I
bloody see in half the isolated little towns on this continent.

'Now look around Unamurra. Do you see any of that? Has Abe
told you that's what Unamurra is like? Nah, 'course not. Because it
isn't like that here. We're safe. Even now, with these two deaths: we're
safe. It's a big ugly world out there, but we're okay in here. Got it
sorted, for the most part; look out for each other. We've made good
decisions, sacrifices, to get to this point and we don't want anyone
wrecking it, thanks. So, sneer if you like. Compare it to Carlton and
find us all wanting – go ahead. But compared to most other towns of
this size, this far from civilization, we're bloody doing okay. We're safe.
You might not set much store in *safe*, but we do.'

He held his hands before him in a tight monkey grip. It took a few
seconds for his breathing to subside, at which point he seemed vaguely
embarrassed by his own vehemence. Dana looked at him steadily,
soaking it up. She'd seen this type of reaction before, in fraud cases.
People who'd been duped and then duped again, lashing out to hide
their own humiliation.

'Anyway,' he said at length, 'I'm bloody busy. So if it's all the same
to you . . .'

Able rose in a rush, tapping Dana's arm as he did so. 'Yeah, yeah. Lots
to do, all of us. Thanks for the tea, mate. Thanks. See ourselves out.'

Able was at the threshold in three strides and swung the door open.
As Dana went to close it behind her, she caught a half-reflection of
Beattie in the glass. He was still sitting in the ragged armchair, his
fingers now scrunched deep into the fabric, glaring as they departed.

Able kicked stones as they walked back to his house. Almost a sulk,
she thought. While it was true that Beattie had virtually thrown them

out of his house when the questioning wasn't to his liking, Dana had no complaints. Interviews rarely went exactly as she wanted: there were human beings involved. Besides, in this case she was coming off a short run. She had only the abbreviated information that Lucy could quickly find and forward. Even so, the gaps between what Beattie revealed, and what actually existed, were alarming.

First – the photos. One framed image of a group of men chugging some cold ones on Mount Panorama. She spotted behind them the famous arched sign over the racetrack. Each of them cast his own shadow, but Dana could infer: the pair possibly holding hands just as the shutter clicked. Another photo in the array, seemingly a pub at nightfall, somewhere in some city. A nice shot – the warm glow of the pub against a purpling sky, light-speckled office towers beyond. But when she examined it closely she'd seen the tell-tale streamers from lampposts: Mardi Gras in Sydney.

Second, the responses about money. Beattie had neglected to tell her – and she suspected Able knew this – that Beattie's wife had left him in penury. Jane had cleaned out the account when she drove away and the divorce had taken half of the rest. Lucy's digging had confirmed: Beattie had sold the house to Annie Ogden five years ago and now rented it back using plenty of his state pension. He wasn't just a little stuck financially; he was on the breadline.

Third – the television. As they'd left she'd made sure they went back a different route, passing closer to the rear of Beattie's house. His television had cables running to the outside but no satellite dish on the roof. There was a rusting relic of one by the greenhouse, though. Someone with Beattie's skills at electrics – he was *handy*, after all – and yet he hadn't put up the satellite dish? It was battered and dented on one side as if it had fallen off the roof, but even so, Beattie struck her as the sort to regard that as an innovation challenge.

Fourth – he'd been adamant there was no need to investigate these

murders. His diatribe about safety was something he could see the
holes in, even as he spoke. In truth there could be plenty of innocent
reasons why the town wanted no more fuss – fear that the publicity
might drive away any future tourists, for example. But Beattie's eyes
had blazed at that point. He wasn't telling her to leave it alone because
he had an objective point to make about economic regeneration, or
because Unamurra felt so safe there was no need to bother. Something
far deeper lay beneath the surface.

'He's a suspect, isn't he?' Able asked almost reluctantly, declining to
meet her gaze and staring instead towards the horizon.

'He would have to be, don't you think? In my position, Able?'

He shrugged, like a small child ordered to tidy his room.

'I mean,' she continued, 'he knows how to fire a weapon, so that puts
him in a broad frame, like most of the town. Then, he knew both victims; knew them quite well, I would think. I bet he's often in the
pub – one of his photos says he played footy when he was younger and
the pub is the only place you can watch all the games. So he knew Tim
Ogden from there, at the very least. He was part of the Council of Feuds,
with you and Annie: he must know Larry Muir from that, if nothing
else. Also, he just specifically warned me off investigating further, and
that's got to raise flashing lights for any detective. Wouldn't you say?'

They'd reached the garage and the security light clicked on as they
drew near. Able chewed his lip and nodded.

'Yeah, yeah. Can't fault your logic, there. Yeah. But . . . I can't see
it. Not with him. If he had a problem, he'd march up and tell you.
Can't see him shooting someone from a hiding place or stringing them
up like an angel. None of that fits with him at all. Not at all.'

None of their previous discussions about forensics had mentioned
shooting from a hiding place, she noted.

'But then, who does that MO really fit, Able? In this town? You'd
say no one.'

She waited for another nod, but it didn't come.

'Yeah, well.' He glanced away down the street. 'Anyone working a station could fit most of that as well, eh? Half of them know Larry from bumping into him in town, or in Dutton. Cattle sales, abattoir, suppliers, that sort of thing. They all know how to shoot straight. Not difficult for them to get into Unamurra from half the stations in the district.' He paused, aware that this foundered because someone would surely have heard them leave and noticed the missing vehicle: it relied on a conspiracy of silence. 'Yeah, maybe a bit weak, but I dunno. And then there's old mate Frenchie. He knew both of them well enough. He might know how to shoot. Knows how to put things up on angel frames, eh? Besides, he's the one that went into hiding when the cops arrived. Didn't he?'

Able pulled his keys from a jacket pocket and turned silently to the door.

Chapter 12

Dana needed a walk.

In Carlton she did this a lot, just switched off the office lights and went for a thought-walk. Colleagues understood – for the most part – though she worried that McCullough would go ape if he knew. There was something about the movement in walking that made her better at calculating angles and strategy. It occupied enough of her conscious mind that the subconscious was able to slip through relatively unhindered and bring forth something useful.

The psychology of this town – she still came back to that. It took a special kind of person to live here. Oh, there could be the occasional visitor staying at the pub for a night. There might even be the odd backpacker – casual grunt on a station, perhaps, or covering annual holiday behind the only bar. But generally there would be the same old faces in the same old places; DuBois' artistry was a tourism epicfail, and Unamurra was neither pretty nor quaint. She could see how the town was not so much dying as subsiding. It was decaying, literally turning – *returning* – to dust.

So the populace needed to be not only comfortable with the familiar but compelled by it. The possibility of any real change must daunt them, she felt, because surely no one who wanted any sign of rapid or

major progress could countenance staying in Unamurra. The longev-
ity, the consistency, the certainty of life's patterns here: they were all
part of the glue holding this town together, fixing its people in every
sense. One facet couldn't exist without the other – the social cohesion
they craved required a conservative and stubborn attitude. They were
more than prepared to pay that price. In fact, she mused, they seemed
scared of any other transaction.

In the first throes of night, the only light came from two homes on
the main street – Able's, and the house opposite him – and from the
pub. In the first-floor window of the pub there was a fierce blueish
light behind the roller blinds, constant and strong. Dana watched that
for a while, thinking. After a couple of minutes she looked down
towards the soft yellow illumination from the bar below, along with
flickering blues and silvers from a giant television screen. She could see
how frequently the TV glow changed to green – they were watching
sport.

She turned the corner into Curtin Street. There must have been a
number of buildings here once, she reasoned; otherwise, the road was
pointless because it faded into desert after two hundred metres. And
yet there seemed no sign of them formerly existing – no stumps, no
desiccated grass eating into concrete slabs, no forlorn markers. Instead
there was one solitary house, at the far end of the street. A home alone,
banished, with a porch at the rear, not the front. The home of someone
turning their back on Unamurra, as if they wished they weren't part of
it. For the locals, a haunted place. There was some faded graffiti on one
wall, too bleached to be legible even when she got closer.

Lucy's data told her that this had been the property of Roger Berry,
one-time school teacher in Dutton and elsewhere. The Roger Berry
who liked to stand in corridors, apparently absent-minded. As the
children brushed past, he'd relish the contact. The Roger Berry who
wouldn't – *couldn't* – stop at that. The Roger Berry who, thirty years

after the fact, had stood in the dock at Dutton District Court, refusing to look at three accusers, each now forty-one years old. The Roger Berry who took his own life in the segregated wing of prison, just before sentencing.

She fizzed torchlight across the property, expecting more recent graffiti, broken windows, vandalism and vented anger. Perhaps, even, signs of a 'mysterious' fire gutting the interior. But no, it seemed solid enough. One wing – a front projection into the unkempt yard – appeared to be brick and render; a rarity out here. The east–west portion was timber and fibro and 1970s construction. The mail box was covered up by a supermarket bag secured by plastic ties, and this was the giveaway. The ties were the same ones used on the angels. This place was now rented by Axel DuBois.

Behind the house she could see a long, low metal shed. It was all pure Colorbond: in the darkness she couldn't be certain of the colour but it looked dark blue, maybe gunmetal grey. More recent than the home, it appeared more liveable: she wondered if in fact DuBois had slept there rather than in the house. Fewer ghosts, if he was freaked by that sort of thing. But his biog details, courtesy of a long text from Lucy while they'd been talking with Beattie, said that despite the artistic calling DuBois was a tough, awkward, obstinate and resilient man. Details were somewhat sketchy and there were missing years, but Lucy had cobbled together a reasonable timeline.

DuBois had grown up in East Germany, escaping in 1985 via Czechoslovakia. He'd found asylum in Canada with grandparents who had been raised in Alsace, so presumably spoke both German and French. His often avant-garde artistic creations, produced over three decades, went hand in hand with extremist politics and flirtations with pseudo-military opposition to the prevailing government: resistance groups, boot camps, scratchy ideological videos and so on. From his childhood and adolescence in Leipzig to adulthood in

Quebec, he'd laid down similar markers. She speculated that DuBois was both a creature of habit and a creature made by habit. He was not, she believed, likely to change tack on a whim, nor be scared by suggestions of ghosts.

She ignored the house totally. She reasoned that, at best, it was a shell that held no meaning for DuBois. He might like the notoriety of it, though. It might amuse him in a twisted way and it would certainly discourage visitors. No, all that was dear to him was in the shed. It had no windows, not even, she saw as she circled it, a skylight. Her torchlight danced on the walls – definitely dark blue – and up onto the roof, where six solar panels formed an oblong block. Undoubtedly the place held the means to make or repair angels; as such, she might want to see inside it at some point. Preferably, she told herself, with DuBois' permission, although that seemed a stretch. Not only was he frequently absent, but she got the impression from Able that DuBois would jealously guard any entry into his working life.

Security must surely feature high on his list: she was unsurprised to find an infrared camera above the only door. The security light blinked on, her shadow stark and large and lurching across the scrub. The spray of light created a cone of artificial brilliance; she could see a huntsman clinging to a wall of the house, make out the patches of brick where the mortar had failed and crumbled. Dana was certain that, sooner or later, DuBois would view this footage. In fact, she was counting on it. She thought back to the warnings she'd had today to leave all this alone – Judge Trent, Cronin and, most recently, Beattie. They would each want her well away from this house, well away from DuBois.

She tore a sheet of paper from her notepad. She couldn't afford to have the indented impression of what she was writing on the next page; the notepad was always near her, but she couldn't guarantee its security. She wrote in big block capitals, like a diligent child, and checked it was easily visible. Her schoolgirl French was limited, but she thought she'd got the basic idea across.

She stalled briefly, feeling disloyal to Able. Perhaps she should share this with him, bring him in and try to tap his local knowledge. She didn't want him to feel shunned, as he surely had with the previous investigation. But no, she told herself. This message was intended for one person only, for very good reason. She needed help, and DuBois might be the one who could provide it. She'd priced in his potential guilt and still felt the transaction was a calculated risk.

She took the note and held it high above her head, as close to the camera as she could, for ten seconds. Then she made sure that she could be seen fishing a lighter from her pocket, burning the note to useless ash and stomping it into the dirt. She nodded once at the camera and headed back to Able.

Chapter 13

The pub was less busy than she'd anticipated. In her mind, it was the social hub and would surely blaze with light and voices until Annie threw everyone out. The bar was split into two rooms. The convivial lounge was at the front, while a more spartan but larger overspill room lay behind. The latter held trestle tables, austere upright chairs stacked in sevens, a pool table covered with a grey dust sheet and a television flush-mounted on one wall.

In one corner of the lounge, two couples played cards while a game show blinked and fizzed on the flatscreen above them. Another pair held beers they intended to nurse all evening, emptied plates set to one side. One elderly lady sat knitting a multi-coloured comforter, the needles clacking and the wool at her feet like an old Labrador. Three men leaned against the bar, their glasses half empty but yet to glisten with condensation: the more determined drinkers.

Dana automatically looked up: she felt certain the ceiling would tell a tale. She was expecting pressed tin from a bygone era, or pinned postcards, or foreign bank notes, or messages left by visitors from around the planet. There was nothing but maritime plywood and six strings of fairy lights evenly spread. She'd anticipated one wall would contain a notice board with a mosaic of photos from past events – Christmas, ANZAC

Day, New Year's Eve, Melbourne Cup. But there was no grinning, gurn-ing, ruddy, laughing, goofy, contented montage to be had.

Instead, the room was understated. The floor was pine and well-preserved. It had some patches of paler wood, but it looked like they washed it every day. On walls of dark green wallpaper were several framed photos of early-century days. Sepia images gave a potted his-tory: covered wagons, thin stern men with pickaxes, a ribbon-cutting ceremony next to the water tower. The lighting was subdued – more like a restaurant – mainly from wall lamps near the corners. It was more restrained and, frankly, more civilized than she'd expected.

Able picked a table in the corner as Dana went to order. The bar-man puffed as he rose from kneeling, kicking the slab of beer he'd been unpacking. He had thick, meaty hands with chipolata fingers. His hair was matted by a sheen of sweat and he stood next to an elec-tric fan when he spoke. He reminded her of a spaniel with its head out of the car window.

'Yeah, mate?'

'A schooner of beer and a bottle of water with some ice, please.'

The water and ice appeared almost immediately. The barman rapped on the bar. 'You hear that? Lady used the "p" word. A lesson for you there, Gus.'

A small, wiry man of about sixty, Gus had ginger hair that stood up like a gundog pointing out quarry. His freckles had formed distinct archipelagos on both cheeks and one temple.

'Ah, yeah.' He smiled at Dana as though she already knew the score. 'They're always bangin' on about that.'

Before she could reply, the barman responded, pulling on the draught as he did so. 'Like Annie always says: read the sign.'

He indicated with an upward nod as he kept pouring. Above the serried ranks of optics was a sign made by burning into a piece of lac-quered timber. Sure enough, it simply read *Manners Matter*.

Gus winked at Dana. 'It's not in my DNA, Macca.'

Macca waited impatiently for the head to subside: he'd forgotten to tilt the glass. Not the regular barman, guessed Dana. He cursed himself. 'What *is* in your DNA, Gus? About thirty per cent dung beetle?'

'You're a national treasure, Macca, I don't care what everyone says. My genetic programming says I drink beer: it's inevitable. Although it's not all DNA, if I'm honest, more of a life skill.'

Macca brought over the schooner, which was still disproportionately froth.

'You know, Gus, they say you can master any skill if you practise for ten thousand hours. Except me pouring beer, obviously. I reckon — *there you go, missus, nine bucks, thanks* — you passed that number around your thirtieth birthday.'

Gus looked both dubious and suspicious. 'Might be true. Could tell you, but then I'd have to kill you.'

'But you still dribble about a quarter of every glass — I'm now the poor idiot has to clean it up.' Macca accepted the coins from Dana. '*Ta*. So either you're more skilful at drinking beer than you're letting on, or you're a really slow learner.'

'Yeah, well. Ten thousand hours to master it, but another twenty thousand to keep up my high standard. See?' Macca drifted away, shaking his head. Gus raised his voice. 'Didn't include the maintenance, did ya?' He turned back to Dana. 'Some people, eh?'

Dana smiled. 'Takes a big man to see the bigger picture.'

She gathered both drinks and left him to it. The reply pleased Gus greatly. He turned back to Macca and jerked a thumb at the space where Dana had been. 'See? Smart, that one.'

Dana and Able settled in the corner and began a companiable silence. It struck Dana that she, just like Able and almost every other cop, always sat in a pub or restaurant with their back to the wall,

facing the room. Even off duty or on holiday, the instinct still kicked
in. Although, it came to her, she couldn't recall the last time she'd had
an evening in a pub or a restaurant. Ah, yes: dinner with Kasparov,
about three months ago. An introverted detective and a heavily jowled
cross-dresser clinking cocktails.

After watching Able drink half his beer and nod to the knitting
lady, Dana leaned over slightly. 'Is this unusually quiet or par for the
course?'

'Hmm. 'Bout average for a night with no major sport. Footy games,
Origin, Big Bash – they fill the place. Only TV in town showing Foxtel, of course. Annie's master stroke, that dish on the roof.'

Dana nodded, then frowned. 'Where did those plates come from?'

She indicated the bar, where, in a matter of seconds, a tower of four
large plates with metal covers had appeared.

'Ah, dinner run. Maybe Annie tonight, although Macca there does
it quite often now. Some of the older residents of our fair town – not
very mobile. Housebound, in fact. Neighbours pop in to make sure
they're okay during the day, do a bit of housework and so on. Annie
has a roster for some of 'em. But the kitchen here makes up some dinners and Annie delivers and collects. Means the oldies get at least one
decent meal a day, no matter what.'

Dana nodded again but squinted as she concentrated. Her radar
was pinging for some reason. She couldn't place why. 'That's very
community-spirited of her.'

Able grunted. 'That's one way of putting it.' He drank some more,
making it clear he wasn't going to expand on that.

Macca came out from behind the counter and picked up the dinners. Annie emerged at the bottom of the stairs and held the front
door open for him. A gentle sway of cool air slipped in from the night.
Annie had a different sweater on now but, as before, the sleeves were
pushed back.

'You did your training at Woolford?' asked Dana.

'Yeah.' Able halted, as though every question Dana ever asked was armed and dangerous. 'Yeah,' he continued, 'the first year it was open. Before the tree fell on the sports centre.'

'Ah, yes. Did you enjoy it?'

'Yeah . . . nah, actually. Didn't like it much. Thank Christ I graduated first time. Don't think I could have repeated.'

He took another sip, as if that would be all the detail he'd provide. It occurred to Dana that Able needed her to prompt. He regarded her prodding as a form of ethical permit.

'What didn't you like?'

'Ah, well, I coped okay. Nothing too drastic. Just I found it . . . a bit . . . well, a bit racist, actually.'

'Really?'

Dana was surprised. Able had gone a few years earlier than her, but she recalled the strenuous efforts during her own training around diversity, respect and race issues.

Able held up both palms. 'Uh, I should qualify that. Probably not what you're thinking.' He took a longer pull on the beer. 'Look, I grew up here, like I told you. There was about ten kids here back then; a teacher came out from Dutton three days a week. We all hung out together: older kids looked after the young 'uns. Parents would tell us to bugger off for the day with a packed lunch – you know: *slipslapslop, don't pick up snakes, come back by sundown, goodbye*. That kind of thing.

'Then we went to high school in Dutton, us Unamurra kids. Scrappy little buggers, but we stuck together. The other kids took the piss at someone who looked odd, had a stupid haircut, weird name – that sort of thing. But it was the same as school in Unamurra in one way. In all those years, never a hint of racism. Nothing. Not one comment, nothing. I was just Able from Unamurra; my mates were Col,

Spicy, Suzy, Ricky, from Unamurra. That was it.' He rushed another sip. 'Oh, I tell a lie. One time some out-of-towner was filling up with petrol here and he called me something. *Lazy little N-word.* Two locals – white, mind – came out of nowhere: smacked him daft, took three hundred bucks for a tank of fuel, told him to get lost. When he's gone, they come over and apologize. They tell me I'm Unamurra first and last, and that bloke was a dickhead. Slipped me a fifty, too. Yeah, that was the only time.

'So while I'm not stupid and I could read newspapers and I had some idea, to be honest, stuff like that didn't really visit me. Oh, I had mob with plenty of stories, I'm sure quite a few were true, more or less. But that's what they were to me – stories. Things that happened to other people, in other places.

'Then I get to Woolford and it's all different. There, my first name's still Able, but my surname is *The Indigenous Candidate.* I'm identified by my race, see; everything else is second to that. It sticks. I start to look at myself in the mirror, wondering. Am I really different to the rest of the class? If I am, is it a problem? Who am I representing, here, beyond myself? Because I was, make no mistake. To them I was an example: look how far the force has come.

'And it showed. It showed in low expectations. Need extra help with the essays, Able? Not used to classes this big, eh, Able? Fifty per cent'll do, Able. We could skip this part and focus on your *other skills*, Able. You'll have great spacial awareness, won't ya, Able? All of that. Subtle, usually. I'm not quite rare china, not quite an exhibit, but close to both. Lower standards for me, lower expectations. I'm the only graduate from that year's intake on the cover of the force's annual report. Why was that, eh? Not the best in my class, not by a long way. Decent, good enough, but not front-cover material.

'So yeah, racist in my book. I know it doesn't fit everyone's definition of racist, but it fits mine. Treated different because I'm indigenous: no need for it at all. A bunch of well-meaning, look-how-liberal types, bending over backwards to improve diversity and show the new broom's results. Low expectations, instead of setting the bar as high as everyone else's and seeing if I could reach it. I didn't want that, Dana, none of it. Not the attention, not the singling out, not the idea that they'd let me slip through with lower grades because I *send an important message*. I was just a bloke trying to become a cop, so I could go somewhere and do some good. That was it. They made it seem like something else.'

Dana nodded thoughtfully. She'd felt something similar, on a lesser scale, herself. Although she'd been preoccupied at the time with the bits she couldn't do well – the self-defence, the physical training she'd struggled over even though her plastic kneecap was a few years away. She'd focused on that, only retrospectively appreciating that she was also an exemplar of some kind, another brick in the quota wall. She'd passed everything – some things brilliantly – and it was all above board. But . . . as Able also noted, those subtle cues that she might be allowed to slide, on account of filling other criteria. It still tainted her impression of, and confidence in, her own ability. It must cast a bigger shadow for Able.

The other point that occurred to her was this: Able had noticed and bristled against low expectations at police college. It had struck at his sense of self and his belief. But twice today – Judge Trent and Annie – people had demonstrated their low expectations of what he might achieve: he'd simply sucked it up. Dana wondered at the difference – perhaps he'd been beaten down over the years by continual denigration. She couldn't see the longer game Able was now playing by declining the chance to stand up for himself.

'You know, it's probably impossible for a large organization to exist without politics. But it would be good if they could. Or even if they tried. I'm sorry, Able, for you going through that. For what it's worth, you strike me as a first-class officer.'

He smiled at his beer, unused to the compliment and unsure what to do with it. She recognized the look.

'G'day Abe. Who's this?'

A hand was thrust into her field of vision. The man was in his fifties, with a seventies vibe to his swept hairstyle, a Skyhooks T-shirt that had seen better days, and some garish Mambo board shorts. His skin hung in small flaps around the triceps, as though he'd lost a lot of weight quickly. The deep tan half-hid a tattoo of a rose and crucifix on his forearm.

She shook his hand dutifully. 'Dana. Dana Russo. I'm a friend of Able's.'

The man stepped back slightly, as though the information was unreliable. 'Reall– uh, Barry. Barry Watson. Baz. Nice to meetcha, and all that. Look, Abe, I really need to borrow that phone of yours. Only take a minute, hey.'

Barry didn't hold out his hand. Able didn't move his fingers away from his glass.

'Yeah, Baz, you know the answer, mate. It's always the same answer; the same anyone in town'll give you. And you know why. All of us want to help you, mate, and this is me helping you. Go talk to Gus about politics, eh. That'll keep you out of trouble.'

Barry nodded at his feet, seemingly chastened, and drifted away. Dana waited until Gus was pouring forth on why no one in this country built dams anymore, then turned to Able.

'Because?' was all she asked.

'Yeah, so, Baz used to be a big noise. Interstate, this was. Had a chain of garden nurseries, doing really well. Then he got into gambling. And I mean got into it mightily. Anything. Greyhounds, pokies, the trots, state elections, two flies going up a wall – anything he could get a punt into, really. Lost the bloody lot. As he's selling off his lovely house dirt cheap, the guy buying it does him a real favour: tells him to go live in Unamurra. Bloke had an aunt here, see – she's long dead now – and he says that's the one place Baz can't gamble.

'Baz was upfront about that when he arrived – enlisted our help. Annie and me put together a plan, got the whole town to agree, Baz included. We strongly discourage any vague notions he ever has about getting a landline. In fact, we'd talk the engineer out of it, if one turned up. We don't drive Baz into Little Big Town, unless one of us is going to sit on him the whole visit. We don't lend him a mobile phone, either, and there's effectively no internet. So he has no real way of getting a bet in – he doesn't have access. Every now and then he weakens and asks us. We have to stay strong for him.'

She took that in. It was an emerging theme from those she spoke to: the sense that this community took communal decisions. It didn't necessarily follow – some communities were linked by geography but remained a collection of individuals and families. There was a common spirit in Unamurra that was, in fact, uncommon. But it had two sides to it, she felt.

'Okay, I'll be devil's advocate. I can see the what and why in relation to Barry, but . . . there's a philosophical question there, surely? Doesn't he have the right to run his life? He's a grown adult – you're taking away his agency. I understand the motive, I really do, but . . .'

'You think we should let him bugger it up again? Mess up his life a second time? Look, three years ago he'd wake up, look at the water lapping against his boat, drive his Maserati to his suite of offices. Then the betting companies got their hooks in. Now he's bumming cigarettes and renting a flimsy house off Annie, living in the outback while his mates keep phones away from him. You think we should just leave him be? Give him a phone and tell him it's okay to set up accounts?

Nah, people need saving from themselves sometimes. We do that here, Dana. We do that for their own good.'

Dana allowed a pause, then said in a quiet, even voice, 'Who's looking after Vince Reynolds' drinking? For his own good.'

Able sat back. The pub's chatter seemed to ebb, like waves retreating into the ocean. He gave her question careful consideration. 'Yeah. Yeah, fair comment I s'pose. Decision like that depends on – well, depends on a lot of things.'

Dana decided not to pursue it. An edge in Able's voice told her it wasn't fertile ground. All the same, the question floated through her mind: *in Unamurra, who decides what's for someone's own good?*

'Are you feeling the pressure?'

Able's question was asked while he stared dead ahead. It wasn't easy for Dana to discern the thinking behind it. Was he warding her off in some way, concerned for her welfare, or genuinely curious about how she felt?

'A little bit. It's not my first rodeo, of course. I'm used to the general pressure from my own boss. In that respect, it's a little easier out here. He can't pay the same attention or look at progress on the shared drive, and I'm cut a little slack because I'm in parts unknown. I don't think McCullough has ever been here, so in that sense he can't really gainsay how I approach it.'

'But he will, later?'

'Oh, God yes, every time. No matter what I do, he won't like it. In fact, he'll begin doing that very soon. He's been granted permission for a District Scrutiny.'

Able turned sharply. 'Jesus. Really? Even Dutton's never had one of those.'

'I know. There have only been four in the last thirty years in this force. Even the Ollie Flynn murder didn't lead to one. So McCullough has a permit to go ballistic, starting whenever he wishes.'

'While you're stuck out here?'

'I'm happy to be here, Able, to solve these crimes with you. So I don't feel I'm *stuck out here*. But yes, they always say the ones who aren't present when a Scrutiny kicks off are the ones under most threat. It's easier to bag and tag people who aren't standing in front of you. Though McCullough doesn't appear to have a conscience, so maybe that doesn't apply to him.'

He shook his head. 'Jeez. Sorry, Dana.'

She shrugged. 'Ah, there isn't much I can do, to be honest. I suspect McCullough will do what he wants, regardless of where people are standing right now. Anyway, the pressure on these two murders really comes from the town. In Carlton I'm trying to solve crimes for the good of the community, but the community is large and disparate. Two hundred thousand people in our policing district; thirty-odd thousand in Carlton itself and twenty thousand in Earlville. So while there's general public pressure, and a more intrusive media than Dutton's, I don't have to look too many people in the eye about it. Victims, families, witnesses, yes, but not the mainstream public. Whereas here? All of Unamurra is invested – the whole town, every single person I meet. Never mind that half of them don't seem to want it solved. The pressure of their existence and their presence is continuous – that's what I'm feeling.'

Able nodded and took another sip. Dana turned.

'Why *don't* they want it solved? It's nagging me that it's significant.'

He shook his head. 'I'm not sure. I'm not sure that they're sure either. If I had to guess, I'd say it's a gut response and not strategy. Something deep down tells them that if they get the answer, they won't like it. I saw the same in a town near the coast years ago, where a kid was missing. He'd been gone for weeks by then and we'd done all the stuff you can reasonably do without an accurate tip-off. The whole squad had that sinking feeling: that all we'd ever find was a body. Everything in that town said the whole town was desperate to find him, and yet . . . and yet, in another way, they weren't. Sometimes it seemed they just wanted to carry on searching for ever. Because if they found him he'd be dead; all hope would be gone and they'd have to turn deeper into themselves about who'd done it. While they were still searching, they might not have to deal with that. So in some ways it was less painful not to know.'

Dana gave that due weight. It was probably partly true, but not the whole story. Unamurra's attitude was more active than mere reluctance or pain avoidance; in some people, it was overt opposition. As if they knew, but didn't want it spoken: a malevolence that was somehow contained as long as it remained unsaid or unproven. Either that, or the cost of revelation was too high to pay.

It was time for a refill. While Able waited at the bar an older man wandered over to Dana. He wore tatty jeans with rips on both knees, and not in a designer way. His shirt was misbuttoned, adding to the sense of benign chaos. His moustache fell unevenly, as if his shaving mirror was constantly tilted and he hadn't realized. In fact, he gave an overall air of getting the wrong end of the stick quite frequently.

'You the detective from away, yeah?' He stuck out a hand.

'Dana Russo, from Carlton, yes.' They shook. 'And you are?'

'William. Billy, actually. Sorry, you made me go all formal for some reason. Billy Golding. Have you got a minute, outside, like?'

Dana nodded and they stepped out. Dana noted that he'd only wandered over when no one was behind the bar. As he left the pub, Billy glanced at the wall and shook his head. The night seemed more profound after the glare of the bar. They followed the shaft of golden light from the doorway along one edge, until their feet passed into darkness halfway across the street. It felt odd to Dana to stand in the middle of the road, but Billy treated it as an extended pavement.

'Yeah,' muttered Billy, 'sorry about the cloak-and-dagger, but, you know. Probably worked all that out for yourself, hey?'

He nodded at her as though she was supposed to join in, but she wasn't really following. Getting no immediate affirmation, Billy pressed on.

'So, look, I tried to talk to those other detectives, the first lot. Dumb and Dumber, there.'

'You weren't impressed?' She sensed he was reticent, so added, 'Don't worry, they're from another station. I won't hold it against you.'

Billy let out a relieved sigh. 'Ah, good. Thought my mouth had got me into trouble, then. Nah, nah, I was not impressed. Those two dick-heads stayed at the bloody pub. *At the pub.* I mean, talk about unprofessional, right? No wonder they got bloody nowhere.'

There was something swimming beneath Billy's words that she hadn't quite fathomed, but would. He was not willing to spell it out.

'You wanted to mention something, Mr Golding?'

'Billy'll do. Yeah, yeah. These two murders. You've got an open mind, is that right?'

'Yes, I have.'

'Good. Good.' He paused for a moment. 'Do they strike you as women's work?'

'In what way?'

'Well, I'm not as expert as you, obviously. But I reckon this sort of thing is, well, a bit fussy. I mean fussy like net curtains, or cushions, or stuff.' He scratched around with his foot and glanced back at the bar. 'Sorry, I must sound like a bloody dinosaur to you. What I'm saying is this. Blokes here would just do it, get it done, then scarper. They wouldn't stick around. Either that, or they'd take the body out and dump it miles away. Then you'd be doing missing persons, not murders, eh? If it was a bloke. All this pissing about with string and art and everything, it's a bit odd, don't you think? So, to my way of thinking, it's fussy like women are fussy. No offence, mate. Who kills someone and then hangs around? Who has to make things *just so*?'

'I understand what you're saying, and none taken. Remember that the original angels were created by a man, so *he* was that fussy. Perhaps some of the men here would take that kind of time and trouble, if they thought it would get them off the hook. If it threw us off the scent and had us blaming DuBois, or *women*.'

'Yeah, yeah, I've wondered about that. I can see the argument but nah, it doesn't fit.'

'To be honest, Billy, not much does. These are two very strange murders.'

'Yeah, and Unamurra is a bloody weird town. So, you know, kind of fits how we are. But all the same, feels to me like women's work and all. Just thought I'd mention it to you. Out here, in the street, like. I'll leave it at that.'

He began sauntering back to the pub, and she let him go. It gave her some time to think, standing in the cool darkness at the centre of the road, the pub's chatter a gentle backdrop. Billy was the first person to voluntarily talk about the murders, so she had to take that as progress. While she thought the gender line was more than a reach, it was true that the way the bodies had been staged – the fact that they'd been staged at all – was significant. She was still unsure exactly why they'd been laid out that way when, as everyone knew, they could have been hidden from view for eternity.

But there was something else that was bothering her about Billy Golding. She couldn't quite grasp what it was, so she walked herself back through the entire encounter. The odd clothing choices, the air of crumpled bemusement? Billy had been sharper than his dress sense, but no, that wasn't it. The dismissal of the previous detectives as hopeless and unprofessional? That was close, but not it either. It would come to her.

Annie collected three empties from the adjacent table, then looked over. Her voice was deliberately loud. 'Huh. Should've known the princess wouldn't drink. You're miles from your big bad boss, hey? He'd never know if you had a few cold ones.'

Dana took a silent breath and held up her bottle of water. 'I'm drinking now, Annie. Here, in your friendly pub.'

Annie took it as an invitation, strolling over and standing needlessly close. It forced Dana to look almost directly up. 'Ah, look, I've got nothing against actual reformed drinkers, not personally. I mean, it's less profit and all, but this is a community centre, eh? So, twelve-steppers and all that? Yeah, power to 'em. But the rest of youse . . . well, I look to you to pick up the slack, know what I mean?'

'I think so.'

'Well, I hope so. I don't mind subsidizing dinner deliveries to the hard of walking – public service, and all that. But I can't have a pub full of people who barely drink, can I? We're not a charity, mate.'

Dana looked evenly at Annie, who eased back a touch. 'Is there anything else, Annie?'

'Nah. You carry on cosying up to Abe. Probably been a while since a woman whispered in his ear. Ha.'

She moved away as Able began to rise. He was stayed by Dana's hand on his forearm.

'That's what she wants, Able. Don't let her bug you. Don't give her the win.'

As he resumed his seat, she was conscious of the hum of conversation renewing. She couldn't be sure everyone had stopped to observe the three of them, but she felt they might have done.

Annie's brief intervention lingered for them both. Able stewed on her little wind-up; he cursed himself for biting, but somehow she knew how to hit the spot. Dana wondered, as she finished her drink, what had just jarred with that entire encounter. It wasn't Annie's abrasion, nor her uncanny knack of getting to Able with just a word. No, it felt as though Annie had done something she shouldn't.

Chapter 14

'Before we eat, have you seen my outdoor cinema?'

Dana frowned. The front door was a metre from the street. The only outdoor space for the property was behind the garage. She'd spent at least an hour there today, pacing around while talking to Lucy. She couldn't recall anything theatrical at all.

'I don't think so.'

'Ah, well, in the interests of spruiking my home town, I should probably show you that.'

Dana ducked into the bedroom and pulled a black puffa jacket from her suitcase. She was hoisting an arm into it as she emerged. Able pointed with a packet of biscuits.

'Ah, Tasmanian tuxedo. Well played.'

Dana smiled ruefully as she zipped it halfway and they descended the stairs. 'I read somewhere that the desert is always colder than you think.'

Able jangled his keys as he held the door for her. 'Too true. People forget that.'

They went around the side of the building as a light snapped on, past a water butt skulking at the base of a downpipe. Dana had a quick glance to confirm that it was empty; dried sludgy lines told of the gradual, inexorable decline of water levels. The town held a thousand such giveaways.

'Tell me,' resumed Able, 'is everything you know something you read?'

Dana smiled and nodded at the western horizon. The light blue had faded now to a thin line; the east had turned to black. She double-checked she had a torch in her pocket.

'Ha, pretty much. Something I read, or something Lucy said, yes.'

'Ah, I'm getting a picture. Here we go.'

They'd entered a dip about eighty metres from the garage. It occurred to Dana that she'd been staring at this exact spot several times today while she rang Lucy, without knowing that the ground slid away at this point. The tawny soil had appeared continuous, but someone could park a car here unnoticed. Another treacherous mis-read. Another reminder that both dead bodies could have been hidden oh-so-easily. But weren't.

Two deckchairs were planted firmly in the soil side by side, tilted up towards the night sky. Old-school design: one elongated arc of canvas and two diagonal frames, like a 1930s seaside postcard. The canvas was a series of candy-pastel stripes. A dust-speckled eskie served as a table between the chairs. She shone her torch, checking for spiders.

'Screen's above you, of course,' added Able, indicating Dana had her choice of seating.

She nestled in her chair and let her neck settle against the top of the frame. Angled upwards, she could see stars beginning to leech through the remaining light. Her mind formed the connections, the lines joining them, like a gentle warm-up for more serious work. The moon was away to the east, low against the land and obscured for now by a cloud bank; about to soar and take command of the sky.

'Do you like it here, Able? In Unamurra?'

He waggled an invitation to take a biscuit. He seemed briefly thrown by the question. Either he wasn't used to social niceties, or he hadn't considered the concept directly.

'*Like?* Hmm. Hadn't – this place . . . it's where I should be. It's home. Feel grounded here, feel like I'm where I'm supposed to be. And *here's* not even where my mob are from. That's another state entirely. So it's not some indigenous thing about being *on country*, it's just my own feeling. Not being funny, but in cities people don't think that way. I mean, they might like where they live – the convenience, transport, whatever. They *admire* their own address, but they don't feel it's their place. Not like we do.'

'We?' she asked. It was the first time he'd gone beyond himself in quite that way. 'You and . . .?'

Able waved a hand. He might have been swatting a fly. 'Well, me specifically. Some of the town more generally, yeah. But I think some of those farmers, especially the second- or third-generation ones, they really feel it too. They have the grounding, I suppose, the hard yards under their belt. They've earned the right to be loyal to where they are, earned it the tough way. Putting in the years, the decades – gives you a kinship with the place. Call it spiritual if you like, but the connection goes beyond practical, or convenience, or even pride.'

She pondered that. The way people connected to this place *was* different from back home. There, they were more transient, more rational. In Carlton they liked the place for specific reasons or stayed because it represented the best viable and rational option. They didn't have *kinship* to the location.

Able qualified his sentiment. 'Look, I don't imagine this is the greatest place on earth or that it doesn't have mountains of problems. I still want a better road to drive on, I still feel the temperature in a heatwave, I still want broadband. Jeez, I still want regular rain. But I wouldn't want to live anywhere else. Wherever I was and whatever I was doing, it would be second best. This place would pull at me, want me back. Yeah, this place wants me here, and I want that, too. Yeah.'

He nodded, more to himself than to her, settling back into gazing at the sky as it eased from colour to colour, gradually draining the final remnants of light. They sat silent for perhaps twenty minutes. Dana liked the way the panorama let her mind drift. It was a form of floating. At length she heard Able shuffle slightly, then cough. She knew there was a question coming.

'What did Cronin tell you, back in his office?'

Able had been quite circumspect about it earlier but she'd recognized, even on the journey to Unamurra, that her time with Cronin bothered him more than her encounter with Judge Trent. At first she'd put it down to mere presence. Able had been in the room when she'd met Trent yet deliberately shunned from the discussion with Cronin. But perhaps his anxiety went deeper than that. She thought again of the written question she'd offered DuBois, and the way she'd hidden it from Able. She'd hated doing that, but she still had an instinct it was the correct approach.

'Ah, he told me these two murders were the Kobayashi Maru.'

'The what, now?'

'The Kobayashi Maru. It's from *Star Trek*.'

She swore she could sense Able frown in the darkness.

'Never saw it. So what's this thing?'

She'd been considering Cronin's warning, off and on, since he gave it. It was, she thought, very specific. It wasn't the same as Trent's general dismissal of her chances of solving the murders. It was more exact than that. She'd felt sure there was a subtext, but it currently sat slightly beyond her reach.

'It's a test they give to prospective captains of spaceships, their last test before they assume command. It's a simulation exercise of their tactics.'

'How does it work?'

'As I recall, they have to rescue hostages from a spaceship. Without sparking a war with the enemy holding the hostages or getting every-one killed, including themselves. There are lots of options about how to attempt that.'

'And?'

'And, it's impossible. Designed to be impossible to win, no matter what strategy you try.'

Able harrumphed and folded his arms. She guessed this from the rustling: the darkness was almost complete. She couldn't tell if Able was hurt by Cronin's dismissal of their chances or just exasperated by a television series he'd never watched.

'Ridiculous. What's the point of that?'

'Partly to remind the captains that they always have the option to retreat – preserve life or resources, live to fight another day. But mainly to teach them humility: that they can't negotiate or batter or strategize their way out of every problem. It teaches them to feel mortal and accept defeat graciously.'

She sensed from the chair's creak that he was leaning forward. Maybe Able thought Dana was giving him advanced warning: that now she was in Unamurra and saw how useless it all was, she'd already given up on the case. Perhaps Able thought she was signalling that her investigation would be simply audit-trail creation; arse-covering and nothing more. Or, possibly, he saw signs she would leave Unamurra without tagging him as complicit, or guilty. She was intrigued about how he might react to those options.

'And Cronin told you these two murders are like that?'

'Yes, he was very precise about it.'

Now Able leaned back, while Dana fiddled with her water bottle.

Something was shifting. Cronin's subtext was starting to float within her grasp. She just needed Able to keep going with the questions.

'So what happened in *Star Trek*, when they took this impossible test?' he asked.

'Every one of the candidates failed. Except one.'

'Ah, who was that?'

'Captain Kirk, the hero of the story.'

'How did he win, with it being impossible?'

'He cheated. Sort of.'

And suddenly, it clicked: what Cronin had obliquely been telling Dana but with plausible deniability for himself.

'Riigghht. And you? Are you going to be like this Kirk?'

Was she?

'Hopefully. And yes, Able, I intend to cheat. Sort of.'

She expected a response, but none came. Able resumed the silence.

She heard a quiet glug as Able took a swig from his water. The moon emerged from clouded shutters and light poured on to the town, glinting off the metal rooftops. Then, just as quickly, the nightscape shifted and the black cloak resumed. It felt darker for having glimpsed the light.

'Able, that Ford Falcon we passed out in the desert, the blue one?'

He paused before replying. 'Yeah?'

This wasn't an easy conversation. She'd been mulling it over for hours. In the end, she'd decided it was better to know. It felt like the kind of thing the locals would already comprehend and she couldn't afford to be behind their curve if she could avoid it.

'The driver who wandered off? That was your dad, Collis, wasn't it?'

Able was silent for a moment, staring at the sky as though it would split asunder and yield something beyond the stars.

'Yeah. Yeah, it was.'

'I'm so sorry.'

Her eyes had fully adjusted to the darkness now. She wasn't sure if she'd offended or hurt him by raising it. His thumbnail flicked at the packet of biscuits, tapping out four-four time.

'You know the worst bit?' He looked at her but turned back to the darkness when she glanced at him. 'I should have seen it coming. Me, of all people.' He nodded to himself. 'Sharing this house with him. In his life, in his space all the time. Too close to focus, I suppose.'

She shook her head. 'No, I disagree. People in that situation? For all that they're overwhelmed by this . . . *thing* . . . they can be consummate actors. It rules their lives and dictates their future, but they can cloak it: that's the paradox, even to them. Honestly, they can hide it from anyone except themselves, for quite some time. Only they truly know.'

Able shrugged, unconvinced. 'Things broke apart. Important things . . . he . . . anyway, his life started going wrong and there was no way to pause it, never mind reverse. Some things can't be put back together, can they? People dig in to where they are, won't back off, won't apologize. It was . . . it was ugly. Something beautiful went to pieces, because of—. And there were other things, not just that. The garage closed down. Easy way to free up the cash flow, isn't it, when your income drops? Just skimp on maintenance. Probably won't come back and bite you on the arse, so what the hell? Dad just lost interest in everything. The town, the footy, me . . . everything.'

Dana found that sequence telling. And the omission from that sequence surprising. His phrase startled her: '*something beautiful went to pieces*'. It came to her: *he'd known*. He'd known the who and how and why of that decay. He couldn't stop it, and the failure still festered.

'Collis couldn't move somewhere?'

Able smiled to himself, partly in reverie, partly cocooned by the

moment. 'Ah, well, there's the interesting bit. I mean, he could, in theory. We've got mob everywhere: he could have gone interstate if he
needed. I begged him to do it. Life here was full of painful shadows.
Town's too small to avoid that stuff. Plus, he didn't have to stay here
on my account. I could have found a house-share with one of the
locals if he'd wanted to go to Dutton, or wherever. Nah. It's not that
simple. I wasn't kidding, mate, about the value of my property. It
really is worthless. Property's only worth what someone's willing to
pay, and in Unamurra that's bugger all. If he'd sold the place, he
wouldn't have got enough for a car to sleep in. Annie wasn't interested
in helping him out. Besides . . .'

He needed the nudge.

'It was all too difficult?'

'Yeah. What's the word? Inertia. It was too much to begin all over
again, somewhere else. Too much. He didn't have the energy, the will.
Take away a man's work – sorry, a *person's* work – and they've got
nothing much to get up for. One remaining slice of family wasn't
enough motivation. Friendships went south, dragged him under. He
drank, for the first time in his life. Put on weight, got sloppy. He could
see it. Knew where it was headed. So he took it into his own hands.'

Familiarity made her shudder. It underpinned her anxiety back
home about McCullough's disdain: that losing the security and identity of her job would be more than disorienting or disabling – it could
be fatal. She had way too much of her sense of self, her sense of worth,
invested in her job. She knew it, but she couldn't escape it. McCullough's
sword would hang over more than her occupation. It could slice right
through her entire life.

'God, that's terrible, Able. You never found –'

'Nah. He was too bright for that. He didn't want anyone finding
him at all. Didn't want the, uh, loss of dignity. Nah. It's not unknown
out here. Dad was the third in a decade to take the long walk. We

don't have cliffs to jump off, freeways to crash on, any bloody water to drown in. All we can do is the walk. A man takes it upon himself to do that? Well, he has a duty of care to those he's leaving behind. Another of our codes – the Unamurra Law of Suicide: *don't leave images they can never unsee.* What Jase Milford did in his garage a few weeks ago; what his kids saw, what he knew his wife would find? Can't condone that, no matter what.' Another swig, just to help him swallow things down. 'I mean, Dad was a lesson to everyone in town. But I don't think any of us took it.'

'Meaning?'

'Meaning we should get out if we can, or get busy if we can't. But, other than Annie, I can't think of a single person in this town who's actually organized their life that way. She was busy; still is. The rest of us sit here, pickled by our own . . . lack of will, I suppose. So, you know. Maybe some of us are headed the same way as Dad: off the highway, start walking, find a hole and finish it.'

There was a long silence. Dana's voice surprised her when she spoke again: soft, almost fearful. 'Don't do that, Able. Don't.'

This time he looked at her almost approvingly, his eyes glinting in the feeble starlight.

'Hmm. I think I'm talking to a fellow traveller, right? Someone back from the brink? I reckon you've been to the edge a few times. So you know how it works.'

She pretended a shiver was the falling temperature and the rising dew. Five months ago she had been literally at the cliff edge, choosing which rock below would smash her skull on impact. A dead man had saved her life that day; she couldn't bank on being that lucky again.

Able turned back to the sky. 'You need one person – just one. The someone whose face you picture when you prepare, the one person you can't bear to hurt in that way. Their face when they find out, or find you, that's all it takes. I reckon you've found that person, Dana. I can see it when your phone rings, eh?'

He switched on his torch but pointed it at the ground. They were both under-lit by a soft glow from the sand. He could see her smile.

'Good on ya, I'm happy for you. But in Unamurra? None of us have that person. None of us. Not even the marrieds, not even the parents and grandparents among us. We don't have that. It's the anchor we're all looking for; it's why we've all ended up here. We're two days' drive from the ocean, but this place is an island of lost souls.'

Suddenly, that vivid grin again. Out of place yet perfectly judged. Saying all things and one thing. He stood up and blatted away some biscuit crumbs from his thighs.

'Anyway. Eggs. Let's have eggs.'

Chapter 15

The clock read 1115. Dana had managed an hour or so of fitful sleep. Lately, she'd had a run of hideous dreams – massacres, brutality, sweeping panoramas of carnage – but tonight she'd escaped that. All the same, she couldn't really settle so sat up to make notes.

The desert held an absence of sound that was startling. Every minute or so she caught up to the lack of noise and was perturbed by the experience. She found herself straining for the kind of extraneous stimulation she knew and understood. She tapped pen against paper, just for the sound it made.

She'd been in Unamurra for six hours – Dutton district for nine hours in total – barely long enough to scratch the surface. Yet she felt issues and potential suspects were firing at her from all sides. In fact, she found it difficult to disentangle the chaff from what she really needed to hold. Kernels of ideas slipped her grasp, arguments and lines rose and fell like flotsam on the open sea. Nothing was quite coalescing, even though it felt at any moment as if it might. Or should.

Her mind flipped through each brush-off she'd been given, each nod to the idea that she should leave these murders alone. Except for Cronin. His advice, she now believed, had been trying to guide her *towards* something. But for the rest? Just pure denial. Either they expected her to perform a perfunctory attempt and announce it wasn't viable, or she was supposed to actively ignore both her instincts and anything that smacked of evidence.

For senior officers like Judge Trent, she could see the goalposts – he wanted Central to stop patronizing him, he wanted serene final years at the helm, he wanted his dead and absent detectives to be vindicated rather than vilified. That made a strategic sense for Trent, even if Dana found it morally bankrupt.

But the atmosphere in Unamurra – that was something else. What sort of town didn't want the murderer of two citizens to be found? What sort of town offered free passes on killing? She *could* have comprehended it, if Unamurra were the kind of place that meted out its own kind of rough justice. If they were a simmering latent lynch mob, waiting for her to leave so the assumed killer could be quietly 'disappeared', as Able had put it; that, she could understand. But there was no underlying sense of malice in town that she could discern. Unamurra's reticence was a deeper malaise – almost torpid, a malarial apathy. It baffled her.

She held fast to the notion she'd had in the car as they drove from Dutton. It said that Unamurra had no exports and no unique selling point to the outside world. In that sense, it was simply a collection of buildings in one location. But it did have a unique psychology. The mental approach necessary to living here, dictated the way people lived here. And that, she was sure, was significant. Though she couldn't tell exactly how it played out.

Likewise, she could see that the impact of the angels went beyond their involvement as props for two murder victims. The tangential kiss of the two curves – murders and angels – was not a coincidence. DuBois was involved in some way, intertwined with what had taken place. She couldn't fully demote him from prime suspect: she didn't have the evidence to displace him. But her instincts shouted that it was more complex than it appeared. She'd asked DuBois a question because she believed he'd give an honest answer, without knowing why she believed that. Again, while she understood that the angels mattered, she couldn't yet fathom why.

And, she noted, Able was a focal point. In this town he was the only public figure, if she discounted an apparently unreliable nurse. For the town, Able represented not only law and order but all public services and their potential to support the people. She reckoned no social worker, no teacher or council officer would set foot in Unamurra without first speaking to Able. Not that he was a tyrant denying access. No, he was simply the obvious gatekeeper and starting point. It was hard to fathom that these murders could occur without him knowing more than he was currently telling. Perhaps he understood something fundamental but didn't consciously know it or had underplayed its significance. Or maybe, he was such a part of this town that *he* didn't wish the murders to be solved, and his opinion influenced everyone else.

Speaking of which – Annie Ogden. The personification of business in the town. Owner of the only premises, the face of commerce. Little could happen without *her* involvement, either. Exhibit A being the Book of Feuds idea. So she and Able together could generate things for Unamurra that the town couldn't muster itself. But equally, Annie and Able at loggerheads pushed the town into stasis, at best. Currently they seemed to be circling in an uneasy truce and it was hard to pick which way they were headed. Like Judge Trent and Cronin back in Dutton station, they would set the mood for everyone and possibly cleave the community in two.

Politics. Even in a town of fifty people, there were politics. *Especially* in a town of fifty people. She shook her head a little, and slept a little.

*

The notepad had slipped to her lap, and the biro had left a faint streak across the sheet where it had fallen from her hand. She wasn't quite snoring, but her head had bobbed to a standstill a few minutes earlier. The noise woke her.

She amazed herself with her speed of response, with its lucidity. She grabbed her holster and had the handgun snug in her grasp before she reached the bedroom door. The stiffness from her kneecap simply didn't exist. It was flooded by adrenalin.

In the near-darkness the only semblance of light was two small diodes from the computer; they gave a pale glow from below the desk. She could barely make out shapes, but she could discern Able's presence by the window. He'd stepped over the table lamp he'd knocked to the floor. Back against the wall, he was sliding open one of the venetians with a finger, peeking out into the night. She could hear his breathing – urgent, needy, charged. He acknowledged her without turning away from the window.

'I thought I saw a light. Just now. Like, one of those laser pens or something.'

The first thought from Dana was a target sight, like a sniper would use. But she could see nothing: no dancing pinprick of colour, no thin beam from beyond the glass. The room remained in darkness, the moon gone and the town without streetlights.

'Is anyone out there now?'

'Nah, not that I can see. Plenty of places to hide, though.'

They both froze, straining to hear anything. This town had none of the noises of suburban nights; no possums, no cats, no slamming screen doors or rumbling cars. It simply had dust and an absence of light.

After a minute or so Able let go of the venetian, which swung a little and tapped gently against the window frame. He moved across to the furthest window from the stairs and peered down the street towards the pub, which was the most likely source of movement or sound. The street was empty.

'I don't like it,' he muttered. 'I mean, can't be sure what I really saw. I just woke up at the tail end of it. But all the same, you know, not good.'

Dana nodded. In theory, it could have been someone passing through town on the highway, but that rarely happened and midnight was just about the worst time to traverse this kind of country. In theory, it could have been nothing at all and Able was the one generating the noise and anxiety, but she trusted his instincts and his experience. He was flustered – that made her worried.

In the silence came an electronic ping. Dana initially thought it was her laptop, or her phone, and glanced back at the bedroom. But Able moved across to his desk.

'Security camera. Got a hit. This should tell us, eh?'

He clicked on a desk lamp and an arc of light erupted. Dana squinted until her eyes adjusted. Able was leaning over the back of the office chair, his hair more unkempt than usual, his gut flopped against his T-shirt. He brought up the screensaver and clicked through to the camera footage as Dana approached. She looked over his shoulder until he realized and made room alongside.

'Thank you. How many cameras do you have?'

'One inside, downstairs. State regulations: I've got public property down there – emergency kit, police radio system, and so on. I can keep prisoners on site for a short spell, too, so it has to be set up like a mini-custody thing. But the one outside at the front, that's what pinged.'

'How can you tell?'

'I set them up with different sounds. Besides, this one has the red marker next to it, see? Means it has movement recorded. Here we go.'

She leaned in further as the camera footage played. Like a dash-cam, it had a constant sixty-second loop going prior to full activation. They both watched the empty street.

'Infrared?'

'Yeah, it has a light sensor. Switches from normal to infrared at sundown. Yeah. Here we go.'

Across the street, a blurred wraith of a figure. They were a light-grey heat transmitter, distinguishable from the darker charcoal of the building. The person stayed back beyond the lee of a veranda; it wasn't possible to discern height, build or gender. Dana searched for inference: the figure wasn't rushed or panicky, movements were smooth and precise. Practised, she felt, well ordered or trained. Nothing ad hoc about it; more a sense of military precision. The figure fussed over something down near their midriff and bent to one knee. There was a brief flash, then the screen filled with visual white noise, a cacophony of fuzzed lines and over-exposure. They watched for another six minutes in silence. Anything could be going on in that street and they couldn't tell – the image was obliterated by excess light.

Abruptly, the light disappeared. As it left, it looped upwards momentarily. They both understood this was the subliminal glimpse that had startled Able from semi-sleep. The camera took a split second to regain its senses, then they were faced with the same street, the same darkness, devoid of people. As though it had rewound to the start and was playing a loop.

'Has that white-noise thing ever happened before?' she asked. 'A technical problem with the camera?'

'Nah. Camera's fine. And no, it hasn't. Someone did something. Shone a laser at it, maybe.'

So, thought Dana, they knew the camera was there, knew it was operating, knew it would record whatever they intended to do, knew it was infrared at night, and knew how to disable it without getting close, being identified or causing damage. That was a lot of knowledge.

'Have you discussed the camera with anyone?'

'Nah. Installed it at night a few weeks ago. Even used a manual brace so there wouldn't be any noise. I know, I know – paranoid, right? Lens is built into the frame of the door. Tiny thing: the exposed bit's about the size of a fingernail. You wouldn't see it unless you were looking for it. The wiring on the inside's above the door frame. Looks like it's an old doorbell or something, in case a visitor sees it. No one would guess.'

'So basically no one should know about it, let alone how to screw it?'

'Nah, they shouldn't.'

'But whoever did, they had a specific reason for doing it, and maybe a reason to do it now.'

They stared at each other for a couple of seconds then moved towards the stairs. Able went first, gun drawn without her realizing he even had it to hand. Dana's knee twinged now, the adrenalin subsiding before a second burst. The desk light illuminated the space above the stairwell, offering a soft pall of light towards the door.

Dana could hear his breathing. He was fighting to keep it under control, but it held a slight wheeze on the draw-in that was disconcerting. He gripped and re-gripped the gun. She stood back and leaned against the wall to minimize recoil.

Able opened the front door slowly, and only a few centimetres. Dana knew what was foremost in his concerns: booby-trap. It flipped through her mind that they were two hundred kilometres from any help.

A thin shaft of light fired out at the street, too slim for her to discern anything except the notion that they were making themselves more visible, an easier target. They waited for something to happen; both had wire-taut trigger muscles and hammering hearts.

She heard Able swallow then slowly ease the door wider with his foot. By now she could see more of the outside: some kind of tall lump, or blockage, to the street. She strained to see better, but that was all she had. She wasn't sure if Able could see it, too.

Once the door was further ajar, Able risked pushing his face out into the street. He let out a quiet grunt, then stepped back.

'Okay. I get it now. Ah, look, all safe. They've done what they wanted to do.'

He opened the door wider and stepped out confidently, certain there was no danger. He dropped his gun hand but held the firearm anyway, more absent-minded than cautious. The cold air struck her fully as she reached the doorway. Able found a torch by the door frame and sent a beam fizzing out into the night. It didn't get very far.

Two metres beyond them, facing the road, were three angels. They blocked the entrance, placed in an arc that protected the door. And the occupants.

They both felt the shudder of adrenalin fading, shaking muscles as it left. Dana ensured her safety was on and gave Able's shoulder a reassuring squeeze. He puffed his cheeks and this time even his trade-mark smile was watery, partial and swamped by relief.

'DuBois, then?' she asked.

'Apparently.' Able swung the beam down and then up again. 'Bloody rubber wheels – I didn't hear anything. Or at least, I might have heard something, but not consciously. I woke up because the light hit the window for a moment. I was half asleep, really.' He turned towards her. 'You probably know more about DuBois than me by now. What is this?'

Good question, she thought. At the very least, another wordless message of protection, to go alongside the Praetorian greeting at the entrance to town this afternoon. Second, it was proof that Axel DuBois was still nearby and not halfway across Belgium. Had he stayed near town specifically for her, or was it coincidental? Third, he'd demonstrated considerable prowess in moving around town unnoticed, able to carry out his business without being seen. It wasn't luck. He was genuinely good at this. As he'd need to be, if he wanted to get away with murder . . .

'Hmm. Well, I'd swear this is a guard. A protection. A warning of danger and a message to be careful.' She wondered whether Able felt it was plausible. They both knew the artist was a major suspect, based on what they currently had. His role as a benevolent influence was far from settled. 'DuBois is worried about our safety in a way that he wasn't a few hours ago. So the questions are: what does he know that we don't, and why is that so dangerous he has to warn us?'

Because, she felt, such a warning could have been given far more easily than this. He could have stuck a note under the door in the night, or rung from the satellite phone she knew he possessed. *That* detail was hidden in an appendix paragraph of the investigation file: another slice that the previous detectives had wished to record but not highlight. But this message was specific, bespoke to her – it carried more than one implication, if only she could work it out.

The breeze rose momentarily and her eye was drawn to a newly visible corner of a fluttering piece of paper. A lurid pink Post-it that stood out against the black of the angel, stuck to its ribcage. She knew not to touch it, though she was sure it was DuBois. She leaned forward until she could read the one word on it.

Stasi.

Dana didn't sleep well after that. She was used to it at home: she averaged three hours a night and that fell in a series of disturbed shards, punctuated by a raft of lock and deadbolt checks that her rational self knew were unnecessary. Here, her mind raced and the strangeness of her surroundings was almost an afterthought.

Stasi.

She'd literally asked DuBois for help: *aide-moi* her note had pleaded. It was exposing – she could be asking the killer for help to find the killer. It might have been the dumbest move she'd ever made, or the key to a breakthrough. It was likely to be one or the other. So she took his response as an indication that it was the latter.

She knew who the Stasi were, of course: the secret police from the communist years in East Germany. A byword for secrecy, subterfuge, cruelty with impunity. She struggled to comprehend what DuBois meant. Was *Stasi* pointing the finger at a corrupt officer? Was it hinting at secrets underpinning what seemed to be police work? No one from Dutton ever seemed to come here, bar the two detectives with their puny efforts. Perhaps, she shuddered, he was pointing the finger at Able. Maybe he was suggesting that Able was involved, either by hiding the killer or by being the killer. It could be self-serving deflection from DuBois; but if she was to take his response seriously – and otherwise, why ask for it? – then she had to consider the possibility. DuBois had risked something substantial, just to reply. Able was a major figure in the town, knew both victims, had means and opportunity. And he had been deliberately held at arm's length by those fellow detectives for both investigations. Able Barella, the local cop, had been shunned.

She wondered about that. When Able was deliberately excluded from the previous murder investigations, how had it actually been done? Had he been called into the office by Judge Trent or Cronin, as she'd been, and overtly commanded to leave the investigation alone? Or had he assumed he'd be involved, until two detectives rolled in from Dutton and told him they'd take it from here, thanks? Or had it been done by omission: by blanking him and the option of him? She cursed herself. She should have found out. She could have pushed it with Trent, or with Cronin: it might have indicated they had suspicions about Able. It could have been – *should* have been – a fundamental part of her starting point, but she only realized that now.

If Able *had been* involved in the killings, he'd been remarkably calm – she hadn't picked up a hint as yet. And she could glean nothing from his reaction tonight. He'd been agitated by the light coming into the room, and genuinely fearful when he'd prised open the door. That hadn't been faked, she was sure of it.

She'd been surprised that he'd merely raised an eyebrow when he saw the note. He had to have guessed that she'd left DuBois some kind of message herself and this was his reply. He also had to infer that she'd deliberately kept him out of that communication. But he hadn't said a thing. They'd returned upstairs and he'd righted the table lamp, shut off the computer and returned to his blanket on the sofa. It wasn't sulking or petulant disappointment, it was compliance. As though he'd expected her to close him off, and this was precisely what he'd anticipated.

She wanted to be wrong. But the notion had first surfaced when she was on the plane. Able had no alibi on each occasion. He knew how to shoot. He knew how to minimize forensic evidence. He knew how to point the finger at others. He knew how the town worked. And now, he was in a position to manipulate her investigation.

Someone with that power had to be on her radar. Had to be.

Chapter 16

'Hi, Luce. Sorry to wake you, chick.'

Dana was skulking near the deck chairs again, comfortable that she was out of earshot. She'd rung Lucy as soon as there was enough daylight to make out the sleeping forms of house and pub. And, hopefully, before the snakes woke up.

'No worries. I was dusting the bookshelves. I totally styled it out; I make it look very chic. If you'd seen me? You'd have wanted to dust too.'

Dana smiled. 'I'd never doubt you.'

'Problems?'

'Yes and no. I wanted to think out loud, basically.'

'Hold on . . . okay, I have coffee now. Fire up.'

'Thank you. Last night I left a note at Axel Dubois' shed. A note I showed to his security camera and then destroyed. I hoped he'd see the footage at some point and reply. The note said "Help me". He replied later in the night, though he did it like a military operation and freaked out both me and Able. Anyway, DuBois came back with one word. *Stasi.*'

'*Stasi*? Nothing else?'

'Nothing else. Apparently, he thinks that's enough. I've been turning it over in my mind.'

'Conclusions?'

'Right. First, he took a risk to answer. He's out in the sand some-where, for his own reasons. I haven't figured out what those might be. But it means any move into town, even in darkness, is a gamble for him. Admittedly, he might do that if he was the killer and this was a way of deflecting blame. That's partly why I dangled the carrot. But if he replies in that esoteric way, it makes me think he's genuine. Makes me *more likely* to think he's genuine.

'Second, he avoids Able. There's no getting away from it: his pri-mary aim seems to be not getting near Able. He avoids the whole town, of course – or, I presume he does – but it seems to me he's mainly avoiding law enforcement. Accepted, that could be because he's guilty. But again, his behaviour doesn't suggest that to me. Plus, he could simply run away if that was the case, rather than hang around, risking capture. It suggests he thinks Able is somewhere between untrustworthy and dangerous. I have nothing from Able sug-gesting that, but I've only known him a few hours, while DuBois had six months of him.

'Third, this note. *Stasi*. If I take it at face value, it means secret police. It means police intent on subterfuge and control. He might mean other officers, but they're two hundred kilometres away and I've no record of them coming here other than during the murder inquiries. Unamurra's a dead zone to Dutton officers – they don't want to trek over here and they leave it all to Able to sort out. So how can I conclude that *Stasi* means anything other than Able's behav-iour? But against that, as I say, he hasn't indicated that kind of behaviour to me, and everyone seems to interact with him as if he's a reliable, solid, decent police officer. So how can he be *Stasi*-like at the same time?

'Fourth, if he is doing something illegitimate, will he undermine my investigation? Did he undermine the previous investigations? They seemed shoddy of their own accord and the supervision was crap, but what if Able was deflecting them? He wasn't involved but he must have been around; nearby, dealing with the same locals. I'm dependent on Able for all sorts of things out here, and I can't go around sulking and not asking his opinion. His view *is* local, and it *is* expert. If I don't include him, I'm basically holding up a flag that I think he's involved in two murders. A flag I have no right to fly, because I have zero evidence.'

'Maybe DuBois wanted to drive a wedge between you and Able and that's why he sent that message. It's very specific.'

Dana nodded. She'd considered an ulterior motive for DuBois, but had no evidence of anything other than cooperation and good faith. 'Yes, that's worth a go. But I can't see how to interpret the message in any other way than pointing towards Able. If that's the case, perhaps I simply haven't dug deeply enough and Able's a good actor.'

'Hmm. I'd trust your instincts, chick. Everyone's got a hundred different tells about what they're like – how they treat others, how they drive, the state of their home, whether they drink a lot, and so on. You've seen plenty of those already with Able – enough to have a gut instinct about him.' Lucy paused. 'I suggest that you think *Stasi* is about something else. But since you can't work out what that might be – not yet – you're clinging to the obvious.'

Lucy had a habit of getting to the centre of Dana's thinking. It was disconcerting and reassuring at the same time.

'Ouch. Yes, I think you're dead right, Luce, damn you. It feels like *Stasi* is slightly oblique, a catch-all or generic rather than just a statement about police. I'm covering myself, focusing on Able, instead of working out the correct answer. Urgh, this case. It gets weirder. It's like trying to catch water.'

'Cogitate, *chérie*. You're good at that. A positive champ at it.'

'Ha! Thanks, Luce. Oh, Able is waving. I think we're supposed to be under way. A six-hour round trip for one interview. Possibly a short interview. It's like that here.'

'Cool. I'm in the office all day, should you require. Live long and prosper, Dana Russo.'

'Bye.'

Now she was thinking about the Kobayashi Maru again . . .

Chapter 17

They set off just before a dawn of grey, milky light and surprisingly low cloud. It looked about to rain, the kind of heavy, persistent pour she knew from her mosquito-infested pocket of the country. But Able had said it was a common deceit: they often awoke to this form of grizzled sky, only to see it burn away in a couple of hours. Almost as though Nature was taunting them. Dana could sense the increasingly desperate air of their upward glances. Every rainless day here was saturated with anxiety.

Dana's sleep had been splintered by thoughts of DuBois' message, and its delivery. In her rush to assess the importance of *Stasi*, she'd neglected the three angels forming an arc beyond Able's doorway; she'd only reconsidered them when she edged past on the way to the car. No doubt the sentries were a warning: she should have felt reassured by their presence. Yet the one-word response felt ambiguous and insubstantial. DuBois could have told her so much more; he could have made himself known to her, available. Although if he was pointing a finger at Able, she understood his reticence. Regardless of his motives, everything DuBois was doing was still deliberate and carefully calibrated. Perhaps he knew the whole story and *she* was the laggard.

Larry Muir's property was away to the north-west, a two-hour-plus trip with the last thirty minutes along loose tracks. It was, no matter what she did, time wasted. Given McCullough's rush towards judgement back home, she could ill afford the whole morning to do one interview, but she had no option. The geography out here was overwhelming – locals sucked it up and took it in their stride, while outsiders like Dana fretted and failed to adapt.

While they still had graded earth beneath them, she read from the laptop. She'd already read potted bios of nine people in Unamurra, and some details of the size and stock of the stations in outer-Belgium. Lucy had set up some kind of manic *send* program overnight, which constantly fired a set of files at the recalcitrant and overburdened internet; at 0337hrs, three of the four files had slipped through. Lucy knew to send accounts because that was Dana's core skill. The state of play for the limited number of businesses in the Unamurra district were now available to her, and she fizzed through the financial statements. In addition, there were records of deeds, mortgages, transfers, liens and criminal records. Dana was mentally building a whiteboard of key facts. Able glanced over occasionally, but she was pretty sure he wouldn't ascertain much from subliminal views of profit and loss.

She couldn't, she mused silently as they drove, dive too readily into actioning the idea that Able might be involved. *Stasi* kept floating in her head, maddening in its insistence and its capacity for multiple interpretations. DuBois could have simply written *Able* if he was so sure. But, if it *was* Able, DuBois would then be taking a chance that he could stay beyond Able's grasp until Dana secured an arrest, assuming she did. That would explain his current AWOL status, but the tactic would be a gamble. So maybe he felt this response was elliptical enough to protect himself while shining a light Able's way. Or, possibly, he was doing everything to deflect attention from himself and on to absolutely anyone else. Or perhaps, he meant something entirely different and she was being obtuse.

No, she thought. Her instincts weren't really headed that way. She had a certain amount of faith in herself and she wasn't getting any feeling about Able that suggested he was a killer. So the idea of Able had to stay in the background, for now. He had to remain a colleague and an ally, unless or until she had clear evidence otherwise. That would maximize his help if the murderer was someone else and minimize the risk if he had any part in the killings.

It took half an hour of pretending to read for that plan to settle in her mind.

Dana wondered who Able considered suspects. He'd mentioned a notion that had gone south. It seemed that he didn't have a favourite right now, but he'd cultivated suspicions at some point in the last couple of months. It didn't matter if his view was right or wrong; discussing it would be a way of keeping their communication and relationship open. She hadn't asked him directly yet. She planned to do it soon.

The silence had begun to weigh a little. Dana sensed Able might be sulking about the extent of her Chinese walls. He'd been sidelined by the first investigation and this must feel the same – worse, perhaps – but she couldn't currently see a way of avoiding it. Part of her wanted to hold all her thoughts to herself, but she understood that wasn't practical here. Able was stoical, though. He might be hugely offended or utterly indifferent, she didn't see a way of discerning.

'Larry Muir and Tim Ogden. There's no connection, is there?' she asked.

'None that I can see, nah. Not mates, not enemies. No business together, no real contact.'

'Phone calls?' She already knew the answer, but it gave them common ground to discuss.

'Nothing in the month before, apparently. Over the past year?

Three, none more than a minute, and those were to the pub, so I guess anyone could have picked up. Records said Larry only had one call around the time of his murder. Original investigation actually followed that bit through – imagine that. He talked to a cattle breeder up near Townsville: some technical questions about artificial insemination. Larry was trying to work out how to rebuild the herd once the drought broke and how to breed more specialized stock. Hence the artificial insemination talk.' He glanced across. 'Forward planning: farmers are always forward planning. Anyway, no sign that he and Tim were more than passing acquaintances whenever Larry was in the pub, which wasn't often.'

Dana was surprised. She'd assumed connections existed between each and every person in town, and beyond. Fifty souls didn't seem enough for one to drift near another without really meeting. Maybe she was in danger of adopting that lazy *they all know each other's secrets* attitude towards rural areas. A private person could still be private here.

'Tim Ogden had never been to the Muirs' station?'

'Nah.' Able disposed of some gum. 'Not according to the workers, or Sarah. He'd have no reason, really. None that I can see. It's way too far for a casual drop-in; isn't on the way to or from anywhere at all.'

'Sarah would be Larry Muir's wife?'

'Widow,' he reminded. 'Yeah. You'll meet her soon.' He smiled, more to himself than to her. 'I'll, uh, let you form your own judgement, eh?'

Dana gave a slight grimace, and scanned some of the records again. In particular, the finances of the Muirs' station, Pelligrini. Given her background in accounting and Fraud, the numbers wove a story.

Able coughed. 'Uh, last night. That note. DuBois left you a message, and you approved of what it said, yeah?'

DuBois had scared them both last night: each knew it for

themselves and for each other, but didn't speak of it. Part of Able's tentative question might be the legacy of that racing adrenalin.

'Yes, he did. I don't know that I approved, as such, but since I'd asked him for his opinion, I have to take that as a positive.'

'*Stasi*. What do you reckon he meant?'

'I've no idea. I know who the Stasi were, but I can't grasp what he's referring to. He's left plenty of room for interpretation.'

'Stasi were cops.' He deadpanned it, but she thought she detected an edge to his voice.

'Yes, they were. But it could be a shorthand for a way of behaving, rather than talking about purely police behaviour. As I said, it feeds into everything else but I haven't settled on a firm view of it yet.'

She hoped that was good enough. It felt weak, and the stretching seconds made it feel flimsier.

Able chewed for a moment. 'So is he your new best mate, or is he still a suspect?'

'Good question. I haven't totally decided. As we've both noticed, he has means and opportunity but, like the rest of this district, it's hard to see a motive. That isn't to say he lacks one, just that I can't see it at the moment. On the other hand, he's sending messages and, given that he's deliberately hiding from something or someone, he's putting it all on the line when he delivers those messages.'

A raised eyebrow from Able. 'Yeah, but if he's the killer, then it's worth his while to risk sending you down blind alleys, eh? That's a good use of his time, buggering up any investigation of him.'

Dana nodded. 'Yes, that's true, and I'm not saying you're wrong. At the moment, it's fifty-fifty. He's implicated in both murders, in my opinion, but it might be an innocent or a benign connection. I'm trying not to assume he's on my side, just because he responded.'

That didn't seem enough either to placate Able or to firm up her own views.

Able slowed as they reached the junction. Four large boulders had been tipped into a loose jumble and given some crude stripes with white paint. There was no signpost. Visitors were simply assumed to know that a station lay sixteen kilometres away; Dana could see nothing on the horizon. She glanced at the map on her laptop, which didn't even show the road they'd been using. Able turned off a few metres and they shared some water and two bars of chocolate. Everything was cold from the refrigerated glovebox and the chocolate gave a satisfying crack when she snapped off a square.

'Nice choccy. German?'

Able peeled the wrapper back further on his bar. 'Yup. The good stuff.'

She shook her head. 'Hard to believe you can get this from the local shop. Expensive?'

He took a moment to swallow. 'Weirdly, no. Lots of things are, but.' He chewed for a second. 'Annie just makes up all the prices. Whatever she says, goes. I mean, it's bit of a run to the next shop, eh? Fruit and veg are cheap: she likes us to have a good diet. Chocolate's a bit of luxury: she lets that through to the 'keeper. But crap like ice cream, white bread, biscuits, chips, and so on? She either ramps up the price or just refuses to stock it. Says none of us would burn off the calories – not us in town, any rate.'

Dana took that in. Her mind was still chiselling away at the information Lucy had provided overnight. No doubt Lucy had read it before she sent it. Dana badly needed to speak to her again and run through some options.

'Hypothetically, Able, you could order all that crap stuff online, stash it at home and eat it whenever you want. She doesn't own you.'

It came out a bit harsher than she'd intended. Able seemed to take it in his stride, but the trademark grin was back and she understood that all types of emotion could skulk behind it.

'Ah, well. A few people tried to buy in a bunch of frozen stuff a couple
of years ago. You know, big discount, half a truck of frozen goods
rolling into town. So Annie's already got wind. She gives the three of
them a real spray, right there in front of everyone at the pub; tears them
a new one. Anyway, within a week they've all got freezer troubles, or
their electrics have gone weird. Cables frayed, or detached, that sort of
thing. All the food gets wasted. Hmm. No one tried that dodge again.
So no, we don't try to sideswipe the only store in town.' He turned to her
and shrugged, as if the conclusion was inevitable. 'What benefit do we
get if we send her out of business?'

Yes, she thought, that made sense. In practical terms.

He shifted the car into drive, and they set off along the beaten-up
track towards Pelligrini. Above the semi-packed earth was a sheen of
tiny, scrabbly pebbles; the Landcruiser shimmied intermittently on
the scree, especially on corners. Dana found herself reaching for the
grab-bar, even though she trusted Able's driving. He appeared
unfussed, however, sawing the wheel occasionally but basically letting
the car drift when it needed to. The engine growled high and low,
seemingly regardless of speed. Dana concentrated on each hundred
metres ahead and barely noticed the station until they crested a small
rise and it hove into view.

She'd assumed Pelligrini would resemble Vince Reynolds' Sorrento; the data suggested it was about the same size. But it was clear,
even as they drove the final kilometre, that the Muirs had a much
more professional operation.

Three sets of curved blades spun and pumped, enough to half fill a
small dam to the right with brackish, beige water from deep in the
earth. The pumps also fostered four brittle palm trees near a barn, as
well as some stringybarks. The roofline of the cattle sheds gleamed;
the fencing and bars that delineated the working area were freshly
cleaned and shining. As the road arced to the left, she saw that the

buildings extended back behind the main farmhouse: some kind of bunkhouse for the workers, complete with solar panels on the roof. Unlike Reynolds' place, Pelligrini had some rises in the ground behind it, shielding it from the worst of the colder winds. The rises framed the buildings and made the whole place seem more settled and less fragile than Reynolds' home.

The sense of order showed in the details. All the utes and trucks were parked neatly perpendicular to the fence, following invisible lines like a supermarket car park. There was an obvious demarcation between family home and garden, and working areas. It was clear that everything had a place, with a place for everything.

'Who's the super-organized one? Larry Muir, or Sarah?'

Able smiled. 'Good question. Sarah, I've always felt. Larry was capable, don't get me wrong, but he was more an instinct guy. Good cattle man, they all say; Sarah was the organizer on everything else.'

A group of four men who'd watched their progress had dispersed as they drew near. Two headed for the back of the sheds; the third made for a tall barn whose open doors showed a beaten ute glowering from within; the other went towards the farmhouse. Able made sure to park his vehicle just like the others: the pattern invited repetition. As he applied the handbrake he spoke in a low voice.

'Sarah used to be my favourite. For the murders, I mean. Just giving you a heads-up.'

He got out of the car without even a glance. Dana wondered why he'd mentioned it, and mentioned it then. Was it supposed to colour her discussion with Sarah? Put her off the scent of something else? Or just fair warning, not to take everything at face value? It was odd both in content and timing, and she felt it was un-Able in some way.

At this time of morning the wind was blustery and the air felt brisk and clean. The cloud had dissipated and the horizon was vivid, an ice-blue snapping crisply into ochre. It occurred to Dana that perhaps the difference between here and Vince Reynolds' place was simply where the cattle were. Vince had sent all but a handful interstate, while Larry had presumably kept nearly all of his stock here. Hence the latter's need for staff and the wherewithal to maintain standards. That would be the compassionate explanation, at least.

As Dana pouched the laptop into her shoulder bag, she saw Able shake hands with Sarah Muir. There was none of the emotional connection that Able had with Vince Reynolds, no overt sympathy for the widow; they were both all-business. Sarah was sharp and scrubbed – jeans over work boots, a plain white shirt with rolled sleeves and a black tee beneath. Her hair was scraped back into a short ponytail. Like Able, her age was hard to gauge; Dana had forgotten to check before leaving the house. Dana's guess was a naturally well-preserved fifty. Sarah looked trim and quick-witted: not someone who suffered fools.

'Sarah, meet Dana Russo. From Carlton, of all places.' Able stepped back as he introduced them.

Sarah shook hands firmly, taking in Dana with one slightly scornful look before turning back to Able. Her features disappeared under an Akubra that was battered enough to be authentic but sufficiently well kept to fit the air of capability and authority.

'Tea's up at the house. C'mon.'

She turned and began walking, clearly used to giving instructions and being obeyed. Her attitude suggested no problems retaining discipline and respect whenever Larry had been absent. Dana suspected little escaped her attention; she probably had a couple of trusted hands who kept her in the loop for whatever she didn't physically witness. The station's work would be hard, but treatment and pay would be scrupulously fair.

Sarah turned at the veranda and walked to a large, covered deck on the west side. It was in shade and a chilly gust whipped around the corner. The house itself was substantial, late nineteenth century and solid. Smoke pulsed from the chimney, and from a short metal stack above the bunkhouse. The home's corner beams and columns were broad and newly treated. Through a window Dana could see, as she sat, a well-ordered office with a wall of pigeonholes intermittently filled with sheaves of paper. Sarah poured tea without milk for the three of them.

It was tempting, given the atmosphere of competence, to assume that Sarah would be far too organized to leave a corpse in full view near Vince Reynolds' property. Without even considering her potential involvement with Tim Ogden's death, it was easy to conclude that if Sarah Muir had wanted to kill her husband, she would have left no trace. She surely wouldn't leave a body to find or evidence lying around; instead, she would be crisply efficient, as she clearly was in her business life.

And yet, Dana could see why Able had considered Sarah a strong possibility. There was proximity, first of all. She'd spent long hours and months on end with Larry. The shared business and the physical isolation from others must have added to that claustrophobia. Couples who lived and worked together always had a potentially murderous closeness that practically defined opportunity.

Second, Sarah stood to inherit a farm that, drought notwithstanding, was in decent shape. When the rains eventually came, Pelligrini would be one of the first back to prosperity. Even now it still had, according to Lucy's data, cash reserves and lowish debts. It was a good proposition and only Larry Muir had prevented Sarah Muir from owning all of it. Probate was probably days from being granted by now: Larry's death meant Sarah was about to become a millionaire. She had clear motive.

Third, she had means. There would be guns kept on the property and no doubt Sarah was one of the few key-holders: perhaps her, Larry, and possibly a couple of staff. Therefore it was likely Sarah was a competent shot at worst; maybe, better than that. The registered weapons had been checked by the previous investigation, but an off-the-books handgun could be easily concealed around this property, let alone out in the bush.

Fourth, Sarah's general air of capability didn't necessarily jar with Larry's body turning up on Vince's land. It may be that she intended it that way, thinking Vince Reynolds would be blamed because of the ongoing flare-ups, all nicely recorded in the publicly accessible Book of Feuds. Alternatively, she could have hidden the body but someone else moved it to Reynolds' gate, either maliciously or because they thought that would help Sarah.

Lastly, Sarah might have simply bungled it in some way, or made poor decisions. Aptitude at running a station didn't automatically translate into competence at murder and subsequent forensics. She might have panicked or broken down; she might have needed help, or left the clear-up to others. Plenty of people were talented at some tasks yet barely sentient about other matters. Dana was her own example of that.

But, all in all, Sarah Muir was currently a good bet. Able had selected wisely. As she took a polite sip of tea it occurred to Dana that perhaps she was looking at this from the wrong direction. Sarah's strong motive for killing Larry, but zero motive for killing Tim, might not rule her out after all. It could be exactly why she should be considered a strong suspect.

'Thank you for taking the time to see us,' said Dana.

Sarah blinked slowly, as if she couldn't care less.

'I'm very sorry for your loss, Mrs Muir. As you'll understand, we have a few questions, ones that the previous investigation might not have covered. I'd—'

Sarah held up her hand, paused and gave an exaggerated sigh while glancing to Able.

'Formality doesn't really work with me. I'm busy. So stop being polite. Call me Sarah, for God's sake, and get on with it. Ask your questions.'

It was one thing to be impatient because there were other things to be done – Dana had anticipated a different rhythm to conversations out here. But all the same, she took a second to take note.

'Thank you. I've never lived somewhere this remote. How do you get your supplies here?'

Whatever Sarah had been expecting, this wasn't the question. She raised her eyebrows.

'Uh, well, we can get anything sent to Dutton; that's not a problem. They won't deliver most of the stuff out this far, though. From Dutton it's two hours to Unamurra, then another two out here: delivering a parcel or two would literally take all day. Sometimes one of the crew's going to Dutton for some reason – spare parts and the like – they'll pick up bits and pieces. But mainly it's me, once a week.'

Dana didn't ask another question, she simply sat and waited for further details. Sarah narrowed her eyes momentarily, as if trying to see beyond Dana's neutral gaze.

'So, I go into Little Big Town every Monday. Sling half a dozen eskies in the back of the ute, go through Coles like a locust. Twelve mouths to feed here, don't forget.'

'That many? I saw the bunkhouse at the back.'

'Yeah, ten to twelve most months. Depends on the time of year a bit. So yeah, eleven other hungry buggers get through plenty of food if we've worked them right. So I pick it up in Dutton, then stop off in Unamurra on the way back.'

Dana nodded. 'You can't get everything in Dutton, then?'

Another glance from Sarah towards Able, as though he would see the ludicrous nature of this conversation and step in. Able appeared happy to sit quietly and watch the palm fronds wave.

'Oh, I could. In theory. But yeah, buy a few things in the shop, have something in the pub. Got to keep Annie sweet. Everyone needs to keep Annie happy, eh, Abe?' Her appeal prompted a non-committal grin from Able. 'Then I bring it all back here. I might pop into Unamurra during the week for something, but otherwise, I'm on station 24/7.' Sarah took a gulp of tea. 'Why are you asking, Detective?'

'Just curious. As I say, I've never lived somewhere so remote.'

Sarah looked her up and down for a second, as though making a fresh but identical appraisal to the last one. 'Yeah, well, it's not for everyone. I grew up on a little island; boat ran once a week to the mainland. So I'm used to all of this. Takes *resilience*, see? Not everyone has the strength.'

'No,' replied Dana, carefully. 'It's rarer than most people think. And more difficult to spot than they realize.'

Able now looked from one to the other, as the silence spooled.

'You clearly have a million and one things to do, Sarah, so I won't waste your time. In your opinion, who should I talk to, about these murders? Who's the most influential person in this area?'

'Abe.'

She'd nodded in his direction and the answer had come immediately, as though Dana were a psychiatrist and they were playing word association.

'Because?'

Sarah paused, toying with the handle of her cup. 'Look, not bagging anyone, but you asked my opinion. Unamurra's a busted flush, assuming it was ever something at all. Most of the population is retired, welfare, whatever. Not exactly wasters, but not, uh, economically productive. Not energetic entrepreneurs: they're *sheeple*. Need nudging, need prodding, don't want to move unless they're told. A few work in the shop and the pub – minimum wage, mind – and that's it. There's no bank any more, no butcher, no pharmacy, no' – she squeezed

Able's arm sympathetically and Dana noticed he didn't twitch – 'no mechanic, either. You can get some food or petrol, have a beer – that's it. All the economic heavy lifting out here comes from the stations. When we do well, Unamurra does okay. When we're doing it tough, like now, Unamurra starves. I don't mean literally. I mean it . . . withers. Perishes.'

Dana found it hard to disagree with the logic. Not only was Unamurra on its knees, but standing again depended on others. Unamurra couldn't rise to its feet – it had to be helped up, with something more substantial than a moving art installation.

'That means the *influence*, if that's what you're really after, Detective, must be with the public services. The private sector's flimsy out here – there's only two businesses for two hundred kays in any direction that aren't farms and Annie owns both. No, public service is funded, stays around, affects people's lives. It's a stable thing in a place that isn't. And, since Nonnie's a useless drunk, the only real public service around here is ol' Abe.'

Sarah had neglected the obvious answer and Dana wondered why. Also, in Dana's view, Unamurra was entirely stable – in stasis, in fact. It seemed encased in the amber light reflected from the sand.

'Really? I mean we all admire Able, of course. But I'm interested that you think this part of the world is somehow unstable. As an outsider, I see very slow change and a reluctance by most to embrace even that.'

Sarah frowned. She swirled the remains of her tea.

'Yeah, well. Looks that way to outsiders, I suppose: you tend to spot the obvious, not the currents underneath. Let's see. We have two people murdered – as many murders as the last forty years for Unamurra – that's unstable. We have farms that have been in the same hands for decades, getting sold – that's unstable. We have a drought they call once-in-a-century but isn't, that takes most of our livestock or forces them interstate – that's unstable. We have volatile prices for our stock, we have to let good workers go, the banks are circling – that's all unstable. Or do you think it's all fine and dandy here, Detective?'

'So people look for a life raft in troubled times? Clutch at what's familiar and appears solid?'

'Exactly. Any port in a storm. They want someone else to sort it all out. People always do, don't they? Abe's the only sober publicly funded person within cooee. So he must be the most influential, eh?'

Dana glanced at Able, smiling. 'Congratulations, Able, you're an icon.'

'Never doubted that,' he lied.

Sarah was hard-edged; there was a flintiness to her answers. She seemed the type of person who would face down cruelty or aggression quite easily but might crack under overt kindness. Dana had already decided that Sarah had a directness that probably stood her in good stead generally, but she didn't evade conflict. Perhaps a quality that drew Larry to Sarah in the first place had turned toxic over the years.

'Before Larry died, Sarah, how did the two of you divide up the work here?'

Sarah swallowed before replying, as though she didn't appreciate being asked. Dana didn't think it was the mention of her husband's name, so soon after his murder. More that Sarah didn't like explaining herself to anyone.

'Larry knew stock: he was fourth generation. From a place near Charleville, but he was third-born son, so he had to build his empire elsewhere. He ran everything to do with the cattle, from insemination to slaughter. All the rest was me. Simple enough for ya?'

Able shuffled on his chair and kept looking back towards the car.

'Thank you. Your turnover is down by two thirds in three years, yes?'

Sarah leaned forward before she spoke. 'Yeah, cheers for captioning our pain. You made it sound like some footy results. Spoken like someone who gets the same pay cheque every month, no matter what. Been checking up? Why is that, then?'

'I'm a numbers person, really, so it's the first thing I do. You have a similar number of cattle to Vince Reynolds, yet even now you have twice the income.'

Sarah gave a wry grin and a shake of the head that didn't suit her. She would always take the shortest distance between two points. Being sardonic looked odd.

'Pfff. Vince? He's a bloody fool. Has been for years. Sorry, Abe, but we all know it. Vince went off the rails after his wife and' – she held her palms wide – 'I'm sure you're across that, seeing as you're so well informed. Yeah, so Vince has been on the slide for a long time. I don't benchmark Pelligrini against him. You don't get to *excellent* that way.'

'All the same,' replied Dana, 'at this time, with the drought, I'm puzzled that you currently get so much more per kilo from Dutton abattoir than Vince Reynolds can manage. More than any other station, in fact. And a further increase agreed for next month. It's in their submission for state subsidy.'

Sarah paused, almost a deliberate attempt to rein herself in. It was clear she wanted to fire back immediately, but something stayed her hand. She tapped the table with her fingertips.

'I suppose in your job it pays to be suspicious of absolutely everything you don't understand. Must be a lot of work for you. Out here, we're a bit more straight-edge. How much do you know about slaughtering meat, Detective from Carlton?'

'Probably nothing.'

'Exactly. Nothing. Put it this way, you roll into a Porsche dealer in a beaten-up Corolla, and I arrive in a brand-new BMW. We both have a *car*, but I get a better trade-in, don't I? A superior product, in better condition, that sort of thing. Abattoir pays based on how much quality meat they can get, in usable condition, at a guaranteed delivery. Most of Reynolds' cattle are interstate so he has less control over their welfare, plus he has logistics problems, can only really slaughter the few local animals he has. No economies of scale, are there? The ones he keeps here are struggling, believe me: I have better stock, in better condition. Plus, the abattoir can rely on me professionally, because I don't piss half my day away sloshing Bundy. Does that clarify it for you?'

'Very much so. Things are getting clearer by the second.'

'Look, I'm sorry for Vince in a way, I am.' She glanced again at Able, who ignored her. 'Can't help but be, can you? But he doesn't bloody help himself, does he? Half the district knows he's on the bottle most of the time. He means well, but things don't get done, people can't rely on him. He's created his own spiral and now he can't get out. Sorry, Abe, I know you're big mates and all, but really . . .'

Sarah had neglected to mention plenty of useful information. Dana tried to read the spaces. Sarah eyed her warily. Able huffed noisily and Dana decided his presence might disrupt her strategy if he hung around.

'I'd like to talk a bit about Larry, if I may,' said Dana. 'About the type of person he was.'

Sarah nodded silently. Dana tapped her pen twice on her pad and Able read their agreed cue. He rose, muttering something about Lee, the foreman, and left them to it.

'What do you want to know?' asked Sarah, finishing her tea in one swig.

'You two met before you moved here, I take it?'

'Yeah. At the Easter Show, actually, in Sydney. One of those few drunken hook-ups that actually goes somewhere. I'd studied Business at uni but I wanted to work in the agriculture sector. That's why I was at the show. Those places, if you show up as a pretty young graduate, there's about a thousand cowboys think they're in. Not quite fighting them off with a stick, but Larry was different, got my attention. Yeah, one night turned to two, and so on. No internet back then, so we actually wrote letters for six months. Imagine that. Half the blokes we employ here have literally never written someone a letter. Christ, I feel old just saying it. Anyway, we moved here just after we married. Started with fifty head, built it up. Larry knew cattle, I have a head for business. It worked, Detective.'

Dana noticed that this was more of a potted résumé than a romantic description of her husband of many years.

'What type of person was Larry?'

'Quiet. Qui-et. Bit like you, I'd reckon. Sometimes talking to him was blood from a stone. Typical Aussie bloke, I suppose. At least, the old-school ones. Lee's the same – thinks one word is the best possible answer. It used to frustrate the hell out of me, but I got used to it. Larry wanted nothing more from life than running this station and dealing with cattle every day. All this? It was his dream since he was a kid. Great with the stock, but with people? Not so good. We worked out early on I was better with staff issues. He usually washed his hands of it. Larry had no small talk at all. If you'd taken him to a party, he'd have stood in the corner drinking, until his obvious misery forced you to take him home. On the other hand, he was a great-looking rooster, reliable, kind without needing eternal gratitude, forgot a grudge real quick – we made a good team. Opposites attract, and all that. Things became stressful lately out here, what with the Dry. But he never took it out on me. Not like some in this district – you ask Abe about that. Larry was a good example to the men.' She threw a glance towards the bunkhouse. 'They take their cue from the bosses, and he showed you could be under pressure and not be a dick. 'Course, they've got me for a boss now, so they've had to learn something new.'

Again, thought Dana, more a character reference than emotionally holed below the waterline.

'Any rocky moments?'

'Pfft. Yeah, sure. We argued every now and then. Used to take a drive out to – see that rise there? Yeah, there. We'd scream at each other there, have it out, decide what was happening, then come back here and get on with it. The crew knew – if we got in the Landy and went up there, they'd better tiptoe around us for a day or two. So it served two purposes, didn't it? Nah, nothing huge most of the time.'

'Can you think of anyone who'd wish him harm?'

'No, no I can't.' Sarah stopped, and Dana felt it was for effect. Sarah didn't strike Dana as someone who chose – or believed she needed to choose – her words particularly carefully. 'Larry was driven where the stock was concerned, but he wasn't one to wind people up for the sake of it. We've had the odd bloke sacked and unhappy, but that would be different scale to this. I did wonder about Vince for a while. Larry's body was on his land, after all. They had this stupid set of arguments they kept going.'

'The Book of Feuds?'

'Yeah, Saint Annie's solution, yeah. The constant sniping – it was deliberate, even if it annoyed the rest of us. It was like going to a game and shouting at the ref. Let them open the pressure valve without anything getting broken. I did wonder if Vince had taken it too far and they'd really fought, but no. At one point, Larry thought Vince had a thing for me, but he never really did. I'm way too full on for him. Vince only ever had a thing for his wife. Which sounds romantic but, you know, that many years after she's dead? Becomes a bit creepy, seems to me. So, no, I can't think of anyone. Can you?'

The last question was thrown as Sarah leaned forward on her elbows, hoping to skewer Dana and force her into a corner. But Able clumped into view at the wrong moment. Sarah couldn't hide her irritation as he hovered near the pair.

'Look, Detective, I've given you the time of day and all. But you said yourself I have a lot of other things to do today, which don't involve gassing to you. So unless there's something *really specific* about Larry's murder, not some crappy chitchat about supermarket shopping and slaughter prices?'

Sarah had half risen and looked to Able, who deferred to Dana. Sarah took that in with a smirk.

'Uh, no, I think that covers it,' said Dana. 'Thank you for your time.'

The handshake was polite from Dana, disdainful from Sarah: barely there and a demonstrable waste of her time. She shook Able's hand more convincingly.

'Oh, Sarah, may I use your bathroom before we go, please?' asked Dana. 'It's nearly three hours to get back.'

Sarah looked skyward, as though the request was unreasonable. 'Sure, why not? Through the front door, there, and it's second on the right.'

Dana was near the door when the coda was thrown.

'Oh, Detective?' Sarah dropped to a flat, aggressive tone. 'Every other room in my house is *not* the bathroom. Yeah?'

Dana nodded. 'Of course.'

The front door was hefty and needed a significant push. Dana wiped her feet on a mat and walked down a wide hallway. Halfway saw a change from slate tiled floor to hooped pine planks. Eight metres ahead of her, double doors had etched glass that withheld a proper view, but she inferred wooden kitchen cabinets and the edge of a dining table. Dana walked slowly, grabbing whatever she could from her peripheral vision and taking in the smell of sizzling bacon from the kitchen. The office to the left was pin-sharp: nothing on the desk except neat piles of paperwork and wipe marks from recent cleaning. The only items on the wall were a large calendar with regular markings in blue and red pen, two certificates that looked like legal requirement not outlandish achievement, and a photo of Sarah and Larry at a torch-lit dinner at Uluru. Larry looked pleased to be there, but Sarah seemed as if she'd been dragged reluctantly: the opposite of Sarah's claims about their party faces.

On the other side of the corridor, a formal lounge of 1920s high-backed leather armchairs in a horseshoe around a matte-black wood burner. The stack of logs was immaculate and symmetrical and the cream carpet was pristine. Above the burner was the prized span of a Texas longhorn: at least two metres from tip to tip, with a delicate, sweeping arc on each side of the skull. The shape reminded her of something but, in that brief moment, she couldn't grasp it.

The bathroom was a long, slender affair carved out of what must definitely be the kitchen on the other side of the wall. Houses like this grouped the water and drainage close together. The cistern was high above her head, worked by a long chain ending in a rabbit's foot. Dana checked the cabinet like every detective would: all first aid and paracetamol – nothing out of the ordinary or indicating significant medical problems.

Four framed photos on the wall occupied her attention: they were out of place with Sarah's demeanour. They didn't suit the rest of the house, either, from what she'd seen, or even the photo in the study. She'd never been to the Whitsundays, but half of Australia recognized that particular view. Her internal radar pinged loudly, but she couldn't tell why. She definitely needed to talk it through with Lucy.

Dana wrote Pitman in her notebook for a couple of minutes. She avoided looking in the mirror. She washed her hands anyway, figuring Sarah might check the dampness of the towel after they'd left.

Able and Sarah had made it ten metres from the veranda when

Dana emerged. Clearly that was far enough for Sarah and a position from which she could see the length of her own hallway. Their discussion was muttered and stopped once Dana opened the screen door.

'All right, let me know if that shows up, yeah?' said Able in a too-loud voice. Sarah nodded once and swept past Dana without looking at her. The cold wind no longer seethed through the trees, but Dana felt it anyway.

Chapter 18

'And you thought you wouldn't make friends out here, eh?' chuckled Able.

Dana kept her eyes fixed on the wing mirror. 'I know, right? She's still glaring at us . . . still . . . still. Yes, all the way until we disappear. Lovely woman. Charming.'

Able swung the Landcruiser through an S-bend as the road rose momentarily. Dana swigged some much-needed cold water; she could feel self-conscious heat swarming through her. 'Be honest, Able. Is she always like that, or was that out of character?'

He paused as the engine lifted. They settled into a longer straight that quickly became rutted and corrugated.

'Would I sound like a pollie if I said a bit of both? Yeah, a bit of both. No offence, but she didn't like you. I mean, obviously, you picked that up, but it was the sort of dislike that comes automatically to her. Nothing personal is what I mean.'

Dana smiled. 'That's usually what people say when it actually is personal.'

'Ha. Nah, she doesn't like people who can't do what she does or can't help her to do it. You fit both those categories – clear to her right from the start. She doesn't think you'll solve either murder, to be honest. She told me while you were having a sneaky look at bits of her house. That means she sets against you before you've opened your mouth. Speaking of which, yeah, she doesn't go much on polite either, so that counts against you as well. Straight talk, no bull: she's happier with that, and Larry was that sort of bloke. Lee's the same: it's how come he's foreman.'

How Dana spoke was clearly a factor. Again. It made her think.

'Anyway, her crew,' continued Able. 'She loves them just as long as they're pulling a proper shift and the station's going okay. If any of them slack off, she's brutal. Likewise with people in town. She's tight as with Annie, I've always thought, but the rest of them are just useless old farts to her, as she said.'

'Yes, I noticed that.'

'Plus . . .' Able tailed off and pretended the packet of gum was difficult to open.

'Hmm?'

'Your questions. They threw her a bit. I mean, I'd said you were a detective brought out from Carlton for the two murders. She'd have been expecting a bunch of stuff about Larry's whereabouts, and about her. How often were either of them away? Any strangers around? How good a shot is she? Where was she on the night of? You know, questions relevant to investigating the crimes. So when you asked her about where she shops, or prices per kilo at the abattoir? Well, I guess it threw her a bit and, when Sarah's thrown, she bites.'

If anything, Dana felt, Sarah had held back: a low simmer, then glad to have the chance to pull the plug and send Dana packing. 'That was partly the idea. She has a temper?'

'God, yeah – ah, wait. Nah, not like that. Not a shooty-temper. Bit like old Beattie: she'd say it out loud. If she thought it needed a slap for punctuation, she'd do that too. I got into it with her once and I ended up with a bruise on the face. Not proud of my part in that. I was heavy-handed and it all got a bit sweary. But it would never occur to her to hold on to that. We both did what we did, and it's all forgotten the moment it's finished. She didn't have a lot of arguments with Larry, by all accounts. But when she did, they mattered: they were humdingers.'

Yes, she thought, they would be. The impression of Larry given by others, including the notes from the previous investigations, was of a laid-back character, except where the stock were concerned. Sarah struck Dana as someone who could escalate then cool off quickly: arguments would be competitions to be won, not embers to be brooded over.

Able seemed to want his last statement to settle with Dana, and it caused him to pause. But then he popped the gum, chewed for a second and continued. 'But nah, that wasn't why I thought she might have done the murders. Neither killing struck me as spur of the moment, so I've never been looking at someone based on a short fuse. The opposite, actually. I think it's someone who plays a longer game.'

That was a good point, she conceded. There was plenty to unpack in Able's reply, and not all of it about Sarah. In truth, she'd assumed that Sarah's hackles had been raised by the questions and their seeming irrelevance. It was a reaction Dana often got; she was used to it. And Sarah's general demeanour – the busyness, the clipped body language and quick movements – said that she wasn't one for the fireside chat anyway. That was why Dana had allowed it to cut so short: she figured all of a small interview was more informative than half of a longer one. Besides, most of the information she'd gained from that interview had been unspoken.

'So why *did* you finger her as prime suspect?'

Able rubbed his cheek, as if the bruise from Sarah were still there.

'Ah, lots of little things, really. Mainly, she'd been spending time with Vince Reynolds in the previous six months or so. They were both tight-lipped about it. She'd nip in to his place on the way back from town quite often. Pretty much her regular Monday routine. She skipped that bit when she told you about the shopping, eh? She'd reach the pub after going to Dutton, have a meal and a few with Annie, then stop at the Reynolds place for a top-up. The slap: I was talking to her about the drink-drive, and she objected. It only occurred to me something else might be going on when Larry was killed and turned up on Vince's property.'

'What did you think she'd done, exactly? And why?'

'Yeah, that was where my theory went south. I don't think she was involved with Reynolds, nothing like that. What she said about him just now is what she's always thought – she sees him as a whiny loser who doesn't face up to life. It's pretty harsh, given what happened to his wife and kid. But Sarah's like that. Nah, no romance or anything, and anyway, I can't see what she would have to gain by putting the body next to his gate. It was more . . .'

'Yes?'

'More a sort of converging, I suppose. Proximity. Sarah's the dead man's wife. Sarah inherits. Sarah was spending time with the guy who owns the body dump spot. Everyone's spread out across Belgium, so how can those three things all link back tightly to one person and that person isn't involved?'

'I see. Yes, I can understand why you went there, and it's a perfectly logical argument. But as you say, it falls at the last hurdle. If Larry had simply vanished – or had *been vanished* – Sarah would be near the top of the list because she inherits . . . eventually. But this whole dressing and staging of the body doesn't seem like Sarah. Plus, she has zero reason to place a body near Vince Reynolds' place. Zero that I can think of at the moment, anyway.'

'There you go. But, like I said, I think she was thrown by your questions and how they didn't relate to Larry's murder. Which is why she got shirty.' Able paused and bit his lip. 'There is a Sarah theory that fits, kind of.'

'Really? Go on, then.'

'Okay. So, it's a bit of a leap. Let's say Sarah and Tim are having an affair. I have no evidence for that, but it's theoretically possible. Sarah confesses it to Larry, because she wants a divorce. Tricky to divorce when you co-own a business, a family home and an investment, all in one. Larry says no; he's addicted to this life and he won't give it up and lose the station. But Sarah's confessed: she's all in now and can't afford to have Larry telling anyone else. She decides the next best option is to kill Larry and she does that, leaving the body at Sorrento. So far, so good. The finger's been pointed at Vince or DuBois and she thinks she's off the hook. Now she says to Tim that, since Larry's gone, they can be together. But Tim's just having a fling, never intended to leave Annie. He shuts Sarah down, and she retaliates by killing him. For spite, she leaves Tim's body where Annie can find it.'

Dana had listened intently. 'It's coherent, but there's no evidence.'

'Yeah, true. And it falls apart for the same reasons as the other one. It doesn't fit Sarah's personality and the whole rigging up of the bodies doesn't feel like her either.'

All the same, she felt, Able might not be totally wide of the mark. She reflected on his description of her questions to Sarah. His comments suggested *he* was perplexed – possibly annoyed – by the approach she was taking. And not just with Sarah; she'd noticed the same after they'd visited Vince Reynolds and, to a lesser extent, after Henry Beattie. DuBois had raised doubts about Able with his *Stasi* statement, but Dana still needed to work with Able and had to take DuBois' apparent opinion as conditional. The air in the car had to be cleared.

'You need to speak up here, Able.'

'Sorry? What?'

'We need to have a discussion. What you're feeling is quite legitim-
ate and you have the right to a decent explanation.' She looked across
to him, but he declined the opportunity, seemingly uncomfortable as
he flexed his hands on the wheel. 'You have misgivings, Able. About
the way I'm handling this case. Please, speak up. I need your input, to
be honest.'

Able frowned, as though he wasn't used to that kind of invitation.
For Dana, it was commonplace. Back in Carlton, she and Mike Francis routinely attempted to demolish each other's ideas and approach
because it helped the overall cause. But Able, whether it was because
he habitually worked solo or because of the febrile atmosphere in Dutton, wasn't prepared for it.

'You actually sure, mate? Some people invite a . . . a question, but
then they don't like it when it happens.'

'I do it all the time with my team: me to them, them to me. Seriously, have at it.'

He slowed the car noticeably as they crested a rise and put the
cruise control on 25km/h.

'Okay. Well. I mean, I trust you and all, and I'm admiring how
you're handling these interviews and everything. In the general sense.
People out here aren't easy. I know that.'

'But?'

'But . . . you haven't asked any of them for an alibi, or who they
think did it, or why, or any of those basics. Or even if they know how
to shoot, for example. You haven't actually asked about the murders.
Not with Sarah, there, even after I said I thought she was a good suspect. And not with Vince or Henry either. It wasn't what I expected
when I was told a new detective was looking at the case.'

He glanced across as though expecting her to tear into him. Again,
the word *compliant* drifted through her mind. But her silence indicated consent, so Able continued.

'And yet, you were so forensically on it at the start, when we were in Dutton. That stuff, when you saw the dead bodies, I loved that. It really felt like progress – like a fresh pair of eyes and a new take on it. Felt like progress, yeah. But now? We've been in Unamurra . . . nearly a day, and I don't know any more. Seems like you go around chatting to a few people about general stuff, or things from years ago. I dunno. Anyway. That's what was in my head.'

'Thank you. I know it's not always easy to say things like that. As you know, I'm against the clock here. My boss is about to invoke that District Scrutiny and I'm not there to defend myself, or others, or what we do. It isn't just that I'm needed there for my own reasons. McCullough could pull the pin on this investigation at any moment and demand my presence back in Carlton. So I'm anticipating maybe another twenty-four hours at most to solve these murders. The time imperative means I can't really afford to cover existing ground; I have to try something totally new. Besides, the first investigation asked those questions – the alibis, the guns – process questions.'

'Yeah, they did. And you really trust the first investigation?'

Dana shook her head. 'No, I don't, not at all. It was sloppy in all sorts of ways. However, before I arrived here, I had to choose one of two approaches. I was tempted to go back over old ground with each interviewee, if only to see if anything different emerged. But I wasn't sure that those interviewees would tell me – an outsider from Carlton – anything more, or different, than they told the first investigation, even with you there. So I didn't think those questions would yield anything better. Maybe, but I didn't think so. Whereas . . .'

'Whereas?'

'My second option on the flight here was this: if I come at them from an unusual angle, I might get somewhere. Especially with those people who *really* know something – who are protecting themselves, or others. If you were preparing a defence, a way to deflect suspicion, you'd prepare for those alibi and motive questions, wouldn't you? Of all the things you'd prep for, those would be top of the list. Imagine if I simply repeated the first investigation's basic questions. Interviewees genuinely wouldn't have anything further to add and we'd be spinning our wheels by asking. Or they'd have readied themselves to stick to what they said and we'd be butting our heads against that.'

Able inclined his head, to say he was willing to consider that. But Dana had more work to do. 'So your questions?' he asked.

'Attempt to slide past their intentions, and come to a conclusion a different way. They answer because, first, they have no reason not to; they're innocuous questions and it would look weird to refuse. Why wouldn't they say which year they moved here, or where they get their food? While they're trying to work out why I'm asking, they're responding and yielding things they don't intend. Sarah gave out quite a lot of information, even though she wanted to give me nothing. Second, they haven't prepped for any of these, so the answers come when they're off balance, which I like.'

'Yeah, all right, maybe. I can see some of that. But if you do that, all you get is some old crap about slaughter prices, or rainfall gauges, or Henry's time in the army. So what do you get? What do you really get out of it, and is it enough? Because it seems flimsy to me.'

'Fair comment. It *is* enough, yes. It feels like progress each time, even if it doesn't look like it. I don't pretend to have the answer yet, Able, but I feel that it's out there and getting nearer.' She glanced at him, to measure his reaction. He looked dubious that she was getting anywhere at all. 'Don't forget, I'm adding these interviews to information from Lucy: all manner of other data is feeding into this. What Lucy's telling me shows up the contradictions, the gaps, the things they're deliberately excluding – that all counts. Or Lucy's data is confirming, giving me detail around the core answers I'm getting. It all plays into the investigation.'

Possibly, she thought, an investigation into Able. Although, apart from DuBois' note, the evidence against Able was circumstantial and similar to that against others in the town. The more she thought about it, the less she liked the notion of Able as the killer. She simply wasn't getting anything to corroborate it. She decided, instead, to see the note as the grit in the oyster shell – troublesome in itself, but a prerequisite to the pearl of solving the case.

Able was somewhere between less than enthusiastic and outright sceptical. He grunted and pointedly stared ahead.

'Sorry, Able, I should have been more upfront about how I work. It's considered a little, uh, *quirky* in some quarters.'

He shook his head. 'Yeah, *quirky* would cover it.'

'Have faith. I swear to God there's a method in there somewhere. When the time comes, I'll need your help to put the pieces together.'

Able shrugged. 'If you say so, mate.' It was the closest he'd come to hostile. He was hurt and saw her reluctance to share as an insult.

He nodded at the windscreen. 'Whatever.'

Chapter 19

They'd reached the 'main road' towards Unamurra an hour ago and the tyres rumble-thumped across the graded dirt as Dana withdrew inside herself. The case was troubling her. No, she thought. It wasn't the case *per se*; it was her investigation of it. Usually, she sloughed off her natural introversion when she got into the interview room: she became focused, socially adept, skilled at moving the interviewee around the chessboard. She prided herself on it.

But out here, with no interview room and no flickering red light or spooling tape, she felt she was floundering. Back in Carlton, she had an innate advantage over someone who was brought in, or coming in, to a police station. The process of offering a lawyer, the implied severity of the circumstance: she could manipulate that. She was comfortable there, when they were not. She had access to support and further information, had the right to investigate and accuse, when they did not. But here she was working within the confines of their homes, their pub, their town: it was a strange environment that eluded her grip. With little small talk at her disposal, she was tending to dive right in. The result was that the interviews were working for as long as they lasted, but they didn't last long. Able must be – apparently was – wondering what the hell she was doing, and how it might lead to a suspect.

The irony was that, as she'd attempted to reassure him, Dana could feel a sense of progress, even if she couldn't point to it. She was missing something important, something she should have grasped by now. It would open up the case and logic would flow from it, but it wasn't within reach yet. It felt on the tip of her tongue – a key fact or puzzle piece she already had, but didn't fully appreciate the significance of. Maybe chatting with Lucy – once they got within telephone range – might dislodge it.

As they neared Unamurra, Dana strained to see the outline of the town. Behind the buildings, the horizon had disappeared into a general white haze. It flattened the perspective and made Unamurra look like a toy town in front of a sheet. She looked to Able, who was frowning.

'Problem?'

'Yeah. Yeah, might be.'

He accelerated sharply, and the unexpected kick caught Dana off-guard. The engine picked up and the ride smoothed out as they gathered speed.

'Dust storm,' he said, pointing ahead. 'What you can see is the leading edge; it's maybe a kilometre in front of the storm itself. We need to get back into the house and tape everything up.'

She'd seen photos and footage of dust storms approaching towns. They were a staple *coming up next* feature of news broadcasts, with their apocalyptic portrayal of incipient doom and threat to life. A sea-cliff of roiling dust, looming over the buildings and streets. The implicit flimsiness of human construction, the unspoken message that life was feeble in the face of Nature's wrath. The lazy link to climate change and environmental vandalism by humans – the inherent insinuation that those about to be engulfed had, in some sense, brought it on themselves. Closely followed by the report of minor damage and no injuries, but here's a picture of a wallaby covered in sand. Those scenes looked, in many ways, like a rainstorm: a rotating, seething mass of cloud flexing its muscles as it barrelled towards town. But this one looked different: an almost misty reduction of depth, a fuzzy loss of sharpness. Dust was in the air, in ever-increasing quantities, but she couldn't yet see the tides within.

They reeled in the scenery. Dana peered at the storm front. Now they were closer she could see the slight curl, like singed paper, as the outer edges rolled and tucked. It was difficult to discern the storm's pace, or whether it might slide past the town without catching it. Able seemed certain it was headed their way.

By the time they reached Unamurra the impending problem was clear. There was no one on the streets, the buildings had no lights and everyone seemed to have hunkered down. They braked strongly, the tyres squealed and the SUV rocked as they turned. Able pressed the zapper on the garage door but all the town's electricity had failed. He jumped out and raised the door by hand, while Dana looked in vain for the satellite phone. In his rush, Able drove into the garage space too quickly, jamming on the brakes but scattering half a dozen boxes. He grabbed two rolls of duct tape from a shelf and passed them to her, along with the house keys. Flutes of dust pirouetted past the open doorway. The roar was incessant.

'You go up and do the apartment. I'll do down here,' he shouted.

'What abou—'

'Nah, I'll stay down here. Lock the front door behind you and tape all the doors and windows. I've got to cover up all this.'

He waved his arm at the police equipment lining the long wall. Half of it would be rendered worthless if it was infested with red dust. He was pulling tarpaulins down from a high shelf and billowing them as he moved towards the back of the garage.

There was no time to argue. Somewhere on the main street something was crashing down from a height; something else was smacking against a wall. When she left the lee of the garage she had to duck and lean forward. The sand whipped her face like hail; she pinched her nose and squinted as larger granules lashed and stung. The key took three attempts to find the lock. The door needed a major shove to close behind her. She blew out to expel the sand about her lips, then set to work. Near the door was a small stepladder she could use to reach up, but her kneecap zinged when she climbed.

She'd thought the noise might reduce once she'd insulated the door, but clearly it was gathering force now; the banshee scream rose. She carried the stepladder with her upstairs and taped the window in the bedroom first because it was the biggest. Behind the garage was a white-out tinged with orange. It seemed more solid than before. The storm had become one giant raging entity, without any elements within or signs of its end.

And the noise. God, the noise. Now the storm was at its height the howl was beyond imagining. Her logical, coherent mind told her it was wind and sand, nothing more. But there was a primeval tap root within her that caught the sound and held it, something instinctive that provoked the shiver, the nameless fear. The storm felt alive, angry. It screamed around corners, moaned as it smacked the roof, whined when structures shuddered and bent. The wind had intent and guile.

She finished the four front windows and the air vent above the stove. Now she was sitting on the floor, clutching a cushion. It was stupid, she told herself, childish and wimpy. Yet it seemed appropriate: the storm felt like something that should be given its due. As though it were a sentient being that would take pity if it was respected but would wreak revenge on the complacent. She stared at the ceiling, waiting for the screech when the Colorbond above would yield and fly away. Her hair was agitated and crackling, the sand whirled into the air as much by static electricity as by wind.

Suddenly the room was plunged into darkness, a black void that was total and absolute. It took seconds for her senses to catch up. She assumed it was a power outage, but no, that had happened before they even arrived in town. Then she realized that it was simply the mass of the storm – dust particles obliterating all the light. With nothing to see, her senses focused on that terrifying, piercing whistle.

She wondered how Able was doing down below. She thought of the old people who were housebound, the rest of the town in their insubstantial houses. The remainder of the world felt a long way away and she sensed again how that might make a town behave. Being pinned down in a storm served merely to distil what already existed – the isolation, the notion of otherness, the idea that the usual rules and norms needn't necessarily apply. This was, after all, a town that apparently didn't want two murders solved. The first investigation had faced obstinate silence and a shrugged insistence that demonstrably feeble alibis should hold. She'd tried to ease around those obstacles with her choice of questions, but she could see the vestiges of them even now. That first investigation had acquiesced, had yielded to the culture of the town in a cowardly, unprofessional way. Whatever else she might get wrong, Dana was determined not to do that. In fact, she mused, it was vital that she didn't.

There was an obvious inference, one she should have made at the start. Unamurra had made murder easy and investigation difficult, and that was the wrong way round.

Another crash of something-or-other. The wind was incessant. It didn't gust, there was no rise and fall, it simply poured through the town. She tried to text Able to make sure he was okay, but the signal was down. It made her shudder: no phone service. She wondered how long that would last, because without phone access she couldn't really pursue the investigation, or summon help. Able had a satellite phone down there, so she prayed he'd charged it. Now that she thought, Dana couldn't recall having seen the sat phone connected to the charger in the car at all that day. Able always had hold of it, had

control; he'd never shown her how it worked. It probably had a security system or PIN, in case it was mislaid or stolen. Right now, she
couldn't contact safety, or back-up. She couldn't get hold of Lucy or
Mike. Able held her only communication beyond Unamurra in the
palm of his hand. The investigation was at a crucial stage – she needed
the outside world at precisely the moment it had slipped away.

Now the darkness held a rumble. More crashes from somewhere
outside, but an underlying vibration had begun to climb through the
blackness. She wondered what that meant. All the cues were wasted on
her. She had no experience of this and couldn't comprehend what the
storm was saying. It sounded like the road train had – for a split second
she had an image of a careening B-double blasting into town in total
darkness, its lights useless, tipping on to its side and skidding straight
for the buildings. She shook off the idea as the rumble became a roar
like an ocean. She braced herself, expecting the worst.

In an instant, the roar ceased. The wind seemed to die in a moment,
as if it had never happened. Light cascaded into the windows, the
eclipse released. It had a sepia tinge to it, like old photos, because dust
was splattered against the glass. The sun made a watery and apologetic
appearance. The calm felt like the eye of the storm, but dust storms
weren't shaped that way, she reminded herself. This was the aftermath.
It was over.

She rose arthritically. She'd been crouched and anxious and her muscles complained about the combination. The massaging of her kneecap
didn't compensate for skipping the morning exercises. She listened for
signs of life, but none came. The silence was post-apocalyptic.

Dana peeled back the tape from the front door. Sand was embed-
ded in the glue where it had attacked from outside. She scrunched
the reels of tape into an untidy ball and the door came open on the
third tug.

The dust storm had gifted the town a bizarre combination of

grit-washed gleam and opaque tide of ochre. Where the wind had whipped past a flat surface, metal shone in the crisp air and wood looked scrubbed and fresh. Where the air was smacked into a corner, dust formed geometric curves into and out of the shade.

The preternatural quiet seemed stranger, now she'd opened the door. A small drift of sand had curled itself against the door and sat suspended like a cross-sectioned dune against the frame. She stepped over it and knocked on the garage door.

'Are you okay, Able?'

A scuffle and three steps. The ripping sound of tape removal on three sides before a slightly sheepish Able lifted the door, crushing the used tape in both hands. He was dishevelled from the frenzy of throwing tarpaulins and taping up. But she thought she detected dried tear tracks as well. She tried not to stare. She'd been worried, but hers had been the concern of a newbie. Able had lived through these and knew more about them. But some things *could* scare Able: things that hinted at a world he couldn't explain.

'That was, uh, intense,' she said.

'Yeah,' Able ruffled his hair. 'Yeah, worst one for a while. They're more likely during the Dry, of course. Roof still on?'

He wanted an excuse to step outside. She noted the way he breathed deeply, pulling in the air. They crossed the street to get a good look at the roof, which was a sandier colour but still intact. They glanced down the street: entirely devoid of life. The only visible debris on the road was a couple of metal signs that normally stood sentry outside the pub and the shop. The dust storm was away to their right, barrelling through open country now and headed for Vince Reynolds. At this time of day, Vince might already be too drunk to notice.

Able squinted into the emerging sun. 'Well, I can't see any major problems. But, uh, maybe you could walk around town for me? Just note anything that looks like significant damage, then we can make a list of what might need doing. Otherwise, it's all brooms for the next hour or two.'

Dana nodded. 'Sure. There are only thirty homes: it can't take too long.'

Able re-crossed the road and she saw him begin to sweep sand into neat piles. She started down the side streets, intending to leave the area near the pub until last. Ransome Street was sufficiently downbeat to have barely changed because of the storm. She saw some of the flimsier chairs had been thrown from veranda to front yard, and a television aerial was creased. As she approached Henry Beattie's house, he stepped out on to the porch. He surveyed the scene with hands on hips – having been a farmer, he was no doubt unfazed by the storm.

'Are you okay, Henry? Able asked me to check all the homes for damage.'

He stared for a moment, as though he didn't believe her and this was some unsubtle form of surveillance. Then he relented. 'Yeah, no probs. Lots of sand in there, came through the bloody siding. Teach me not to fix it, eh? But nah, nothing that won't sweep out. Wasn't the worst I've ever been in. Bet it scared the crap out of you, though?'

Dana nodded. It was stupid to pretend it hadn't been frightening. Henry seemed surprised she'd owned up.

'Yeah, anyway,' he continued, 'I can help anyone on this street. Dust storms are mostly noise; never much actual damage. Surprises townies, that. Yeah, nah, back on the main road, almost opposite Able: Mary Gosling. She's in a wheelchair and all, might be worth a knock.'

It was the nearest she'd get to Henry's overt assistance: a throwaway remark that spoke of concern while cloaking it.

She headed back towards the main road, still slightly freaked out that so much wind, noise and dust could produce such little damage. Henry was right. She'd expected blown roofs, scattered vegetation, maybe broken windows. But other than a beige wash to every colour, there was almost no sign of impact at all. Perhaps Unamurra was more resilient than she'd thought.

The house opposite Able's garage had a large window at the front, as though it was a converted shop. The window had battered venetian blinds that were askew at the top, but with the sun behind her all Dana could see was her own reflection. She knocked on Mary Gosling's door. While she waited for a reply she looked down the street towards the pub, expecting Annie to be already out and clearing up. There was nothing. In fact, no sign of anyone in town at all; as though they were waiting for some mysterious second hit and knew not to venture out. She was wondering if she should ask Able about a dust storm equivalent of aftershocks when the door squeaked ajar.

'Who are you?'

The door had been answered by a tall, thin man with a butterscotch moustache. He had two small scars across one cheek and held the door delicately by one hand. His T-shirt was ragged from years of laundry, but she could still make out the remnants of the words *Back* and *Black*.

'Oh, hello. I'm Dana Russo. Helping out Able, there.' She pointed to the garage and then realized it wasn't necessary. She thought about reaching for a handshake – her usual greeting – but quickly appreciated that the man wouldn't respond. 'Um, Henry Beattie thought Mary Gosling might need some help after the storm?'

The man looked skyward, then smiled. It didn't move his moustache or reach his eyes. 'I'll bet he did, interfering old bastard. Tell him from me, Gary says get stuffed. She's not leaving him anything, and that's the end of it. She's fine. We're fine.'

Gary stood implacably. Dana couldn't hear any sounds from within the home: the television would be off, but there might be a radio. Or a cry.

'You've seen the roof, then?' she asked, trying to goad him outside, or at least gain access to Mary.

He glanced up and considered moving. Instead, he doubled down and sank a little further back behind the door, his wedding ring scratching against the latch as he did so. He looked Dana up and down for a second, as if surprised that she might have any tactic against him. There was still nothing from Mary.

'It'll be okay. I come up here every week to check on Mum, so you and Henry bloody Beattie don't need to be worried about her. Do you?'

Actually, thought Dana, *I am now*. She'd ask Able, and she wondered if it was even feasible for Social Services to make a trip from Dutton on the off chance that someone was being controlled by their son. Gary's sulky belligerence felt like more than a mere wish for privacy or dignity. She couldn't shake a sense of coercion about his body language.

Gary seemed to snap to a better focus. 'You're that new detective, hey? From miles away. Carlton, or somewhere?'

'Yes.'

Gary stood a little straighter. 'All right, so you can bugger off as well. No one in this town invited you, did they? Nothing for you to *detect*, Detective.'

They stared at each other for several seconds.

'Two people were murdered.'

'Yeah, but now they're both in the ground.' He waved at the street. 'And hey, look, town's still standing.'

She tried to move forward surreptitiously, still concerned about Mary. 'Don't you want to know what happened to them? Don't you worry it might happen again?'

'Nah. And nah. That would be stuff it would be nice to know, I guess, but I don't *need* to know.' He shrugged. 'It's basically gossip, yeah? The ins and outs. Annie would know, anyway, wouldn't she? Pub landlady in a one-horse town, they know anything worth knowing, eh?' Now he shook his head, his fringe flopping towards one eye. 'Nah, not worried it might happen again. Only two murders in the thirty years Mum's been here. If I thought it was dangerous, I'd move her, wouldn't I?'

Possibly not, floated through Dana's mind. The evidence equivalent of a false note was somewhere in this conversation, but she couldn't grasp it.

Gary gave a humourless grin. 'So, like I said, Carlton, get lost.'

He tried to slam the door theatrically, but it was badly bowed and clattered twice before it clicked shut. Dana automatically looked to the window, in case a distraught Mary was signalling for help, but saw nothing.

Reminded once again why she'd hated her years in uniform, Dana turned, contemplating going back to Able and asking more about Gary. She still had two streets to cover, however.

She'd intended to leave the pub until last. There were probably plenty of helpers hunkered down there; possibly the shop staff had sheltered there once someone warned them and they had closed the store. She veered off to the left. Something had caught her eye and she couldn't quite believe it. She half ran – as much as the kneecap could allow – towards the ANZAC monument. As though it were a mirage that would fade at any second.

At first glance, the ANZAC memorial seemed miraculously spared. Aside from a blood-orange dust drift at the base, it appeared untouched. The names on the obelisk were unsullied, kept legible not by the chance of capricious wind but by a cloth that had wiped each stroke of the stonemason's chisel. Close up, Dana could still see the trail of the cloth's creases in the slight residue. A solitary set of footprints wandered up to the memorial and back to the roadside, then disappeared. The Good Samaritan had revealed the names of the fallen to a freshened day, then seemingly disappeared.

Beyond the memorial, the parade area of green grass was mottled by the storm's residue. She wondered whether the town would sacrifice more of its precious water to clean the grass, whether they'd make the restoration of that miraculous patch of green a bigger priority than their own homes. She half hoped, and fully believed, that they would. The ANZAC memorial was not only a shrine to the fallen but also a testament in other ways: to the resilience of the town, to its cohesion, to its difference to any other place. Unamurra would want its lawn back, no matter what.

The sun was stronger now, making her squint. It was too high to cast much shadow. As the sunlight grew she discerned a set of footprints just below the mottled beige surface, in a dark strip from the obelisk into the grass.

On the speckled lawn, ten metres in front of the memorial, was an angel. It had its back to the monument, as though unimpressed by the sacrifice of others. Dana absorbed the details. A thin layer of sand obscured the trails that the angel's wheels would have left behind. The backs of the wings had a slight trace of dust, but little more. As she stepped around the figure she could see that the menacing, obsidian black of the head was completely unblemished. Once again, someone had taken exquisite care to polish it in the few minutes when that became possible. She needed a second to percolate the thought, but she could find no other explanation. She hadn't seen the memorial since yesterday evening, yet the evidence was clear.

The angel had been placed here *during* the storm.

As had the other twelve.

The dozen were curved around the first in a radius of a further ten metres inscribing a half-circle. She let the meaning of the art seep into her. DuBois had created something that surely spoke to her, if only she'd let it. An arc of twelve angels. Numbers always mattered to DuBois. All facing . . . the *accused*. She could see it now – the artist's intent. The angels were a jury: one that had met in the screaming wind and cruel darkness and now glared its verdict for all to see.

The message was clear to her. One person was guilty. Just one. DuBois was telling her to act. To act now. He thought she had the answer, clearly thought he'd already supplied it. So he must have done. Why, then, couldn't she see it?

Dana turned at the sound of a shoe scraping on the tarmac. To one side was a small, round woman with a blue shawl wrapped around her. The woman's hair was long – almost to her waist at the back – a series of streaks in silver and grey. A thin headband held it in place. Her face was creased deeply, more by sun than age; she had heavy eyelashes and a slightly hooked nose.

'He's a nutter, hey? I saw him, middle of all that wind. Moving his . . . whatever they really are. Everyone's hiding indoors, and he's cocking about doing that. He's looney tunes, that one.'

She waved surprisingly long fingers at the angels. Her thumb was hidden under several chunky silver rings.

'Do you think so?' asked Dana.

'Yeah. Only met him twice, Frenchie. When he first got here, he actually talked to us. Before he disappeared up his own backside. I thought he was an old backpacker or hippie or something, 'till he announced he was in town to make angels. Bunch of us rolled our eyes and let him get on with it. Bloody state government – *you don't have enough water, but we can give you some art, is that okay?*' She gave a sarcastic thumbs-up.

The thought had struck Dana, too. It was hard to see how DuBois' work – and she did admire it – could actually help this town. The bottom line was that no one came here. No one would traipse a four-hundred-kilometre round trip for an art exhibit.

The older woman didn't appear to need an interlocutor. She barrelled on.

'Anyone who's happy living in that paedo house – well, bloody hell, you'd stay away, wouldn't you? Jesus, the ghosts there must be in that place. Second time I met Frenchie was the, uh, *grand opening.* We all get dragged from the pub, whole town's expected to turn out for our big moment of civic pride. Photographer from Dutton takes a happy-snap, there's a two-minute speech from Annie, and that's it. That's our *economic regeneration*, hey? Bunch of netball posts and things that don't look human.'

Dana understood that the real civic pride lay in the grass she was standing on, not in pieces of art moved around the streets. But she thought that maybe the people of Unamurra had that wrong. Perhaps the angels did have worth to the town, but it wasn't economic. And perhaps the town had a loftier view of its civic pride than it warranted.

Dana stepped forward and offered a hand. 'Detective Dana Russo, from Carlton. You're the famous Nonnie, I'd guess.'

The woman's handshake was as reluctant as it could possibly be; a wary lean-in, a brush against the jewellery and it was gone.

'Yeah. Abe mentioned me, hey? Don't believe everything that bloke says, will you?'

Someone else happy to cast Able in a poor light. Dana folded her arms. 'Why wouldn't I, Nonnie?'

Nonnie gave a sly look, as though unsure whether Dana was wilfully naïve or quietly savvy and looking for Nonnie to make some kind of mistake. It took the older woman a few moments to choose her words.

'Yeah, Abe. He's a bit slow on the uptake, if you know what I mean. Bit slow to make sense of it all. Stuff going on here he should have copped on to, but never has. Covers that up by telling yarns. Always a lot of truth in them, to be fair. But in amongst all that truth is where he's adding a bit of mayo. You can't always tell what he's made up and what's spot on. Not easily, any rate. Abe's nice enough, I suppose, but not the sharpest. Dull, in fact.'

Nonnie wafted her hand, as if to usher her last statement into the background.

'Don't they say,' asked Dana, 'that the most dangerous thing in the kitchen is a dull knife?'

'Ha. Good one. Yeah, yeah, they do. Look, Abe's never done anything to me. But he bulls like it's an Olympic sport, is what I'm saying.'

Dana nodded quietly, as if this was unsullied wisdom that she was absorbing gratefully. 'You don't think the angels are beautiful? Or powerful?' she asked.

Nonnie shook her head. 'I think they're . . . clever. But creepy. A bit, uh, *sacrilegious,* to be honest. Not as important as he likes to think. I don't get why he's still round abouts, Frenchie. He must have moved them angels to every part of town by now – not that big a place, is it? Don't know what message he thinks he's sending.'

'Perhaps that's why he's still sending it.'

Nonnie grunted and stuffed a hand into her pocket. The rings clanged against glass. 'Come to mention it, I don't get why *you're* still here, Detective. Getting nowhere, are ya? Could have saved you the bother. We're not fussed, see? We're not hiding in our houses in case a serial killer pops up, are we?'

'What makes you think it's all over?'

'Huh. If you lived here, you'd know. Can't work it out just waltzing in from wherever. Got to know a place like this to work it out. Got to be in your guts. Nah, all over now. Been and gone. Forget it.'

Nonnie looked up the street, where someone had emerged from the shop and was looking for the errant sign that had somersaulted forty metres away.

She turned back to Dana. 'Anyways, last blokes couldn't find the killer, so why would you? Everything that was there when they investigated is here now. Nothing's moved, no one's done anything different. All where it was.' Nonnie paused. 'So if they didn't get anywhere, how are you going to do it? I'd have thought a few days banging against a brick wall would be enough. As a nurse, my advice is – it stops hurting when you stop butting your head.'

As a *former* nurse, thought Dana. As a former nurse kept pickled each day by a stipend that was created by, and depended on, the police officer she'd just insulted. Nonnie had the air of being both impervious to others and believing herself a protected species. Dana wondered why Nonnie felt that, when her circumstances in fact appeared precarious. All the same, Dana tried to remember the older woman's phrasing *verbatim,* because she sensed Nonnie had let slip something significant.

'So what do you make of this particular formation, Nonnie? *As a nurse.'*

Nonnie gave a smile that resembled a wince and turned back to the angels. 'How many?'

'Twelve in the curve, plus the one here nearest the frustum.'

Another twitch in Nonnie's features, as if Dana's final word was odd, or inappropriate. *'Frustum?* Oh, the monument, yeah. Jeez, you do talk weird. They all said you did. Right. Thirteen, then, in total? Unlucky, isn't it, thirteen? Wasn't Judas the thirteenth? I think he was. Frenchie thinks there's betrayal in the air; someone's gonna turn their back on someone. Or maybe it's a question mark. If you look from above, like. Frenchie, admitting he knows bugger-all? Bloody hell, that would be nice. And unexpected.'

Dana glanced again at the angels and, when she turned back, Nonnie was already on her way, shuffling towards her street with a roiling gait that suggested a hip operation was overdue. Nonnie paused to flip the finger to Gus, who was coming out of the pub, holding a broom. Gus gave a sarcastically over-happy wave in response.

Dana nodded as she neared the pub. 'Hello, Gus. Is everything okay in there?'

He nodded, laughing. 'Top, thanks. I was smart enough to get "stuck" here when the storm hit. Annie tried to shoo us off to our homes, but we stayed 'till it was too late for all that. Had a little crisis of faith when the power went off, but all good now.'

Dana could imagine the look on his face when someone told him the barrel pumps wouldn't pull. 'You have electrics now?'

'Yeah, whole town came back a few minutes ago. Mobile reception should be on its way any minute. Apparently the storm cut across the main road about halfway back to Dutton, so that's where the breaks were. You and Abe good?'

'We are. He sent me around town to see if anyone needed help.'

'Well, there you go, missus. Unamurra community spirit, and all that.'

In the pub's saloon Dana could see at least six elbows cleaning, scrubbing and pouring errant dust into black bags. Gus watched Non-nie's disappearing form, then glanced back.

'So? Volunteering, water-lady?'

Dana smiled. 'I'd love to, Gus, but I have to report back to Able.'

'Ah, I think we got off light, to be honest. I've seen worse. It's all sand, this one. Which I know sounds obvious, and all. But, you know, the sandstorms that do the damage are the ones with debris in them. Fencing, stuff people left in their yards, that kind of thing. That's what buggers a roof or breaks a window. I mean, a glass window's basically sand, isn't it? So – sand hitting sand, really.'

'Ah, I hadn't thought of it that way, professor.'

He grinned and turned back to the bagging operation. Dana leaned against the door jamb, hair brushing the wall lamp, and switched on her phone. She was waiting for the signal bars to appear when an app lit up. Unreasonably. Unfeasibly. She frowned.

The click came. The one she'd been praying for.

It flew in and felt like a physical blow to the chest. She whirled around as if someone had punched her. Realization sent her off-balance.

Nothing's moved, no one's done anything different. All where it was.
That was precisely what Nonnie had said. It struck Dana as true.
Which meant that the reason for the murders must still be here, still
be extant, still be a motive. It must be dominating the town in some
way. Now she knew. Now she understood. DuBois had been right.

'Oh,' she said softly. 'Oh, oh, oh. Crap. Christ, I'm stupid.' She
shook her head and walked in a tight little circle, fists clenched. 'Jesus,
I was stupid. Idiot, idiot.' She slapped her temple with the heel of her
hand. 'Could have solved this by now, could have done it. Idiot.'

The solutions barrelled in and through her, like a sequence of explo-
sive charges cleaving away a mountainside. One idea got her two, got
her three; she could barely keep up and hold them all in her mind.

She stared at her phone, praying for a signal. Four bars. Good
enough. She stepped away to mid-road and could see her fingers shaking as she swiped to Lucy's number. Lucy picked up on the second
ring.

'Hey, Dana.'

'Luce, Luce, I've got it. I've been so stupid, but I've got it now. Got it.'

Her voice was higher, more urgent, than Lucy was used to.

'Seriously? Right, what do you need from this end?'

'A lot, Luce, a lot. God, I missed every turning there was – every
one. Sarah's photos, Collis' suicide, DuBois' note. Christ, his note.
Stasi. Sidetracked me when it should have pointed the way. Voices.
People talk. Henry's dish. Freezers. Billy, lampshades. Those hopeless
detectives, the sale of Vince's place. What else? Oh, Kobayashi Maru,
let's not forget that.'

There was a pause at the other end. 'Er, I may be a bit behind you
here, chick.'

Dana took a breath. 'Oh, crap. Sorry, Luce. Thinking out loud. I'm
rushing it. All right. Let's get this in the right sequence. Sequence
matters.'

For the next thirty minutes, as various people struggled in and out of the shop and pub with brooms and bags of blown sand, Dana leaned against a fence and outlined her case. She danced around the chronology, feeling the pieces slide together and the whole mechanism build into something solid. Dana talked and Lucy's fingers flew – not just recording the details but pulling in relevant data at lightning speed.

Eventually she paused, if only to reconsider whether the sequencing worked. 'Does that sound coherent, Luce? Possible?'

'Yes, it does. But I'm hearing it in the abstract; just a list of data and supposition. Only you know if that all works in reality. I can store it all on the cloud until the right moment. It's all secure. Are you sure you want us to make these phone calls?' Lucy paused, gathered herself. She could practically see Dana out on a limb. 'You'd want me to spell this bit out, I think. Right now, you could be audit-trailing your last few hours as a detective, chick. If you're wrong, that is. I'll always back you, but I might also be writing the evidence for your dismissal. You do know that, right?'

'I do know, I know. But yes. Make the calls. Get Mikey to make the calls. Please. And text me as each bit comes through – I need to know what I can back up. Thanks, Luce.' Dana took a deep breath. 'I need to have words with Able Barella now.'

When Dana returned to the garage, Able was almost finished. There was still a partial sheen of dust particles on the concrete floor, but she assumed he'd hose it when they were certain the water supply would be sufficient. They counted every litre in Unamurra, Dana understood. There would be more pressing needs for water use in the next day or two.

'Any storm damage?' he asked. He was hefting several boxes to a high shelf and waved his hand to indicate he didn't need help.

'Not that anyone can see. Henry Beattie was sorting anyone on Ransome Street; the pub and shop have people taking care of them. Henry suggested I look in on your neighbour, Mary Gosling? I got short shrift from her son when I knocked.'

'Ah, yeah, sorry, should have remembered he was here. Gary. He's a tosser.' Able shrugged, as though it barely needed stating.

'I got that impression, yes. The way he was, the way he denied entry – I wondered. Maybe he's a bit controlling, there?'

Able stopped the shelf-packing and turned. 'Coercive control? Mary? Same thought had occurred to me. She wouldn't talk to me if it was – she'd be mortified by the whole thing, wouldn't want the likes of me knowing her shame. Henry tried, but Gary's, uh . . .'

'A tosser?'

Able grinned. 'That sounds totally un-you, when you say it. But yeah, Gary acts like everyone's after Mary's money, not that she has a lot. Gary's got cheque-fraud convictions himself and he sails close to the wind back in Dutton. Annie takes Mary her dinner during the week, seeing as Mary's in the chair. Annie says it's all good; Mary has all her marbles and she gives her son just enough sugar to keep him sweet. So, watching brief, really.'

Dana stroked some of the dust particles around with her foot. Almost like a small child about to ask permission from a parent. Able folded a tarpaulin and pretended not to notice.

'Able?'

'Yeah?' He stopped folding.

'I know who killed Larry Muir and Tim Ogden.'

Chapter 20

Able began walking towards the deck chairs. Dana fielded a phone call from Lucy, hunkering down by the water butt.

'Howdy, Dana. All done at this end. Extra info on a *really* long text to you now. Dealt with Able yet?'

Dana tried again to run through the sequencing in her head.

'I'm just about to; good timing. Confirming that data from overseas – is that locked?'

'And loaded: we have copies with the requisite signatures and seals. They didn't make it easy to find.'

'Hmm. For a very good reason. They aren't supposed to be anywhere near that kind of thing. That stuff from the professional advisers: have I seen all the data?'

'Everything I could get, yes.' Lucy paused. 'They said they're happy to be formally interviewed. They didn't strike me as having anything to hide. It's all a normal day's work for them. Same with the clerk of council, for that matter.'

'And Cronin – Mikey's certain of that?'

'You have his word on it, yes.'

'Good.' Dana squinted at the horizon and tried to control her skittish breathing. She needed these things to launch, but they were a means to an end. They weren't enough to close the case on their own, and that left Dana twisting in the wind if they didn't prise open Pandora's box.

'Ah, Jesus, Luce, this is a biggie, isn't it?' They both knew the question was rhetorical. 'Is Mikey primed?'

'He can duck out and speak to you whenever; has what you need on speed-dial. I've talked him through it, so yeah, he knows verbally what's coming. Happy?'

'Not happy, not yet. I need to take Able through it, step by step, to see if he's in agreement. It doesn't work if he kicks against it.'

'Fair enough. I'll wait for your call, chick.'

For the next two hours they sat in the deck chairs and focused entirely on Dana's laptop, phone and notebook. The extra computer records – which had filtered through from Lucy on a scrolling text – were mainly more financial and legal statements. Dana's notes were useless to Able as they were Pitman squiggles, but they helped Dana frame her argument. He seldom interrupted, except for clarification.

Eventually they sat back and guzzled at water bottles. Courtesy of Sandy's wife, Able had some sponge cake wrapped in kitchen roll, like two trophies from a little kid's birthday party.

'So, what do you think?' asked Dana. 'Am I crazy, or does that make sense?'

Dana's question sounded like a plea. As she'd laid it out for him – the facts and figures, the confirmations, the suppositions – she'd waxed and waned.

Able spread his hands. 'I'd be lying if I said it made total sense. I mean, it can't, can it? Something that . . . *outrageous*? I reckon that's the word. It's freaky, it's from left field. Not the identity of the killer, perhaps, but their reasoning, the motive, the background – it's wild.

So in that way, no, it does not make sense. But if you're asking me if you have enough evidence, if you have the right person? I'd say yeah.'

What he'd agreed was momentous for him, she understood that. He'd lived in Unamurra most of his life, so he didn't simply know the people and know them well, he also understood the history of the place, the likely legacy of what they were considering: the potential repercussions and how they would ripple outwards. Able comprehended that this would shatter the whole district in a very particular, very frightening way. He would be dealing with the fallout for the rest of his career – maybe, beyond. So his agreement was no small thing, for the case, or for him. It was a Rubicon crossed.

She sat forward. It had been exhausting, recounting her ideas and how they'd formed: twenty-four hours distilled into two. The original notion hadn't taken root until late this morning because of her near-total lack of knowledge of the town and how it worked. Was she now putting her faith in an outlandish idea because it made her outsider status an asset, rather than a liability? She couldn't truthfully answer that; she had to rely on people she trusted. Lucy had said it wasn't a fig-leaf, and the theory held water. Mike had felt the same. Since he was currently risking his professional credibility for her at Central, he was trusting she was correct.

Able shifted in his chair and stared at the sky, still featureless even though the storm was now miles away and decaying. Dust clung to the air and to the roof of his mouth.

'What do they call it?' asked Able. 'Those theories about everything?'

Dana frowned. 'I don't understand the question.'

She looked towards the pub, past the rear ends of several houses. Macca was edge-walking a tarnished silver barrel through the pub's rear gate.

'You know, theories that explain everything, get to the guts underneath.'

She snapped back to the conversation. 'Oh, *critical theory*, I think they call it. Like Marxism, feminism? There's something about power structures as well.'

Able nodded. 'Yeah. Yeah, thought so. That's what you have here, isn't it? A critical theory of the two murders?'

'Hmm, I suppose so. Yes, good point. I have a theory that looks below the waterline. It certainly speaks to power, one way or another. If my idea of motive's correct, then yes, we have a theory that describes what took place and why, and how that *why* came to be. So, yes, I suppose it is a form of critical theory.'

'Yeah. Exactly. And it is *critical*, as well, isn't it? Of me?'

She jolted, hadn't seen it that way. 'Ah, I see where you're going, but—'

'Nah, it is. And it's fair enough.' Able sat forward. 'Because now you've laid it out, it's clear that most of that has been going on right under my nose. On my own patch, in Belgium. In fact, I sort of knew about half of it, some way or other. I *knew* but I didn't know; didn't put the bits together.'

He was right. But Dana couldn't afford to have him thinking that way. She needed him: now, more than at any time since she'd landed at Dutton. This probably wouldn't land at all without Able. If he opposed it in some way, or even stood aside, it was impossible.

'No, I think that's inaccurate. And unfair to both of us. I'm not criticizing you over this, Able, I'm not. It's a radical idea and it might still be wrong. In which case, I'll be the laughing stock of the force. We haven't . . . *I haven't* . . . proven anything beyond reasonable doubt yet. Or, we could be completely right but totally unable to make it stick. Worse yet, we could end up with everything I've found so far being true but our theory of the murderer being wrong. That happens, sometimes. But you're being unfair on yourself as well. I think it's the kind of idea that only an outsider could have.'

Able was clearly unconvinced, but he settled back and they lapsed into silence for a few minutes. Dana felt he needed that time for certain ideas and ramifications to percolate. He took another swig of water and turned back to her. 'So, was that cheating? Your Kobi-whatever? You said you would cheat, but does that count?'

'Sort of cheating but not cheating? Yes, as it turns out. Ignoring half of the things detectives are supposed to pay attention to, that's a kind of cheat. I didn't focus much on alibis, forensics or witness statements, as you noticed. Now I've got the theory first and I'm hoping that having the theory leads to the evidence that supports it. That's also a kind of cheat. I form the idea and then see if the evidence backs it – so my whole approach has been back to front. Don't feel bad that you didn't reverse your way towards the same theory, Able. It's a stupid way to travel generally. But occasionally, like now, I think it's justified.'

He raised an eyebrow. 'So, Detective from Carlton: you want to carve up this town on a theory from out of left field, based on poor investigation technique, while seeing your lack of local knowledge as a key asset?'

They shared a watery smile.

'Yes. Yes, I do. Are you up for that?'

'Hellish risky, Dana.'

'Yes, I know.' She nodded at the ground. 'It's a greater risk for you than for me, really. If I'm wrong, I probably screw what career I have. However, I don't really put my personal safety at risk. But you do, Able. I've tried to assess that risk on your behalf. Now it's your turn to assess it. If I'm right, we have a small window right now to prove our case and bolt everything down. If we miss that window? Well, you have to live here afterwards – that would be somewhere between uncomfortable and fatal. Probably nearer fatal. I can't demand you do that. It's still not too late for you to back out, even now.'

There was a terrible, silent wait. She wouldn't blame him if he put self-preservation above her semi-formed theory. As she'd said, he'd face the worst of the repercussions, and that was no small thing to ask. Plus, if he agreed, he was essentially fessing up to his own mistakes and the inadequacy of his awareness.

'Nah, your idea makes sense. I mean, it's mental, don't get me wrong. But sensible-mental.'

She smiled in relief. 'You're not the first person to call me that. All right, some logistics. We aren't going to pull this off without the help of the Scorpions.'

Able sat back in the chair and puffed his cheeks. 'The Scorpions? Jesus, you weren't kidding, were you? For one murderer?'

'Well, not just the killer, some others, too. It has to be a timed and coordinated takedown. If we give any party breathing space they can destroy evidence, warn others and generally make life very difficult. We need some helpful people on tap, us here, and a fast means of getting certain people away from here. I can't predict exactly how this will go and I need the potential for significant back-up if necessary.'

Able shook his head. The Scorpions were a special taskforce reporting directly to the Federal Minister of Justice. Primarily aimed at corruption, they operated from the back of an RAAF base and had a record of cutting swathes through opposition. Highly trusted by the public, they had an all-or-nothing approach that was widely seen within the force as a high-wire act.

'Christ,' he muttered.

'Look, I might be gilding the lily a bit, but I figure better safe than sorry.'

'Yeah, yeah. Nah, I can see what you mean. How do we even do that?'

'I call Lucy, then I call my colleague Mikey. He's at Central today, but he has the Scorpions on speed-dial and they're waiting for my signal. They know what you know – I've been feeding them this theory via Lucy. Once I give that signal, Able, there's no going back for either of us. Are you in?'

She stretched out. He shook her hand, rewarding her with that grin.

'Yeah, all in, mate,' said Able.

Chapter 21

Able headed off to fetch the car. Dana paused for a moment, trying to run through what she needed to do and, more importantly, the sequencing. Now she was committed to running full pelt at this, it was clear that doing things in the correct order was paramount. The first and vital step had been securing Able's active cooperation.

She considered again why Able had been held back from the previous investigations. It would have stood out to those who viewed it from any kind of distance. It was strange that Central hadn't immediately flagged it up on the compulsory twenty-eight-day review. Every homicide or rape case in the state was independently reviewed by detectives at Central twenty-eight days after the crime was first reported. Crimes in or near the city would get personal visits from the review team. Sometimes they were welcomed, sometimes not. For a crime out in Dutton district it would be a desktop review. But such a distance would only make omissions like Able's sidelining all the more obvious. Yet Dana had read nothing about it, and Lucy couldn't find anything either. Presumably the up-tops in Central were somewhere between relaxed and indifferent about it.

Able's lack of involvement had created two problems. First, he couldn't give her an inside track into the thinking and actions of the previous investigations, the off-the-record discussions and options. That meant she had to rely on a politically careful, finely calibrated and largely antiseptic report. Second, it had made her wary of Able himself. She'd used her personal instincts and confided in him as far as she dared, but it would have been less of a leap of faith if she'd felt that Dutton district had trusted him from the start.

Now, in the light of what she'd discovered and what she was about to do, she felt she understood Dutton's reticence about involving Able. It made a loose kind of sense, viewed from a certain angle and with a cynical tint to the glasses. It had strategic and political logic, even if it was stupid from an investigative point of view. No one had known where Able's loyalties really lay, or how much he might be immersed in what was being investigated. Cronin had been spot on about that.

Dana made more use of the regained mobile phone signal while Able ran a necessary errand. The wind whipped up occasionally but, when it died, the town had a peaceful, sleepy repose. She should, she reasoned, try to remember it this way. She'd probably never return and, anyway, it would never be like this again.

'Hey, Luce.'

She could picture Lucy at her desk, almost picture what she was wearing; certainly anticipate Lucy's slightly anxious edge. It was rare to be involved in something like this and it inevitably led to an adrenalin rush.

'Hey, you. I take it you told Able?'

'Yes. It was a lot for him to take in. Especially for him – I've sort of overturned his world. But yes, he's in.'

Lucy's sigh of relief was audible. 'Okay, good. I'll secure the files at this end.'

Lucy's previous career on the edges of tech security had come into play. Everything Dana had uncovered, read, asked Lucy to find or discussed was held on a secure file in the cloud. Lucy was the only person who could get to it. Even Mike couldn't access it – he'd simply discussed verbally with Lucy and had no tangible evidence at all. As soon as Lucy put down the phone, she'd send an encrypted access code to the Scorpions. The fact that it had to be this way made Dana's heart skittish.

'I'll update the log,' continued Lucy, 'then it's down to you. Anything else you need?'

'Some courage. Large slice of luck. That kind of thing.'

'Wishing all that your way. Go bring 'em down, chick.'

Dana smiled as she signed off and dialled Mike Francis. He was supposed to be at a conference, but he'd gladly ducked out and was sitting on a park bench across from Central.

'Ahoy-hoy.'

'That definitely isn't catching on, Mikey.'

'I'm a patient man; I'll grind everyone down. How did Able take it?'

'Oh, hard not to blow him away with that kind of thing. He's very tightly connected to this town – born and raised – and I'm about to make the place implode. He'd be within his rights to call me everything under the sun and refuse to participate. It was good to tell him, though. Not just because he had a right to know what I've been thinking, or because I need him badly for the next bit. It also meant I had to work through the argument and my line of reasoning, which gave me a chance to see how it held up.'

'And how did that go?'

'Yes . . . it held up, I believe. Some of it is, uh, *contingent*, rather than established. Which makes me nervous. But yes, Able's on board, and he'll be professional about it.'

'Good.' The pause was at Mike's end, building up to something. 'Are you double-double sure you want to do this?'

It was a good question. She was dragging a number of people into a maelstrom on the basis of her theory: a hypothesis they had no real access to, in terms of reviewing the available evidence. There wasn't the time for that, and logistics counted against her. She was asking them to jump based on blind faith in her, and she'd never been enough of a networker to ensure that kind of loyalty. In fact, she was trading off Mike's credibility within his own web of contacts. It meant she was risking the reputations and careers of others, along with her own.

'It's your last chance to pull the plug yourself,' she reminded him. 'Or talk me out of it. You think I'm ahead of myself? Or up myself?'

'Neither, obviously. No, as it happens, I think you're right on the money and this is the way to handle it. But, you know . . .'

'It's a career-finisher if I'm wrong? Yes, I knew that. If you invite the Scorpions on a play date and then embarrass them, it doesn't end well. But thank you for making me pause. Yes, I know that it all goes south if I'm wrong about this. But I believe I'm right and I have to back that. If you're okay being along for the ride? I can't promise you won't become collateral damage.'

'Ah, Barb married a crazy, risk-taking yet charismatic hero – of course I'm in. But once we set these wheels in motion, they won't stop.'

That was true. The immediate consequences would barrel through and take everything with them. The longer-term implications would rumble for years, for myriad people, while Dana was home on the other side of the state. It was akin to lighting a fire and then driving away.

'Agreed.' She took a deep breath. 'Then you can set them in motion, please, Mikey.'

Dana wandered over to the garage, almost dragging her feet like a recalcitrant teenager. She felt a sudden and dramatic loss of energy, a hollowing out. She'd never been less sure of a murder theory in her life. *Actually*, she thought, *scratch that*. She was sure of her theory. But

she had doubts about whether she could prove it or not. She had misgivings about the implications, if she was right. And, if she was totally
honest with herself, she had to question whether the damage was
worth the prize. For the first time, she began to comprehend the
town's reticence about wanting to know the identity of the killer. It
was clear that some of them had known – *must have known* – and had
made a moral choice. They wanted their local spirit intact more than
they wanted justice. She disagreed, and would deny them that. But
she now understood why they'd thought it.

She cut through the alley to the main street. Able's garage door was
raised to knee height. She heard the clink of keys in a lock. Footsteps.
The door rolled up and there was Able, attaching the keys to his belt
loop. She purposely didn't glance inside at the temporary jail cell, but
she could feel the murderous stare from that direction. A look tinged
with gold.

'Any problems?'

'Nah, nah. All done quietly.' He pulled the door closed and locked
it. 'I think there was a bit of relief, when I actually came to call. Nah.
Left some food and water, and the radio's on: test match from Sri
Lanka. So, you know, welfare's been considered and all.'

'I meant for you. With all this.'

Able squinted and looked up and down the main street. His street,
his whole life. His eyes glistened. 'Nah, not really. I mean, not looking
forward to it. But it's got to be done. Can't leave things like this and
just hope they get better.'

The pub was half full. The clean-up crew were getting a free thank-
you drink, mingling with the usual lunch crowd, who were grateful
their place of rest had been restored. Able stepped up to the bar.

'Annie around, mate?'

Macca pointed at the stairs separating the lounge from the shop's
store room. They were barred by a draped, chained sign of *No Entry*.

Dana stepped forward, unhooked it, and let it clatter noisily to the floor. It was a deliberate act, a statement of intent. Macca raised a hand, as if meaning to intervene, then pulled back. The bubbles of conversation in the room subsided and the only sounds were the scrapes from chairs as heads turned. Able shuffled uncomfortably, then followed Dana up the stairs.

Chapter 22

They turned left at the top of the steps. Able had been this far, but no further, a couple of times, helping Tim Ogden to carry furniture. Some old stuff, probably antique, and worth a buck in an upmarket shop when Annie sold. The last load Able shifted with Tim had been a nineteenth-century sideboard, the curves of the mahogany inlays contrasting with walnut burr. A beautiful piece, but it couldn't have been heavier if it had been made of mercury.

Able pointed wordlessly at the door to Annie's private apartment. The light from under the door was muted. Annie kept the translucent blinds drawn all year round; she'd never taken the chance that someone could see in from across the street. It was a private, hibernation mind that Dana recognised and admired. She knocked solidly on the door, which was warped at bottom right and rattled.

'Whoever it is, piss off.'

It rang out with an air of both weariness and habit. No doubt the staff occasionally had to knock, one of them drawing the short straw and being ushered upstairs by the glowers and relieved smirks of colleagues. The unlucky one would scamper back down after getting a bad-tempered spray, happy that they'd done their duty and now held an indemnity the next time someone pointed their way.

'Annie. It's Detective Dana Russo and Constable Able Barella. We'd like to talk to you, please.'

Able raised an eyebrow at the last word. If Dana meant to impose herself – and marching up to Annie's private sanctum suggested she did – then being polite was surely counterproductive. Perhaps courtesy was such an ingrained habit with Dana that she couldn't drop it, even when she should.

'Yeah.' The voice was muffled – more so than previously – as though Annie was now across the room, or bending down. 'Yeah, I'll pop over in a few minutes. Ta.'

Dana leaned in. 'Now, Annie. And here.'

The silence signified not only that Annie wasn't answering but also that she wasn't moving. She'd stopped, mid-whatever, at Dana's words and tone. *Impudent*, that's surely what Annie would call it. Impudent and stupid, not aware of the lie of the land, blundering about thoughtlessly; careless. Just two steps – she'd been that close all along – and the door swung open.

'What? Where's the fire, eh?'

Annie's hair was more unkempt than usual. One of her sleeves had fallen down to the wrist, giving her a slightly lopsided look.

Dana's voice was even and controlled. 'This is probably better inside, Annie. Unless you want the whole pub to hear. I doubt you do.'

Annie glanced at Able. 'You part of this, Abe? Or just tagging along behind a girl?'

Able gave his best dazzling grin. 'Now, if I were you, Annie, I wouldn't be winding up the detective. Can't see how that's in your best interests, eh?'

One raised eyebrow from Annie, as though Able would regret that remark in a day or two. She glanced behind her; over her *left* shoulder, Dana noted. There was a flicker before Annie gathered her composure.

'Yeah, I guess. Look, a couple of ground rules. If you're gonna need the lav, you can go downstairs. I don't share my bathroom. And, uh, we'll be sitting in the dining room and nowhere else.'

'Of course,' replied Dana, 'That sounds fine.'

They entered the apartment. Able had lived seventeen metres from this place for eight years but had never been in it. There was one main room with a line of Shaker-style kitchen units along one wall, headed towards a door leading to the laundry. At the end of the counter was a collection of old-school flasks and pipes: Annie's own cold-filtered coffee set-up. One corner of the room was sectioned off by a series of tall bookcases. Two chairs – one a nineteenth-century rocker, the other a well-padded Barcelona chair from the 1950s – sat either side of a wood-burning stove. There was a pricey German hi-fi and an enormous television on one wall. Nearer the kitchen, a round dining table had three austere-looking chairs, each with vertical ribs, that to Dana's eye looked vaguely Mennonite. The floorboards had been sanded and stained, but most of the room was covered by a huge and opulent rug. The drawn blinds gave the light an opaque, dreamy feel.

They sat silently at the kitchen table and waited while Dana carefully took two recorders, a notepad and a shorthand pen from her bag. Annie watched, pretending to be amused. Able gave the room a second look, stunned at the luxury and implied cost. Dana started the recorders.

'It's monumentally hard work for you, Annie. It must be exhausting.'

Dana's voice sounded sincere.

'What is? The pub?' Annie scoffed and sat back. 'Nah. Easy as, once you're used to the buggers.'

'No, not the pub. The voice. *Your* voice.'

'What about it? Not as fancy as yours? Let me tell you, Miss Detective, people here are laughing behind your back. Please and thank you, every five minutes? Your magnificent knowledge of words? What was it you said to Nonnie? *Frustum*, was it? Bloody hell. You sound like a snob, love. No disrespect, of course.'

'Hmm, I doubt they are laughing. This is my natural voice and my natural vocabulary. People in rural areas generally take you as they find you; they don't care how you normally pronounce words, but they don't like being misled. What would they make of your voice, do you think?'

'Mine? They hear it every bloody day. Probably sick of it, but. Especially when I shout *last orders*, eh, Abe?' She winked at Able but jolted when he didn't return it.

'Not that voice, Annie,' replied Dana. 'Not your pub voice. Because that's fake. It's a construct, isn't it? You don't really speak like this, not at all. You fake it. You act the landlady and the shop-owner, give it the whole gruff *rough-and-ready woman in an outback town* shtick. No doubt they found it convincing. But I *know*, Annie. I've worked out that bit. So you can drop it, have a rest. Spend a little time among adults who don't mind hearing your true voice.'

'You're crackers. She's crackers, Abe. Is that what they do, send the weird ones? Get 'em out of their hair for a while, give themselves a break? Are you doing respite care for the police force, mate?'

Able glowered. 'You should listen, Annie. Listen very closely. *Mate*. She's not mucking around here. Neither am I.'

Annie tried to shuck it off, but it was clear that Able wasn't playing by the usual rules.

'Pfff. Didn't take long to have you running around like a puppy, did it, Abe? Been short of female company, eh? Told you I could sort you out with some, uh, talent in Dutton. There's lots got bills to pay, over there. Should've just tipped me the word, instead of embarrassing yourself like this . . . uh, Jesus.' Annie turned back to Dana. 'Go on then, hotshot. Tell me about my own voice, for God's sake.'

Dana took a breath. 'You were born Anne Blakely, in Melbourne, and grew up in South Yarra.'

Annie looked up sharply. Her mouth opened for a moment before she covered her concern with a weak smile.

'A beautiful home,' continued Dana, 'Arts and Crafts style, tennis court; lovely. Your father was a very successful businessman, your mother was a one-time fashion model. As nice a gilded cage as a child could ask for. You went to a private prep school, then a private college in Bendigo. You graduated from the University of Melbourne with a law degree, became a lawyer, and you were headed for the silk when your parents divorced. A bitter fight, with their only child in the middle. It became, in your eyes, necessary to choose a side and, when you did, it was decisive. You took your mother's maiden name – Merrin – and helped her to clean your father out of every cent he had.

'A colleague of mine found him. It's a top-dollar nursing home, specialists in Alzheimer's, so you've made sure he has the best of care at the end, if only he knew it. You did have at least a pang of conscience after your mother died, didn't you, Annie? Some remorse for the way you laid waste to all that he'd created, brought down his chemical company with environmental lawfare, made him crumble. There was a sliver of regret – that maybe you'd taken it too far. Your mother had spent money like water, despite your best efforts – she tore through most of the fortune with almost nothing to show for it. When your mother died you had a little money left, and no family that would touch you. So Anne Blakely, now Anne Merrin, married in haste. You became Annie Ogden and bought this pub and shop in little ol' Unamurra. You ran away from what you were, but you didn't run towards something. No, you had to make that *something* out of thin air. And you did, fair play to you.

'I heard a recording, Annie, of you on the radio. My colleague played me a slice. It's from the year of your parents' divorce. You're talking about changes in rental management legislation. Would you like people in Unamurra to hear it? Because it doesn't sound remotely like you. Yet it is. Very much you – the real you. Not the fake that you've been projecting, very convincingly, since you moved to Unamurra. Would you care to comment?'

Able's expression said that this was all about-face. Everyone, since her arrival at Dutton station, had been deriding Dana for the way she spoke: the good manners, the diction, the precision. They'd all done it – Judge Trent, Sandy, Vince Reynolds, Henry Beattie, Sarah Muir, Annie herself. Yet *Dana's* voice was authentic. No one had ever questioned Annie's voice – but that was the fake.

Annie hitched up her sleeves and rested her elbows on the table, dominating the space. Attack was her best form of defence.

'So what? So, I was a different person before I came here. So what? My voice changed a bit? Big bloody deal. You hang around with people, you pick up how they speak. You adapt, you fit in. Well, *you* don't. No biggie, is it? Used to be one thing, now I'm something else.'

Yes, thought Dana, *you're really something else.*

'You're free to do as you choose, Annie, within reason. But you can see how astonished Able is, now he knows your backstory. That's how most of the town would react, I imagine: bewildered that you'd create a persona instead of simply being yourself. They'd wonder why you felt the need to construct such an elaborate facade. Three different surnames weren't enough camouflage for you? I mean, you employed a specialist company from San Francisco to bury your electronic footprint, such as it was. No one's looking you up on the net easily, are they? Luckily, my colleague is very talented and got past that company's best efforts: they'd shoved your past names so far down the Google trail you were near impossible to find. There has to be a reason for that, doesn't there? Beyond, for example, a wish for privacy, or a sense of starting over.'

'Lots of people here looking for a fresh start. That's why half of them pitch up. Old Abe, he's one of the few that's born here.'

'Yes, that's true. Although, of course, if you've buried your own past with an enormous shovel but others' lives are just lying there in the sun, you might use that to your advantage. If you're in a position to exploit the weaknesses, the past, the regrets of those around you, it pays to bulletproof yourself against any attempt to retaliate. If you were unscrupulous and wanted leverage and control. Viewed through that lens, the scrubbing of your online records makes perfect sense, doesn't it? As a prelude to blackmail, or worse.'

'Only if I'm actually unscrupulous.'

'Yes.'

'Which you can't remotely prove.'

'Really?'

Annie leaned forward. 'You come at the queen, you'd best not miss.'

Dana returned the glare. 'I haven't.'

The stare lasted seven seconds.

'I had no reason to look into your background that way, not initially,' continued Dana. 'But when I did, I was surprised that you'd led such a life, then came here and began faking another. I thought that trajectory was a one-off, until I met Sarah Muir.'

The merest twitch told Dana she'd struck a nerve. Annie feigned indolence. 'Uh, really. Dragging Sarah into this crap as well, are we? Do tell. I'm mesmerized by your intellect and all.'

'Sarah used a phrase about "benchmarking excellence", in relation to comparing Pelligrini with Vince Reynolds' farm, Sorrento. Such an MBA-type phraseology. I had Sarah checked and, sure enough, she has one; got it before she met Larry. Nothing conclusive in itself, of course, but again I was surprised by a deliberate burial that seemed unnecessary. Here was a second example of a woman who had brains and qualifications to spare, but hid them behind a no-nonsense, rough-around-the-edges outback persona. The same artifice to the voice, the same bristling manner, the same downplaying of the education. And the same descriptions of your respective departed husbands, as though you were each giving a job reference:

no passion, no hollowed-out soul. You're two peas in a pod out here, aren't you? No wonder you get along so well.'

Annie tapped the table with an index finger, as though her point would be telling. 'It's a tough world out here, love. You've clearly had a pleasant little path your whole life. Out here there's no mercies, none of the nice little courtesies you have where you are. Unamurra's a blunt town in an unforgiving desert. All that emptiness means there's no reason to tiptoe around. Us women have to make the best of it.'

Of all Annie's possible retorts at this point, this was the one Dana had predicted most likely.

'Nice try. If I'd never been here and never met you, I might believe it. No doubt you can bull for Australia about the male-dominated nature of the community, the hidden or not-so-hidden misogyny, the *need to be twice as good to prove you're equal,* and so on. I'm in the police, Annie. I hear that line of reasoning all the time, and sometimes it's true, sometimes it's not. I won't be following the sisterhood trail this time, I'm afraid. It doesn't stack up: the evidence is too compelling. You're the most important person in the entire town, Annie, and Sarah runs a station of a dozen men without a hint of backwash. I can't see either of you being *subjugated by the patriarchy,* which means you weren't playing down your abilities and background because others demanded it. No, it was a deliberate strategy – one you each chose, independently, and both needed. That sort of coincidental deception sparks a detective's curiosity. In fact, for a while there I had a little theory that the two of you had run some sort of *Strangers on a Train* routine. You're familiar with the film?'

'Oh, films now?' Annie sat back, spreading her hands wide. 'Please, showcase your knowledge. It's a great substitute for actual evidence.'

'As I'm sure you know, the film hinges on two murders. Strangers meet in a railway carriage and seem to agree that each will carry out the other's murder for them: the police will be baffled because each

stranger can't possibly have a motive or connection to the crime. I considered whether you and Sarah might hatch a similar idea. You kill
Larry, but you're discounted by the investigation because you have no
reason to kill Larry. She kills Tim, but she's never considered a suspect
because she has no motive for killing him. I only dropped it because
one thing made it unlikely. You're an arrogant control freak, Annie.
You wouldn't leave the act of murder to anyone but your impeccable
self.'

Annie gave a theatrical glance at the ceiling. 'You're saying I . . . no,
really? I killed Larry Muir? What, and Tim as well? My own husband?
Jesus, you've lost it. I don't even *need* a lawyer for this crap. It's just
garbage. Why, why, why, would I kill either of them? I run a pub and
a shop in a no-horse town, love. At best, I fleece 'em on the prices a bit
and use some inside knowledge for a bit of entertainment. Happens in
every small town in Oz.'

'Well, let's step back a bit, and I'll explain your motive. I think we
can all agree that Unamurra faces one huge problem. But we might
not agree on what the problem is.'

Annie couldn't wait to dive in, trying to grab the steering wheel.
'Pfft. *The problem is the Dry.* It's the almost total lack of rain, obviously. I thought you were smart, Detective. Abe promised you were.
But sometimes, when I speak to you, it feels like you have yawning
great gaps in what you can understand. You strike me as someone
who's bright when it comes to things you've actually experienced, but
dumb as a rock when you haven't.

'Look, when the Wet rolls through here, it's good times. People pay
off loans and get the banks off their backs. Farmers have stock, have
work. *Winner, winner, chicken dinner*, eh? But you wouldn't get that,
would you? Not coming from Carlton. All swamp and mozzies over
there, isn't it? I'm not surprised you can't see what's obvious to the
locals. Everything here is strapped to a rain gauge. *Everything.* People

in towns don't get it. They turn on the tap – water comes out. They don't see beyond. Unamurra's problems would all disappear with one year of heavy rainfall. Only a moron would think it's anything else.'

Dana could sense the acceleration in Annie's words, the need to push them out as though they'd have more force that way, more truth.

'Hmm. None taken. It's an interesting observation, Annie. When I first arrived in Unamurra I felt like the outsider I was. I assumed that would hold back my investigation.'

'It did. You're fumbling around like a perv at junior soccer. This is crap, and you, Abe, should be bloody better than this.'

Able sat back in his chair, astonished and relieved that Annie could be so much on the back foot. He'd never witnessed such a thing.

'Best listen to the nice lady, Annie. Dana?'

'Thank you Able,' resumed Dana. 'I thought being a stranger would be a hindrance, but I believe it's actually the other way around. When you live somewhere, you get used to it. More than that, you come to see everything as natural, inevitable. If you live in the outback, you're accustomed to the space, the light, the peace. If you live in the centre of Sydney, you're comfortable with the traffic, the bustle, the people. You habituate to wherever you are, but more importantly, you assume that kind of life carries a certain logic: it's that way because it should be. That's what people in Unamurra have done.'

Annie gave an exaggerated sigh. 'Is there a point?'

'Oh, yes, very much so. If there are fifty people in a town and two are murdered, there's a serious problem with the town. Not with one person: it's not an aberration, a one-off. No, with *the town*. It's comforting to them to imagine, or to pretend, it's a lone-wolf act, a lunatic, and better yet, a lunatic from somewhere else. But that's just burying their heads in the sand. Besides, if most people then behave as though they don't want the murders solved, there's *definitely* a problem with the town. That's what we have here. An entire community with a problem.

Although they've been blinded – allowed themselves to be blinded – to the true nature of that problem. Thinking this way has been a comfort for them, but not a solution. It's made things worse, culminating in two homicides.

'You see, there are two factors at play in this town, and the second one is the real problem. People are getting them mixed up, or only seeing one. It's understandable, really: they look and feel the same. The symptoms are, at first glance, almost identical. But they're very different.'

Annie grabbed a banana from the bowl on the table. 'Don't mind me, mate. You think you're on a roll. I'm just tryin' to stay awake.'

'On the one hand, Annie, you're right – you do have a drought. It's slowly squeezing the economic life out of the town. Fewer trucks, poor prices for stock, no tourists, Dutton dying on its backside and less able to help Unamurra out of the predicament. The heart and life of the town are evaporating and leaving a hollow husk in their wake. That's something people comprehend. It makes sense to them, and it's what they've been told constantly: *the town is crumbling because of the drought.*

'On the other hand, there's a second factor. It overlays the first. It's camouflaged by the Dry, and it's the real problem with Unamurra. It's doing the same things: choking hope, syphoning off spirit, bending the town to its will. People who stay in Unamurra all the time, I'd bet they can't even see it. In fact, I know they can't. To notice what's really going on, you need to have arrived from somewhere else: you need the perspective to discern what's happening here. Someone like Axel DuBois. Or me. We've both arrived at the same conclusion. Another, bigger factor is killing this town. It's you, Annie.'

'Me?' Annie stopped, mid-peel, faked a bitter chuckle and looked to Able, seemingly confident he'd act as nonplussed as she was. 'Have I stopped the rain falling, then? Bloody hell.'

'The issue is you, Annie. When I first came to Unamurra I thought there would be a special mentality to living here, a unique psychology. And there is. But I misjudged what that psychology would be. I thought it would be about resilience, character and stoicism. The land-scape, the life, seemed to demand that. But the mentality of this town is actually acquiescence and surrender. Congratulations, Annie – you made them surrender. Pretty much every one of them – Able, too, to some extent. The only real hold-out was Axel DuBois, but you were trying to deal with him when I arrived. Then I became a problem and, by extension, so did Able. Luckily, we've reached our conclusions before you took drastic action. Which is why we're here now.'

Annie plucked a segment of banana and rolled it in her fingers. 'Jeez, for a quiet little mouse you sure love the sound of your own voice once you get going, don't ya? Still waiting for that point. Whenever you're ready, genius.'

'The point is, Annie, that in this town you're the Stasi.'

Annie stopped just short of a bite. She flicked a glance to her left – the same left as her glance when she'd opened the apartment door. 'I'm what?'

'The Stasi. From East Germany.'

'I know who they bloody are, thanks. What are you talking about?'

'Not just me: Axel DuBois thinks the same. In fact, he confirmed his view in writing.'

'Frenchie? You take the word of that nut? You're officially crazy, Detective.'

'I don't think so. Perhaps you don't realize: Axel is Québécois now, but he was born and raised in East Germany – Leipzig, to be precise. He escaped in 1985. I don't imagine he's discussed that early part of his life. It wasn't a happy time; the regime he grew up detesting was big on social control. They did all sorts of things, Annie. Things that might be familiar to you.'

Annie popped the first segment of banana. She chewed thought-fully and Dana gave her the time. This would work best if all the implications gradually sank into Annie's consciousness. Dana needed Annie to get so rattled she made a mistake.

'Great. I like the History Channel, myself. Bit too much about Hitler, but all the same. It's educational, isn't it? Enlighten me, then, oh wise one.'

'For example, the regime owned the houses people lived in; they set the conditions to keep them in permanent penury and obligation. They owned all the shops where people bought food and necessities, and how they bought them. That way, they controlled the supply of vital items, as well as the opportunity people might have to acquire anything else. They blocked supplies from anywhere they didn't control; they punished transgressors. They controlled bars: the alcohol served and the access. Meanwhile, they kept the finer things in life for themselves. The luxuries they denied others became routine to them.

'They barred as much communication with the outside world as they could. There was no internet back then, but you can be sure they'd have interfered with that as much as possible – regimes like North Korea do that now, so the trend is clear. They even stopped people watching certain television programmes without their express permission.'

Able knew the bare bones of this reveal before they walked into the apartment, but Dana knew the flesh of it would be appalling to him. Not just what Annie had done – slowly, with a python's squeeze – but what Able had allowed. Missed.

'To make sure people stayed under their thumb, the Stasi mounted surveillance. Sometimes they bugged public places or people's homes, or they placed tiny cameras. Often, they simply recruited citizens to keep watch on other citizens. They had a rough rule of thumb – a known ratio of informants that meant everyone would likely have a spy among their family or friends, or believe that they did. The whole thing operated on fear of discovery, or of accusation. The Stasi didn't need to recruit everyone – just *enough*. And of course, they did so by blackmailing people into working for them. This coercion relied on exploiting others' shame: their secrets, their regrets.

'In return, they promised . . . well, they promised the world. There would be security. Everyone would have a job and everyone would have a home. The state would prop people up if they fell too far, but block them from rising. The Stasi stoked fear about the outside world. They made people feel that if they ever escaped, they'd perish. They promised the state would continue inexorably; there would be no need to adapt to change because there would be no change. And there would be equality – everyone on the same level, all the time, against a common foe, and demonstrably on that same level. Does this sound familiar, Annie? Because it sounds like Unamurra to me.'

Annie smirked. 'Well, that's very nice and all. If I ever have to lecture on East German history to keep my liquor licence, I'm set now. Thanks, genius. Pfft. Me and a communist regime, the same? Talk about a long bow.'

'I don't think so. You own every house in this town, bar three, and I suspect you're one stroke or heart attack away from Mary Gosling's place, aren't you? Able's home is another target, but he refused to sell. Those houses were purchased when people were at their lowest ebb. You bought them dirt cheap and now rent them back. You present it as a favour, a benign gesture to keep the town together. But really, it yokes them to you: it makes them beholden and therefore compliant. The longer they stay, the more impossible it becomes to afford a life anywhere else. It gives you control.

'You own the only shop, which sells the only food. When people in town tried to buy in frozen food from elsewhere, you stopped them. Cut their electricity supply for a few days; broke their freezers. You only had to arrange this once, for a few rebels, before the message hit home. Everyone in town has to buy all their food at Annie's shop. You portray this as common sense: if the shop closes, the town is on the skids. But you decide what the shop supplies and how much it charges. So really, you're a one-woman state when it comes to basic essentials like food and shelter.'

Annie moped across to the rubbish bin like a petulant child, dropping the banana peel from a height into the bin.

'You exacerbate that, Annie, by taking meals across to some of the older residents. Oh, it's a charitable gesture and Annie is looking after the needy. But they're eating your food; no one else's. They're still paying you something, and they're not only dependent on you for the food, they rely on you to deliver it. Everything you do is calculated odds; making a population more compliant, more reliant.

'Meanwhile, this apartment quietly collected things that were out of reach for others, or were deliberately blocked by you. The Bang & Olufsen stereo, the antique furniture everywhere, a genuine Persian rug. Most importantly, an aerial next to the satellite dish on the roof: proper internet for you, but not for your people. Hence, several computers in your little hidden office over there. Bad move: they give off a stable blueish-white glow – different to a television – and at night that's easy to notice, believe me.'

Now Annie was at the window, still silent, easing back one of the blinds and squinting down the street.

'Three times, Annie, according to the council minutes, you've objected to the infrastructure upgrades that would actually bring the internet to the rest of this town. You don't want it because it would boost independence in all sorts of ways. You also own the only satellite dish in the town and therefore anyone wanting to watch most sport has to come to the pub to watch it. When someone tried to set up their own dish – Henry Beattie, let's say – they found it vandalised the next day as a warning. No. Everyone has to come to the pub and watch what you choose for them, while drinking beer you supply at a price you decree.'

Annie turned back towards the table. 'I provide a bloody service to this town. Why should I sabotage myself? Do you know how much it costs to have bloody Foxtel in a pub? Do you? An arm and a friggin' leg. I don't get that money back, Detective from Carlton. Not from a few oldies hanging on to a beer all night. It's a loss – a loss I bear for the town's quality of life.'

'It's a ruthlessly enforced monopoly, Annie. You know it. Don't insult my intelligence that I can't see it. You enforce your own power. You have a network of people who feed you information. People who, over the years, have let slip information, divulged secrets, told of regrets. You store that information: I'm willing to bet you literally have a note of it. To control the town you don't need to know everyone's secrets: just enough people that anyone has an informant within their orbit. In a town of fifty souls with nowhere to escape to, that number is quite low: maybe six or seven, at most. You blackmail them into cooperating, then sit back and watch the intelligence roll in, supplemented by your own digging online. That's how you know who's trying to buy frozen food in Dutton, or who might want their own satellite dish. Knowledge is power.

'Just to shore up that information, you bug the pub. Yes, I did notice eventually. Many haven't. In each wall light there's a little extra bit of kit; the same with the smoke alarms. I have a phone app that scans for basic devices like that. I'll bet the accommodation rooms are the same – you probably couldn't believe your luck when detectives Milford and Carver stayed here, chatting away about what they'd found and what they might need to do. You had a front-row seat to the investigation: it's why you got huffy that I was staying with Able. It's also why I chose to stay with Able, just in case. Someone said Milford and Carver were unprofessional to stay at the pub, and initially I thought that meant boozing while working, but no. They were telling you everything they intended to do. It wouldn't surprise me if you had bugs in the homes you own: the ninety per cent of homes in this town. So the bugs, plus the network, plus the welfare visits to the housebound – they give you all the data and leverage you can handle.'

Dana couldn't bear to look at Able. She could picture his face, though. The hours he'd spent at the pub, unwittingly feeding Annie what she needed. The monstrous intrusion, the threat that his own home might not be safe even though he owned it.

Annie sat down carefully.

'Taking dinners to housebound oldies, that's your pitch? That's my disgraceful, outrageous behaviour, is it? Pardon me for giving a toss.'

'It's all about cementing your control. No good deed goes unrewarded – you get insider gossip in spades, and you use it. And what does Unamurra get for its feeble acquiescence? You would be the benevolent mother-figure. You'd kick their backsides into communal do-gooding: the Book of Feuds, the ANZAC lawn, housework for the housebound, sensible water management, the clear-up after a storm. You'd buy their homes when no one else would, when they were in dire need. You'd put some money in their pocket and charge them what they're told is below market rent – but you're the only market. You'd police their diet by refusing to stock trashy food. You'd keep the beer flowing and the footy on and provide the warm focal point of the town. You'd make sure they had petrol in the tanks – when you decide to, for the only five vehicles in town, two of which are yours. You'd deliver meals across the road to the elderly and stay for a debrief— sorry, for a cosy chat. You'd be the upholder of standards: no bare feet, no swearing, no aggro. *Manners matter*, right?'

'My crime is giving them a better life? A better life than any of these useless bastards could manage on their own? A better diet, access to a car, a place to go each evening instead of staring at their own four walls? Wow, what a toxic influence I am, eh?'

The sarcastic tone wasn't working. It wasn't aggressive enough to be the familiar Annie. It wasn't barbed enough to be the forensic former lawyer Anne. She was in transition, neither one nor the other. She was getting there, though, Dana could see it.

'What life does this give everyone in Unamurra, Annie? They almost never leave it. They have no access to representation, because there's no council here and you're the queen bee. Their post and their medication are delivered to you, and doled out by you. An essential such as water? You dominate the committee of three that dictates how much water they can use each week. All the while, the rest of the world is slipping further and further out of reach. But you tell them they're *safe* and that the world is wicked, so that's okay, right?

'So, yes, Annie, you *are* the Stasi. Worse, you're also the state that supports it. You're a one-woman empire that plunders people's lives and strips them of basic liberties. All in the name of some maternalistic catch-all: *give me your freedoms and I'll keep you safe in an uncertain world. You'll be limited, but you'll be safe. Always safe.* These people have never knowingly signed up to that trade-off. I don't see any vote or plebiscite. They've simply succumbed to it over time: frogs in the saucepan. They've gradually assumed that it's better the devil they know. You've made them fear the outside world, while manipulating their lives to make it almost impossible for them to re-join it.'

Annie was nearing her own boiling point. It seemed for a moment she'd rise sharply, knocking over her chair and darting at Dana. Instead, she managed to rein herself in and, fuming, reached to Able for an intervention.

'Still sitting there, Abe? Not walked out yet? This is crap. Total crap. Apparently, I'm a communist dictator because I own a pub.

Whatever she's smoking, you should take it off her. I'm forcing people to stay? The McGregor widow, last year. Reese Baines, before that. Harry Mountfield, before that.'

'Oh, yes,' replied Dana, 'I know. I had the records checked. Five people have left in the past seven years, not counting those who've died. All taken in by their children, who came here and physically took them away. Some came from interstate; one came all the way from Europe. To rescue loved ones who were unable to leave, or unable to perceive that they could. I bet you despised them for it, didn't you? Let me guess: talk them down to the others, gleefully inform the crowd that two of the five died within months? *Yes, people can leave, but look what happens to them.*'

Dana continued. 'And you were quite content with that . . . *empire of dirt.* For a while, that was enough. Oh, the warm glow of it, Annie. You wallowed in the praise and the influence. The dependant who were fearful but grateful – exactly the balance you were aiming for. You'd rolled into this town by buying a lame pub and a half-empty shop, and now look. You were hooked into people's lives; they were doing your bidding and they didn't even know it. The control proved what you'd always thought – that you were smarter than all of them put together, and you could demonstrate just that fact.'

Chapter 23

Annie smirked. 'Let's say this crap is all true, every word of it. Let's say I'm some kind of human Stasi, for Christ's sake. Answer me this: why didn't I leave it there? You say I wanted the town, and you say I had it – why would I do anything else? And what's this garbage got to do with two murders? If I'm the all-singing, all-dancing dictator, why would I need to kill anyone? Jesus, you haven't thought this through.'

'Fair enough. We're coming to that. What gnawed away at you was this sense that your kingdom-building had come to a halt. The stations were a roadblock: they'd get most things from Dutton or beyond and you were powerless to stop them. Autonomous and impervious to your control, run mainly by skilled business owners who were adaptable, flexible, smart, resilient. Our farmers are some of the best of us. There seemed no way in for you.'

'Why would I want to? Bunch of dried-up farms? I didn't need the extra money, Detective. Right now, I'm loaded.'

'Yes, you are. But all this was never about money, Annie. You could have stayed in Melbourne, remained single, and made a mint as a lawyer. You were highly regarded, the pickings were there. I don't know of any barristers on the breadline. Do you? This was always all about control: dominating and manipulating lives without anyone spotting what you'd done. A delicious superiority, that you could dictate and shape an entire town and they'd do nothing but thank you for it. It frustrated you that you couldn't do the same to the stations. Their independence was an affront, a rebuke, a suggestion that your abilities were finite.

'You became desperate for quick leverage, because you knew the drought would end sooner or later. It was survivable for people like you, who had the reservoir of capital to withstand the pain, but those stations out there would be juicier assets once the rains fell and they were so cheap right now. You wanted leverage via desperation – because that's your stock in trade – so you started with Vince Reynolds, a shell of a man. Ironic, really. You battled to keep the people of this town in place, but you fought to get rid of the farmers. They were a bit too much like trouble.'

Annie glanced across to Able, to see if he was still behind Dana or was having doubts. She sighed and looked back at Dana. 'I've done this all on my own, no doubt? You're not saying Tim was part of this fantastic conspiracy you've imagined, are you?'

'Up to that point you were solo, yes. But the farms were a different matter. Sarah Muir seemed like your ticket into owning stations, precisely because she wanted out. It's not apparent, and I'm sure she'd deny it. She was convincing – until I used her bathroom. There, on the wall, are four framed photos of the Whitsunday islands. Those classic shots of Whitehaven Beach – literally the purest sand in the world, the turquoise water, the tropical foliage. Having those images in a drought-ridden station is like making a thirsty man watch a waterfall, isn't it? It's either masochism or daydreaming. It got me pondering. Sarah looked miserable in that photo from Uluru in her office, so she didn't strike me as someone who simply liked to travel. The Whitsunday photos represented something else for her. She told me Pelligrini was Larry's dream. She never mentioned her own. My colleague uncovered the trail. Sarah made nine visits to her solicitor in the twelve months before Larry's death. The first investigation thought *maybe divorce*, but I say it's more complex than that. Sarah had talked to three financial advisers as well. They supported my intuition: my colleague spoke to them all and confirmed it. If I were Sarah, I might become sick of a landscape that never changed, a life scoured by the seasons, a future contingent on something as mundane as rain. She wanted out, yes, but with her rightful share in her pocket. But Larry was wedded to farming: it was his lifeblood and he saw no reason to give it up. He would never yield. Perhaps, you both felt, he would change his mind if the landscape altered, if he felt he was facing obvious headwinds.'

'You deduce this from a photo in the toilet? Seriously?'

'That was the catalyst. It goes to state of mind. Sarah dreams of somewhere else, somewhere opposite to this, somewhere she's never been – somewhere Larry would never want to live. The photo kick-started the idea.

'To create the necessary momentum to acquire Pelligrini, you offered Vince Reynolds a way out from Sorrento, time and again. With Sarah's connivance. That's why she kept visiting Vince on her way home each week. He was supposed to be the first domino to fall. Those regular little digs of hers at the foundations, sympathizing over the inexorable drought, raising the option of escape. Eventually, Vince signed; you and Judge Trent co-purchased via shell companies and assumed no one would work it out. We've found the paperwork, despite the attempts to hide it. The Vanuatu government plays ball if the right person leans on them. You induced and rewarded Sarah's actions by cutting her a special price at the abattoir – you and Trent quietly own a quarter slice of that, so creating extra revenue solely for Pelligrini was a temporary sweetener you could afford even in a drought. It also reminded Larry of the power you held over stations, being the only abattoir within reasonable distance.

'You thought Larry would give up, once he knew Vince had caved. But Larry doubled-down and looked to the future. Sarah couldn't convince him to sell to you. Legally, she owns half of Pelligrini, but without his signature, there'd be no deal. That was why Larry Muir had to go. By which I mean *dead*. Simply *missing* would place the station in legal limbo until he could be officially declared dead. It would be years. You had to get your hands on the deeds before the Wet came: the banks might become more conciliatory if the place greens up. No, Larry had to die and die soon; just as important, it had to be proven that he'd died.

'You needed certain hardware for the task. Judge Trent could have organized that for you, but you baulked at that. I wondered why; it took a while to percolate. Although you're partners with Trent, you don't own him. You each know secrets which provide mutually assured destruction. You wanted a gun – and a silencer – but you wanted the supplier to be under your thumb. You chose Henry Beattie.'

Annie blinked too much. The veneer was cracking, buckling under the strain. She'd obviously never imagined anyone could get this close.

'You chose Henry for three reasons. First, he's very handy and has a workshop: he could fashion a silencer that would do the job. Since it was bespoke, it couldn't be traced and was a forensic dead-end when we got hold of the fatal bullets. Second, he had old army contacts and procuring a suitable weapon wouldn't be a problem. Third, you'd had Henry on the hook for years. His relationship with Able's dad, Collis: you'd driven Henry Beattie into the ground, blackmailing him over that. Not just the relationship itself, but his disavowal at the crucial moment. I believe Collis had wanted to go public about their affair at the last, but Henry chickened out. Collis took the Unamurra Long Walk; Henry never got over his guilt. You never let him.'

She flicked a glance at Able, who swallowed hard but nodded silently.

'So Henry manufactured a silencer and procured a gun from old mates of old mates; it doesn't matter who. As it turned out, you didn't really need the silencer for Larry Muir, but you probably did for your husband. So, an investment well made.'

Annie sat forward. 'This is a silencer you don't have, for a gun you don't have, that no one can report seeing. Used in murders no one witnessed, which happened at a time you can't confirm, at a place you can't confirm. Juries think this sort of mess is amateurish. For good reason.'

'It goes like this. You invite Larry to Vince Reynolds' station, Sorrento. Oh, you're careful, you don't ring him up: that would leave a trail. The next time he's in the pub, you have a word. To everyone there, it looks like you and him chatting over a beer. It's a throwaway little thing really, so he doesn't realize the significance. You probably dress it up as something to do with the Book of Feuds, a grown-up attempt to solve the water argument, perhaps. At your request, he doesn't mention it to Sarah or anyone else; therefore, no one supposedly knows he's going to be there. You ask to meet at the entrance to Sorrento, and you'll travel on to the house together.

'I doubt you explain it. I very much doubt Larry had any real idea what was going on. Not like the television or the films – no elaborate explanation of your motives or how you're about to do it. No, it's cold. You simply walk up to him, make sure he's off his guard, then shoot him in the heart from maybe five or ten metres away. You can't miss: no special skill needed. He drops where he'd stood. You have all the equipment in your car, and you've watched DuBois' videos before. Larry's hoisted up like an angel in a few minutes, on the empty frame DuBois had left there before. Larry's ute? You found a suitable crevice and then scratched out the tyre tracks to it. The initial investigation "forgot" to even look for it. That was the first note I ever made about this case, before I even got to the airport. It was so glaring, so telling. We'll use a drone to find the ute. It won't take long.

'You know Reynolds' schedule. You know he won't be leaving Sorrento for a few days and it's unlikely anyone will visit him. Sarah's been forewarned to stay away and already knows why. Those few days will muddy the forensics and time of death. You're back in town twenty minutes later – behind the bar or mingling, establishing an approximate alibi, being your usual self – just in case Larry gets discovered early. Sarah won't raise the alarm on him going missing because she knows: when Larry doesn't come home, it's because he won't be coming home. You'd already agreed all this between you. So Larry hangs there until Vince comes looking for more booze. Poor guy gets the shock of his life. Fair play to him, he runs straight to Able – no panic, or trying to do the wrong thing.'

'Supposition. Speculation. Is this worth your career? And Able's?'

'It fooled me, at first, your hoisting Larry's body up onto the frame. It took me a while to see through the fog of it. Oh, I never suspected Vince Reynolds. No, he's as ruined a human being as I've seen with a beating heart. Not just from the drought, either; that soul-breaking swing in his front yard. He's smashed to pieces by it all. I knew he had nothing to do with Larry's death, but the placement next to his station still meant something. It spoke because the body wasn't hidden: the messaging was deliberate. It told me that the stations – not the town – were at the heart of motive. You tipped me off, Annie. Being a smart-arse began your undoing.'

Annie gave a shudder. She seemed perturbed by the mere mention of her making a mistake.

'Once I finally realized that DuBois, far from being a suspect, might actually be aiding the investigation, it all began to come into focus. The murderer for both killings had to be someone with a reason to kill Larry Muir. Since he died first, the motive around him mattered more than the reason for Tim Ogden. That motive was more likely to be related to the stations than the town. The murderer also had to have some reason for wanting to put DuBois in the frame. To most of the town, he was a harmless nut moving angels around. The murderer needed to be smart enough to know DuBois' predilection for mathematics, so that the staging of the corpse was convincing. They had to be smart enough to make it *just so*, and it had to matter to them that the fakery was exact. The murderer had to be someone with a reason to kill a second time: Larry would have been a one-off for almost everyone. Those assumptions narrowed the field considerably: Able, Sarah Muir, possibly Henry Beattie. And definitely you, Annie.'

Annie sat back with an air of resigned amusement.

'And we're back to Frenchie as a key part of your "proof". God, it gets worse. As you say, Detective, I'm a qualified lawyer. Even after years away from courtrooms, I know enough to see your ideas are just hot air: there's no *prima facie* case here and precious little in the way of evidence. Holes joined by supposition and conjecture – that's the most benign description I can bring. I see also that you're quite content to label the people of this town as stupid. Apparently, to you they're a bunch of sheep who'd act against their best interests time and time again. A jury in Dutton would see a snotty detective from somewhere else explaining to them why the locals are thick. Good luck with that.'

'Hardly. Though I imagine that will be part of your defence. I've never said the people of Unamurra are stupid. Far from it. They've moved here, and stayed here, for perfectly rational reasons. Most are retired or were unemployed. They can't afford anywhere else. Most have come, one way or another, to rely on you. It would be foolish for them to move somewhere that would bankrupt them. And it would be naïve for them to think they could go against you without repercussion. So, consciously or not, they've made a sane and reasonable decision to go with your particular flow. The trade-off is safety versus liberty. For some, it's perhaps a more overt pact; for others, it's something that happened to them. In fact, they've all made the best of it – they've built some social cohesion and they have admirable qualities of helping each other in tough times.

'No, the answer isn't that simple, Annie, as you well know. The problem for this town is that each time they acquiesced, they made you a little stronger. As the saying goes, *An appeaser is someone who feeds a crocodile, hoping it will eat them last.* When Larry Muir was killed, half the town probably thought it was you – simply because they can't conceive of something occurring in this town without you knowing about it and approving of it, or doing it yourself. They thought you had to be involved. So what did they do? They hunkered down and hoped it didn't happen again. And when it did, they buried themselves deeper. They gave the investigators a blank wall, said they didn't want the murders solved, talked of *getting on with life* and *moving on.* Because that was the only way to assuage the person they knew they had to placate. It was a rational assessment of their position, and a logical decision. But it's morally and ethically wrong. It simply emboldens a murderer to think they can act with impunity.'

Annie had calmed a little, found her way to icy contempt. Again, the low, quiet voice from Annie was her most sinister.

'You're very quiet, Abe. What's the matter, detective got your tongue? For someone who's lived here most of his life, you've given up the steering wheel pretty quickly. I'm surprised you've decided to risk your career on the meanderings of this one's mind.'

Able held his hands wide open. 'I trust her with my career just fine, thanks. With my life, come to that. You, Annie – I wouldn't trust you as far as I can spit. Dana's right on the money, mate, I can see it in your eyes. And she's right about your voice. Lower tone, longer words, wider vocab. It's all changed in twenty minutes, hasn't it?'

Annie flinched, then recovered.

'Ha, now you're seeing what you want to see, Abe. It's a sign of desperation – your mind is clinging to a life raft. Sad. Pathetic, in fact. You're chucking it all away for a stupid little conspiracy theory. Well, go ahead, Carlton, you might as well finish your fable. Just so you know, I'll be chucking you both out in about ten minutes. I've got a barrel delivery coming. The people's beer matters more than indulging your creative selves.'

Dana double-checked the recorders were still operating. 'You don't need to worry about deliveries, Annie. Your diary won't look the same for a very long time. So, you've killed Larry Muir and everything seems to go smoothly. The police arrive, but of course you can hear every word they say in their rooms and you have Judge Trent in your pocket, so they don't go too hard. As we said, they manage to ignore where Larry's ute might have gone and, of course, Sarah's not going to remind them to look. There's no search of this apartment, no involvement from the local officer who knows you all too well. You face two out-of-town detectives who are at loggerheads with each other and half of Dutton station. One of them is emotionally on the edge before he even starts. The weak questions begin and Unamurra does what Unamurra does: acquiesces to you and says nothing. Sarah Muir applies for probate and, when she gets it, she'll be able to sell Pelligrini to you and Trent. I believe Trent wasn't suspicious about you buying Sorrento, and if he has future qualms about how Pelligrini came to be up for sale, he'll swallow them. If anyone remains a murder suspect at that point, it's Axel DuBois, because the hoisting of the body perfectly mimics how he'd do it. And I mean *perfectly* – golden ratio and all. That's another reason why I'm sure it was you, Annie. Any other suspect would have approximated and left it at that. Happily for you, DuBois disappears into the outback, returning only occasionally to shuffle the angels. That disappearance makes him look more guilty.'

A sound rose from the pub below. More than a murmur, slightly less than a clamour, it was a rumble of agitation. Annie raised an eyebrow. Perhaps, thought Dana, she feels forces are mustering in her favour. Yet again, the notion that they were two hundred kilometres from any support flooded her mind. Dana re-gathered.

'But, then. Hmmm. Something happens a few weeks later, doesn't it? Something shifts. You were hair-trigger at that point, even though you'd essentially got away with it. I'm sure we'll find the evidence of what happened next when we take your apartment and computer system to pieces, but I'll run with a line of best fit. Tim found out the full extent of what you've done to this town, and/or evidence that you intended to buy Pelligrini to add to Sorrento. He put two and two together and believed you'd killed Larry Muir. You couldn't take any chances: Tim knew all your background and just how much of your current life was artifice. He could have blown the whole gig, couldn't he? So you murdered him, too. But at the precise moment when you killed him, for some reason, you couldn't deal with the body. Maybe you hid it, intending to work out the forensics later on.

'One of two things happened next. Either you decided to give the second murder the same MO, to implicate DuBois further, then pretended to be surprised at dawn by the corpse of your husband. Or DuBois stole the body and hoisted it himself, genuinely surprising you that morning. Either will do. I'm sure DuBois will come forward now and help to explain which it was. The bottom line was that Tim had outlived his usefulness. So, Annie being Annie, you casually killed him. The only headache for you was the logistics of dealing with a second body.'

Annie sat back and rubbed her fingers through her hair, as though her scalp was tingling. 'Well, wasn't that nice? Cluedo without the board. It was me, in the billiard room, with the candlestick. Or was it me, in the study, with the lead pipe? Whatever. Your ten minutes are up, kids. It's been nice for you to indulge your ego, Detective, but I have work to do. Apparently, so do you, since you don't appear to have anything to back up your comprehensive guesswork. A weapon, for example, would be nice.'

'It won't us take long to find the gun.'

Annie's lips twitched. 'Yeah, good luck with that. Assuming I was the killer, I have half a desert to hide one tiny gun. You drove here yesterday. Big, isn't it? Feel free to drive two hours in any direction you like and start digging. Then just work your little trench back until you reach the pub. Then go out again, et cetera ad nauseam, for each of the three hundred and sixty degrees on the compass. That can't take more than ten or fifteen lifetimes, can it? A gun you could fit in a pocket, in thirty thousand square kilometres? Jesus. You should have held her hand better than this, Abe. It's like the two of you didn't think this through at all.'

'On the contrary, Annie,' replied Dana. 'We thought it through very carefully. I considered what sort of person you are. To have shot two people dead, at the first time of asking, in cold blood, one of them your husband? No remorse, no guilt, no giveaways? I thought about that.

'Then I examined what someone with that pathology would do with the murder weapon. You see, this level of sociopathy – because that's basically what you are – means you don't think like most people. It's an asset when you're carrying out a murder, or even planning it. There's no semblance of self-doubt: you don't hesitate, you don't get distracted by angst or morals. It's clean and it's linear and you never think for a second that it won't work.

'But the trouble is, the aftermath. Sociopaths aren't as good at that part. Because cleaning up doesn't just mean making sure the forensics are gone, or ambiguous. It isn't merely pointing the finger at the nearest conceptual artist. It requires you to work out what others might think and do. It takes empathy. The perspective of others is really a theoretical concept to you, where you have no true idea whether you're

right or wrong. You can fake it in small and frequent doses, or where
the stakes are low, but *in extremis* your mask slips. So, instead, you
considered the aftermath in terms of what *you* wanted, and nothing
else.'

Annie flinched and wiped her mouth. 'It's a wide brown land,
Detective. And guns are little things – that's why you can hold them
in your hand.'

'In theory, you have, as you say, half a desert to hide the gun, but
the reality is very different. You'd want the murder weapon to remain
within reach. Because if you got away with two murders, you'd see
every reason why a third would be possible. So, no, you wouldn't drive
hours away and bury it in a crevice. Nor would you anticipate anyone
finding it at all, because that would mean they're smarter than you
and that's an idea you can't entertain. Hence you've been sloppy about
where you put it. Also, you wouldn't expect to be searched, and you
weren't. Twenty-two buildings in this town were searched during the
first investigations – including the pub – but not your private apartment. You'd believe that if it came to it, you could fake righteous
indignation, call in favours, intimidate, garner support. Not forgetting that you had Judge Trent, the biggest cheese in Dutton police, at
your beck and call. You felt you had weapons that could hide the
weapon.

'So, the gun you used to kill Larry Muir and your husband? It's still
on this property. In fact, it's about three metres from where we're sitting.' Dana looked carefully around the room. 'Everything in this
room is *just so*. That's a phrase I heard yesterday, and it's truer than the
speaker realized. You were precise about faking DuBois' artistic calling cards, and you're precise about your interior design. This room is
admirable. Congratulations. I like the symmetry – no doubt you find
that soothing. It's all very tasteful. A little haven in the outback, isn't
it? But I feel you should have made it messier, more haphazard. I've

seen people make this mistake before. The room is so flawless that anything out of place really stands out.'

Dana continued to look Annie in the eye but pointed across the room to Annie's left. 'Here's the error I've been looking for since we arrived, Annie. That walnut sideboard. You've glanced at it three times: once when we arrived, then later on when you became rattled. And again a moment ago. So fast it's like a reflex. I doubt you're even conscious that you did it. That's your giveaway error, Annie, your *tell* – thank you. I noticed the marks on the floor where the sideboard's been moved out and back about ten centimetres. Now, it's possible you simply dropped something behind it and needed to retrieve it. But I don't think so. I think – in fact, I'm *certain* – that's where you taped the gun.'

Dana turned further to her right. 'Don't forget your gloves, Able.'

Annie gave a smile that was half-hearted and forced. There seemed a moment where she would rise and physically try to stop Able, but a raised eyebrow from Dana stayed the movement. Able had a perplexed frown as he donned the gloves, as though he couldn't quite believe Dana would be right. He rested his shoulder against the window ledge and looked down the gap between sideboard and wall. The sideboard was slightly recessed at the back: he saw the shadow of something, but not the object. He gave a grunt as he shoved a little further out. The rubber feet squealed as they yielded grip.

'Jesus. It's—'

He reached in, and there was a rasping sound as the tape was ripped. He pulled a bag from his pocket and slid the weapon into it carefully, holding the middle of the barrel as he did so. He held it up like a fish he'd just caught.

'Why didn't she – why didn't you hide this, Annie? Out in the bush? Jeez.'

Dana swivelled back to Annie. 'Are you going to answer the nice man's question?'

'Do it your bloody self, smart-arse.'

'Oh, Annie, don't *manners matter* any more? The reason Annie didn't bury the weapon where we'd never find it, is . . . she fully intended to use it again. A third time. Maybe a fourth, as well.'

Able returned slowly to his seat. 'What? Who?'

Again, Dana looked back to Annie, as though she might care to explain. Annie blanked it and glared at the Barcelona chair.

'Third?' said Dana. 'That would have been Axel DuBois. If she ever got hold of him, he would have been next. He knew it, too, hence his hit-and-run tactics for the past few weeks. It turns out he's had years of training in subversion techniques and off-the-grid survival, courtesy of some dodgy left-wing activist groups. He knows his way around a laser pen, too. I believe he knew Annie was the killer and he was undermining her, working away at her foundations. He couldn't go to the cops – even to you, Able – because he didn't know who was on Annie's side. He could see from the standard of the first investigations that she had friends in high and low places. It was his lucky break that someone from so far away pitched up to investigate. If he was going to risk telling anyone, it would be me. Even then, he hedged his bets and stayed out of sight. He kept using his angels to send subtle, wordless messages. Until I asked him openly, using a format that he could see left no traces – that reassured him that I understood the need for discretion. Then, he got bold enough to communicate directly. Truth be told, if not for his artistic hints, I can't say I'd have got this far. Not in this time frame, that's for sure. He pointed me in the right direction.'

Able looked towards Annie, who was pulling her sleeves down. Her body language was regressing towards childish by the minute. 'Christ, Annie. Christ. What the bloody hell, eh? And the fourth?'

'You, Able,' replied Dana. 'She was prepared to kill you if the investigation got too close to the truth. Which it has.' She put a hand on Able's forearm, sensing the shaking that had begun. 'I couldn't bet against anyone in this town blowing the whistle to the killer. That was partly why I used all the apparently meaningless chitchat in those interviews – elliptical questions that would mean nothing if someone spilled. It turned out I was right to be so circumspect. Annie was – *is* – desperate. She goes to extremes, trying to protect her power.'

'Jesus crap. Let me think, let me think. What . . . what else?'

'The silencer, Annie, that would be the cherry on top.' Dana looked to Annie. 'You could tell us, to save your lovely apartment getting ripped apart.'

Annie summoned a superior smile and said nothing.

'Ah, you think we can't find it?' Dana paused, and began thinking out loud. 'Hmm, this fits with your sociopathy again, and how poorly it serves you in hiding evidence. Since you must know that we'll find it eventually, then I assume that smile was because you think we won't find it quickly. You're very pleased with your hiding place. There are some obvious parameters. It's a cylinder about ten to fifteen centimetres long, diameter around two centimetres or so. You could hide something that small almost anywhere, Annie. Inside the casing of the television? Within the extractor fan on the stove? False ceiling or floorboard? No, wait, you'd want to use it again and you might need it quickly. For example, you could spot Axel trying to get some things from his shed and you may only have a minute or two. So, it's within the same easy reach as the gun itself: you won't be undoing screws or bolts or climbing into lofts.' Dana considered for a moment. 'Able, please go through there and check Annie's bedside tables. You'll be looking for something you'd, uh, prefer not to pick up. Something that unscrews or unfastens.'

Able frowned again but moved into the bedroom. Dana could see Annie visibly flinch when the door opened.

'Awful isn't it,' said Dana, 'when police officers go through your dearest, most private possessions?'

Annie fixed a glare in defiance. 'Not. Over. And when I get past this stupid garbage, I'll be coming for a chat with you. Don't think I won't.'

'Actually, I *do* think you won't. I think you'll never set foot outside prison. You'll die there. Larry and Tim deserve at least that much.'

Able appeared at the bedroom threshold, clutching two plastic evidence bags. One contained the silencer, glinting in the diffused sunlight. The other contained an electric-blue vibrator.

Dana tapped her pen on her pad. 'Do you still think we have no evidence, Annie?'

'Planted. Nothing to do with me. How do we know Abe didn't have those in his pocket all the time? There was no one in the room with him when the search was conducted.'

'Well, I'm pretty sure we'll find your fingerprints on one or both items. Obviously . . . DNA as well. But to answer your concern: when he walked into this apartment, Able switched on his bodycam. He has contemporaneous, continuous footage of everything he's done. Along with a further recording of our conversation. Don't be daft, Annie, you're smarter than that.'

For the first time, Annie gave a flicker of defeat. Just a split second, before she lifted her chin. 'What now, genius?'

'Now we take you a long way from here. Stand up, please.'

Chapter 24

Dana waited patiently until Annie relented, and stood. 'Thank you. Able will search you and then we'll go downstairs. At this point, I'm not minded to handcuff you. Someone else will be formally arresting you and reading your rights. But one semblance of a risk to Able's safety and I'll taser first and long, pepper second, hogtie third, and first aid will come last. Are we clear?'

Able moved forward and carried out a hand search, including pockets. Annie bore it all with an undignified fuming breath and resolute gaze at the ceiling. Able placed a small webcam on a shelf with a clear view of the entry and hid all but the lens behind two piles of books. Dana had emphasized the risk of the scene being compromised the moment they left it.

They stepped out of the apartment, and Dana blocked further progress while Able locked the door and double-secured the entrance with police tape. He sealed the edges of the doorway for extra protection, took a notice from his inside pocket and taped that to the door itself. The warning was stark: breaking the seal without permission was a $10,000 error. Plus prison time.

Now, thought Dana. Now was the moment where this whole investigation would either be delivered, or fall apart. Help should be on its way, but for now she had the kind of logistical headache that officers in vast empty regions were used to solving. It was sheer numbers – Dana and Able were only two people and there was a whole town out there. She had her suspect. She had an apartment, and a pocket, full of evidence. But if fifty people in Unamurra took up cudgels, they could wipe all that away in a moment.

Everything they'd done in the apartment was, in Dana's eyes, a known quantity. She'd been sure the evidence she already had would rattle Annie and lay the groundwork for the case. She'd had a reasonable bet that the gun, or the silencer, or both, would still be there. It had been a gamble based on Annie's pathology, and Dana felt she had a good hold of that. But the reaction of Unamurra – she couldn't be certain how they'd respond

A town revolt wasn't such a strange idea. Ever since she'd arrived in Dutton, a slew of people had told Dana to do the minimum and walk away. Yet here she was, taking away Unamurra's emotional and financial crutch. It would be immediately obvious to anyone what would happen if Annie left town. If they so chose, the town could take Annie back and free Able's other prisoner. They could take the computer drives, the gun, the silencer, and bury them all where they'd never be found. Then Unamurra could do what Unamurra had done twice already – close ranks.

As she strained for distant sounds, Dana could hear something else. Whispering. Sibilant noises. The lone cough in an expectant group. Dutton station was still two hours away.

Dana reached the top of the stairs and saw, at the foot of the steps, a throng of people. Their muttering rose briefly and faded immediately as they all stared upwards. At least ten at the bottom of the stairs, hunched in the little hallway before the pub's front door, but her sixth sense inferred others in the lounge. Most of the town was here, summoned by excited knocks, frantic texts and salacious calls about police in Annie's private domain.

Dana led the way down the stairs. She flicked her jacket as if it was a casual reflex, but it allowed the throng to see the edge of her holster. They backed up as Dana descended but, even so, it was claustrophobic. If they wanted to jump her, she wouldn't be able to reach the gun and use it: they were too close. She mentally prepared to reach for the taser, then the spray, in the hope that it would give her enough shock-time to draw her gun. As she reached the bottom step, she swore she heard the noise she was hoping for in the far distance.

The crowd had created a two-metre circle for the three of them. But the silence of thirty-plus people in an enclosed space was unnerving. All eyes were on Annie. It was only to be expected, thought Dana: their leader was being taken away. They wanted to know what they were supposed to do, how they were supposed to feel, what they were supposed to be.

Annie smiled and addressed her people.

'Just so youse know, this clown is arresting me. She thinks I'm the killer, because she doesn't like me owning a pub and a shop. Some people can't deal with a strong woman, eh? Even another woman. You wouldn't believe the crap she's come out with, up there. I don't blame Abe, and you shouldn't neither. He has to go along with this joke, 'coz she's the senior one. But here's the bottom line, people. If I have to go to Dutton right now, the pub closes. My name on the licence, so it has to shut. The shop as well – it's me's got the combination of the safe. Petrol pump's goin' off, too: my safety certificate, so I can't have accidents on my conscience, can I?'

Dana looked around at the group, who glanced at each other and mumbled quietly under their breath.

Annie raised her voice. 'And that's just for starters. If she keeps on with this garbage, none of that will be opening any time soon. The pub, the shop, the pumps – they stay closed for ever. I'll have legal bills to clear my name, so after that, I'll have to raise some cash. Whose house shall I sell first, eh? I own your houses, see – the bloody lot of you. I've been nice and quiet on that to give youse a cosy life, but no more. I'm landlady to everyone in this room except two. Yeah, think on that. Everyone here's gonna be out on their arse. Who's volunteering to be out on the street? Who'll take the hit? Any of youse got lots of money? 'Coz I'm happy to start with you, to spare the others. But in the end, I'll sell all of 'em if I have to. Can't not, can I? This moron's staked her career on this. It's not gonna be pretty and it ain't gonna be quick. Unless, of course, you persuade her otherwise. So let's see ya. All the people I've helped over fifteen years – every last one of you – let's see what you're made of, eh?'

Dana anticipated an awkward stand-off. Annie had made her pitch. Support her, or go without food or petrol, lose your home and go broke. Most of these people had no buffer, no means to be resilient. Dana's hand drifted closer to her taser; Able's hand to his.

Gus was first. He shouldered his way out of a group that parted for him. He came within a metre of Annie, hands clasped before him like a penitent schoolchild. Annie smiled and softened that adaptable voice.

'Well done, Gus. First of many. I won't forget it, mate.'

Something died in Gus's eyes. The light, the intensity. He turned and showed her his back. And stayed there.

Someone near the far end of the room whispered, *Christ*. Baz, the semi-reformed gambler, stepped up. He twitched and fidgeted and couldn't look Annie in the eye. But he did the same.

Macca, Annie's new deputy and pub manager, raised an arm, and the crowd let him through. Annie turned and smiled uncertainly. 'Us two against those two cowards? We'll walk it, Macca, you'll see.'

Macca turned his back.

It was enough. As one, the rest of the room shuffled awkwardly and silently until everyone in the place had turned away from Annie Ogden.

She was speechless. Her lips moved, but no sound emerged. She frowned at the impossible concept. She seemed to be mouthing *why*, but her voice had gone.

Dana moved in front of her and stared her down. 'At the end of the day, maybe there's no real loyalty in fear, Annie.'

Chapter 25

The trio emerged into the blazing light. Dana had forgotten quite how dazzling it was, and took a second to put on her sunglasses. She tilted her head for a moment and smiled to herself. Yes. She could definitely hear it now. The air some distance away was being chopped; the echo of it pummelled her senses. The helicopters were near. The Scorpions had arrived.

Able could hear it as well and gave her a thumbs-up as they loaded Annie into the car. Dana sat in the back with her, Able driving, as they prepared to pull away. Dana risked a glimpse back at the pub, somehow fearful that the crowd had changed their mind and were about to swamp the car, rock it on its suspension and reclaim Annie. What she saw was a cowed, regretful line of people spilling out on to the veranda. There was a quiet nod from Gus, which she returned. To his right, behind his shoulder, she briefly imagined she saw a face she recognized.

They made their way out of town, passing the ANZAC memorial. All the angels were gone. DuBois must have shifted them the moment Dana had gone into Annie's apartment. For that brief time, he'd known Annie couldn't get to him and he had a chance to move the angels. The lawn still looked tawny beneath the haze of dust from the earlier storm, but the memorial caught the sunlight as they passed and seemed to glint at them.

After three kilometres, Able pulled over to the side of the road. Ahead of them was a wide, flat space the size of a football oval. Two black helicopters, floating like giant wasps, were approaching the landing space. Annie remained silent, boring a glare into the back of Able's head before returning to the window. They all watched the helicopters land and the rotors gradually slow, morphing from a frantic whirl into solid blades settling in the sun.

'Step out, please, Annie.'

Annie complied, holding her hands in front of her as if already cuffed. A man in a black jumpsuit was half jogging towards them. He had short, scrubby hair and broad shoulders, a grim look behind Aviators.

'Detective Russo?'

They each flashed ID before they shook hands, conscious that everything here had to be a perfect process beyond legal reproach. The man's bodycam blinked a red light from his shoulder. 'Hi, I'm Captain Tom Billings, deputy head of the Scorpions. You've set up quite the scene here.'

Annie raised her eyebrows at the word *Scorpions*, then frowned. She might have been expecting cops from Central, though the helicopters would have been a reach for them, even with the logistics of the outback. The Scorpions, however, indicated another level, and emphasized that the corruption angle was almost as important as the killings. She would guess, thought Dana, that Judge Trent was going under as they spoke.

'Thank you for coming, Captain. Able can take three of your men to Unamurra, to protect Annie's apartment. He'll pick up Henry Beattie from the temporary cell and bring him here.'

There was a snort of derision from Annie, behind her, who'd been unaware Henry had been arrested earlier. Perhaps she was starting to think that it was only right that others should fall with her.

'Sounds fine. You have the rest of it?' Billings signalled three of his team to join Able and the Landcruiser executed a U-turn and headed for town. The helicopter motors ticked in the heat, but other than that the scene was strangely muted.

Dana produced the evidence Able had collected – the gun, the silencer, the vibrator. Billings raised an eyebrow, but he understood that it must relate somehow: Dana didn't give the impression of some-one who messed around. She handed over another plastic evidence bag – the flash drive of what she held on her laptop, the two interview recorders, and her notebook of Pitman.

Billings grinned. 'We'll get a stenographer to officially decipher this. Thanks. Morton?'

Officer Morton scampered out from the second helicopter.

'We searched her, but I didn't cuff her or read her rights. You'll probably want to,' said Dana.

Billings raised an eyebrow. 'Oh, hell yeah. Morton? Wrists and ankles before we set off. And read her rights when you've listed the charges. I'm sure you know your legal rights backwards, Mrs Ogden, but . . .'

Morton nodded and grabbed Annie by the arm. Dana waited for a defiant final comment, but Annie merely glared, until Morton pulled again and she was on her way.

Billings looked around the area, hands on hips. 'I bloody hope you're right about this, Detective. We just spent a hundred thousand to do the set-up, secure this place, tie down the station at Dutton. Got law-abiding police officers standing around in the motor court there, phones taken off them, wondering what's going on. The district's effect-ively got no police response now for hours, minimum. Got the media ringing already. Got a district commander in custody, for Christ's sake.

Got a whole town here with no more food, looking down the barrel of being homeless, starved or destitute. All on your hunch.'

Yes, thought Dana, *I've been aware of that for hours now.* 'I believe I am, Captain. I wouldn't call out the Scorpions on a whim.'

'That's what Mikey said. Your evidence so far is solid, I'll say that. It's why we went at it. Here – the mobile number of the guys guarding the apartment. In case you need to liaise. We'll be airborne for the next thirty minutes. Need anything else?'

'No, Able will take me to Dutton airport. Thank you.'

They shook hands and Billings turned back to the helicopters, conscious that they cost almost as much on the ground as in the air. The engines took a couple of minutes to fire up fully. Able had returned, and Henry Beattie was already cuffed, presumably by one of the Scorpions. Henry nodded to Dana before he clambered aboard. Able swung the car around to pick up Dana, and the helicopter rotors were swirling dust before he even got to her.

She turned away from the billowing sand and swallowed hard. The helicopters ascended with a cacophony of noise, the air so viciously sliced she could feel the ripples on her skin. She and Able watched them slide away through the air, headed for Dutton and a rendezvous with four other units. The Scorpions had indeed gone all in. She couldn't fault their commitment once they'd made a decision.

Able had his dazzling grin again. 'Guy said they spent seventy grand just to start the op. Bloody hell, Dana.'

She smiled. 'Their boss just told me a hundred. The cost is coming down by the minute.' She turned towards town. 'Oh, crap, what's that?'

Hidden by a rise in the ground, they couldn't make out details. But they could see the smoke – black pulses and dark grey clouds frothing into the still-milky sky. Something was burning fiercely back in Unamurra.

Chapter 26

Dana shuddered as the car launched from the sand and slewed onto the tarmac. Able had the lights firing as a visual warning to any other cars. He was coming straight down the middle of the road.

Dana wasn't quite praying, but not far off. As the idea of Annie and the Stasi had built, she'd been acutely conscious of preserving all that she'd uncovered. The motivation for the crime was so outlandish that it needed every sliver of evidence she could muster, both here and in Dutton. Even finding tangible proof that Annie and Trent had bought Sorrento required a huge effort.

So protecting everything in Annie's apartment, especially the computers, was critical. Dana hadn't thought that Annie would have had time to set any booby traps, any timed devices. But now she wasn't so sure. Perhaps she'd set them before she opened the door to Dana and Able: a couple of small incendiaries just to get things going, hooked up to a timer and needing her to shut them off to prevent a fire. When Annie had walked out of her apartment, she hadn't looked back wistfully. She'd had a relative serenity Dana had found surprising. Perhaps this was why: she knew most of the evidence would be smoke and the rest was circumstantial. Or maybe, despite the turned backs at the foot of the stairs, Annie had someone loyal enough that they'd set the blaze anyway.

From this distance, the smoke and the buildings seemed intertwined. It was impossible to discern the source of the fire. She didn't
need to speak to Able – they both knew what each was thinking:
Annie skating, or convicted of minor infringements, knowing where
Able lived.

As they passed the town sign and came up the slight rise, they got
a better view. The fire was behind the main street – off near the deckchairs of Able's outdoor cinema. Dana could see Able visibly relax
when he saw no one's house was aflame. Just as important, Annie's
apartment hadn't been torched.

Now they were within mobile coverage, Dana spoke to one of the
Scorpions guarding the apartment, who'd also seen the smoke and
gave an update. 'Yeah, none of the buildings, apparently. Some empty
area out the back, locals are saying. Maybe someone burning some
rubbish? Can't imagine you get the garbos here too often.'

They passed Able's place and drove down a wide alleyway between
two other houses, skidding to a dusty halt as they emerged back into
the sunlight. The smoke was still billowing from a pyramid-shaped
pyre, tended by a robust man with a hefty beard and a red checked
shirt. He pushed at the pyre with a broom handle, seemingly aware of
their presence without having turned around.

Dana and Able got out of the car and scrunched the hundred
metres to the edge of the fire. It gave off a constant pulse of heat.

'Monsieur DuBois? I'm Dana Russo.'

She extended her hand as he turned and smiled. There were smudges
of ash across his features and his hair was unkempt and slanted to the
right. His hand was large and meaty and he gave a mashing but not
aggressive handshake.

'We meet at last, Detective. Because, finally, we can, non?'

'D'accord. I never expected to see the angels like that.'

He turned and regarded the pyre he'd created. The metal frames were in a loose group beside it, cascading down to the bottom of the dip. The angels themselves lay at crazy angles, wings beginning to melt, faces dripping, limbs fusing into other limbs. She couldn't swear there were twenty-eight ablaze, but there might be.

Able was hanging back, his body language a facsimile of his reticence when they'd encountered the Praetorian guard yesterday. *Wow*, she thought, *yesterday*. Only twenty-two hours ago.

'He won't bite, Able,' she said.

Axel laughed. 'That's easy for you to say, ami.'

'Yeah, Dana,' muttered Able as he stepped gingerly forward. 'That's easy for you to say.' Able extracted himself from the handshake at the earliest opportunity.

'Monsieur DuBois isn't a biter. He's a freedom fighter, aren't you?'

He shrugged. 'Axel, s'il vous plaît. Where I can, or when I must.'

'In other circumstances,' said Dana, still observing the fire, 'we might be on different sides. But today, I thank you for your help. It was vital.'

'Merci. I have to say, I think you would have got there in the end. But maybe, with my help, a little faster, non?'

Dana nodded. 'Much faster. And for the good of everyone, it needed to be quick. As you'd already calculated.'

The three of them stood for a moment, entranced by the flames. Then Able turned to Dana. 'So the murders *weren't* impossible, then? Weren't the Kobi-thingie?'

'Ah, yes, well, they kind of were. So, some background. The feud between Trent and Cronin: it's partly about Annie. My colleagues Lucy and Mikey have filled in a lot of the blanks. Annie counts Judge Trent as an ally; they have surreptitious business dealings, some shared company ownership, and she's funded part of his lifestyle. Lucy did a stand-out job connecting dots. It's low-volume but high-impact corruption, really. It gives Annie leverage and power. Cronin is the antidote to that, according to Mikey's intel; he's outside her loop and despises her influence. Trent tries to get rid of Cronin, but Central has people who like Cronin being there. They fear a free-for-all for Annie and Trent, if Cronin isn't there as a counterweight.'

'If Central know this, then why not dump Trent? Or prosecute Annie?'

'Evidence. Until now – until all this – they had no clear evidence. Even the shared ownership documentation was tricky: Lucy had to look down rabbit holes, through tax shelters and the like, to find it. Thank God I used to work in Fraud and knew how the dodges worked. Cronin was trying to get genuine leverage, but he was struggling. All he could do was fight the symptoms, not prove the cause.'

'So they kept Cronin there to keep Trent in check? And Annie?'

'Exactly. Or, more accurately, as much in check as he could, because he's barely kept a lid on it lately. When I met Cronin he couldn't lay all that out for me, because he didn't know which side I might be on. I could have gone back to Trent and spilled, for all he knew. And likewise, with you. He couldn't bring you into his confidence because he had no way of knowing if you were batting for Annie or not.'

'Or if I was just plain terrified of Annie?'

'Quite so. You're good at this stuff, Able, don't kid yourself you're not. Anyway, Cronin wanted to tell me that solving these cases wasn't impossible, if I followed a particular and oblique direction. So he said they were like the Kobayashi Maru, knowing that it was such an esoteric label that I'd mull it over and work it out.'

'But the Kobi-thingie *was* impossible. That was the point of it, yeah? So Cronin *was* saying it's impossible.'

'But Cronin could have just said *it's impossible*, like Trent did. He didn't say that; he specifically pointed me towards something odd and memorable. His reference was precise and accurate – an apparently impossible scenario that Captain Kirk solved. That meant the case was solvable, if I did what Kirk had done.'

'Yeah, how exactly did that cheating thing work?'

'In the story, Kirk sort-of cheated: he reconfigured the computer program of the Kobayashi Maru roleplay so that there was a solution. He explained it in the film as "I don't accept the no-win scenario". What Cronin was telling me was that these murders wouldn't be solved by being orthodox, by following standard procedure. He was telling me the solution lay in redrawing the parameters.

'And he was right. Once I stopped trying to battle with forensics, timings, alibis, and so on, the answer started to come into focus. I needed to understand what Annie was doing to the town before I could work out what she'd done to her husband and to Larry Muir. I wouldn't have got there without Cronin showing me the way, in his own oblique fashion. It was smart thinking on his part – plausible deniability for himself if I turned out to be part of the Annie/Trent complex, but a nudge towards what would work.'

Able took some time to chew on that. They all did. The fire danced again. Axel leaned forward and prodded at a torso. It collapsed into a molten wing and the flames flared again.

Dana struggled to turn herself away from the pyre. There was something majestic, something nobly sacrificing, about the image before her.

'Axel, the angels. They're magnificent, you should be very proud. Unfortunately for you, two dimensions doesn't do them justice. Publicity photos wouldn't tell people what they'd experience by seeing them. It was a privilege to witness them close up, Axel, a real privilege. And they saved a town. I hope you've kept some, or you'll make more?'

'Non, et non. There is no need. They exist for a purpose. That purpose is not to be something only to stare at: angels are warriors and messengers, always. They have done their task, mais merci bien.'

'Fair enough. And for my own personal curiosity – their silhouette with wings and head: does it mimic the outline of a Texas longhorn?'

'Aha, well played. Very close, ami, very close. Texas longhorns come first from European stock; I see the European *criollo* when I make the angels' outline. So, very close. You get the general idea, oui. My hommage to the farmers here: they are very tough, very creative people. They deserved better than Annie Ogden.'

'So, Tim Ogden – your role?' She showed him she was recording with phone and camera.

He coughed and then nodded. 'Bien sûr. When I first came to Unamurra I was going to move the angels for a few weeks, then leave. But I saw. Almost from the first day, I saw the control she had. At first, I think maybe it is good: she leads, the town wants her to lead. It behaves like a real community, yes? It cares for those who struggle; it feels like a team. Maybe you feel the same at first but . . . merde, it changes fast, non? The more I learn, the worse it was. It dragged me back, you see – Leipzig, all of that. Clearly you know, Detective. I had to go . . . what is the word? *Guerrilla*. I couldn't go away and leave all these people to Annie. They were so . . . *pacifique*, yes? So calm about what was happening. I couldn't understand why they did not know, or did not care.'

He shook his head, still in disbelief.

'I knew she had killed Larry Muir. I saw her car coming back into town that afternoon. I had a bad feeling, somehow. I thought, maybe she had moved the frame, or damaged it. After she'd passed, I went back up the highway to the entrance to Reynolds' farm and saw for myself. It was terrible. And Annie – she had put the body like that to make me the suspect. She stole the wings from one of my angels – she plans it this way. I could see her mind working, non? Everyone blame the stranger: I think this works in some small places. I could not change anything for Larry, could not give him some dignity. Someone might have seen me near the body already, or maybe I leave finger-prints, or whatever. So I had to leave him. Hated to do it, but Annie, she had made a bigger problem. I was a suspect, and she had the power to keep up the pressure. I had to move into the desert. I place lots of food and water in hiding places, and I go.

'I could watch her home from very close, at night. The ground is very strange there: it looks flat, but lots of places to hide. If you are trained, you can keep watch. I see her on the computer for hours: the silhouette behind the blinds, a certain colour of the light. Artists and the quality of light, eh? I imagine she fishes for secrets, like a good Stasi. One night, she stays up all night. Tim drives back from Dutton very late and this time, for the first time that I see, he is in the apart-ment. Maybe you do not know: they live in separate apartments up there. She has her own space always, but this night he is there, too. The silhouettes, they argue; she throws a punch. The lights go off and I am getting ready to leave when the two of them – Annie and Tim – come out of the back of the pub.'

He paused, stoked the pyre again, and wiped his mouth with the back of his sleeve.

'Halfway to dawn, now. She has a gun. Tim is walking ahead, maybe ten metres, and they come towards my hiding hole. I cannot move; I am stuck. Closer. I can't believe she doesn't see me because I cannot get low enough. He sweats, he looks for a way out. He sees me, half buried in a hole. Maybe he will point to me, huh? I don't move; we just connect with our eyes. I wait for him to betray me, because that is the only way he might stay alive. But he walks *away*, Detective. He pretends to trip and goes to the left. He saves me, saves my life. Even when he knows what will happen to him, still he looks to save me, eh? When he turns to face her, she shoots. Bang – no hesitation, nothing. He just drops. Poor man, poor man. She pushes him with her foot, like rolling a log that is in her way, like he was never anything to her. He flops down into a hole. She thinks for a moment. I guess she wonders if she has the time to deal with the body now. But – headlights. A truck near the edge of town, daily food delivery. The headlights, they spray everywhere. I think she must see me now, with the extra light, but she rushes inside and I see my chance. Tim was not big – I can carry him. I get him away to a better hiding place. He is dead, of course. I thank him for saving me.'

Dana swallowed. One of her biggest problems had been her inability to sense exactly what the crime scene had been like at the time: the light, the sounds, the tension in the air. She was feeling it now.

'Now what, huh? Now what can I do? What I must do is to make Annie pay. For both of the men but, most of all, for Tim. He was a good man, a good person. I must make her pay. All day long she frets about the body. I see her come to the back gate many times but she chickens out, gets called inside, whatever. She comes back later; she holds the phone and kicks the sand for disguise, because she is not talking. She is looking in the hole, wondering why he isn't where she shoved him. Maybe he's not dead? Maybe he crawled away and he will live and tell everyone? I hope she fears this, worries about this.

'I know the milk delivery is the next morning. It is every three days, at the same time. I want the milk guy, Declan, to see Tim first. He will raise the alarm and Annie will have no choice but to fall into line. She will have no time to destroy the evidence of what she has done. I get Tim to a frame, and I hoist him up. I say sorry, because this is undignified and he deserves better. I wheel it into place and hope the timing is right.

'I see the lights of the milk truck. He has to arrive before Annie gets there – it is a race, but he doesn't know it. Closer, closer, but Annie is like clockwork – the lights come on in her apartment. Now

I worry. The truck, it seems so slow. I underestimated how far away when I saw the headlights. Really slow. Now I think it will fail, Annie will see Tim and get him out of sight. She makes her fancy coffee she thinks we don't know about, she comes out to the back yard.

'Now. Now I hear the truck braking – the *ptshh* it makes – and I know it will work. It is perfect. She sees Tim, she puts down her cup, she opens the gate, et voilà! The milk truck comes around the corner to the back of the shop. Parfait. She has no choice – Declan also sees Tim and she must pretend to be amazed, horrified. She is trapped.

'I thought that they would arrest her straight away. But they come, they go; nothing changes. I see lives go back to normal and I'm crazy about this. Why? Why do they live like this, huh? The town says nothing, does nothing. Because of her power, of course. Because she says that if they trust her, they will be safe from this terrible world she tells them about. Then, a rendezvous with a friend who helps me. He washes clothes, gets messages, this kind of thing. He says that you arrive – a new cop, a fresh chance. So I begin again with the angels. And I pray you hear them. And you do. You do. Oui.'

His eyes were misting up. Dana rushed to reply just to stem a flow of tears. She could feel her heart rising.

'I did, Axel, I did. It took until this morning to work out those messages, but I got there. The guard of honour at the entrance to town – welcome, but be wary. The three sentries outside Able's place – look out, Annie's suspicious of you. And the response to my message – Stasi. The jury, after the sandstorm – the one you think is guilty is guilty. Strike now. Yes, Axel, your messages were perfect. Under the radar, yet out in the open.'

Able pretended to have some grit in his eye, but then turned and tapped his watch. Dana nodded.

'Ah, yes. Axel, I have to go now. Able will need a formal statement from you this evening.'

'Bien sûr. I am at Gus's house now. He will let me shower and stay over. You can find me there, monsieur.' He turned to Dana. 'I can tell you are someone who hates to be hugged, ami, but there is nothing else for it. You saved lives, including mine. So, prepare.'

It was, of course, a bear hug.

Chapter 27

The drive from Unamurra to Dutton seemed shorter than the trip out. They passed the halfway marker with Dana lost in thought, staring out of the window. Lucy had texted just before they'd left, congratulating her. Now she was missing home: her own place, the chance to snuggle down in an armchair this evening and talk to Lucy on the phone. She wanted to telescope the time and simply be there, now. The loss of adrenalin had left her feeling weaker.

'Hmm? Sorry?'

Able grinned. 'Ah, you were miles away. I said, I have a question, if you're up to it.'

Dana shuffled up from the slumped position she'd lapsed into. 'Yes, sure, go ahead.'

Able frowned. 'So I know what you just did, and I get why you did it. But I don't get . . . how you knew to do it. How you got from A to B, so to speak.'

'Ah, what was the process? Good question. Okay, well I arrived here without preconceptions, or much hope, to be honest. As everyone was very quick to tell me, all the odds were stacked against a win. McCullough was already pressuring – this was before he got permission for the District Scrutiny – and I felt a failure here would give him the ammo to send me across the state. It seemed I'd been set up to fail.

'But once I saw the two bodies in Doc Mangold's magic freezer, I started to think that there could only be a few people in Unamurra who could, or would, do that. It's not really a question of brains or strength or ability, you see, more an issue of will. Most people don't kill at all, but if they do it's usually a panicky, desperate thing. It's messy; they don't know what they're doing before, during, or after. That's because everyone's entire moral life includes *thou shalt not kill*. It's hard-wired not only into individuals, but the society they're raised in. Kicking against that stricture is seldom something people do in a calm and reasoned way. It's a rare mind that can be so calculating while killing: those people will give themselves away by being callously indifferent in the rest of their lives. Less sociopathic killers will give themselves away by being stunned, traumatized or overcome with guilt at what they've done.'

'So you were focused on the psychology?'

'Partly, but not entirely. As you saw in Doc Mangold's lab, I wasn't ignorant of the forensics, or physical evidence. But yes, the psychology had to be front and centre because it was the only resource I really had. So, the killer or killers are either guilt-ridden or sociopathically indifferent, but no one displayed either of those traits in Unamurra, not even close. No one even hinted that they were involved. For all that I could have suspected Axel, or Sarah, or Beattie, or you; none of you had left a hint that there was a trail to uncover. So I had to be realistic: either there was a conspiracy among several people who were remarkably calm, or it was the work of one person. That person had to be socially adept enough to pass muster but brutally cold and selfish on the inside. That iciness might make them arrogant, contemptuous of the idea of being caught, and therefore ultimately careless. That was what I was looking for.

'Second, the property data from Lucy told me which path was most likely. Annie had quietly bought up almost every property in town. From what she said when we took her away, half the town didn't even know the other half were tenants, let alone that they shared a landlady. Annie would have pitched her discretion as part of the deal for most people – the tenant avoided embarrassment, humiliation – but it also kept her empire under wraps even as it grew. She would no doubt have claimed it was altruism: it certainly didn't make financial or commercial sense. The homes hold no intrinsic value and, even if she squeezes the tenants tightly, there's a limit to how much income they can generate. The money she'd have got was small fry compared to the turnover of her businesses. No, unless she knew they sat on a mother lode of gold or something, the reason to buy those places had to be personal. I concluded that the reason for Annie owning them was simply to own them. It was a power thing. And sociopaths are interested in power.

'Next we went to Reynolds' station and, again, I saw a dilapidated place that had found a buyer. Even in the good times, farming is marginal out here; there are richer pickings elsewhere that carry less risk. Rational purchasers wouldn't necessarily rush to buy somewhere that had decent revenue three years a decade, and near-zero revenue four years a decade. Sorrento was a poorer investment than almost any other station in Belgium. So again, the purchase was less like a sound business venture, more like ego indulgence. Therefore, it was likely to be the same person as Unamurra's houses, though possibly with a business partner, given the size of the sale price.'

'So by now you're onto Annie: she's become favourite?'

'Not entirely. I'm suspicious of her motives at this point. Her financial and business behaviour is odd, that's all. It's probably true that half of Australia's sociopaths are in boardrooms, but that doesn't mean unusual buying patterns indicate a murderer. Annie had raised a flag with me and that needed to be followed up. Lucy came through with Annie's bio – her more general behaviour became harder to justify as natural or normal. She'd hidden an entire life, and was play-acting now in front of all of you. I might have given her a pass if she was running from a terrible trauma, or hiding from organized crime or something. But she wasn't; it was a deliberate choice. I filed it away, but Annie was looming larger in my thinking.

'Then we went to see Beattie and other pieces began to fit. The photos on the wall told me that he and your dad had been involved. The possibility of him being blackmailed started to come into view. Since he was stony broke, the pay-off being leveraged by blackmail couldn't have been monetary: it had to be about controlling and making use of him. I was struggling to see what use he might be to the blackmailer, although I had thought previously about his workshop and a hand-made silencer. Even so, the men's shed could have produced that and anyone could use that space. I had no evidence for Beattie making the silencer; without finding the silencer, I never would.

'Then Beattie went apoplectic about safety. It really was odd – here was a capable man who'd seen active service, who seemed a reasonable judge of risk, and he was absolutely paranoid about the world outside the town. It really jarred with me: he had to have been taught – *finessed* – into that level of fear. I'd been wondering why people seemed so keen to stay in Unamurra at all, particularly after two murders, and Beattie's rant showed me why. He was demonstrating the town's mentality. They were all fearful, all willing to place safety – or the appearance or promise of it – above everything else. Objectively, Unamurra was a ridiculously safe place, yet paradoxically it was where the fear was ramped. Someone had to be doing that: either you or Annie, because only you two had the influence to shape a whole town's attitude. I didn't think it was you. That was why I asked Sarah Muir

about influence – and when she ignored Annie in her answer it suggested deliberate evasion. She had to know something to have played
down Annie's influence in the town, and had to have a motive for
doing so.

'When we visited Sarah, I already knew about Annie's background
from Lucy. What I saw in Sarah was a mirror-image of Annie. Someone capable, yet hiding part of it. She gave away that she had a high
level of education, that she felt superior to Larry in many ways, that
she wasn't happy. Here was a second woman sublimating her intellect
when there appeared no reason for doing so, someone steeped in a persona that was an act. This morning I tagged in to Lucy's data about
Annie's background and her joint purchase of Sorrento: it struck me
that Sarah might be looking for a way out. She'd need a divorce, or
Larry's signature on the deal, or Larry gone. Lucy found the financial
and legal data to back up the theory. A divorce looked a no-no: nothing to indicate Larry would agree. So while Sarah's main option was
to sell to Annie, she could only do it if Larry relented, or died. And
there was the plausible motive for murder. Taking everything to that
point: it was Annie. It had to be Annie.'

Able shook his head. She could tell he was thinking this was somehow obvious; that he had been a fool not to see it. She put a placatory
hand on his arm.

'I could only get to that conclusion by mixing what I heard from
those interviews with the evidence Lucy was uncovering: either half of
that wouldn't have been enough. Once the overall idea took root, I
realized there was another source pointing me in that direction.'

'Which was?'

'All the direction of the evidence was being underpinned by
DuBois' actions. I was sure, even before I arrived in Unamurra, that
he had something to share. At first, of course, he was a potential suspect, but I started to downgrade him. The messages from the angels,

and their positioning, spoke of someone who wouldn't point the finger at themselves. Axel would have disappeared those bodies if he'd been the killer. Instead, he had to be the person pointed at, not the pointer. So I began to trust his messages, and they dovetailed with what I was learning and thinking.'

'Hmmph. I never trusted him, see? Even now, I just can't connect with the bloke, and that made me doubt him. I can agree with your logic about him, but my gut won't let me run with it completely.'

'Fair enough. He was coming out of left field. But he didn't know if he could trust you, hence, he didn't run to you and spill his story. He tried to communicate using his angels, but it wasn't really working. The first investigation ignored him; he needed a second investigation, from someone with no previous skin in the game, before he'd take a risk.'

'Okay,' agreed Able. 'So you have Annie's weird financials and hidden life, Sarah is like-minded and wants out, Vince and Axel are not suspects, Henry's involved but probably not a killer. How do you connect the dots?'

'I needed other little nuggets, each minor in themselves but adding constantly to the picture. I only really worked it out this morning – that was my breakthrough. Billy Golding had pointed me to the recording devices in the pub, though I was slow to recognize it. Annie's knowledge about Mary Gosling gave a malign view of the dinner runs; the wilful destruction of Henry Beattie's satellite dish told of Annie's control over what the town could do for itself. At that point, Axel's message – *Stasi* – started to make perfect sense as a reference to Annie. Once I saw everything through that lens, it all made sense.'

Able smiled. 'When he said *Stasi*, you must have wondered if he meant me, yeah? I did.'

'It confused me at first, yes, I have to admit. I think of Stasi as secret police, and no officer was a regular visitor from Dutton. So yes, at first glance I thought he meant you, and I thought he was mistaken.

It took a while to filter – that he was talking about Stasi behaviour rather than Stasi police per se.'

'It's fair enough. In your place I'd have done the same, I reckon. Got to say, of all the things I thought might happen to me in Unamurra, being accused of acting like the East German police was not one of them. So, what was your thinking once you'd bottomed that out?'

'So now all I had to do – ha, *all* – was to pull the threads together. I was sure that if I got into that apartment, I'd find something that would lead me to the evidence. As I said before, it's a back-to-front way of doing it, but in this case it was justified. Annie needed to be undone first, then she'd buckle. She has too much ego to sit silently and say nothing. Especially if you were there; she'd want to show you how superior she was.

'Coupled to that, the legal and financial data told me that Trent was involved. Possibly, he'd dragged others into it as well, but that was beyond what I could explore. I was fairly sure Cronin would be the counterbalance to that – it explained their animosity, but it also explained why Central insisted on keeping Cronin in place. Mikey knows far more about the politics than I do – he confirmed it. If a district commander was taking slices of the action, and especially if he was smothering murder investigations to protect himself, then I needed a higher power. The advantage of the Scorpions is their reach: they can bring the hammer down on everyone at once. Without them, I would be undermined by some of those involved getting a warning and disposing of evidence.

'That request to the Scorpions was the most awkward decision, but not the worst. Personally, I could handle accusing Annie – I could even accept being wrong about it – but my career would never recover from inviting the Scorpions for a non-existent dance. Their power and reputation depend on them being right all the time: if I screwed their batting average they'd never forgive me, and neither would the up-tops.

'But the biggest call I had to make was about you, Able. Keeping you safe. I was thinking that if it *was* Annie but I couldn't nail the evidence, I would essentially leave you in a small town with a killer. One who'd see you off, sooner or later. Either I got it totally right, or you'd perish. Even if I got it right, if I told you too early or you inadvertently tipped our hand, you'd be at similar risk. I can cope with putting myself on the line – it's my decision to do that – but putting you in danger was much heavier.'

Able swallowed and gripped the wheel tighter. 'Jesus. You carried that? I mean, all on your own. I know you had your Lucy to talk to but, even so, that's a heavy load. I'm . . . I'm sorry I didn't help.'

'No, no, don't be sorry. I couldn't have done it without you. I needed your balance. Not least, once I had my ducks in a row I needed a sane human being to hear it and judge if it made sense. Out here . . . out here, there's no perspective. At least, I don't have one. It's so alien to me, as a landscape and a life. I had to know if a fellow police officer who lives here thought my idea was crazy. You could have shot it down, Able, even if you felt it had merit. That would have been the easy path; it might have seemed to you the road to self-preservation. You put your career – *your life* – on the line, because I suggested that you do. That's profound. That's courageous.'

Able gave a watery smile, and looked away.

Able scored a bench while Dana checked in for the flight. The seat was a collection of uncomfortable wooden ribs that invited the sitter to reconsider.

'Here.' He handed her a pack of gum. 'It's for the . . . ears . . . pressure . . . thing.'

'Ah, for the thing,' she replied as she sat. 'Thank you, Able.'

'No, thank *you*. I mean, you solved two murders in my back yard.'

They both considered for a moment, mesmerized by the ride-on polisher that spooled between benches and pillars while it buffed the floor tiles – an airport Zamboni.

'Well,' she said quietly, 'I had a lot of help from the king of Belgium, don't forget that.' They both smiled. She couldn't look at him directly and spoke to the floor. 'You're a good man, Able. Doing a good job. They need you. Now, more than ever. They respect what you do, what you are.'

'Yeah, well, maybe. But thanks, hey.' He paused, embarrassed. 'I, uh, I didn't spot any of it really, did I? I live in a town of fifty people, yet I couldn't see what was growing right in front of me. Like you said, frog in a saucepan.'

'It was exactly that. No one in Unamurra could reasonably have worked out all that was going on. Don't beat yourself up about it, Able.' She glanced at him, and he looked sceptical. 'Okay, *try* not to beat yourself up. It took Annie a long time to gradually turn the screw. It relied initially on shame and secrecy to leverage the power; it depended on the town taking the path of least resistance and not considering the consequences; it needed everyone to trade personal freedoms for the promise of safety. That was Annie's advantage, and her Achilles' heel. You needed to be coming in from outside to have a point of comparison.'

'We really gave everything away to Annie, didn't we? Kinda betrayed the ANZAC spirit, there.'

He was right. A town that sacrificed precious, life-giving water so that the ANZAC memories could be surrounded by fresh grass, had yielded those hard-won freedoms without a whimper.

'I think,' she said carefully, 'that sometimes we lose our collective marbles. When we come under pressure we aren't as principled as we think we might be. We turn into frightened pragmatists pretty damned fast. Especially if we think the same bad thing is happening to all of us. We think it's random chance and therefore we could be next.

'Annie picked at the golden thread: we lead comfortable lives for the most part, so we're vulnerable to persuasive lines about risk. Someone says we're unsafe, but they can protect us if we do what they say. If they can make that argument stick, we throw our principles out of the window. We just want to be *safe* again – it's a primeval human need – and we become less particular about the consequences. We throw away risk assessments, values, ethics, all our previous plans, because we're caught up in the fear – the fear people like Annie stoke.

'The further we go down that road, the more we've invested in it, the more we double-down and won't countenance an alternative. I've seen it with Fraud cases. We just can't accept we've been wrong. We start *othering* those who query the prevailing direction; we take pride and solace in being with the herd and so we don't question; we degrade those we think are undermining the new cohesion. Annie saw that, used that. Some leaders create power for themselves by trading on that vulnerability.'

Able stared at the tiles. 'With no checks and balances to that, eh? Not even from the cops. Trent was all in for the same result, and I was bloody useless.'

'No, Able, you're misjudging yourself. Don't. If a leader convinces a community they will only be safe if they do what the leader says, all other voices become irrelevant. The community can't – *won't* – listen. They'll justify their own behaviour, couch it in terms of legitimacy. Once they hear the word "safe," then ideas like proportionality, evidence and accountability just seem like empty concepts. You couldn't have stopped Annie, not on your own. You couldn't. It would, uh, *take a village*. And the people who grab power that way? They always overreach: they can't help themselves. And they never want to give back the power.'

Able nodded, but wasn't convinced. 'Another thing came to me, on the ride in. Something else the town never noticed. I never noticed.

Annie – she didn't want the drought to end, did she? We were all busting for rain, she was saying all the right things at the right time, but that was another lie. She wanted the Dry to go on.'

'Yes, she did. It's completely amoral, but in Annie's world all that matters is Annie. It suited her for the Dry to continue; it maximised her chances of buying stations and buying them cheaply. She'd traded on the desperation of others for years. Cheering on the drought was just another manifestation. If the rains came, the banks would ease up and the farmers would have cash and cash flow, and in that scenario they'd never sell. So every day Annie was praying for dry weather, while you were all praying for rain.'

Able thought about that as they stood. He nodded at the runway, where a small aircraft had taxied to a halt. 'Good luck with that thing.'

Dana turned. If anything, it seemed smaller than the one that had brought her to Dutton. 'It does look ridiculously frail, doesn't it?'

'I hate 'em. It's like a *Flintstones* plane.' He held out his chubby hand and they shook. 'It's been a pleasure, Dana.'

'Likewise. Goodbye, Able.'

'Bye.'

She watched Able head for the exit, his feet splayed slightly as he walked, like almost every police officer she'd ever met. Dana followed the three other passengers and stepped through the double doors into the scorching light and cool breeze, Lucy's last phone message still in her head.

Come home, chick. I miss you.

Acknowledgements

This is my third published novel. My first two, *Hermit* and *Prisoner*, were both born during the Covid pandemic. In the UK all bookshops were closed, in Australia there were widespread restrictions. To have been published at all was a miracle of hard work and dedication from everyone at Headline in the UK, and Hachette in Australia. I owe them a huge debt. Hopefully *Red Dirt Road* will have an easier pathway to the readers.

This book has been through the loving hands of my editor, Toby Jones. His wise counsel has, fortunately for readers, prevailed. And none of this would be possible at all without my agent, Hattie Grunewald of The Blair Partnership.

My books are also available in the Czech Republic, courtesy of Host and the translations of Radka Klimickova. Their books are little gems, beautiful objects to hold in your hand. I'm privileged to be part of that.

I'd also like to mention my copy editor, Sarah Day. Many people don't know much about copy editing, so let me just say that Sarah is halfway between a human safety net and a forensic scientist. She spots my absurd errors with good grace, sees anomalies, and generally makes this book smoother and more impressive than I had. *Red Dirt Road* is about ten per cent more enjoyable solely because of Sarah's work.